The Contractors

A Novel

by

JOHN B. KEANE

MERCIER PRESS

Mercier Press
PO Box 5, 5 French Church Street, Cork
24 lower Abbey Street, Dublin

© John B. Keane 1993

ISBN 1 85635 058 4 *(paperback)*
ISBN 1 85635 067 3 *(hardback)*

A CIP record for this book is available from the British Library.

*To Gerald and Chris
with love*

The Contractors is a work of fiction. All the characters and situations
in this book are entirely imaginary and bear no relation to any real
person or actual happenings.

Printed in Ireland by Colour Books Ltd.

THE
CONTRACTORS

1

ALTHOUGH THE conversation was less than a half an hour old he felt he knew more about her than any other woman he had ever met, his mother apart. She was freckled with an overglow to her cheeks but this might have been the wind which blew directly into their faces. Her auburn hair was straight and skimpy but it was well cared for. She was short, but not stubby with large blue eyes. She had a certain vivacity and there was invitation of a kind in her glances. This was new to him. At home in Kerry a girl would never dream of opening a conversation with a stranger.

'What are you looking at?' she quizzed.

He brushed the question aside with a shrug.

'You're a deep one,' she said. 'Still I'd better tell you my name. Do you want to know?'

He nodded.

'It's Patricia Dee. My friends call me Tricia. To what part are you going?'

'Bertham,' he answered.

He explained that he was going to work on the buildings. A neighbour of his to whom he had written had promised to fix him up with a job and digs.

The boat drew closer to the harbour. Soon they were looking down at the customs sheds through which they must presently pass. She looked at him wistfully.

'We'd better see to our bags,' he said.

'It was nice meeting you,' she told him. 'I don't suppose we'll see each other again.'

'You never know,' he answered solemnly.

'Look here,' she put it to him suddenly, 'I'll give you the number of the nurses' quarters at the hospital. It takes time to get used to things over here. You might feel you want to talk if you get lonely.'

He waited while she searched her handbag for something to write on.

'There,' she said handing him a slip of paper on which she had hastily scrawled the number. He took it and put it in his trousers pocket without looking at it.

'Don't forget,' she reminded him.

Before he could reply she had gone. He withdrew the slip, looked at it and folded it neatly. Then he took out his wallet and carefully secreted it in a stamp pocket. He felt lonely. Even though he was twenty it was the first time he had spent more than one night away from home.

He located his one large suitcase and went towards the customs. A deep feeling of self-pity welled up inside him. In a moment he would be crying. He shrugged off the feeling and gritted his teeth. For the first time he fully understood the meaning of the word homesickness.

It was March of 1952. Of the classmates with whom Dan had gone to school in the two-roomed schoolhouse of mountainy Ballynahaun none now remained behind. Most were in England. The rest were in America, Australia or Canada. To emigrate was the traditional thing, the most natural thing in the world, and there was no alternative for most. It solved many of the country's economic problems and created none. At the time of Dan Murray's disembarkation at Fishguard there were already one million of his fellow-countrymen in Britain. The majority lived in ghettos, drank in pubs where the barmen or landlords were Irish, frequented dance-halls and clubs which were Irish-owned and rarely if ever mixed with the English. The others were made up of two main classes the first of whom were the exploiters, contractors, sub-contractors, dance-hall owners, flat-letters and so forth. The second consisted of those who had professions, principally doctors and dentists. There were thousands of these, attracted by the huge earnings in an England still chronically short of medical personnel so soon after the war.

He knew something about London from listening to other young men who had come back home to Kerry on holiday. If a fellow worked his head he could get on in England, be promoted to chargehand or foreman or even become a sub-contractor. This was where the real money was.

Dan's mother had given him a few inadequate shillings to tide him over till his first pay day. She had also given him new Rosary beads and made him promise that he would never miss Mass. His father had told him to look out for himself, no more. His one younger brother had told Dan how lucky he was. He would be forced to stay on in the small farm until he was old enough to emigrate himself or until the parents died and he could inherit the place.

Before leaving home Dan Murray had been warned about England and the likely evils that would confront him in that pagan place. His parish priest often referred to it from his pulpit. Sometimes he called it a gigantic whorehouse, unconsciously whetting the healthy sexual appetites of the lustier young men in his congregation, making them all the more eager to go there. Missionaries who came to give the annual retreat were more expansive. English-run dance-halls were iniquitous sin palaces where couples danced belly to belly and abandoned themselves to thoughts most foul. Belly to belly dancing or close dancing as it was sometimes called was, according to the missionaries, the most degrading public practice to which young boys or girls could possibly submit themselves. England, they said, was also noted for its homosexuality, rape, incest, sodomy and all forms of lechery but bad as these were worst of all was to turn Protesant. No words of these practised performers could adequately describe the enormity of such a sin.

DAN WAS fortunate to find a seat on the train and still more fortunate to get one near the window. One of his companions was a moustached man of forty or so who slept soundly. There was an unmistakable odour of stale liquor on his breath. From their accents Dan could tell that most of the occupants of the carriage were Irish. Before long, however, his interest was completely taken up by the passing scene. They followed the coast for a time and then proceeded through hilly country. The sea kept reappearing. In contrast to the craggy shores of his immediate homeland, there seemed to

be no end to the beaches. The train sped past countless cara-
van parks and after a while the face of the Welsh industrial
belt began to show itself most clearly.

From Llanelly to Cardiff to Newport the countryside
was defaced by ugly industrial complexes. These appeared
almost non-stop until Bristol. After Bristol the countryside
was a delight and, it seemed to Dan, the English had pulled
a monstrous confidence trick on the Welsh.

The man beside him sat up suddenly, muttered a few
unintelligible words and fell asleep again.

Onwards they sped past Bath and Chippenham towards
Swindon where there was a delay while some extra carriages
were coupled. Dan stood up, opened a window and looked
out on to the platform. There was an unfamiliar air of bustle
and quiet efficiency – none of the happy-go-lucky atmosphere of Irish railway stations. His neighbour sat up a
second time and from partly-opened, bloodshot eyes looked
about him in bewilderment.

'What are we stopped for?' he called out weakly to no
one in particular.

'Just a few extra carriages,' Dan explained. 'We should
be on our way any minute now.'

'You a Paddy?' the man asked.

Dan nodded. The moustached man was about to frame a
second question but changed his mind.

'My name is Sylvester O'Doherty,' he said. He thrust out
a hand for Dan to shake.

'Dan Murray,' Dan said.

Sylvester O'Doherty produced a noggin bottle of whiskey and handed it to Dan.

Dan uncorked the bottle and swallowed. Then he returned it to Sylvester who emptied it in a series of gulps
punctured by gasps and grunts.

'That was badly wanted,' he disclosed breathlessly.
'Normally I'm a beer drinker but this holiday has exhausted
me beyond belief. I need something more essential to sustain
me. Eleven years since I saw home. Eleven years and nothing's changed. I'm a Maynooth man,' he went on. 'I would
have been ordained a priest if I hadn't met this girl. Just as

8

well. I wasn't cut out for the priesthood. I could never close my eyes to the fact that I have here between my legs, hidden from the eyes of the world, one of nature's recurring miracles. I'd never be able to suffer the celibacy. How I endured it for so long is still a mystery to me. It broke my poor mother's heart. The neighbours looked at me as if I were some sort of freak. There was nothing for it but the boat to England.'

Dan suspected he would be less forthcoming when sober.

'What sort of work do you do?' asked Dan.

'Ever heard of the Reicey Brothers?'

Dan nodded.

'I work for them. I'm a cross between an accountant and an unconvicted forger. I do the contracting books by day and act as cashier in the dance-hall at night. The Reicey Brothers are millionaires but you probably know that. They pay me well. I'll say that for them. What do you do yourself?'

'Just a labourer,' Dan said. 'It's my first time here.'

Sylvester O'Doherty appraised him carefully. 'You won't be a labourer long my friend,' he said.

Dan pressed him for further information about the Reicey Brothers. Sylvester produced a second noggin. He swallowed copiously. Then he talked. The three brothers Tom, Joe and Pat had come to England from Mayo in the early war years. They worked around the clock and saved their money. Gradually they drifted into sub-contracting and after the war took on some sizable projects. They had no labour problems. In the beginning most of their workers were Irish speakers from Connemara who had difficulty in speaking English. To men like these the Reiceys were a Godsend. Most of them could not conceive of departing the confines of Kilburn when their day's work was over.

In a short time they became known as Reiceys' Volunteers. They were clannish in the extreme and so were feared and avoided but they were steady workers, proud of their strength. It was said of them in Kilburn and Hammersmith that if one was stabbed every man-jack of them bled. Their ignorance of the London scene was a handicap which bound them body and soul to their employers. These labourers had to have some place to go on Saturday and Sunday nights when the pubs closed so the Reicey Brothers built a dance-hall. They called it the Green Shillelagh. The Irish in the district swarmed to it, and were encouraged by their priests. After all the Reiceys were Catholics.

'If you want to meet the fighting Paddies,' Sylvester continued, 'the Green Shillelagh is the place to go but after Mass on Sunday mornings is the time to meet the real Irish. You'll see them in the clubs or pubs nearest the churches, decent folk. If you'll take my advice which you won't, you'll give the Green Shillelagh a wide berth. If you're in any way sensitive or different from the pack in any sense whatsoever they'll sniff you out and tear you apart. Those they don't understand they hammer down. Men have been done to death near the Green Shillelagh. A drunken Paddy in an RAF uniform strayed there one night last year. For no apparent reason he was kicked to death. I understand this type of Paddy. He's best left to his own ilk. There are other Irish dance-halls and there are countless Irish clubs. Most are frequented by honest, God-fearing people but if you have any sense you'll avoid the lot till you know mutton from goat.'

Dan wasn't sure he fully understood but he did not interrupt.

'Today,' Sylvester continued, 'the Reiceys own race-horses. They drive Jaguars. Their sons will be engineers or doctors or priests, most likely engineers. There's only one sour note.'

'What would that be?' Dan asked.

'They never learned how to enjoy money. They have mansions. They have racehorses and they have Jags but they haven't learned how to live.'

Dan found Sylvester to be a most informative and entertaining companion all the way to London. It seemed there was nothing he did not know. He would only reveal so much, however, about his employers.

'They are the people who pay me,' he told Dan, 'and it's not fitting that I should discuss their business with outsiders.'

Dan accepted this and was quite content to absorb whatever he was told. Sylvester drained the last of the whiskey after Dan had refused his offer to try another swig. They were now in the suburbs of London.

'Yours is the next stop.'

The voice came from behind him. He turned to see the girl he had met on the boat, Patricia Dee. 'It's in a few minutes,' she said.

'Thanks.'

'Don't forget the number I gave you. Ring if you get a chance.'

'Sure,' said Dan. She waved a casual farewell and returned to her own carriage.

'Looks like you've made a conquest,' Sylvester complimented. 'She's nice and plump, the kind that tormented me when I was a student.'

'Does that mean they torment you no longer?'

'Oh they torment me all right but now I can do something about it,' Sylvester grinned.

Dan rose and took his suitcase from the overhead rack. 'I don't suppose I'll see you again,' he said.

'You will,' Sylvester assured him, 'you'll be over to the Green Shillelagh the same as the rest. Just look out for Reiceys' Volunteers.'

Dan promised he would and turned to go towards the carriage door as the train slowed down. As he was on the point of lowering the window to locate the door handle he was tapped on the shoulder. It was Sylvester O'Doherty.

'You want a sub?' he asked. The puzzlement on Dan's face brought a smile to that of the older man. 'A sub,' he repeated. 'What you look for when you're broke, a subvention till pay day.'

'You mean a loan?' Dan was still vague.

'Do you want a few bob to tide you through?'

Dan nodded and turned the handle to hide his embarrassment. Sylvester thrust something into the pocket of his overcoat. Dan mumbled a thank you and stepped on to the platform. A number of other passengers were alighting. From a window further down, Patricia Dee waved at him.

11

He waved back and looked around trying to locate the man who had been his neighbour. There was no sign of him. The train had pulled out immediately.

In a matter of moments the platform was deserted. Dan became a little apprehensive. Suppose his contact did not show up. He had the address somewhere in his suitcase but he sensed the place would be hard to find unless he met someone with a knowledge of the locality.

The only building open along the entire length of the platform was that which housed the toilets. He entered the one which invited his own gender, not daring to relinquish his suitcase. Taking off his overcoat he withdrew two crumpled pound notes from one of its pockets. He would repay Sylvester in due course. He washed his hands and face thoroughly and then combed his hair. He drew on the coat and returned to the platform. It had grown colder. There was a pricking east wind that sent a shiver through him. He had never experienced anything so bitter.

Again came the loneliness and homesickness, like a foul-tasting potion forced upon him against his will. For the first time in his life he was really alone, really away from home. The station proper had all the haunting loneliness of a poor-ly lit, unfrequented chapel. Having placed his bag under a light standard where he could keep his eye on it at all times, he proceeded determinedly to the furthest end of the plat-form. He walked quickly throwing hasty looks over his shoulder now and then to ensure the safety of his bag. As he walked he took stock of his surroundings. He passed a man-sized weighing scales and a ticket office hermetically shut-tered. He knocked faintly, hardly expecting a reply. There was none. In vain he looked for some office or store hoping to meet a human who might give him directions. From the entrance to the station he looked out on to a deserted road-way. Beyond it there were lights and a mixture of noises. He decided to wait a while before venturing forth.

The neighbour who had promised to meet him was a long-time exile of forty-odd years of age. Eddie Carey had a wife and seven children. They lived near Dan in Ballyna-haun, in a small cottage dependent on whatever he could afford to send home each week.

Dan had always liked Eddie Carey and it was to him he had thought of writing when he finally concluded that he had no future in Ballynahaun. Stating his case in the simplest possible terms he wrote that he wanted a job, anything that would make him some money. Eddie's reply had been through the medium of his wife when he sent her the weekly portion of his wages. Yes. Come on. There was work galore and the money was good. Come any time but let him know in advance so that he could meet him when he arrived. Well, he had arrived and there was no sign of Eddie. He paced the platform from one end to the other for the best part of an hour. Then, when he had almost given up hope, a small, uniformed man appeared out of the darkness carrying a lantern. Dan hailed him and the man stopped.

'Wossup mate?'

Dan told him where he wanted to go and the man listened carefully.

"'Ere's wot you want to do, lad.'

It was Dan's first full earful of Bertham English. Patiently the man with the lantern revealed the steps Dan must take if he was to reach his destination safely. The instructions were clear and simple as though it were his job to relate them regularly. Dan was amazed at his cheerfulness in that cold and lonely spot at such an hour. He thanked him.

'G'night lad,' the man said. 'Look sharp now.' With that he changed the lantern from one hand to the other and proceeded with his inspection.

Dan decided to wait another quarter of an hour before acting upon the instructions he had received. Again he paced the platform, despairing completely now of Eddie Carey's arrival. Then he saw a man with a cap silhouetted under the faint light of the lamp near the exit. It was Eddie Carey all right. There was no mistaking him. It was the way he wore his cap. It leaned altogether to one side. The exposed side of his head exhibiting a tuft of bristle which, one could see at a glance, was impossible to control.

'That you Danny?' he called softly.

'Here Eddie.'

13

Dan lifted his case and went forward hastily to take the welcoming hand of his fellow countryman.

2

ON HER arrival at Newsham General Hospital, Patricia Dee found herself on the roster for night duty. Two of the night nurses were out with flu and the only others available were students. In an emergency one or more of these might be called upon but it wasn't an emergency. Patricia was tired and not a little irritable from the long journey.

She would have the assistance of the two student nurses till her round of duty finished at nine o'clock in the morning. It was now five to twelve. Hastily she made her way from the nurses' quarters to the hospital.

She wondered how Dan Murray was faring. They all looked like that when they came first, bewildered and apprehensive but trying almightily to conceal it. No matter how hard they tried it showed like a fever or an illness to the experienced eye. She wondered why he had made such an impression on her. He wasn't in the least gallant nor was he even colourful. If anything he was a little dull although he was attractive. There was no denying that. He didn't take advantage of this undeniable asset and maybe this was why she found it so hard to get him off her mind. Whatever else he might be, he was decidedly a young man who left an impression.

In the nurses' room she checked the roster. The girl Patricia was to relieve was also Irish, Nurse Cullagan, a few years her senior from the same county but at the other end. Tricia sat down and went through the ward lists of the wing where she would be holding sway till morning. There was nothing really that would demand her constant or undivided attention apart from a few cases of pneumonia. The rest were on the mend or chronic cases who knew the ropes and never caused any difficulty. Often they provided light relief from the tedium.

At ten past twelve Nurse Cullagan appeared. She was a tall, soft-faced girl with an uneven mouth and a good figure.

'Tricia!' she exclaimed with some surprise. 'I certainly didn't expect to find you on. You don't have to you know.'

'Oh it's all right, Margo. It's only till nine. I'll get over it.'

'You sure now because I can stay on?'

'Quite sure.' Then realising that she might have sounded a trifle gruff she asked, 'How're things?'

'Nothing exciting,' Margo Cullagan said dreamily. 'There's a new intern in casualty but everybody says he's engaged.'

'That shouldn't trouble you.' Tricia said it to herself.

Both girls were products of the same background and the same type of Catholic schools – the Presentation Convents – which were often the only kind available to Irish country girls who wanted a classical secondary education and whose circumstances put boarding schools out of the question. Both had come as students to the same hospital, qualified after the prescribed period and stayed on as staff nurses. Here the similarities ended. Physically they were distinctly different. Margo Cullagan was four inches taller, and had dark, close-cropped hair. The trim uniform did not fully tone down a rebelliousness of manner and character. There was a carelessness to her which would seem to be inconsistent with her profession.

Margo had no particular ambitions beyond being a staff nurse. She enjoyed life whenever possible. When she had passed her Leaving Certificate, she could not get out of Ireland quickly enough, out of the 'sexless morass' as she called it, out of the 'dreary strictures of nunneries', a phrase she had picked up somewhere and of which she had wholeheartedly approved. She wanted escape from the unnatural physical restrictions as she had so often confided to her best friend in the convent. She was forever delighting and shocking this fascinated listener with threats and promises of what she would do as soon as she established herself in England.

Margo Cullagan was but three days in the English capital when she was bedded by her first man. He was a bus conductor from Salford, a gentleman of vast experience by the name of Henry Wilkes. He weighed Margo up at once and correctly interpreted the message in her eyes. It stated unequivocally that she couldn't wait to get started. He was a practised performer with little else in his head save the seduction of all and sundry who wore skirts. He maintained a single room in an apartment house just off Hammersmith Broadway. He believed in precautions and had an ample stock of these. It lasted a fortnight. He lost his place unexpectedly to a young intern from Dublin. But he would be remembered when all the others were forgotten. This was followed by a brief affair with a police sergeant of fifty who often visited the hospital on business. He later confided to his inspector that she went near being the death of him.

She never dated any of the Paddies she met frequently at the Green Shillelagh on Saturday nights. With these she displayed a distant and deliberately dreamy attitude which gave the impression that she was virginal and inaccessible.

For her part Patricia Dee could never countenance an affair or any sort of intimate relationship outside of marriage. She was brought up to believe that nothing really mattered apart from preserving one's chastity. She felt she would be lost, even damned forever were she to betray her upbringing. The idea of sleeping with a man before marriage appalled her.

She had many relationships with men. She had gone steadily with one and had been proposed to by another. All of them, with the slightest encouragement and without qualm would have ended forever all her claims to virginity. She accepted this as part and parcel of the nature of man. She had heard her mother refer to it often enough when she was younger. A man couldn't help being what he was. That was the way God made him the cratur and it could not be changed. You had to be eternally vigilant when dealing with a man. The reverend mother of the Presentation Convent had told Patricia's Leaving Certificate class that once a girl yielded to one man she would yield to all men and that total trollopy would follow in short order. A girl beside her had whispered, 'How the hell does she know?'

She wondered yet again about Dan Murray. A pity really that a boy like that should have to work as a labourer on a building site. Not that she looked down on builders' labourers – far from it – but the Murray boy had a refinement and gentility which had registered with her. She felt he could better himself without difficulty.

The man to whom he had been talking on the train she knew quite well by sight. He was the cashier at the Green Shillelagh. There was an air of mystery about him. It was said that he was an unfrocked priest. Others insisted that he was within days of being ordained when he ran off with another man's wife. Nobody knew where he lived nor did he frequent the Irish pubs. She had never seen him at Mass in any of the local churches but this did not mean that he had abandoned his religion. It was more likely that he went to a church where the congregation was almost entirely English.

IN THE Colorado Hotel a few blocks away Margo Cullagan sat in the dim light of the residents' lounge with a glass of gin in her hand. Her other was entwined around that of the new intern. He drank Scotch. He had waylaid her in the main corridor of the hospital and invited her out for a drink.

'Where,' she had asked innocently, 'could one get a drink at this hour of the night?'

'Oh dear,' said the new intern, 'I'm new here but there's surely a club open somewhere.'

'We might try the Colorado.' She told him she had been there on a few occasions and that it was possible to get a drink after closing time. She did not tell him that she was well known to the night porters.

The lounge of the Colorado was empty save for two elderly gentlemen who spoke in whispers at the furthest end from where they were seated. The intern whose name was Angus McLernon was a native of Alloway where his neighbours and friends proudly referred to him as a buirdly man. His only other visit to London had been two years previously when he travelled as a member of his university's boxing

18

team. He had been nervous on that occasion but now he was more nervous. He did not know how to broach the question which was uppermost in his mind or even if he should broach it at all. After all she was a staff nurse and he might easily lose a newly-acquired and valuable friend if he gave offence. He called for a second round of drinks.

'I find London very lonely,' he told her.

'It can be when you're not used to it,' Margo agreed.

He judged her reply to be sympathetic and decided to take the bull by the horns.

'The only real cure for loneliness is a beautiful girl,' he tried.

'You ought to know,' she replied. 'You're the doctor.'

When the night porter returned with the drinks, he told him to keep the change out of the pound note he handed him. He could sense Margo's approval.

After a while he spoke. 'I'd give my right arm to make love to you,' he told her.

'You mustn't say things like that,' she reproved. But she gave him a playful nudge nevertheless. There was a long silence.

'I'd dearly love to go to bed with you,' he announced limply. When she did not reply at once he asked if he had offended her.

'No,' she said, 'it's just that I'm not that kind of girl.'

'Oh,' he said flatly.

'I've never gone to bed with anyone before.' She sounded aggrieved.

'I'm sorry,' he said, 'I didn't mean to offend you.'

'You didn't. You said what was on your mind and I like a person for that. I suppose you're a Protestant?'

'Yes. A Presbyterian.'

Margo smiled to herself. She had never gone to bed with a Presbyterian.

'Why don't you ask the night porter if he has a double room with a bath?' The question caught him by surprise.

'What did you say?' he stammered uncertainly.

She repeated the question. Like an unleashed greyhound he sprang from his seat and collared the night porter who

led him to the reception desk where he signed the visitors'
book. The porter handed him a key which he pocketed nervously.

3

FOR THE first few days Dan Murray found the new job difficult. It was wholly demanding and all but exhausting. His hands suffered most. He would have liked to wear the canvas gloves which were available from the charge hand but none of the labourers on the site wore them. It was all right for the bricklayers or blocklayers but a traditional ignorance demanded that labourers should forego such luxuries. A few unfortunate men who broke with tradition were targets for jibes.

On the site was the foreman's shed with a shelter attached for the charge hands. The foreman's shed was a corrugated-iron, makeshift affair with cement blocks on the roof lest it be whipped off by the wind. It was erected on a minor elevation from which vantage point the foreman had a commanding view of the greater area of the site. The charge hands were constantly on the move, ever on the lookout for dodgers or malingerers. There were other foremen, each one supervising for a particular sub-contractor and, finally, for the main contractor there was the general foreman.

When charge hands saw something amiss they reported to the foreman. With him and with him alone lay the power to dismiss workers. As a rule he was guided by the recommendations of the charge hands. They were better informed and more in touch with the labourers. Only serious or habitual cases of negligence were reported. An experienced charge hand never reported a good man. A good man always compensated with extra labour when found out. Neither were known fist fighters reported. The site suffered them and they usually backed up the foreman by way of gratitude if there was trouble over a dismissal.

As far as Dan was concerned the foreman was God Almighty and the charge hands his avenging angels. He need not have worried. Already he had been the subject of discussion between the foreman and his immediate charge hand. He was regarded as a good man and it was axiomatic to all building sites that a good man was seldom wrong and never late.

He worked alongside his friend Eddie Carey who was a bricklayer. It was Dan's job to supply Eddie with bricks and to remix the mortar which he drew in barrows from the giant automatic mixer in the site centre. The accurate appointment of brick heaps on the scaffolds was important too. There were other minor chores all requiring a certain amount of experience but in this respect Eddie was like a father to him and his lack of know-how was no disadvantage. He was able and willing and he was possessed of considerable strength. These assets did not go unnoticed. After a few weeks he was as good as the best. It was at this stage that Eddie started to give him tips about bricklaying.

'Watch me. Watch what I do,' Eddie would say. 'There are Paddies on this site and they don't even know what we're building.' This was true of some. They were content to labour without curiosity. They never asked questions for fear of receiving a smart answer. A building site was a great place for mickey-taking and practical joking of the crudest kind. Most of the labourers were poorly educated. Most of those who were not were over-educated alcoholics and were known as builders' barristers. Others with some education worked at labouring till they found their feet. They used it as a stepping stone.

On the night of Dan Murray's arrival, Eddie Carey took him directly to the house where he boarded. It was a modest, two-storeyed affair, part of a long terrace about half a mile from Bertham Station. There was nobody awake when they arrived. They sat in the kitchen for over an hour while he unfolded all the news from home. He had some cigarettes, a gift for Eddie from his wife and a flitch of home-cured bacon from his own household. It was two in the morning when they retired. It had been decided that Dan would go to work at once. There was no future in idling around for a whole day when he might be earning good wages.

'Nobody will expect miracles from you the first day,' Eddie told him. He explained that they had just passed the foundation stage of a new block of flats being erected for the Newsham Borough Council. There would be three months work at least and after that there would be no scarcity of jobs. Everywhere the English were rebuilding. The country seemed to be on the brink of a Utopian era with new factories popping up everywhere, a flood of American investments through Marshall Aid pouring in, better housing, better schools, no unemployment and, most important, no serious competition as yet from the European industrial theatres. The prospect was a good one in every respect.

Upstairs in the boarding house there were three bedrooms and a bathroom. With Dan's suitcase in one hand, Eddie noiselessly opened the door of their bedroom. Rather than switch on the room light he allowed the door to remain ajar so that the landing light threw a faint glow about the room. Dan could distinguish two beds. One was occupied by a pair of sleeping forms. The other was empty. Eddie had explained that it would be necessary to share a bed. In spite of this, the house was regarded as one of the best digs in Bertham. In a whisper Eddie intimated that the pair in the bed were bachelor brothers named Maguire from County Cavan. They were heavy sleepers and there was no danger that they would awaken unless some loud noise intruded. They were plasterers and worked on the site. The second bedroom was occupied by four other boarders, two English men from the Midlands and two Dublin men. The Dubliners also worked on the site. They were carpenters. With a minimum of noise the pair prepared for bed.

Still in whispers Eddie explained that they were lucky to be accepted into such digs on account of their being Irish. There were not many boarding houses which would admit Irish labourers. Neither would they admit coloured workers. The proprietors of the boarding houses were not altogether to blame. In many cases the Irish labourers misconducted themselves, often beating up other boarders and even the landlords.

Eddie went on to tell Dan that there had been no trouble so far in the digs they now occupied. They were the first Irish to be accepted and it was imperative they preserve a good image. The landlady Mrs Hubbard was a decent soul who understood the needs of working men. Full board was two pounds, seventeen shillings and six pence a week. This included laundry.

Asked how he managed to gain admission to such a place Eddie confessed that it had been pure luck. He had been sharing a room with three other Irishmen, one from Kerry and two from Galway. One night there was a bad fight in which the occupants of the other rooms became involved. All were Irish. Eddie managed to keep out of it although this had proved difficult.

The upshot of the melée was that a man was kicked to death. He was an innocent man who wanted no part of the fighting, a married man with a wife and family back home somewhere in County Limerick. No one suffered for it. The police tended to look upon Irish rows as purely internal affairs and after a preliminary investigation the whole thing was quickly shelved. Eddie left the rooming house the day after the fight and searched for alternative accommodation. In a pub one night he fell into conversation with the two Midlanders who slept in the next room. He became involved in a darts foursome. The Midlanders, one from Leicester and the other from Northampton told Eddie that he spoke like a Welshman. This was true. In the south-west of Ireland many country people spoke a form of English almost identical to the English spoken in the Welsh countryside. This may have come about as a result of the importation of Welsh miners to the south-west of Ireland in the latter half of the nineteenth century.

'If,' said the Leicester man, 'you was able to make us believe you was a Welshman, why not Mrs 'Ubbard?'

They brought him to the digs and introduced him to Sid and Gillian Hubbard. She had vacancies but he would have to share a bed. They were convinced he was Welsh and after a few weeks when it transpired that none of the household had been murdered in their beds he made a clean breast of

24

his nationality. This occurred one night after he had been to the local with Sid.

'I reckon it's all right,' Sid had said. His missus accepted Eddie too. He was quiet and scrupulous.

On the morning after his arrival, Dan rose with the others at half-five. He did not feel in the least tired. All of the eight boarders sat around a large table in the kitchen. It was a warm spot with a gleaming Stanley range the showpiece. From an adjacent scullery Mrs Hubbard brought in the breakfasts. These consisted of goodly sized plates of beans and toast. In the centre of the table was a large dish of sliced bread already buttered.

Earlier he had been introduced by Eddie to Mrs Hubbard. She had welcomed him explaining that her husband had gone out to work earlier. He was employed by the corporation as a driver and was usually gone out before the others came downstairs. These welcomed him too, the Cavan men reservedly and the Dubliners with a joke about a Kerry take-over. Because he was a friend of Eddie's the Midlanders received him warmly.

As the weeks went by and the weather turned softer with the advent of April, Dan Murray began to feel his way about the site. He was working for a firm of contractors who took the bricklaying on lump. These were the Reicey Brothers. He had never met any of the legendary trio although he had caught a glimpse of one talking to the general foreman. Dan's foreman was a morose, red-haired Kerryman with a short temper and a mean streak. The general foreman, a withdrawn uncommunicative fellow, worked for the main contractor. All the bricklayers on the scene together with their mates, worked for the sub-contracting Reiceys. It was one of the Dubliners who had pointed out the Reicey brother to Dan during a tea break.

'There's Dicey,' he said, pointing to a tall well-built individual who wore a white gansey, corduroy trousers and a pair of wellingtons. Dicey's real name was Patrick. He was the only unmarried brother. He had a reputation for being a ladies' man. No doubt he was handsome in a leonine, florid sort of way but Dan felt he would run heavily to flesh the moment he took life easy.

'Guess what he's doing?' said the Dubliner.

Dan indicated with a shake of his head that he had no idea.

'He's droppin' the buckshee,' said the Dubliner knowingly. Again Dan conveyed his ignorance. The Dubliner elaborated.

'You and me we work for the Reiceys and the Reiceys pay us. See them labourers that help out the brickies like you do?'

Dan nodded.

'Them labourers don't get paid by the Reiceys. They get paid by the main contractor only the main contractor don't know the men he's paying are doing Reiceys' work. The general foreman sees to that. Whenever the Reiceys run short on labourers he obliges.'

'But suppose he gets found out?'

'General foremen don't never get found out.' The Dubliner, whose name was Willie, spoke as if he were quoting from the gospel.

'Why does he do it?' Dan asked puzzled.

'For the buckshee, the dropsy. Every week Dicey comes along and parts with maybe thirty pounds.'

'But surely,' Dan protested, 'somebody's bound to inform the contractor sooner or later?'

The Dubliner laughed. 'You want a broken jaw, maybe two broken legs, maybe get the boot between your shanks till you got no cobbles left.'

'Indeed I don't,' Dan assured him.

'Well then don't you never tell on the foreman.'

Dan nodded.

'Even if you did tell on him,' continued Willie, 'nobody would want to believe you. The general foreman's got to keep the job going. It don't matter how.'

Dan made it clear he understood perfectly.

That night after they had finished dinner Dan invited Eddie out for a walk. Not far away was a small park and it was towards this that they inclined their steps. Dan wanted to talk. There were certain things he had to know.

'There's something you want to make up your mind about shortly,' Eddie said solemnly. 'You must decide to accept what seems like dishonesty on building sites for what it is, just a way of life. If you have a rigid conscience you'll never get anywhere. You have to bend to survive no matter what outfit you join. Always remember the job's got to be finished in the time so it don't matter how.'

'All right,' Dan put it to him, 'how did you become a bricklayer?'

In the park they sat on a wooden seat. It was a pleasant evening and there was more than a cock's step in the lengthening of the days. All around them was the song of thrush, linnet and blackbird. Rhododendrons were bursting into bloom and a row of flowering cherries in front of them capped their slender trunks with clouds of curdled pinkness. Dan had seen sweeping vistas of mountain, moor and sea in his native place but of order he had seen none. He was not blind to it in Bertham Park.

'When I came first four years ago I worked as a labourer for eleven pounds a week,' Eddie opened simply. 'I worked overtime for that amount, fifty-six hours a week. Out of it I sent home six pounds a week. It cost me nearly four pounds to feed and clothe myself and pay for a share in a filthy room. I kept my eyes open. I achieved my one ambition, to be what you are now, a brickie's mate. I watched everything. I missed nothing. I was shown nothing by my master brickie because nearly all the brickies are English and like to keep the trade to themselves. Still I picked up a lot. I would arrive at the site an hour earlier in the summer mornings and I'd start laying them dry. I began to get the hang of it but I would have to be given the chance to work with real muck. That's what we brickies call mortar in case you don't know. Have you ever stacked a rick of turf?' He shot the question suddenly.

Dan nodded.

'Well that's what it's like, clamping a rick of turf, only for turf you don't need a level and a string. Still, there's not all that much between them.'

'Yes.' This from Dan impatiently. 'But how did you finish yourself off?'

'Bit of luck. One day my gaffer was bricking up a deep trench which was dug for a petrol tank. In the house there was a good looking pusher and there didn't seem to be any sign of her husband. At four o'clock she invited the gaffer in for a cup of tea.

'"Paddy," he said to me, "you finish off 'cos I'll be some time." He was in good form at the thought of the cup of tea.

'I was on my own and I could make mistakes because in an hour my work would be covered forever. That was the evening I first got the hang of it. After that it was easy. I can now lay a brick with the best. On the lump I do 600 a day. I've laid 800 for a bet. I've heard of a man who laid 1,000 in a day. It was wall work but it's the best I've heard.'

Dan nodded.

'Come on,' said Eddie, 'I'll buy you a drink.'

They walked back to the local. Eddie Carey called for two pints of beer and they sat in a corner out of the way. For a while no word passed between them but Dan sensed an excitement in himself that was foreign to him. It was possible for him to better himself, to move up in the world. The thought made him giddy for a moment. He composed himself and resolved to listen carefully to Eddie.

After the third pint Eddie confided that he was earning nearly thirty pounds a week, although it meant working overtime on Saturdays and occasional Sundays.

Dan gasped.

'Watch me. Watch me carefully and do all I tell you,' Eddie counselled, 'and you'll be earning the same in a year or two. Never give way to your emotions. If you do you'll be just another Irish buck-navvy and you'll never amount to anything. The Reicey Brothers, with the exception of Dicey, are men without emotions as anybody who worked for them will tell you. They may not be household words like the Murphy Brothers or McAlpine, but they're on their way.'

Shortly before Dan's arrival the Reiceys' workers let it be known that they were no longer to be called Reiceys' Volunteers. It sounded too like a substitute for McAlpine's Fusiliers – it was to be Reiceys' Rangers. Not everybody who worked for them had the right to the title of Ranger. At the insistence of the brothers only loyal workers qualified, simply being from Mayo was not enough. A man's county mattered not at all. What mattered was blind loyalty.

The Dubliners had just come into the pub. Dan and Eddie acknowledged their presence with waves of the hand. If it were a Saturday night they would have joined forces, but long sessions involving large rounds were out of the question on week nights. Their names, Eddie had informed Dan, were Willie Hunt and Neal Rohan. Both were married with families living in Dublin. Asked why they could not get jobs in Dublin where there was a limited amount of building going on Eddie explained that they were not real chippies, that they were not able to turn out joinery or other delicate work. They were builders' chippies all right but there were still too many first class joiners available in Dublin. Maybe when the building expanded in the Irish capital they would find jobs.

Dan was intrigued by the difference between a builders' chippie and a real chippie. It was made clear to him that high class joinery had virtually disappeared from building sites. Factories supplied whatever was wanted in that respect and all that now remained were first and second fixings such as door frames, skirting and door-hanging, stair-casing, windows and floors.

A first-class joiner was a luxury and a rarity except in a joinery works. When the Dubliners first arrived in London it was doubtful if they knew a hacksaw from a brace-and-bit but like Eddie they had looked and learned. In their case it was easier because carpentry was not the closed shop that bricklaying was.

Eddie decided they would have a last drink. This was the fourth but neither showed the slightest sign of being intoxicated.

'There are a hundred fiddles on every site,' Eddie informed him. The Reiceys according to Eddie were in the concert class.

Not long after the three brothers arrived in England Tom, who was the oldest, was made a foreman by a firm of housing contractors. Apart from possessing an innate cunning Tom Reicey sported a frank and honest face. It was the sort of face that inspired confidence, that caused wavering bank managers to reconsider and the sort that was to drag Tom Reicey from the bottom to the top in a few short years. When the firm's general foreman died suddenly on the site the directors were in a dilemma. If they were to advertise for a general foreman valuable time would be lost. They looked over the likely candidates in their employ. Tom Reicey was the least experienced but he impressed the directors more than any of the others. They pondered and they argued. The managing director consulted his wife. Discreetly and, without giving the impression that she was doing so, she carefully took stock of the likely candidates when they came to the office seeking directions after the unexpected death. Tom Reicey left an indelible impression. Of all the candidates he was the only one who guessed why she was there. His visit to the office was to suggest that they hire a general foreman immediately.

'What's the hurry?' she had asked her husband at the time. It was Tom who answered the question.

'Because missus,' said he, 'you must have a boss man on a site. The men know when there's no leadership and you can see the effects in their work. There's no one to crack the whip. Honestly sir,' he addressed himself to the managing director, 'I'd rather jack up than be held responsible for mistakes that might happen. When there's no cat the mice will dance.'

Ten minutes later he was asked if he would be willing to act as general foreman in a temporary capacity.

Eddie Carey worked as a labourer on the same site. As the houses neared completion Tom Reicey pulled off a coup which was to be the first of many brilliant money-making gambits. There was a touch of genius about his maiden fiddle. At a corner of the site was a huge mound of topsoil which had been removed from the surface before the sinking of the foundations.

Starting at six o'clock of a Saturday evening Tom Reicey made a canvass of the estate. He took Eddie with him, not that Eddie had any function in what followed. Maybe it was that Reicey considered a delegation of two to be more impressive than a delegation of one. The first door on which he knocked was opened by the man of the house. Reicey explained that the excellent topsoil from the site was to be removed early during the following week. It had been bought in bulk by a market gardener from Croydon. It was none of his business but he felt that the gardener could be prevailed upon to sell again at a modest profit. It would be ideally suited to the front lawns and back gardens of the estate. He figured it could be delivered at five pounds per five ton truckload. Two truckloads per house would be sufficient to cover the back and front areas involved. He went from house to house with the same proposition, always taking infinite care to disclose that it meant nothing to him but it would be a pity to see the soil go. There was no immediate hurry. He would call again on Monday. Unfortunately it would have to be cash on the line. No need to make up their minds at once.

The new householders had grown to like him. His rough competence and open countenance gave the impression that here was an honest, reliable man if ever there was one.

His suggestion was well received all round. Everybody was agreed. On the following Monday he called again and collected ten pounds each from the 104 houses. He personally supervised the unloading of the trucks which were company property. Then he pulled a dozer off the road-building and saw to it that the mounds of earth were properly spread. This was not part of the bargain and he received a large number of cash gifts from grateful householders.

The removal and distribution of the earth was done under the eyes of the company's senior engineer. As far as he was concerned nothing underhand was being perpetrated. The contract clearly stated that the topsoil was to be replaced when the houses were erected. He would have no way of knowing that the foreman with the honest face had made house to house calls on Saturday night and that he subsequently succeeded in criminally talking 104 ratepayers out of one thousand and forty pounds not to mention the sixty-six pounds and fifteen shillings in gifts.

They finished their drinks and walked slowly homeward. Dan was deep in thought. It was a matter of taking one's chances and remembering that there was no immediate hurry. When he spoke it was to ask another question.

'How much did Tom Reicey give you?'

'He gave me fifty pounds and told me to go and have a drink.'

'That was decent of him.'

'If you knew him like I did you'd mean that. Tom Reicey looks after his own whatever else.'

Certainly Tom held sway over his Mayo brethren but, if he did, he exacted the same loyalty from other counties. He was their guarantor, their father figure. He knew the highups in the police force. Didn't he go on fishing holidays back to his native Mayo with chief superintendents and once with a member of parliament! When the Black Marias gathered their weekend harvests of drunken Paddies and deposited them in a variety of London jails, the men who worked for the Reiceys were the first to be released.

Tom Reicey could squeeze work out of a man far beyond that man's normal capacity. The more ignorant the navvy the easier it was to work him into an early grave. Eddie went on to tell Dan that he was once digging foundations for one of Tom Reicey's first independent contracts. Digging with him was another Kerryman and in the next trench were two Mayo men. His fellow Kerryman was illiterate. The pair from Mayo were no better. At the end of the first day Tom Reicey surveyed the work done by both pairs.

'Christ Almighty,' he roared, 'the Mayo boys has the Kerry bucks dug out of it.'

Eddie's mate took this to heart and was determined that the honour of Kerry should not be besmirched a second time. The following day he dug like a man demented. He did more work in ten hours than a normal man would do in three days.

He did not last long but what did it matter? There were others to take his place. Ireland was a brimming labour pool.

4

SYLVESTER O'DOHERTY lay awake. All his efforts to sleep had for some hours now been thwarted by his troubled thoughts. The woman with whom he shared the bed in his twin-roomed flat slept soundly. She breathed gently and evenly and although she stirred occasionally he could tell she was fast asleep. Sylvester was worried. He had stayed on that evening an extra two hours in the offices of Reicey Brothers, poring over a particular ledger. All the other account books, and there were many, were of the sort that are commended by inspectors of taxes. They were models of book-keeping, with concise, neat entries never overflowing. Everything was readily acceptable even to the most critical eye. All of these ledgers could withstand any sort of analysis, except the ledger which prevented him from joining his fair companion in sleep.

In this problematic book was an account of daily, weekly and monthly payments to one Sylvester O'Doherty. The total ran into thousands. In one week alone in July 1950 there were 25 different payments, each of twenty pounds. This money was supposedly being paid by the said Sylvester O'Doherty to migrant labourers, fleeting craftsmen who did unusual work, specially hired emergency men, here today and gone tomorrow and to assorted roughs and toughs who worked short-term and strictly for danger money. The cheques were signed by two of the three Reicey brothers. As soon as he was handed the cheques Sylvester went straight to the bank where he cashed them. It was then that the money was allegedly paid over to the mysterious, unnamed workers. What happened was that when Sylvester returned from the bank he went directly to the office of Tom Reicey and handed over the cash.

He was never given a receipt and why should he be

33

given one? The cheques were given to him by the Reiceys. It was their money, their concern. He was a humble clerk. It wasn't that he hadn't asked for a receipt. The first time it happened he said to Tom: 'Don't you think it would be better if you gave me a receipt for that?'

'Look now Sylvie,' Tom Reicey was the soul of patience. 'As far as the tax people are concerned you paid this money to casual workers. So why should I give you a receipt?'

'I know, I know,' Sylvester was patient too. 'But suppose the tax people get suspicious. I'll be in serious trouble. If I had a receipt for the money everything would be all right.'

'Well I can't give you one because if I did I'd be in trouble. You just stick to your books Sylvie. Do what you're told and let me worry about the tax people. Why don't you make out receipts yourself?'

'What sort of receipts?' The suspicion in his tone came across clearly.

Tom Reicey was most explicit in his reply. He spoke like a teacher who is trying to impress a simple solution on a dull pupil. 'Receipts from the workers you're paying with the cheque I gave you.'

'You want me to forge receipts?'

'Now I never said that Sylvie. It was you who used the word "forge".'

'Is that what you want me to do then?'

'You suit yourself. You're the accountant.'

'It can't be done.'

'Why not?'

It was now Sylvester's turn to be explicit. He spoke slowly, stressing every word. 'Because I would have to forge too many names and the similarities in the writing would be easy to spot.'

'I see,' said Tom Reicey thoughtfully. 'I'll tell you what Sylvie. You just forget about it for the present. If anybody asks you, just say you paid the money to my workers and they refused to give you receipts. That way you'll be blameless. Off you go now like a good man.'

Uneasily Sylvester turned over on his side. The girl's hair shone bright under the yellow beams from the street

34

light. Of late the invisible force of labourers and craftsmen was increasing. Sooner or later somebody would be called to account.

The buckshee or dropsy money was different. The tax inspectors were forced to concede that it was sometimes necessary if a job was to be completed in time. As long as it wasn't overdone they allowed it to pass. They would have no idea of the other ways the buckshee benefited the Reiceys. For instance, a foreman in another company might divert several loads of high quality gravel to a Reicey site. It paid dividends in earnest when the Reiceys had the sub-contract for all the brickwork on a site. A clever general foreman might see to it that free casual labour was always available from the main contractors' work force. Expensive materials which could cut down profits might be available also. There were a thousand ways in which a general foreman could be helpful.

Sylvester O'Doherty rose silently and went to the window. He looked down into the deserted dimly-lit street. He wore nothing. 'If mother could see me now,' he thought. He turned, looked at the form in the bed and smiled. Sandra Felby was ten years his junior. They had been to bed before. She was, in fact, one of the typists in the office. She would have liked to get married but Sylvester had no time for anything so conclusive. She hailed originally from Luton where her father ran a small greengrocery.

Every time they slept together she would ask him if he still held the same views about marriage. At first he blamed his religion. Uncomprehending she sought an explanation. He told her that it was the *Ne Temere* decree. This seemed to satisfy her but after a while she asked what it meant. He told her it was a Papal decree binding on all Catholics who married partners of a different persuasion. They were bound to raise the issue of such a liaison in the true faith, to wit, the Catholic faith.

'But it don't matter,' she said.

'No,' Sylvester had responded nobly. 'It wouldn't be right to ask you to do such a thing. We'll just have to go on the way we are.'

35

SYLVESTER O'DOHERTY was an only child. At eighteen he had entered Maynooth College direct from his local seminary to study for the priesthood. He was born in Ballyrooney in County Mayo in the year 1921, the only issue of Walter and Hannah O'Doherty. Both parents were teachers in Ballyrooney National School, his father principal of the boys' division and his mother principal of the girls'. The outlook of both parents was narrow in the extreme. They were strict Catholics and very early on when he was at his most impressionable, his mother planted the seeds of a vocation in his young mind. Both parents were daily Mass-goers and receivers of Holy Communion. It was difficult not to be holy in such a household.

In 1932 when Sylvester was eleven, Eamon de Valera came into power in the then Irish Free State. The same year saw the beginning of the economic war with England. In America Franklin Delano Roosevelt was elected president but at home in Ballyrooney there was to be a spectacular happening which would help propel Sylvester into the priesthood more effectively than all his mother's prayers.

In the month of January their housekeeper died. His mother advertised in the local paper for a replacement and from a host of applications, because of wholesale unemployment at the time, selected a girl who had been trained as a cook in a convent in Dublin. She had excellent references and after a month, when they were growing used to her, Hannah O'Doherty decided that she had chosen wisely.

On the evening of 15 August the inevitable happened. Sylvester's father not without premeditation suddenly found himself making advances to the housekeeper while mother and son were on a visit to the seaside. He had complained of a headache and insisted that they go without him. The girl had come into his study, polishing and dusting. Having long since been denied comprehensive intercourse by his over-religious wife he simply was not proof against the quivering, barely-concealed buttocks of the younger woman. She resisted at first but his pleading was so woebegone and distraught that she relented.

Thereafter whenever an opportunity presented itself

they had a session of lovemaking. Within such limited confines it was almost certain that they would be caught sooner or later.

Shortly before the Christmas break Walter O'Doherty complained of having a head cold. His wife advised him to stay in bed. Taking Sylvester's hand she set out for the school which was less than two hundred yards from the house. At eleven o'clock Hannah sent Sylvester home for a book which she had forgotten and from which she had promised the children she would read a Christmas story.

When he opened the door of his father's room he was bewildered by the animal noises and the profusion of white flesh. He cried out in horror. He ran from the house at once and back to the school where he handed his mother the story book.

He never told his mother but the exposition he had witnessed alienated him from his father until that parent was on his deathbed.

From where he stood near the window Sylvester could see the sky lightening towards the east. It would be dawn in a few more minutes. 'The poor oul' bastard,' he said aloud. Walter O'Doherty died when his only son was fifteen years of age. Relations between them had been strained despite every effort by Walter to restore the boy's former regard for him. Sylvester rued the fact that he had been too young to forgive or to understand.

Conscience-stricken, Walter had confessed to his wife a few days after his son had surprised him. She dismissed the housekeeper at once and was curiously sympathetic to him for the remainder of his life. It was as if she were carrying his weakness on her back, a back buttressed by the steel of ten thousand novenas.

It was this experience that strengthened Sylvester's resolve to be ordained a priest. There was in him a new hunger to belong to something that was above and beyond things carnal. He believed that the priesthood was the answer. His first year in Maynooth was a relatively contented one. His second year was different. When he came home for the Christmas holidays his mother suggested that he enjoy himself. She made sure that he was invited to the various Christmas parties and Wren dances.

It was at one such occasion that he met Rita Cuddy. She was on holiday from Dublin and was staying with an aunt, a sister of her mother's who was childless and a widow. Rita was an attractive girl of twenty-five and was not reserved or restrained with him the way the local girls were.

'I like you,' she had said at once. 'You're pale and interesting.' She had made him laugh at once without difficulty. They spent the remainder of the holidays in each other's company.

Back at Maynooth he missed her terribly. There was no Easter vacation and he went through the tortures of the truly smitten waiting for the summer to come around. Towards the end of term his confessor took him to one side and asked if all was well, if there was anything he would like to talk over. He stiffly denied that he might be floundering in any morass of uncertainty or that he might be demoralised by any external obsession.

The reality was that he could not wait to get out of the college to be reunited with the object of his dreams. Instead of going home when the holidays came round, he went to Dublin. He wrote to his mother and explained that he wanted to do a paper on a deceased bishop of the diocese and that it would simplify matters if he could encamp himself in the National Library. He went first to the main office of the Bank of Ireland where, after identifying himself, he withdrew a sum of one hundred pounds from an inheritance of five hundred pounds willed to him by his father. He went to a popular hotel where he booked a room overlooking the Liffey.

Rita worked in a solicitor's office on the other side of the river. At six o'clock when she emerged from her place of employment he was waiting. She was only mildly surprised.

'Oh, it's you,' she said.

They stood talking a while, he indecisive, she impatient. At length she told him she was hungry and had to go home for supper. She did not invite him to accompany her. Despairingly, he suggested they have dinner somewhere.

'I'd love to,' she laughed, her whole manner changing.

During the following weeks their habits followed a fixed pattern. There would be dinner after she finished work followed by a visit to a cinema or the theatre.

During all this time he corresponded regularly with his mother, reporting on the progress of the non-existant paper. She advised him against touching the inheritance his father had left him and sent some money. The weeks dragged into a month until one morning he received a short letter from his mother telling him to come home, that if the paper wasn't finished he was to abandon it.

He replied that the paper was almost complete. He also sent a request for more money. She refused. That night he acquainted Rita with his dilemma. She advised him to go home.

'Will you come with me?' he begged.

'That would be out of the question,' she answered curtly.

'Why?' he had asked in amazement.

'You forget I have a job. I can't just walk out.'

'Let's get married,' he said in a sudden do or die effort to salvage their romance. He thought this was what she wanted. She shook her head and sighed.

'You're going to be a priest,' she said.

'No I'm not,' he made it sound adamant. She looked in his face and knew he meant it.

'Now will you marry me?' he asked.

'You haven't got a job,' she said.

For a long time he pleaded with her but his entreaties only strengthened her determination to refuse him. In the end he knew it was no good. Later she complained of a violent headache and begged to be allowed go home. He could hardly say no. The next evening she did not appear. A letter awaited him when he returned to the hotel.

Dear Sylvie,

There is no use in putting it off any longer. I will not be seeing you again. It is over between us. Do not try to contact me here at my home as my mother and father would only savage you should you call. Do not call to my place of work again. I would not like it. I mean I would not like it. You should go home at once to your mother. It is not fair to her. You are the only person she has.

SYLVESTER TURNED from the window to find Sandra sitting up in the bed.

'A penny for your thoughts,' she said. He located his trousers, fumbled in the pockets for cigarettes and handed her one. He lit them both and told her he had been thinking of home.

'Your mother?'

'Yes,' he said, 'and others, but principally my mother.'

He sat on the edge of the bed.

'In the Midland Bank,' he told her, 'there is a sum to my credit of thirteen hundred pounds. Would you mind if I redeposited it in your name?'

'I wouldn't mind,' she said.

'You won't draw it out and go on a spree?'

'Not unless you come along.'

'When the time is opportune, I'll put it back in my own name again.'

'Why are you doing this?'

'I want to see if you are trustworthy.'

She drew on her cigarette. 'Are you in some kind of trouble?'

'No.'

They lay in bed watching the day break. His mind went back to the time immediately after Rita Cuddy's rejection of him. On his way back home in the train he resolved that he would not go back to Maynooth. Telling his mother would be the hardest part. That night they sat together in the sitting-room listening to the radio. Steeling himself he rose and reduced the volume.

'Don't you like it?' she asked.

'There's something you'd better know,' he declared. He could not fail to notice the mounting alarm which started to register on her face. He had the feeling that she somehow anticipated the dreadful disclosure he was about to make.

'I'm leaving Maynooth.'

'Jesus, Mary and Joseph!' she cried out. 'Say you're not serious.'

'I'm serious.'

'But what about me? The neighbours?'

'I owe the neighbours nothing. I'm sorry about you.' He turned his back to her relieved that the terrible pronouncement had been made.

'We'll never live it down. We'll be the talk of the country.' His mother's voice was high pitched now. 'Oh sweet Jesus, this is a nice answer to a mother's prayers. A spoiled priest after my years of devotion.'

'I'm sorry Mother.'

She was suddenly silent. After a while she tried a different approach. 'I daresay there's no student didn't say the same thing some time or other. I knew men that left and went back again. Those that leave for good are never the same. They never know a moment's happiness till the day they die. It's flying in the face of God. Put all thoughts of leaving from your mind this minute. I swear to you it will be the death of me if you leave. The mortification and the shame of it would put me in the grave years before my time.'

'You might as well get used to it, Mother. My mind is made up. I'm not going to be a priest.'

The argument swung back and forth for an hour. She refused to concede. In bed that night he slept soundly. Nothing mattered now that he had told her. It was all over. He was free.

His reckoning, however, did not include his mother's unwavering faith. There was a visit the very next day from Father Slater the parish priest. After two hours of intense effort Slater left in deep disappointment. Two days later, the bishop's chauffeur-driven car drew up outside the door. Sylvester's first impulse was to make a dash for the hills. On second thoughts he decided to endure it. It would be a small sufferance for the freedom that was sure to follow once this final fence was cleared. His mother stayed on in the room while the bishop told Sylvester of his own early doubts while a student. There was a note of levity in the beginning,

41

this to suggest that Sylvester's change of course was no more than a passing whim. Turning to Hannah O'Doherty, he declared that he was gasping for a cup of tea. She took the hint. Alone now the bishop opened in a serious vein.

'I have seen mothers pine away after hearing that their sons were abandoning their vocations. I have seen them wilt and wither and ultimately decay. I hope you realise you may be signing the death warrant of your own Mother.'

'I have no vocation, my Lord.'

'Don't say that. How can you be sure?' The bishop looked towards the ceiling. 'Let the man above decide,' he said persuasively. 'You had a vocation when you started out. You may think it's gone now but believe me my son you are only divorced from it temporarily.'

The bishop was proving to be a tougher adversary than his mother.

'God called you once. You must not expect that your creator will call again. One summons from the Almighty should be command enough for a lifetime. To be beckoned once by God should convince any man that his vocation is enduring beyond human comprehension.' The bishop was cantering on his favourite course. In vain Sylvester tried to interrupt. The prelate raised a hand ablaze with sapphire.

'My son, I now want you to forget you ever thought of leaving. It's purely a matter of organising your mind and searching for the strength to carry through in prayer.'

'My Lord!' Sylvester had to shout to claim the bishop's attention. 'My Lord, I am finished with Maynooth. Nothing anybody says or does will ever make me return. I have no vocation.'

The bishop pretended he had not heard. When Hannah entered with a tray he was still holding forth about the power of prayer. She stood still, nodding her approval. These were the things she had wanted to say but could not.

The final result of the bishop's call was that Sylvester promised to reconsider, to pray daily for the strengthening of his vocation and to receive the Blessed Eucharist each morning.

This was what he promised.

What he did was to call old Mrs Reicey who lived at the westernmost bounds of Ballyrooney parish. From her he received the address of her son, Tom, who was reputed to be a big contractor in London. Next, he crammed into a suitcase a few shirts, an extra suit and a half dozen books. He wrote a letter to his mother in which he explained that he would not be coerced into the priesthood, that he would only make a bad priest.

In London he had no bother locating Tom Reicey. Sure, Tom could use him. Actually he was just what Tom wanted, an educated man to do the paper work and look after the books. The firm was small in those days, just getting off the ground. Tom Reicey was grinning when Sylvester left him. It was incredible. From now on he would have Master O'Doherty's only son working for him, for Tom Reicey who left Ballyrooney National School in the fifth book, Tom Reicey to whom Sylvester's high and mighty mother would not bid the time of day the last time he was home to see his own mother. On his payroll from now on would be the son of the man and woman who gave him the only education he had ever received.

It was a quare turn in the world. He grinned savagely. Did he ever dream and he going to school in Ballyrooney, that things would turn out the way they did?

5

DAN IMPROVED steadily at his work. Eddie had encouraged him to lay bricks whenever the foreman was out of sight. He was still far from understanding the finer points of pointing, plumbing and bedding. Only with the aid of experience would he master these aspects of the trade. Eddie already had a substantial sum saved. He was also generous with his weekly contribution to his wife. His long-term plan was to buy a modest farm in Ballynahaun. The present time was inappropriate for a number of reasons.

Many of his contemporaries were living with women or at least having part-time affairs unknown to their wives. Licentous and mortally sinful in Ireland, no notice whatsoever was taken of it in England. If Irish women prayed for the moral welfare of their menfolk they also prayed for McAlpine, for the Murphy Brothers and the Reiceys and for the other big contractors who never refused a good man a day's work. In England a man in search of a job was never asked about his religion. Nobody knew or cared about his politics.

Consequently, the wives and mothers of Irish emigrants had reason to be grateful. There was the story of a woman in West Kerry who wrote to her son for a photograph of Tom Reicey. She wanted it to hang between pictures of the Sacred Heart and the Last Supper. Her five sons, from money earned as labourers with Reiceys were able to save enough in ten years to buy a farm apiece.

After five weeks on the site Dan Murray prevailed on Eddie Carey to take a half day off on Saturday. They both needed new outfits. Burtons provided the suits, light greys, shimmering, creased and spotless.

In another shop they purchased shoes and socks, in another shirts and ties. Laden with their purchases they took a bus home for supper. It was the first Saturday they had

44

taken off since Dan's arrival. Saturday was time and a half and for men who were unused to money it would have been an outlandish extravagance to waste it. Later that night Dan would make his first visit to the Green Shillelagh. His guides would be his fellow-boarders, the Maguire brothers from Cavan.

The brothers never missed a Saturday night. It was the highlight of their week, the most important happening in their social calendars apart from the annual trip home. In preparation for the occasion they would start to get ready at least an hour before. In the bathroom upstairs they would bathe so thoroughly that they literally shone when the ablutions were over. Wearing trousers and no more they would shine their precious low shoes till they gleamed under the light of the scullery bulb. It was a time in rural Ireland when low shoes were used only for dancing or Mass-going or maybe to answer a summons in court. It was considered a profanity to wear them at work.

When the shoes were polished to the satisfaction of both Maguires they placed them in a corner of the scullery and went upstairs to don their best suits and comb their hair. Dawdling and talking would come after. They would stand around, hands in pockets, admiring each other and proud of each other. It was the best part of their night-out. Neither drank but they agreed to go along to a pub with Dan.

In the new suit Dan looked like one of Burton's models.

'By God,' Eddie Carey said to him, 'if I didn't know you I would say you were somebody else.'

Gillian Hubbard was another to be impressed. She made him turn round to see if he looked all right from the back. The Dubliners who had seen the suit earlier had expressed their admiration and the pair from the Midlands, never given to excess talk, cooed their approval earnestly.

When the Maguires decided it was time to go, Eddie came as far as the front door of the digs with them. 'Look out for yourself,' he said to Dan.

They took a bus into the city centre and from there to Hammersmith. The pub they selected was crowded and, after one drink, they tried another. Dan was surprised to hear so many Irish accents. The Maguires drank glasses of orange juice. Dan drank pints of beer. At half-nine after three drinks each, they decided it was time to go to the dance-hall. It was a short bus trip from where they were but it was agreed that a walk wouldn't do them any harm.

The Green Shillelagh had once been a garage but the owners closed it during the early years of the war. It was sold cheaply to the Reicey brothers after a few years of closure. Its conversion to a dance-hall had been an easy matter and it was an immediate success because around Hammersmith there were Irish boys and girls in their thousands, occupying rooms and small flats. In the Catholic churches of the district the priests would announce forthcoming dances from the pulpit because they were being run by Irish Catholics. In addition, most of the curates and many of the parish priests in London were Irish by birth or descent. Only those parishes which had Irish clubs of their own with small dance-halls attached failed to advertise the Shillelagh dances.

The hall was only partly full when they arrived. Turlough, the older of the Maguire Brothers, purchased the tickets. They cost four shillings each. In the box-office Dan caught a glimpse of Sylvester O'Doherty. He was assisted by a girl. He looked vastly different from the individual Dan had met on the Fishguard train. He was cleanly shaven and his sparse hair was combed carefully. He wore a neat blue pinstripe suit. Not only did he conduct himself as if he were a cut above his customers he also looked it. He did not lift his head when he handed over the tickets.

At the entrance their tickets were collected by the burliest doorman Dan had ever seen. He looked almost freakish with his immense barrel chest and long arms. He had close-cropped hair and a carefully trimmed moustache.

'There's a one,' Turlough Maguire whispered, 'I'd prefer not to meet on a dark road.'

'Or any kind of a road,' Dan whispered back.

'He's an ex-commando,' Shay, the younger of the Maguire brothers, informed Dan when they were safely past. 'They say if he wanted he could kill you with a blow of the hand.'

In the hall a band played. It consisted of a drummer, a pianist, an accordionist and a saxophonist. There were no more than twenty couples on the floor. Most of these were made up of girls.

'It'll be lively enough soon,' Shay Maguire predicted.

Dan excused himself a moment while the brothers took seats. He returned the way he came and addressed himself to the doorman.

'I want to see the man in the office,' he said. The doorman without a word weighed him up from head to toe finally concluding that he meant no harm. He advised Dan to knock on the door and wait. Dan did so. It was opened at once by the girl.

'Yes?' she asked.

'I want to see Mr O'Doherty,' Dan informed her.

'He's busy just now,' the girl replied. She assumed Dan was displeased with what was on offer inside and wanted his money back. It happened all the time.

'All I want him for is to return some money I owe him,' Dan explained.

'Wait there,' she ordered curtly. In the space of a few moments Sylvester came to the door. At first he failed to recognise Dan. When he did he smiled.

'Ah!' he exclaimed. 'It's you is it? So you've come to pay me back.'

Dan nodded.

'Come in. Come in,' Sylvester invited.

Dan followed him into the small office. 'Maybe you're busy,' he said.

'I'm never too busy to collect a debt.' He accepted the two pounds which Dan handed him and produced two bottles of beer from a crate covered by a mackintosh in the corner. 'We don't start to get busy,' he confided, 'till they get kicked out of the pubs. Then we get too bloody busy. They all come at the same time like a flock of rooks before nightfall and just as noisy. This you might say is the calm before the storm but tell me about yourself. How are things with you?'

In a few sentences Dan told him about his digs and his job with the Reicey Brothers.

'What I prophesied for you came true. Here you are at the Green Shillelagh in spite of my warning.'

'It doesn't seem too bad.'

'It isn't really but it could be. That's the unpredictable part. Fortunately we haven't had a bad scrap in months. Nothing's likely to happen inside with old Crazy Horse around.'

'You mean the doorman?'

'We call him a chucker-out. The Paddies christened him Crazy Horse because of his close-cropped head and after he lost his temper one night. There hasn't been a real row since then. It's when you get outside afterwards the trouble starts and believe me my friend if you're looking for it you'll get it. Even if you aren't looking for it you're likely to get it unless you look out for yourself.'

Sylvester handed him a second bottle of beer.

'Maybe I should go,' Dan said.

'What's your hurry? Wait a few minutes and have a free peek at your fellow-countrymen. You'll be all the better for it. This here is Tilly Atkins. Her mother is Irish. Tilly, say hello to Dan Murray.'

The girl nodded politely.

'The chucker's real name is Dick Daly. He's from Mayo but from which part I never found out.'

Sylvester pulled the door open. 'Dick I want you to meet a friend of mine. This is Dan Murray.' From where he stood with his hands behind his back Dick Daly nodded inscrutably. Sylvester closed the door.

'Does he ever smile?' Dan asked.

'Not since his wife ran away with a house painter from Aldershot. He's a decent type of man, believe me, too bloody decent. He could be making a packet on the side flogging pass-outs but he'd sooner die than do anything dishonest.

48

The sad thing is that the Reiceys will never pat him on the back for it. Here comes the first of the deprived.'

'Deprived?'

'Deprived of his seat in some pub, expelled by the management,' Sylvester explained, pointing to a youth of no more than eighteen who was staggering drunkenly towards the ticket office. There were traces of vomit on the lapels of his coat but he would, more than likely, notice these when he went to the toilet which was the first place he would visit when he entered the hall. His eyes were somewhat glazed. He looked with considerable perplexity and with a fully opened mouth at Tilly Atkins.

'Four shillings please.' She made her voice sound metallic.

He reeled a little and blinked his eyes. After a search he produced a ten shilling note. She snatched it and handed him his ticket and change. 'Move along now please!' The same metallic tone but it was a tone which penetrated the layers of drunken fogginess and succeeded in temporarily unglazing the eyes of the youth.

'You might say,' Sylvester said with a rueful shake of his head, 'that he is the shape of things to come.'

'Isn't he too drunk to be admitted?' Dan asked with some alarm as the youth, holding on to the wall, made his way to the main entrance.

'He is,' Sylvester said, 'but if I was to refuse him the Reiceys would want to know why. Worse still his brothers would want to know why.'

'His brothers?'

'Yes. There are four of them by the name of Morrikan and by comparison with any one of the other three, our drunken friend is nothing but a runt. He fulfils a role, however. His brothers will want a row later on and he's the bait. If somebody belts him unwittingly or bumps into him accidentally during a dance or pushes him out of the way in annoyance he'll tell his brothers who'll beat the bejasus out of the innocent or innocents responsible. These innocents are almost always new boys who don't know the ropes, chaps not unlike youself. It's part of their education, and you must remember that in any country a thorough and all-embracing education is somewhat expensive.'

From time to time taxis drew up and disgorged several drunken revellers at a time. Then suddenly the business slackened. There were stragglers but the big rush was over. Sylvester shook hands with Dan and told him he was welcome to visit the office at any time.

In the hall which was now full Dan explained to the Maguires that he had gone to see a friend. He sat with them a while, watching the dancing couples. Near the door the crowd was at its densest. Many would stand there for the night content to watch or spot form as the dancing couples passed by. Shay Maguire whispered into his ear. He indicated a beautiful red-haired girl who stood aloof from all the others.

'See her!' Shay said. Dan nodded. 'If you dance with her you'll get beat up.'

'Oh!' Dan exclaimed. 'By whom?'

'By her boyfriend,' Shay whispered. 'That's him over there.' Shay nodded his head in the direction of a powerfully made man at the other side of the hall. 'He don't like nobody to dance with her.'

Dan was beginning to understand. To pass through this sort of set-up peacefully it was imperative to learn the rules and, having learned them, to abide by them. Trying to understand them would be a waste of time. Every community has its taboos. The ones that confronted the newcomer to the Green Shillelagh had nothing to do with tradition or antiquity. They were still in a state of evolution. A stronger force could change or influence the existing ones; the only force capable of exercising such an influence was violence. A tall dark-haired attractive girl, different from the others, waltzed by in the arms of a young man who never took his eyes off her face. She pretended not to notice.

'Who's she?' Dan asked.

'She's from Newsham General,' Shay informed him. 'She's a nurse. I think she comes originally from Wexford.'

Dan followed her movements with interest. She was quite a beautiful girl in a tragic sort of way. He thought of a print of the Madonna which hung over the big double bed in his mother's room.

'Her name is Margo Cullagan,' Turlough put in, 'but you're wasting your time because she has never left the hall in the company of a man.'

'That's true,' Shay added. 'On the stroke of twelve she'll walk out that door either with another girl or on her lonesome. You watch for it and you'll see.'

The girl still danced dreamily. Her partner addressed her with considerable animation to no effect. She took not the least notice of him. Her face showed no emotion of any kind save complete indifference. Dan was puzzled.

'Why does she come here?' he asked Turlough.

'Because she's Irish the same as you and me,' he answered. 'Where else would she go if it wasn't here?'

No, Dan thought. There has to be more to it than that. He decided he would dance with her at the first opportunity. It presented itself almost at once. Two strapping, red-faced girls, obviously sisters, came straight from the ladies' cloakroom and sat with the Maguires. They were introduced to Dan as Rose and Bridie Mulvanney from County Leitrim. It was at once evident that there was an understanding between the brothers and sisters. They swapped questions about each other's families and seemed relieved to have met.

When the band started to play the Maguires claimed the sisters. Dan saw that Margo Cullagan was standing alone only a few yards away. At a respectful distance stood a number of young men. They were hesitant. Dan approached and invited her on to the floor. Without a word she offered him her outstretched hands. He held her lightly at arm's length trying not to start on an erratic course. They moved easily around the hall, Dan not saying a word. She had not even looked at him. She wore that dreamy faraway look which seemed to captivate so many of her admirers. When, after several rounds of the hall, Dan made no attempt to start a conversation she cast a glance at him. 'You're new here.'

'Yes.' They put several more circuits behind them before she spoke again.

'Where do you work?' She put the question as if she did not care whether it was answered or not.

'On the site at Bertham.'

'Oh there,' she said.

'Yes,' he answered. The ensuing silence lasted till the dance was almost over.

'Tell me,' she asked, 'are you always as talkative as this?'

'Always,' he said. She took a longer look at him and smiled.

'Spare another dance for me.' There was no coyness in the way she asked nor could it be interpreted that she was bestowing a favour on him. As Dan understood it she was merely enjoying herself. He was part of that enjoyment. Deep down he felt that she was waiting for something to happen or for someone to arrive. For all her dreaminess and detachment there were times when she cast a glance in the direction of the entrance. He couldn't be sure of this, but why else should she come, constantly as he was told, to a dance-hall like the Shillelagh when, to the most inexperienced eye, she belonged elsewhere.

When the dance resumed Dan stood at the back of the hall with a throng of other spectators, all male and all unwilling to take the floor. Dancing awkwardly with a partner who looked as if she might be twice his age was the drunken youth, the youngest of the Morrikan brothers. He was a comic spectacle but then Dan remembered what Sylvester had told him and the laughter died on his lips. He was quick to notice that nobody else was laughing. The youth stumbled and bumped into numerous other couples. He contrived with a rolling, swaying movement, in which he utilised the weight of his heavier partner, to knock another couple to the floor. These were a gangly youth hardly out of his teens and a young girl of the same age. When the gangly youth recovered himself he helped his partner to her feet and looked about him belligerently. The youngest Morrikan was laughing loudly, holding on to his sides and pointing a wagging finger at the youth who had risen from the floor.

Morrikan stuck out a length of tongue and slapped his chest in an effort to control his laughter. The gangly youth looked about him unresolved. He didn't know whether to treat the matter as a joke or to have it out with his tormentor. His girlfriend decided for him when she pouted for his pity and produced the semblance of a tear in one of her dark brown eyes.

Morrikan laughed all the louder and suddenly seizing his partner in a manner which wasn't in the least drunken danced her away from the scene.

Dan found himself dancing with Margo a second time. It hadn't been easy to isolate her. She was always in demand. She had given him the advantage over several others for as soon as he started to walk towards her, she moved towards him.

'You're not a bad dancer,' she told him after a while. 'You want to hold your partner a little less tightly, as if she were a delicate article like a woman.'

Dan nodded. He held her less tightly.

'That's more like it,' she said.

Dan was enjoying himself immensely. Of all the girls he had ever danced with this demurest and dreamiest of creatures was the easiest by far to look at. Then suddenly for no reason that he could immediately fathom, he felt her body go tense. He found himself being steered towards the entrance and did not have to look round to know instinctively that whoever might appear at the entrance was the sole reason why Margo Cullagan had been frequenting the Green Shillelagh.

The newcomer was Dicey Reicey. Significantly, Dan felt, she made no effort to look in his direction. It was the opposite with Dicey. His mouth opened and his eyes followed her hungrily when she passed.

'Do you know him?' Dan asked.

'Know who?' It came out so innocently that he almost believed her.

'He's Dicey Reicey,' Dan informed her. 'I thought everybody knew him.'

'Oh is that who he is?' Again the almost perfectly feigned guilelessness.

In spite of feeling a little aggrieved at the thought of losing her, Dan found himself smiling.

'What are you smiling at?' she was quick to notice.

'Nothing much except that I think you've found what you came for.'

'Don't be too sure.'

'I'm sure,' he said with finality. She had the grace to avert her head. He could not be sure whether she blushed or not. When she looked at him again she was smiling.

'What's your name?'

'Dan Murray.'

'I like you Murray. You're different.'

He nodded his head without smiling. At this precise moment he felt himself being tapped on the shoulder. He turned to find a smiling Dicey Reicey nodding politely.

'It's not an excuse-me,' Dicey said unctuously, 'but I know you won't put me to the trouble of making it one.'

'You're welcome,' Dan told him, and with that he handed over his partner.

'You're a sound man,' Dicey commended. 'I'm thankful to you.'

'Not at all,' Dan said withdrawing to the rear of the hall to join the other observers.

From this vantage point he was able to see without being seen. Margo's face was animated now as she exchanged pleasantries with Dicey. For his part Dicey showed none of the overpowering confidence which was part of his trade as a lover of some renown. There was obeisance in his every gesture and deference in his attitude. He seemed to be aware that he was holding something of value, something far different from the run of the mill partners of his coarser entanglements.

Twelve o'clock came and went but Margo Cullagan did not go home. Nobody commented on this, nor was there any of the usual cutting-in by outsiders despite the fact that

Dicey was monopolising the most attractive and most available dancer in the ballroom. He was one of the Reiceys, maybe the least powerful of the three but he was a Reicey nevertheless.

At half-twelve the bandleader announced that the last dance was about to begin. Before the music started Dicey and Margo Cullagan left the Green Shillelagh together.

OUTSIDE THE dance-hall was a concrete forecourt once occupied by petrol pumps and showrooms. A solitary naked light overhung the area and cast a pallid glow when the electric discharge lights in front of the ballroom were extinguished.

These were still on as Dan and his party were leaving the Shillelagh proper and the forecourt was still a bright bustling place filled with talk and laughter. The moment the ballroom was empty the neons were put out. As they stepped out on to the street Dan noticed a group of grim-looking men huddled in a ring around two others. One was the youngest of the four Morrikans. The other was the youth who had been involved in the earlier embroilment in the hall. Morrikan was insisting that the youth defend himself but an animal instinct forewarned the young man that the moment he lifted a hand the odds would be heavily against him.

'Forget about it,' he was saying.

Morrikan's answer to this was to unleash a flood of expletives one or two of which Dan had not heard before. In the distance he could hear the Maguires calling him. He ran a few steps after them and called out that they should go on without him.

'Come away out of it,' Shay called back. 'It's none of your business.'

'It's all right,' Dan called. 'I'll be along after you. I'm only a spectator.'

This seemed to satisfy the Maguires who continued on their way. Dan returned and became part of the crowd. The

Morrikans, he discovered, were from Kerry like himself. He searched the crowd for sign of the older brothers but they gave no indication of being present. The youngest had now dispensed with his coat and was freely striking his opponent. The blows were more provocative than hurtful but a few carried a sting, and there was a trickle of blood visible at the side of the victim's mouth. The baiting continued for a long time until the youth decided he was having no more. Wildly he lashed out and caught Morrikan on the chin with his right hand.

Suddenly three figures, animal in their fury, erupted from the crowd. Dan stared spellbound, unable to move. The first blow from the biggest of the three felled the youth at once. He rose quickly, only half-conscious, afraid to stay on the ground. The other blows came in rapid succession. The sound of each was sickening. When the young man fell to the ground completely unconscious the youngest Morrikan kicked him in the side and manoeuvred himself so that he might kick him in the head.

'Jesus Christ!' Dan shouted, surprised at the timbre of his own voice, 'stop it or you'll kill him.'

The other brothers who were positioning themselves for kicks looked about in surprise. They ignored the plea and turned their attention to the lifeless object on the ground. Dan threw himself across the body. At that precise moment he lost consciousness. An hour would pass before he opened his eyes.

'Sylv,' the Sandra Felby called, 'he's coming to.'

Sylvester joined the girl at the end of the bed. Dan looked from one to the other searching for an explanation. Sylvester left the room and returned at once with a glass containing some brandy.

'Drink this,' he said, lifting Dan's head so that it rested against the pillows. Dan swallowed and almost vomited.

'Don't worry,' Sylvester smiled, 'you're supposed to react like that.'

Dan swallowed mouthful after mouthful till the glass was empty.

'What happened?' he asked.

'You can thank Crazy Horse,' Sylvester told him, 'he dragged you to safety. Nobody else cared and nobody else dared.'

'What about the boy?'

'The last time I saw him,' Sylvester replied without emotion, 'he was dead.'

Dan looked at him, the horror radiating from his face.

'Oh God!' he groaned. 'He reminded me of my brother.'

'Be thankful that you yourself are alive.'

'Those animals, what happened to them?'

'Sweet bugger-all.'

'What will happen to them?'

'Sweet bugger-all.'

'But they murdered him. They beat him to death for no reason.'

'That may be,' Sylvester sounded matter-of-fact. 'The important thing is that nobody will report them.'

'But that's terrible.'

'Don't I know?' Sylvester sounded resigned, as if it were an everyday injustice.

Dan covered his face with his hands and moaned.

'It's best this way,' Sylvester tried to sound reassuring. 'They'll get theirs some day. There's nothing surer than that. You must believe that. It's a vicious circle. The boy's body has been found by this time. Naturally it was moved to another location. It will take a few hours to identify him. The police when they discover he's Irish will shake their heads. Another Saturday night, another Paddy. The last time the person was only maimed for life, and the time before that it was a case of smashed ribs. There will be a preliminary investigation but after a while the whole thing will peter out. Being a Paddy has certain advantages at times.'

'Not for the boy who's dead.'

'I don't want to harp on this,' Sylvester said, 'but remember what I told you on the train. I told you not to go to the Green Shillelagh and I told you I knew you would. It's part of your education. Be glad that it's over. Write it off.

You don't seem to have suffered any hurt apart from a prize black eye and a few bruised ribs.'

'Where am I?' Dan asked.

'You're in my flat and this here is a friend of mine. Her name is Sandra. Sandra meet Dan Murray.'

'Would you like a cup of tea?' she asked.

He shook his head and got to his feet. 'What time is it?'

'Four o'clock. It's also Sunday afternoon.' Sylvester smiled at Dan's reaction.

'I've missed Mass,' he cried.

'Don't worry,' Sylvester told him, 'it was through no fault of your own so you won't be damned for it.'

6

EDDIE CAREY took his annual holidays in the middle of July. So did the Dubliners and the Maguire brothers. Dan had long since decided to forego any break until Christmas at the earliest. The marks on his face and side had disappeared. The Maguire brothers knew of his involvement in the fight outside the Green Shillelagh but never once did they mention it to Dan or to anyone else. The others heard it in time but the subject was never aired.

Dan had told Eddie all about it. 'Let it be a lesson to you,' his friend said. There had been no admonition in the comment although Eddie said at the time that it would be a shame if the Morrikan brothers were allowed get away with it altogether. Dan told him what Sylvester had said about fate catching up with them.

'Oh sure,' Eddie retorted 'but what about the other innocent young lads that are likely to run into them in the meanwhile?'

Dan thought the Morrikans would lie low after the murder or at least be more cautious for a period.

'The fact that they got away with it,' his friend countered 'will only encourage them.'

Eddie had decided to travel first class on the boat from Holyhead to Dublin. It was an unprecedented move.

'I've always wanted to do it just once,' he told Dan. It had been with great difficulty that Dan had prevailed upon him not to wear his cap with the sports-coat and flannel pants. Seated comfortably in the lounge bar of the tourist deck he sipped a whiskey and read a newspaper. The ship's engines were a drowsy beat in the background, comforting and relaxing. A steward in a white coat approached and enquired if everything was to his liking. Eddie was taken by surprise but he made a timely recovery to reply that there was nothing he needed. The steward withdrew obsequiously. Eddie, unused to such attention, fingered inside his collar and looked surreptitiously about to see if anybody was looking at him. 'Shag the lot of 'em,' he said under his breath. 'My fare is paid.'

He took an express train from Dublin to Limerick where his wife was waiting. On his instructions she had hired a car, the only one for hire in Ballynahaun and brought the children with her. They all sat quietly on a platform seat waiting for the train to arrive. None of the children had seen a train before. The younger ones drew closer to their mother when the monstrous engine puffed and hissed its way into the station. The youngest started to cry but the older ones comforted her.

Noreen Carey's eyes nearly popped out of her head when she saw her husband's regalia. When the other women of Ballynahaun, particularly the farmers' wives saw the finely-dressed man she had they'd be giddy with jealousy. On the way home later she whispered to him, 'I declare to God, when I saw you stepping from the carriage I thought it was a bank manager or a schools' inspector.'

In Limerick, Eddie bought a leather football for the boys. For the girls, the oldest of whom was five, he bought cloth dolls. He persuaded Noreen to buy a new frock and a pair of shoes. She kept insisting it was a waste of money but Eddie knew only too well that she never bought anything for herself and that if he didn't insist she would go without as always.

In bed that night, after they had made love, they smoked cigarettes and talked about the future.

Noreen had been barely eighteen and Eddie twenty-four when they left Ballynahaun parish church as husband and wife. She came from the south of the county to work for a farmer. Her mother collected the thirty pounds which was the hire for the eleven month period and returned home the day she delivered her daughter. Noreen had no easy time in the house. The farmer was over-attentive and if the wife noticed she neglected to reprimand him.

Eddie lived then with his widowed mother in the cottage he now occupied about four miles from where Noreen worked. They met first at a cross-roads dance on a Sunday night at the beginning of April. It was the only time she made any sort of journey from the house since coming there early in spring. They danced together all night long and when it was announced that it was time to go home he asked if he might walk as far as the farmhouse with her. She argued that it was four miles but he declared he would walk a thousand with her. She said she was with a friend which was true. This was an older girl who worked on the next farm. This would be no obstacle either. As far as he was concerned the whole parish could accompany them as long as he was allowed to stay by her side. She liked him. He brought them to their destinations using a short-cut which he often took when hunting for hares or fowling for snipe and grouse in the heather-covered hills. It was a pleasant night and the ground was springy and dry under their feet. They sang most of the way and he left only when she promised she would meet him on the next Sunday night.

The following Sunday broke wet and cheerless. Visibility on the hills was poor and the rain clouds that rolled westward in unchanging patterns seemed to be endless. There were but a few at the cross-roads dance but the musicians had shown up. There was a fiddler and a concertina player. All that was wanted were the couples to man the wooden platform. As the evening wore on there seemed no likelihood of Noreen appearing. Those who had come to dance lay huddled against the hedges under the shade of bushes or stunted trees. As the evening darkened Eddie's dejection grew. It was the most depressing Sunday night he had ever experienced. Slowly he wended his way homeward vainly looking behind him from time to time hoping to see the slender dark-haired girl who was beginning to haunt his dreams and fill his every waking moment. The driving, rain-weighted mist fastened to his clothes and soaked him through. He could not care less. He felt no discomfort only an overpowering desire to see her.

The following evening when he finished work in the quarry he took the road which led to the hillside farmhouse where she worked. Rounding a bend in the road he focused his eyes far ahead and there she was before him, wearing a light frock, her hands behind her back, her head in the air and the dark hair flowing freely in the wake of it. They walked across the hills together to the source of a mountain stream where the water was clear and musical. They sat on a boulder exchanging stories until it grew chill. On the road back he removed his short-coat and covered her shoulders. At the gate which opened on to the avenue which led to the house he took his leave of her. He sensed she was unhappy and perhaps frightened but when he asked her if all was well he could get nothing out of her. On his way to his own home he was worried. He knew the man for whom she worked. He did not know him well but he knew that Noreen would want to take good care of herself under his roof.

'Your strong farmer,' Bill Murray, who was Dan's father, had said to Eddie once, 'mounts his serving girls, spares his wife and makes priests and doctors of his sons.' Eddie knew that this was true of only a few and in all fairness the same could be said of other interests all over the country. Still Bill Murray was an astute judge of the local scene.

'M'anam ón diabhal,' his mother said when he lifted the latch on the door, 'but 'tis you that has the black face on you.'

Eddie laughed. 'I have a touch of a pain in the head,' he said.

'Or a touch of a girl in the heart,' she teased.

In bed Eddie was as restless as a whin bush in a March gale.

Tom Joe Scanney, the farmer to whom Noreen was bound for the eleven month period, was a man of substance. Married to a meek wife who came from much the same stock as himself, his farm covered a hundred acres of healthy pasture and several hundred acres of mountain and bog-land. The land supported sixty milch cows, a fair quota of calves and bullocks and two pairs of workhorses. Tom Joe Scanney belonged to a type of Irish farmer common to every poor parish at that time. He employed a full-time serving girl and two male agricultural workers. For the saving of his hay and for the annual threshing of his corn he would employ casuals or he would have the service of men who might have borrowed one of his horses for a day or a piece of machinery, such as a plough or a harrow. His wife worked hard all the time. Tom Joe's only function was to issue orders for the day and put in an appearance in a supervisory capacity whenever he felt like it.

He could be compared in no way to the half-sirs or squireens who unsuccessfully aped the so-called ascendancy classes for generations. Tom Joe Scanney and his equals were of the people. They drank with their workmen and were on friendly terms with the cottiers, small-holders and labourers who were their neighbours. These strong farmers as they were called could be relied upon to secure a man for the purchase of a bicycle or part with a loan of ten pounds or even twenty pounds if a man met hard luck and could not meet his rates. They were liked and respected. Where was the point in going to a poor man with a hard luck story when all he was likely to offer you would be sympathy or the fill of your pipe?

Tom Joe Scanney was there and he was accessible and he was one of their own with no foolish airs or graces. If he liked to pat a serving girl's buttocks or knock a labourer's wife between the turnip drills wasn't it well known, although the priests would not hear of it, that God was soft on sins of the flesh?

If a woman took sick in the middle of the night who was one to turn to? Was it to a Holy Josie with a big Rosary beads or to a sinner like themselves who had a motor-car? Tom Joe was all right. He might have his faults but he was where a man expected him to be when he was needed and he was a man who found it hard to say no. The more he had and the better his luck the better for everybody who knew him. You had to ask, that was all. A poor man might be as good a friend but he would never have the means to show it.

Eddie Carey fell into a troublesome sleep. When he awoke again he could hear the voices of his mother and another woman in the kitchen. He listened intently but could not be sure. His heart thumped violently like the drumming of a hare's feet on hard ground.

Holy Mother of God it was her voice. But what was she doing in the house? He looked at his watch. It was only seven o'clock and barely light out of doors. He groped for his shirt and trousers and dressed himself hastily, pausing every minute to listen so that he might reassure himself that it was really she.

He was never to know the real reason why Noreen came to the cottage that April morning. He might guess but he was prepared to forget the matter when she told him once with finality that she would rather not talk about it.

She had told his mother. When she had parted with Eddie that night she had gone straight to the kitchen of the farmhouse where she poured herself a cup of milk. Mrs Scanney sat by the open fire knitting. They spoke for a while but Noreen realised that she would have to be first up in the morning. She therefore excused herself. In her room she knelt by the bedside and said her prayers. No sooner was she in bed than she fell sound asleep. Some time later she woke drowsily. Things were not as they should be. In the room was the unfamiliar figure of a man. She lay perfectly still, afraid almost to breathe. There was something else wrong. There was a hand gently stroking her, tending to probe insistently between her thighs. She overcame her drowsiness with difficulty and tried to scream. No sound would come. Kneeling by the bed in his bare and hairy pelt was Tom Joe Scanney. There were sounds coming from his mouth.

'Easy, easy now,' he was saying. She lay rigid and tensed, terrified lest some movement of hers might give him the impression that she was responding. 'Steady, steady,' he whispered soothingly. It was the way she had heard him address the black mare which was always tackled in the morning to take the milk to the creamery. She shivered all over with fear. Misinterpreting this he forcefully tried to prise her thighs apart. She leaped suddenly from the bed and confronted him on the floor looking wan and waifish in her night-dress.

'Steady now. Steady girl.' There was a fearful monotony

about the words as if the act of seducing her was a formality that needed only patience and common endearments. Keeping an eye on his every move she snatched her dress from the end of the bed and evaded him easily when he endeavoured to place his arms about her. She guessed that he might be drunk or at least that he might be heavy in drink. He was lumbering towards her again but this time the door was behind her and groping in the dark she found the doorknob without difficulty. In a flash she was in the kitchen pulling the dress on over her head. She did not feel the morning cold where she stood with her back to the remnants of the fire. He appeared in the doorway of the kitchen.

'You're flighty,' he said, 'come on back to the room and don't have herself wake up.'

'No,' she said, 'and if you come near me I'll scream.'

'Come on,' he persisted, 'no one will ever know except the two of ourselves.' With outstretched arms he advanced towards her.

'Easy now like a good girl.' When he came within arms' reach of her she could smell the stale drink. He paused for a moment breathing heavily all the time.

'Stand now,' he said, a measure of triumph in his voice. 'Stand now like a good girl.' He stretched out a hand towards her shoulder and this time she screamed.

'Blast you,' he said, 'what in hell did you want to go doin' that for?' He stood perplexed not knowing how to proceed. There was a mixture of lust and bafflement on his face.

'There was no call for the screeching,' he said.

'If you don't go,' she threatened, 'I'll screech again.'

'I don't know what to make of the girls that's goin' these days,' he pouted. 'One of 'em is giddier than the next. Quiet yourself now and when you're leaving here for good I'll slip you a handy fist of notes for yourself.'

'What ails you Tom Joe?' The voice came from behind him. He turned in some surprise to see his wife standing there.

'What do you think ails me?' he grumbled.

'Go away to bed now Tom Joe like a good man,' his wife told him. 'We'll talk about it in the morning.'

65

Reluctantly he turned and without a word left the kitchen. Mrs Scanney placed a chair near the fire and bade Noreen take a seat. She drew up another chair for herself and started to probe the great ash heap with the heavy iron tongs. In a short while she had a glowing heap of embers separated from the ashes. Noreen shivered, grateful for the heat. The older woman placed a hand on her knee.

'You don't have to tell me what happened,' she said, 'for indeed I know well. Still we can't be hard on the poor man. He's only what God made him and he can't help the way he is.'

'I can't stay here,' Noreen answered and she began to cry. 'I'm afraid of him. I might not be able for him.'

''Tis a bad time for him with me the way I am,' Mrs Scanney went on as if she hadn't heard. Then she forced a laugh. 'If the two of us can't manage him sure we're no use at all.'

Noreen could hardly believe her ears. Without another word she rose and went to her room. She gathered her scant belongings and began to stow them in the calico flower bag she had brought with her. Her task was almost complete when Mrs Scanney entered the room.

'What in God's name are you doing?' she asked.

'I'm leaving,' Noreen said.

'You can't leave like this. There's the money we paid to your mother. If you attempt to go I'll have the civic guards on you. Where is your mother going to raise thirty pounds to pay us back? You'll wind up in jail if you don't come to your senses.'

Noreen was taken aback but only for a moment. She was resolved to get out of the house whatever might happen.

'I'll go to jail if needs be,' she cried out. 'Isn't anything better than what's in store for me here?'

Mrs Scanney was unused to such determination. She tried a new tack. 'All right,' she agreed with simulated resignation, 'but wait till the end of the week till we find someone to replace you.'

'No,' from Noreen.

'In the name of God wait till morning itself,' Mrs Scanney implored. Buttoning her coat Noreen slung the calico bag across her shoulders.

'I'm not staying another minute in this house,' she said. Mrs Scanney suddenly flopped on the side of the bed and covered her face with her hands. Her sobbing was genuine. For an instant Noreen felt sorry for the woman

In the kitchen of the cottage Eddie's mother, Nonie Carey, listened without a word while the girl sobbed out her tale.

'Very well,' she said when Noreen had finished. 'Whatever else you did the right thing but you must never breathe a word of your story to anyone else. The man is a good neighbour whatever about his failings and moreover he's a man poor people wouldn't want to be on the wrong side of. I'm sure his wife and himself will be content to let it lie.'

The following day they managed to send word to Noreen's mother to come for her and to bring the balance of the wages which she had collected at the beginning of the agricultural year. Word came back after three days by way of a poorly-written letter. The mother would not countenance Noreen's return home under any circumstances. They were in a dilemma in the Carey household but it was solved easily enough before the month was out. After a visit from Nonie Carey, Father Ferris the parish priest of Ballynahaun consented to marry the young couple.

He had hummed and hawed but when she presented him with three pounds there was no difficulty in persuading him to perform the ceremony. A single pound would have been sufficient since the recognised charge for a marriage ceremony was a pound per cow but Nonie foresaw that there might be difficulty. Consent came at once from Noreen's mother who wrongly imagined that it had to be a marriage of necessity.

With a ten pound note borrowed from Bill Murray and six pounds which he had spared for a rainy day they spent a three day honeymoon in the city of Cork. They stayed in a guesthouse on the Western Road and were as happy as a newly-married couple could be.

After the arrival of the first child Nonie Carey took ill.

67

She ailed for a year and despite advice that the old woman would be better off in the County Home Noreen would not hear of it. She nursed her to the end. From the beginning their relationship had been a happy one. This would be unusual anywhere but in Ireland it was exceptional.

Usually when mother-in-law and daughter-in-law were forced to live in the same house the atmosphere was charged with a tension that needed little to release it. When they lived in separate houses and could not claw verbally at each other all the time or hinder each other's movements the relationship wasn't too bad but where they were forced to endure each other for years in a small dwelling they had unwittingly consigned themselves to hell upon earth until the expiry of one or the other. They were truly the victims of tragic circumstances. Some of the torment might have been alleviated if only the mother would remember that she herself was once young and flighty or if the daughter-in-law would only realise that she, one day, would be old and grey. There were some exceptions and without doubt the Carey household was one of these.

A few years later after the death of his mother with three children to support, the quarry where Eddie worked was closed down. He was forced to go on the dole. Dolers were often taunted by those who were fortunate enough to have jobs. Local employers held them in contempt. They would have preferred them to work for a pittance than to draw money for doing nothing at all. The dole was never sufficient. In England a man of Eddie's years and ability could earn ten times more in a week than he drew at home.

Lonely as she might be without him Noreen wanted education for her children. She did not want them pressed into service the way she had been. They kept putting it off from week to week but one day the final humiliation came.

On a Sunday at a local football match when the teams were level and excitement ran high Eddie had an altercation with a man who came from the next parish. One word borrowed another but the climax came when the man said, 'I never drew the bloody dole anyway.' The statement had the effect of completely deflating Eddie. Humiliated he left the field. It was the fierce injustice of it that rankled and embittered him. He was known far and wide as a man who liked to work. There would be no more dole for him. Let others draw it if they had to. Many of his neighbours and friends were in England. He would write and ask one of them to fix him up with a job. What the work might be like was no consideration. It was the amount of money he could earn that mattered.

After his third week in England Eddie Carey started to send his wife six pounds a week. It was a change from the weekly dole which consisted of thirty shillings. Out of the six pounds it was no trouble to Noreen to put aside three pounds. In the space of three months she bought a new cow through Bill Murray who sold the old one for a fair price. She missed Eddie beyond words but she was only one of many who endured the absence of husbands for a new dignity and a brighter future for their children. There were hundreds of thousands of her ilk in Ireland.

Around this time and for years to follow untold millions of pounds crossed the Irish Sea in the weekly consignment of registered envelopes. The money made life bearable in Ireland for many who might have otherwise lived like paupers or even starved through pride and ignorance. Those responsible for the economy were never publicly to acknowledge this flood of money.

Shortly before Christmas during Eddie's first year in England Noreen resolved the one problem uppermost in her mind for many a long day. Borrowing a bicycle from a neighbour she cycled the four miles to the farmstead of Tom Joe Scanney. Mrs Scanney asked her in and made her take a chair by the fire. Noreen explained that she dare not delay on account of the children. She withdrew an envelope from her pocket and handed it to Mrs Scanney.

'I want you to check that it's all there.'

Limply Mrs Scanney accepted the envelope and withdrew the contents. Slowly she started to count the bank notes and silver.

'You'll notice,' Noreen was saying, 'I deducted for the time I worked. I must go now. A Happy Christmas to you and yours.'

Before Mrs Scanney could reply she had left the warm kitchen and was wheeling the bicycle down the avenue. When she mounted the bicycle and started to pedal homewards the cold wind numbed her fingers and chilled the tips of her ears but it brought the colour to her face. Inside the bare hedgerows Tom Joe Scanney's fields were green and dry. The cows still grazed them contentedly. Noreen, in spite of her loneliness for Eddie, experienced a new elation as she cycled. A few short years and they would be in a position to better themselves. They were independent and that was worth it all. A little waiting was what was needed and then all would be well with the help of God.

On Christmas Eve night there was a surprise knock at the door as she was preparing the turkey. She called out bidding the knocker to come in. The door opened and Tom Joe Scanney stood there.

'Can I come in?' he asked. 'I mean no harm.'

'Of course,' she said. She did not offer him a seat, however. He laid the money which Noreen had earlier that month given his wife, on the table.

'There was no need to give it back. It's yours. Keep it and a Happy Christmas to you.'

Tom Joe sounded contrite.

'It's lawfully yours,' she told him.

'Let's have no more of it now,' he smiled. 'You're welcome to it. I'm sorry that what I did turned you out of my house that night.'

She bent her head not wanting to discuss it. He stood in the centre of the kitchen wishing in vain that something worthwhile to say would come to him.

'Will you have a bottle of stout?' she asked.

'No,' he replied, 'but thanks. I have enough drank and anyway I'm not to be trusted and that's the truth of it where women are concerned.'

Noreen laughed.

'You're not too bad,' she said.

'I'd better go,' he announced awkwardly. He stood there trying to think of something more to say. Nothing would come. He placed his big hands on her shoulders, squeezed gently and kissed her on the forehead. Then releasing her he walked out into the night.

Now years later with Eddie beside her in the bed, Noreen wondered how much money would be required to buy Tom Joe Scanney's farm. Rumour had it that he proposed to sell within a few years. His two daughters were in convents and his only son studying medicine.

She would plot realistically when Eddie left. Whatever else, she must think in terms of bringing her husband home for good as soon as possible.

7

WITH HIS friend in Ireland Dan Murray was no longer accorded the status of bricklayer's mate. This did not worry him at all. Already he knew as much as many of the bricklayers on the site but he did not know enough and he did not possess the assurance or the experience to try some other site on his own. Before Eddie left, Dan, acting on his advice, went to the office of the general foreman and asked for a job as a labourer on the main contractor's force. 'Would you be prepared to work twelve hour shifts from Monday to Friday and a half-day on Saturday?' the general foreman asked.

'Yes,' Dan had said.

'You won't have to work the whole time,' the general foreman told him, 'but I'll want you around. Don't ever leave the site because you never can tell when you'll be needed or what you'll be needed for. Just hang around till I call you. If you're not around when I want you I'll sack you without notice and you'll forfeit whatever wages are due to you. I'll also personally see to it that your arse gets broke.'

'I'll be around,' Dan promised.

'I'm sure you will,' the general foreman agreed. He knew Dan to be a capable man who got on well with the others on the site.

'You'll get twenty pounds a week. That includes 24 hours overtime.'

Dan tried to conceal his surprise. Twenty pounds a week. A thousand a year, the same salary as the dispensary doctor back home.

It was holiday time and labourers were scarce. The overtime money was to ensure he stayed on the site. Only a very reliable man was offered a position as site factotum. He spent the first five days, from eight in the morning to eight at night, assisting a team of plasterers from Clare who were

72

working on a sub-contract. Two of their labourers were on holiday and because of this Dan was made available to them. The work was drabbishly hard and the amount accomplished in the period at their disposal had to be seen to be believed. Dan was unused to the square-headed English shovel with the T-piece at the end of the handle. It was a far different proposition to the tongue-headed shovel so common in Ireland and with which he was familiar. Still he mastered the use of it and towards the end of the fourth day overheard his praises being sung by one of the Claremen.

When they quit the site at the end of their term they paid him the singular compliment of asking him to join up with them. He told them about his relationship with Eddie and they were forced to agree that it would be foolish if he were to abandon his apprenticeship when it seemed that he was beginning to master the trade.

The following week there was next to nothing to be done. Dan used his time to mooch around the site. He tried to grasp the mechanics of the entire contract. There were so many facets that he almost gave up in despair. One morning he saw a labourer wheeling a barrow in which were deposited 4 new shovels. In Ireland a man brought his own shovel to work as if it were the tool of his trade. In England shovels were supplied by the employers. The man lifted a finger to his lips invoking Dan's silence. He deposited the shovels behind a hoarding a hundred yards from the site. When Dan saw him again the man was pushing a load of bricks towards the same destination. The third journey he made was with a barrowful of expensive tiles.

Dan felt responsible and no matter what Eddie told him he felt it was his bounden duty to report the matter to the general foreman. This he duly did and the answer he received did not surprise him.

'Just do what I tell you, Paddy,' he was informed, 'and never mind the others.' Dan was later to discover that the materials were for a new house being built by the general foreman who every evening took a company van, loaded it with the materials dumped behind the hoarding and drove unashamedly past the main entrance to his own site. Not the slightest notice was taken by the other workers. Towards the end of the second week it was Dan's turn to contribute to the building of the new house.

This time the use of a two-ton truck was involved. Trucks arrived on the site regularly with loads of cement, gravel and sand. One evening a truckload of each was diverted to the general foreman's proposed home.

'Get aboard Paddy,' he had called to Dan when the driver of the cement truck obligingly opened the door of his cab. Dan got in. They drove into London and right through the city till they came to a pleasant area overlooking the Thames in Woolwich. They stopped near a particularly well-appointed clearing bordered by trees and shrubs.

Two houses were being built. One was to accommodate the foreman and his family. He would sell the other. Dan recognised a number of workmen from the site.

One of them helped him unload the cement. Everybody connected with the project worked at a furious pace. The foreman was liked and he could do things for workers with closed mouths who worked hard. All the injected materials and those strewn around had come from the main site. If the foreman was found out it would mean jail but there wasn't the remotest likelihood that he would be caught.

Only the choicest materials were being used. When the cement was unloaded Dan helped with the mix. All the foundation trenches were filled the day before and now the walls were going up. Hour after hour went by yet there was no slackening in the pace. By this time he was well-used to the speed. All present worked silently and with a will.

At nine o'clock an old Ford van drew up near the building. From it the general foreman emerged followed by a fat woman and a good-looking girl of eighteen. The females carried baskets. They commandeered a carpenter's bench for use as a table. On it they placed a selection of quality food. There was a whole cooked ham. Dan remembered that the foreman had the week before received a gift of two hams and a bottle of whiskey from a paint contractor. There was a leg of mutton, several pan loaves, sliced and buttered. There was a dish of cold, cooked sausages, a jar of pickles and a jar of beetroot. Nothing had been overlooked. From the van, assisted by one of the workers, the foreman bore a barrel of beer, tapped and ready, to a block pile where he set it up.

'Dig in boys and drink up,' he ordered.

This was the life, Dan thought. It was a pleasant July evening with a cloudless sky overhead and the surface of the river burning just below them as if it had been caught by fire. Everybody was eating heartily. The foreman came and sat by his side.

'Paddy,' he asked, 'what's your full name?'

'Dan Murray,' Dan replied.

'Real ole Russian monicker that,' the foreman laughed. 'Murray, this here's my missus and this is my daughter.'

They exchanged pleasant nods and when he managed to swallow the mouthful of food he was masticating Dan touched on the pleasantness of the evening.

The girl's name was Sally. Dan discovered that she was studying economics at Cambridge University. They would be occupying one of the houses as soon as it was ready. After that her father planned to retire. Dan imagined that this would not be difficult when he remembered the numerous stories he had heard about buckshee.

He accepted a pint of beer from the foreman's wife. She asked him a number of questions and listened attentively to his answers.

She went around to each of the workers in turn and spent a short while with everyone, always listening attentively. When the barrel of beer was exhausted Dan was given a lift to the digs in Bertham by the driver of the truck. Between them they figured that the foreman would have his two houses built for a quarter of the true cost – it never occurred to the driver to suggest that wholesale robbery was involved. It was normal practice and therefore none of their business.

For the remainder of July Dan spent every other day working on the Woolwich houses. The foreman would arrive in the evening around nine o'clock. Usually he brought sandwiches and beer but there was the odd time when the wife and daughter would accompany him. When they came the fare would be much better. It was their way of showing their appreciation for the extra hard work.

When Dan drew his weekly wages he discovered that instead of drawing 24 hours overtime he was getting paid for 36. He asked no questions.

'Satisfied with your packet this week Murray?' the foreman asked and winked knowingly.

'Yes,' said Dan.

With the long hours he found little time for pleasure. On the main site there was little to do except to stand around where the general foreman could locate him without difficulty. On the first Friday in August he asked for a half-day off. This was granted unconditionally. In his room in the digs he changed into his new suit. Downstairs he asked Gillian Hubbard for his wallet. He had asked her to look after it for him while he was at work and she had locked it away in an ancient safe with her own valuables. Every week he added to its already bulging contents until at last he felt the time had come to entrust his savings to the bank. Dan had never seen the inside of a bank in his life and for this reason he asked Sid Hubbard to recommend one. Sid suggested the Midland where he had an account himself. In the four month period since his arrival Dan had managed to put aside a sum of one hundred and thirty pounds. None of his wages were whittled away by deductions for income tax. Every second Irishman who came to England claimed for a non-existent family back home. One of the first things Dan did after his arrival was to claim for a wife and two children. There was no point in claiming for more. He was too young and there might be an investigation. Even when there was an investigation it was a relatively simple matter to contact the clerk of one's parish. He it was who kept the records of births and marriages and it was unlikely he would answer a query which might land a neighbour's child in trouble without first consulting with the neighbour in question. One perplexed senior official in the income tax department could not correlate the published census report which showed the population of Southern Ireland to be two and four-fifth millions with his own findings of three millions. Either the

76

extra quarter of a million children being claimed for did not exist or the government of Southern Ireland was keeping it a close secret for reasons best known to themselves.

The Catholic Church in Ireland and Irish confessors in England took a liberal view of tax dodging. It was regarded as a venial sin, a preliminary contribution before the confession of major sins of the flesh and other evil excesses.

Dan was warmly received at the Midland Bank. The manager shook his hand and told him his account was appreciated. He was given a deposit book wherein was written the amount he had lodged. He refused the offer of a cheque book but promised to bear it in mind. The truth was that the thought of having a cheque book frightened him a little. He doubted if anybody back home in Ballynahaun had a cheque book excepting maybe Tom Joe Scanney or the creamery manager or possibly one of the national teachers. If he had any strong feelings about the transaction they were not ones of elation. If anything he felt guilty. One hundred and thirty pounds was a huge amount of money for an investment of a mere four months of unskilled if unremitting labour. He thought of his father and the other small farmers back in Ballynahaun. If they earned that amount in a year not to mind saving it they would consider themselves fortunate beyond words.

While extracting the money from his wallet he came across the slip of paper which Patricia Dee had handed him before she left the boat at Fishguard.

After supper he decided to visit Sylvester and use the phone in his flat. They had met several times since the affair at the Shillelagh. It was Sylvester who filled him in on the happenings after the discovery of the body. There had been an inquest. There could have been no possible verdict other than foul play although Sylvester cited similar Irish killings before the war when death by misadventure was recorded.

Sylvester had been in the ticket office of the Shillelagh going over the accounts with Tom Reicey when the police inspector called. There had been a resounding knock at the main door of the ballroom.

'Go and see who that is like a good man and for God's

77

sake try to get rid of them if you can at all Sylvie.'

When Sylvester opened the door he guessed that the caller was from the police. The man wore a light mackintosh and seemed most affably disposed. He showed some identification and asked if he might have a word or two with the proprietor.

'If you care to step in,' Sylvester said, 'I'll go and see if he's available.'

Tom Reicey came from the office at once and shook his caller's hand.

'Inspector Reeze,' he boomed. 'It's been a long time. I hope I'm not wanted for anything.'

'I should think not, sir.' The inspector laughed at the idea of Tom being wanted for anything.

'I'm investigating the murder of a youth,' Reeze said. 'His body was found some short distance from here. So far my investigations lead me to believe that he may have been here on the night he was killed.'

'Come to my office at once,' Tom Reicey said. 'This is a serious matter.'

Tom knew for some time that the lad had been murdered and where and how the crime had been perpetrated. If the police could prove that the youth had been killed in the forecourt of the Shillelagh he would have trouble holding on to his licence. Tom guessed that the inspector knew the truth and that the source of his information would have to be an anonymous telephone call or letter. Proving it would be another matter. He knew Reeze and his connections and made a quick calculation as to the amount it would take to blunt or divert their investigations. In the office the three of them sat down together. Reeze declined the offer of a drink. He put a number of formal questions to Sylvester who assured him that there had been no disturbance of any kind on the night in question. Some nights there might be a scuffle but this was always a natural development, quite harmless.

'Paddies are apt to be naughty on Saturday nights,' the inspector quipped. Tom and Sylvester laughed dutifully.

In answer to further questioning they assured him that they had neither seen nor heard anything which might be tied up or linked in any way with the crime. Tom Reicey acted as if he were most perturbed. Actually he was congratulating himself that the inspector was Reeze. It might easily have been a troublesome individual who could make things awkward for everybody. On their promise to notify him in the event of any helpful information coming to hand he rose to take his leave. At this exact moment Tom Reicey addressed Sylvester.

'Like a good man will you excuse us a moment,' he said. 'I have a personal matter I want investigated.'

Sylvester went outside, closing the door behind him. The lightly built wall of the ticket office was poor proof against the deep and powerful voice of his employer.

Sylvester distinctly heard the words: 'tickets for the policeman's ball'.

This was more often than not a mythical affair and the money went to less deserving recipients. On his way out the inspector said goodbye to Sylvester. He seemed satisfied with the result of his investigations.

They finished the accounts that evening. As far as Sylvester could make out there was exactly the sum of a hundred pounds missing from the safe.

'Who's that good-looking bird Dicey's knocking around with lately?' Tom shot the question out of the blue while Sylvester was in the middle of a long tot.

'She's a nurse in Newsham General. I believe she originally hails from Wexford.' He started the tot a second time.

'I see,' Tom said, 'and do you know if she's a Catholic?'

'She certainly is.'

'Seems a respectable type of girl?'

'Seems so all right.'

'I'll tell you something straight and fair Sylvie.' Tom Reicey was anxious to confide in Sylvester. 'That bloody brother of mine has my heart broke. When he isn't on the jigs from drink he's exhausted from women. He's bound to get a right dose sooner or later. 'Twould be a great ease to me to see the scoundrel married to some decent girl.'

Tom only half-meant what he was saying. Nobody could be more indulgent than he to the youngest of the three brothers. There was a hint of pride in his tone when he spoke of Dicey's prowess as a philanderer. Still it was clear that he was concerned about Dicey's habits and that he would not look with disapprobation on a liaison of permanence with a respectable Catholic maiden.

Sylvester's personal opinion of Margo Cullagan was that she was a nymphomaniac but that her marriage sights were set on Dicey Reicey who for all his dealings with women seemed to be utterly captivated by the virginal illusiveness which she seemed to radiate. In Margo there would always be that frenzied but carefully concealed yearning for the unattainable. Dicey would be temporarily satisfying while at the same time he would provide her with the status of well-off wife and possibly mother. The only hope Dicey would have of sharing a bed with Margo was through the purchase of an expensive engagement ring and a conclusive walk in the direction of the nuptial altar. Sylvester foresaw this clearly.

Dicey's knowledge of the opposite sex was confined to an outsize and probably record-breaking collection of pornographic magazines and photographs portraying incredibly agile couples in every conceivable and inconceivable form of nude pose. He also had the telephone numbers of the prettiest call-girls in the city and was intimately acquainted with scores of other females who copulated with him for no material gain. What he was experiencing with Margo Cullagan, although he would be the last to admit it, was his first introduction to the disease of calf love.

Sylvester had a very low opinion of Dicey. He had some regard for Tom and Joe. Whether they meant it or not they never showed him anything less than respect. He was well paid and generally speaking, well looked after. He had continual misgivings about the cheques he was made to cash by Tom Reicey. Tom's assurances helped allay his fears to some degree but there was the nagging worry that the deception could not last forever.

WHEN DAN'S phone call was put through to the nurse's

home at Newsham General Hospital Patricia was just leaving with another nurse. They planned an evening at a local cinema and a drink or two afterwards at the Colorado Hotel. Patricia's most recent outing with a member of the opposite sex was with an intern from another hospital. He expressed keen disappointment when she refused to go to bed with him at once, going so far as to suggest that there must be something serious the matter with her such as frigidity or perhaps some form of pernicious sexual irresponsiveness.

The latter was partly his own composition and while he told her he had the only cure for both maladies she declined. She refused to go out with him again.

She was leaving the hospital grounds as she was being paged. When she returned just before midnight the girl at the switch-board told her that there had been a call.

'Oh!' she exclaimed with some surprise. 'Who was it?'

'I believe he said his name was Murray,' the girl replied.

'Would it have been Dan Murray?' Patricia asked.

'I think it had the name of Dan all right,' the girl answered vaguely as she toyed with one of the switchboard plugs.

'Aren't you sure?' Patricia demanded. The girl shrugged.

'Did he leave a message?' Patricia asked, rapidly losing patience.

The girl shook her head.

'Well did he leave a number where I can call back?'

Again the annoying shake of the head.

'Didn't you ask if there was a number which I might call?'

'I should think not,' the girl answered.

'Damn you,' Patricia whispered fiercely and stalked off.

In Sylvester's flat Dan put down the phone. 'She's not there,' he said.

'Well if she's not on duty,' Sylvester said, 'you can hardly expect her to stay inside on a Friday night. She's out somewhere or she's no use at all.'

Dan was forced to agree.

'It doesn't matter,' he said.

'The mood I'm in at the moment needs a large quantity

81

of intoxicating drink before it can be disposed of,' Sylvester suggested. 'Do you feel like coming along?'

'I suppose a drink wouldn't poison us,' Dan concurred.

'Nor affect the general tenor of our lives to any alarming degree,' Sylvester asseverated.

'Oh sure,' said Dan.

'And so long as we don't make pigs of ourselves. That's most important.' Sylvester sounded so serious that Dan looked to see if he meant it.

'I mean,' Sylvester spoke convincingly, 'it's all right for a man to have a drink or two but any more is an affront to those saints and martyrs who thought up the seven deadly sins. A man who stuffs himself with intoxicating liquor is no better than an animal. Better his right cobble were cut from where it hangs with its fellow or that his penis be guillotined at its maximum erection. I say to you,' and here Sylvester pointed an apocalyptic finger at Dan, 'I say to you put your appetite behind you and go forth in the nude to the well of the spring water or a day will come when you will call from the flames of hell to the holy in heaven for a drop, a single drop of water. Now let's go forth and get truly pissed.'

'What about the Shillelagh?' Dan asked.

'I have every third Friday night free,' Sylvester assured him.

'And Sandra?'

'Sandra is babysitting for a friend. I can see you are determined to put obstacles in my way.'

'You are already half drunk,' Dan reminded him.

'That's a terrible state to be in. Let's go.'

They started off at the Crown in Cricklewood but the place became crowded in a short time so they left and took a taxi to a pub in Kilburn High Road. This was not so crowded but it was noisier and there were two sing-songs going at the same time.

'These are not my normal haunts,' Sylvester told Dan, 'but I imagine it will appeal to you with your tender years and your appetite for life. This is alleged to be the best pub in London for the "crack" as the Paddies euphemistically call that vulgar mixture of Irish gossip, dirty stories, news of cushy jobs and the silent migrations of the ever-transient whore population of this great city. In short it's the buck navvy's paradise. Here he can drink and mate and fight. What more does a red-blooded man want? Here he will hear the sagas of the legendary long-distance men and the tough tales of the present-day ones who cannot stay for more than a season in the same place. If you are a buck navvy and want to stay a buck navvy this is the place to be. If you never want to possess the price of a down-payment on a decent house for your wife and family let this be your hang-out because your fellows are here.'

Sylvester did not sound bitter but it was obvious that he was not happy in their present surroundings.

'We can leave if you like,' Dan suggested.

'No. No,' his friend was adamant, 'tonight won't be too bad. We'll stick around while we can. Enjoy the scene. These are our own people and yet they are a people apart. I wouldn't come here tomorrow night for all the money in the Bank of England.'

'It seems all right,' was Dan's rejoinder. 'They may be a bit rough and ready,' he went on defensively, 'but they seem to be a good-natured lot.'

'You will insist on learning the hard way,' Sylvester smiled ruefully. 'Listen Dan, the odds are ten to one on that there will be a serious fight in this pub tomorrow night. A number of people will be hurt. Most of the customers come here for no purpose other than the settling of old scores. Here they are away from the supervision of parents and parish priests. In their own townlands and parishes they numbered only a handful. They were suppressed easily and the violence rarely surfaced. Here they number hundreds. They are a force to be reckoned with. They fight amongst each other for recognition the same way a colony of artists might try to outpaint or outwrite or outsculpt each other. The art forms here are the fist, the duster and the boot. Tomorrow night when they have exhausted themselves the Black Marias will haul them to jail.'

They stayed till closing time. A somewhat intoxicated Sylvester held forth on matters relating to the building industry, 'I don't know what I'd do without the bustle of a site now and then. I need it to sustain me, to comfort me. Whatever else there may be on a building site there is no loneliness. There's camaraderie and there's pride and there's life but, best of all, there are the sounds.'

He swallowed from his glass and would have said no more but he noted Dan's intentness. The younger man had been listening, really listening.

'Sounds of the site,' Sylvester spoke half to himself, half to Dan, 'the song of the site I call it,' Sylvester continued. 'It's not to be heard at its best on the site itself or too near the site. Like the bagpipes.'

Sylvester's hands were extended now as he forgot his surroundings, 'the chorus of the site is enhanced by distance. It is a chorus beloved of contractors. They spend all their waking hours with their ears tuned to it, ears that have been developed for nothing else. You too Master Dan will develop an ear for it as I have. In the early days on my way to work I would park the van at the requisite distance. Then, in with me to the nearest field where I would listen in peace to the opening notes, the jibes, the catcalls and the whistles of the labourers setting up for the day, then the chippies joining in with tipping, tapping and thumping of hammer on joist and beam and hardboard. Every hammer-blow says we're here, we the chippies are here, the cockerels of every site, we begin, let others follow. Then the deafening drillers now muted by distance, then the churning mixers and the scraping shovels and the clinking and the clanking, and the chugging of the dumpers and the dying of human voices as the chorus strengthens and all the sounds are one.'

Dan turned his ear to the pub noises, the singing, the bustle, the drunken staggering, the joviality of the various groups, the apparent good-fellowship at every table. Behind the counter a squad of coatless barmen were pushed almost beyond their capabilities to meet the demand for pints of black and tan, mild and bitter and in-between nips of the hard stuff. Not once did Dan hear anybody question the price of a round of drinks. Every so often a charge-hand swept the tills clear of larger notes. In jig time the tills were filled again. Dan had never seen the equal of it.

In the toilet there was a man with his coat off and his shirt outside his trousers. The coat was wet from the urine which spattered from the white-tiled channels. He did not seem to notice. He stood swaying with his legs apart.

'I'm rough,' he was saying. 'I'm tough. I'm Irish.' He kept repeating the phrase.

'Bait,' Sylvester whispered.

'Hardly,' Dan was inclined to disagree.

'Bait,' Sylvester whispered secondly, 'although I doubt if he's party to it.'

'Let's get out of here,' Dan urged, 'before one of us brushes against him accidentally.'

'Excellent idea,' Sylvester assented. He led the way, carefully avoiding the swaying drunk.

'O, sweet memorable John Joseph Jesus!' The exclamation came from Sylvester when he opened the door of the toilet and looked into the bar.

'What's the matter?' Dan called from behind him.

'What isn't?' from Sylvester.

Dan peered over his shoulder. The bar was a broiling mass of crazed humanity. Women screamed and men yelled. Bottles flew and glasses were smashed. A man came staggering toward them with a broken corrugated glass clutched by the handle in his hand. It was discoloured with a mixture of beer, foam and blood.

'Get out of my bastardin' way,' he shouted.

Dan and Sylvester moved to one side. The man with the glass disappeared into the toilet.

'What are we going to do?' Dan asked.

'Follow me,' Sylvester said. With his back to the wall he edged his way towards the door. Dan followed close by.

When they were half-way towards their destination a man dashed from the outskirts of a rough and tumble where everybody was trying to strike everybody else. He recognised Sylvester.

'You're the dirty bastard that had me barred from the Green Shillelagh,' he shouted. He swung a powerful fist which caught Sylvester on the side of the face. Sylvester covered his head with both hands as his assailant made ready to strike him again. Before he had time to deliver a second blow Dan struck him a flush on the jaw. The man dropped without a sound.

'Come on,' Dan called, 'before his pals get us.'

He pushed Sylvester towards the door and out on to the street where the fighting was worse. Several of the combatants lay on the ground or were crouched in a huddled position holding their stomachs. Some moaned with pain. Others were unable to do so. Dan warded off a blow from a youngster who was determined to fight someone so that he could make a name for himself. Sylvester slumped against the balustraded window of the pub. His hands still covered his head. Dan was forced to turn his full attention to the youth who was endeavouring to strike him.

'Go away,' Dan said, 'I don't want any trouble.'

'Fight you coward,' the youth called mockingly.

Again Dan was forced to move quickly in order to avoid the swinging fists. Then suddenly and quite unexpectedly the youth turned and ran. Dan was mystified. At the same time a crowd came pouring out of the pub. They did not seem to want further fighting. Their only aim seemed to be to get as far away as possible from the disaster area. Dan was perplexed by such odd behaviour but when two large black vans drew up at the kerb, from opposite directions he guessed that these must be the infamous Black Marias. He lifted Sylvester to his feet as about twenty policemen with drawn batons emerged from the vans.

Suddenly he felt his left hand go limp. He turned to see a policeman with a baton in his hand attempting to strike him again.

'I'm only trying to help this man,' Dan explained and pointed at Sylvester.

'Effing Paddies,' the policeman snarled, 'can't take a drink like civilised people.'

He struck Dan a sharp blow on the head. The blow made him lose consciousness. He reeled for a moment or two and then fell to the ground alongside Sylvester.

The powerfully-built man Dan had seen in the toilet

seemed to be immune to the baton blows that rained on his head and shoulders. Eventually they managed to hold him down. Sylvester, who saw what was happening, was certain that the man was in for a terrific beating but the police seemed content to lift him bodily into the van.

When Dan came round and opened his eyes he discovered that he had an excruciating pain in his head. Sylvester lay beside him but he was fast asleep, snoring drunkenly in much the same condition as when Dan first met him on the train from Fishguard. They were in a cell. That much was obvious from the iron bars in front of him. There were two other occupants. One was the man Dan struck in the pub and the other the burly fellow the police had been unable to render unconscious. Both were sleeping soundly. There was some congealed blood on the big man's face but otherwise he looked in good shape.

Dan was unable to sleep. The pain in his head was a real discomfort. The hours passed. From another cell, in another part of the building came a drunk singing 'Down by the Glenside' and in the circumstances Dan found it weird. It affected him in the oddest manner possible. He felt as though he must weep. At first he put this down to drink but as the verses dragged on he found it was something more. The song rang out hollowly, eerily and lamentably. It literally chilled him although really it was no more than a lonely, poorly-sung melody but Dan felt an overpowering loneliness for his home, for his brother and his parents. Suddenly the singing stopped. It was followed by a grunt and he guessed that his captors were less appreciative of the song's value.

In the morning they were whisked away to a courthouse where a magistrate was disposing of similar cases at a speed which left Dan somewhat giddy.

Sylvester, before they left the cell, told him that they would be charged with being drunk and disorderly. If the charges were anything more serious the jails of England would not contain the great numbers of Irish prisoners. Unless a policeman was seriously hurt or property damaged the proceedings were always cut and dried. Dan found himself standing before the magistrate. He was a small, thin-faced, grey-haired man. He did not raise his head from the papers in front of him when the charges were read. The policeman who brought them could not have been more respectful or kindly. The incidents of the night before seemed to have been completely forgotten.

'Drunk and disorderly.'

The constable reeled it off as if he were passing the time of day.

'Thirty shillings or seven days,' the magistrate announced. Dan quickly signified his intention of handing over the money. The magistrate looked at him bleakly.

'Haven't seen you before, Pat?' he said.

Dan shook his head.

'Let's not have you again Pat all right?'

'Yes sir,' from Dan.

Sylvester was next in line. Unwashed and unshaved, as were the others, he looked a pathetic sight, by far the worst of the unkempt assemblage.

'Thirty shillings,' the magistrate said tonelessly.

As they were leaving the burly man now far from being rough or tough was explaining to the magistrate that his money must have been stolen in the pub or when he had become involved with the police on the street.

'Let it be a lesson to you Pat,' the magistrate advised sarcastically, 'when you get out in a week's time stay away from pubs.' The attendant constables laughed obligingly.

Quickly Dan stepped forward and thrust the thirty shillings into the big man's hand.

'There's no call for that,' the big man said although he seemed to be deeply affected by the gesture.

'That's all right,' Dan told him, 'you can pay me back.'

'Yes. Yes,' he said eagerly. 'I can do that. I can pay you back.'

'I hope they never hear of this back home,' Dan said in the street.

'I'm a jailbird,' Sylvester muttered half to himself.

'You look like one,' Dan was remarking on his friend's wretched appearance.

'Let's go somewhere and have a drink.'

'I'm game,' Dan agreed, 'where would you like to go?'

'Let's call a taxi to the Ritz. The change will do us good.'

'Sounds like a solid idea but let's stop off first and clean up.'

IN ONE of the maternity wards Sister Dee sat talking to a young mother who had, a week before, given birth to twins. Together they were going over the feeding charts upon which the infants' survival would depend when the pair left the hospital. It wanted only four days for Christmas. In less than 24 hours Patricia would be going home to Wexford for a week.

In the corridor she was informed that somebody wanted to speak to her on the phone. She looked at her watch. It was almost twelve noon. At six o'clock she would be free for a period of nine days. At the main reception she was directed to a cubicle.

'Yes?' she said when she had the phone in her hand.

'Is that Nurse Dee?'

'Speaking.'

'I don't know if you remember me,' the voice said. 'I rang once last summer but they said you were out. I met you on the boat to Fishguard. I suppose you've forgotten.'

'I'll say one thing for you Dan Murray.'

'Oh?'

'You're a great warrant entirely for making phone-calls'

'Amn't I though? I suppose everyone has a turn for something.'

'Oh indeed. Two in ten months!'

'Listen.'

'I'm listening.'

'Will you see me tonight?' There was no plea, no entreaty in the request.

She decided to gamble and make it more difficult for him. It just wouldn't do to give him a walkover.

'I'm leaving for Ireland early tomorrow,' she said.

'So am I.'

'What way?'

'I'm driving to Liverpool'

'Driving?'

'Yes. A friend loaned me a van.'

'But you have to do a driving test.'

'I did it.'

'And you passed?'

'Yes I passed.'

'I'm not sure I believe you. You're sure you're not having me on?'

'What good would that do me?'

'Sorry. I believe you. It's just the surprise. The last time I saw you, you looked like a lost sheep and now you're able to drive a van over one of the busiest roads in England.'

Dan did not say anything for a while. Patricia grew worried but she decided to wait and see if he would ask for a date a second time.

'What about tonight?' Dan reminded her.

'I suppose so.'

'Where?'

'Meet me at the main entrance at half-six.'

'I'll be there,' he said.

She hung on expecting him to say more. When she realised he was no longer on the line she replaced the phone. It was all so sudden. The last time he called was late in July yet he hadn't forgotten. So he was able to drive. She had been right. He was different. He would never have a great deal to say for himself but he knew where he was going.

What to wear? She had lost weight over the autumn months. It hadn't been easy but now it seemed well worthwhile. All right Dan Murray. I'll be nicer than any girl you ever saw, for tonight at any rate. You won't go home by Liverpool either. You'll drive us both to Fishguard and you'll be seeing a lot more of me from now on.

8

TOM REICEY sat up in his bed, his broad back propped by an assortment of pillows. The weak December sunlight pierced the lace curtains of the big bay window and high-lighted the lines on his drawn face. He would never get used to this damned room. It was seldom in use. Originally it was meant to be a visitor's room but the Reiceys never had guests. It had been his wife's idea to transfer him to this room when he took ill a week before. It was warmer and quieter and since he was the worst of patients he would at least have as much peace and quiet as a detached abode in outer Chelsea could afford.

The house was an old one. Once it had been the property of a famous actress. In the early nineteenth century extensive repairs were carried out on all its three floors and the brewer who owned it spent a small fortune on elaborate wrought iron to adorn its interior. He spent still more on marble, mahogany and every conceivable decorative embellishment in an effort to gratify his wife who was but half his age. When he died she sold it to a wealthy Australian who wanted his son and two daughters educated in England. After five years he sold it to a retired hotelier and when he passed on after a further ten years his widow disposed of it to Tom Reicey.

Tom's wife who came originally from Kerry was struck by the house at once. He had not been so keen but then he shrewdly realised that the antique fixings would always make a good price separately. He was recovering from a heavy bout of flu but there were urgent matters which claim-ed his attention. On chairs at either side of the bed sat his brothers Joe and Dicey. Sylvester O'Doherty sat on a chair near the bottom where he had spent two hours reading fin-ancial statements. It looked as if it were going to be a record-breaking year for the Reiceys. On one medium-sized contract for the erection of a five-eyed concrete bridge in Kent there would be a profit of £20,000 despite having to buy a convenient gravel pit in the North Downs. At this stage it looked as if the pit was going to be worth ten times what they paid for it. It was only one of many such pits. There was one in the Chilterns, inexhaustible in relative terms and currently worth a hundred times what Tom originally paid for it. In the early war years hillsides with gravel deposits were to be had for a song. The red brick was the basic material for all English building but nothing is so subject to sweeping changes after wars as general building. Later when astute builders sought their own gravel pits they found that Reicey Brothers had the richest deposits. No one was in a position to compete with the Reiceys as far as concrete was concerned.

Tom Reicey was sometimes nicknamed the Cement God. He did not take exception to the title. There was no reason why he should. Every day of the week aeroplanes from all over the world were landing on the concrete strips his Rangers had laid down. Children played on his playgrounds. Trucks, buses and cars trundled and sped over his concrete roads. Although few firms had expanded so dramatically he was yet the soul of caution and had uncanny foresight.

He never gambled or trusted to luck in any operation. He had to be absolutely sure before he started. Every single facet had to be checked and rechecked before he submitted final figures. It was an industry that had a higher incidence of bankruptcies than any other and he always made certain that his name would not figure among the forgotten giants of the building trade.

The flu which confined him to his bed so near Christmas had proved to be sapping and insidious. He blamed it on his most recent visit to Ireland to see his mother. At eighty-one she was as hale and hearty as many women half her age. Having spent a week in Mayo they had gone to see his wife's mother in Kerry. His wife would not give it to say to the neighbours that they stayed in a hotel. It had to be her parents' home or nowhere. God knows he was no snob but it was a thatched hovel of a place, cold, windy and damp. There was no doubt in his mind as to where he picked up the germ. Typically his wife blamed his mother's home in Mayo but this was not true. He had rebuilt the ancestral cot and installed hot and cold water, added a bath and flush toilet.

Tom had found no change in his mother, and had begged her to come back with him but she would not hear of it. Tom's wife pretended to find her somewhat vulgar.

'There's young wans in the town wears no drawers at all these days.' The old woman made this claim one night as they were going to bed.

'No doubt, no doubt,' Tom said hoping she would shut up. Every time the old woman said something out of the way it compensated hugely for the shortcomings of his wife's parents.

"Tis true,' Tom's mother went on. 'Not as much as a stitch of drawers and the men going around wearing their low shoes every day like 'twould be Sunday.'

'Yes. Yes mother,' Tom said not unkindly. 'Don't you think it's time you were going to bed?'

'Low shoes,' the old woman looked in his wife's direction as if she were to blame for it all. The younger Mrs Reicey bore the rebuke silently.

'Some of the straps wears no corsets. They have the young men driven out of their minds. 'Tis all drinkin' and eatin' and whorin'!'

Fond as he was of his mother Tom was glad when they left for Kerry. His happiness was short-lived. His wife seemed to think that his only function was to take her father to the pub morning, noon and night. Not once during the four days did the old man put his hand into his pocket to buy a round of drinks and this despite the fact that she had given him twenty pounds as soon as they arrived. Not only that but Tom was expected to stand to the friends and relations too.

Of the three Reiceys Sylvester liked Joe best. He was neither greedy nor grasping and Sylvester knew that there were times when he wasn't happy with certain aspects of the business. The workers liked him and in this capacity he was indispensable to the firm. Sylvester got on especially well with him.

'Boys,' Tom Reicey said and he sat up in the bed, 'my mind is made up. We must buy more property in Ireland. It's a coming country.'

'What have you in mind?' Dicey put the question.

'Everything and anything. Land is cheap at the moment. Let's buy the good stuff while the Ascendancy boys are on the run from taxes and merchants. After we pay our taxes we should have £100,000 to kick around with. That will buy a hell of a heap of good land. Better buy places not too far from the sea. In ten years Ireland will open up. I feel it in my bones. In twenty you won't be able to buy land there. It's a good place to live. There's peace there and there's scenery. There's labour. It's wide open boys so let's invest in time.'

'We already own a hotel and a farm.' This from Dicey.

'I know what we own but I also know that a time will come when England will expand no further. The English are sick and tired already of the income tax dodge and the lump system. In the building trade there are only a handful of Irishmen stamping cards. It won't last forever.'

There was murmuring of assent from Joe and Dicey.

'Anyway, I have no intention of spending the rest of my life here. There isn't any gravy for the likes of us in Ireland yet but there will be. I'm just making certain that we have big spoons and that we get a place near the pan.'

'Who would buy the land and who would own it?' Joe asked.

'A fair and honest question,' Tom said in assent. 'We'll get our solicitors back home to buy it but of course we'll want to see what we're buying. I'll go over myself before any deal is closed. With the kind of money we're offering we can pick up ten of the best farms in the west of Ireland. There's mighty land for the asking in the county of Limerick.

The Kerry cuties are buying left, right and centre, going to their necks in the banks but if they are their land is doubling in value every three years.'

'By God, that's so, that's so,' Joe Reicey said.

'We can clean up if we move now,' Tom swept on. 'There was never a better time. You hear talk of golden opportunities. Believe me boys these opportunities are everywhere in Ireland at this present time. My advice is buy now and worry later.'

'I'm inclined to agree with you,' Joe said. 'You didn't say who would own the land.'

'I'm coming to that. We will own it, the three of us. Fifty per cent for me and twenty-five per cent for each of you.'

'I have no objection to that.' Dicey rubbed his hands together, a huge smile on his face. This news would bring a glint to the eye of Margo. It might be the sort of announcement to soften the way for the proposal he had in mind.

'What say you Joe?' Tom rearranged the pillows at his back.

'I'd be a fool if I complained. There's no doubt but it's a famous deal for a country boy who hadn't a second shirt twenty years ago.'

'You're agreed then?'

Joe shook his head slowly. 'It's fair all round and you're entitled to the largest share but isn't it time Sylvester was included in one of our developments.'

'Your heart is in the right place Joe but the Reiceys are the Reiceys and while I'm at the wheel that's the way its going to stay. I like Sylvester as much as you do and I have a great wish for him. Didn't I give him a job when no one else would? Did he ever have to ask for a rise? Did you Sylvie?'

'No,' Sylvester said. 'I'm well paid and well looked after. I appreciate your thoughtfulness Joe but Tom is right. The Reiceys made this company what it is. It would be wrong to bring strangers into it.'

Tom Reicey swung out of the bed and pulled on his dressing gown. He walked across the richly-carpeted floor to the window. From the tiny bay table he took an envelope and handed it to Sylvester. 'Don't open it now Sylvie. It's a bonus for Christmas. There'll be no tax on it. I think you'll agree later that I have a good memory for good men.'

Sylvester thanked him and put the envelope in his pocket.

'Is there anything else boys? I find a tiredness coming on.' He returned to the bed and made himself comfortable.

'There is a matter,' Joe said, 'which must come to light.'

'Now's the time,' Tom Reicey encouraged him.

'There's an increasing number of firms giving the five-day week with the unions discouraging overtime in some cases. Some of our lads are starting to crib too.'

Tom Reicey laughed. 'I don't believe you'll ever see the day that a Paddy will turn his back on overtime. It's his beer money and if he's paying tax it's his tax money. It's his whore money and his landlady's money. It's the money he puts in the wife's registered letter and it's the money he gives to the priest who forgives his sins.'

'Well it's not widespread,' Joe conceded. 'But a few of the single lads are starting to get fond of their Saturdays. There's muttering going on by some.'

'A man muttering under his breath is the best bloody man you ever had,' Tom said. 'I never cared for men who are well contented. A mutterer will work the temper out of himself without ever knowing what he's doing.'

'I don't know Tom,' Joe shook his head.

'All right then sack the bastards. There are thousands more in Ireland.'

'I think sacking them would be a good idea,' Joe agreed. 'I think they should be sacked without notice and moreover if they give any trouble we should have a few five-eights handy. These fellows are the wrong kind of latchikoes to have on any site and it might do no harm to make an example of a few of them.'

'Do you think the rest of our workers will go along with the idea?'

'The rest of the workers want overtime, all the overtime they can get.'

'Make sure nothing happens on any of the sites.' Tom raised a hand to make sure he was understood.

'Nothing will unless they start it themselves. If it goes to that I'll call in the law. They owe us a turn.'

'There's no need for the law,' Dicey put in, 'the rangers are bursting for an outing. Just make sure the law don't get to the pub till our lads are clear.'

'I think I can promise that,' Tom grinned. 'Now if there's nothing else I'm for sleep. I'm as weak as a whore of a Sunday morning.'

Joe and Sylvester left the room together. On the stairway they chatted for a while. Normally Tom's wife would ask callers to have a cup of tea or a drink but she could not and would not understand Sylvester, neither the things he said nor the words he used. He knew she did not understand and this made it worse because out of politeness he spoke down to her. This infuriated her to such an extent that she tried to pretend she wasn't listening.

Politely she showed them out baring her teeth into what she hoped was a disinterested smile. It went unnoticed by both men, the curse of the crows on the pair of them. She would have a laugh when Dicey came down. He would fill her in on his latest conquests and excite her a little as he always did.

Maisie had first met Tom Reicey at a dance-hall in Kilburn exactly one week after he had arrived in England. At that time she was Maisie Greynie and she worked as an assistant cook and chambermaid in the house of an Irish doctor in Kilburn. She was immediately taken by the powerfully built, ruddy-featured young man from Mayo. She inveigled an introduction to him through the girl with whom he had spent most of the night dancing. The rest had been easy. Tom Reicey had always imagined himself to be a good-looking fellow with a future brighter than most. Maisie Greynie convinced him that both beliefs were strongly founded. Up to this he had met no other human being who shared these high opinions of himself. Maisie understood Tom from the start.

Their backgrounds were almost identical. Both knew poverty from birth. Sometimes they had known hunger. They were a frugal pair from that first night to the morning of their wedding breakfast in the Swan and Cygnet in Hammersmith. During a year of courtship they avoided pubs and spent most of their time window-shopping or walking in the parks. On rare occasions they went to the cinema, never aspiring to any form of luxury beyond a pair of four-penny seats. After the pictures they would purchase bags of chips and ray and catch the last buses home. They saved assiduously and were one of the few couples of their kind to start off in life with their own house. Granted they were forced to let rooms to Irish labourers but there was none of the trouble associated with like situations. This could be attributed to the fact that Tom Reicey and his brother Joe who stayed with them were not a pair who liked disturbances.

A year after the marriage they were without issue or signs of issue so to occupy her spare time Maisie decided that she would dispense with all room tenants and declare herself open to fulltime boarders. She succeeded from the outset. If a man wanted a quiet life Reiceys' was the place to stay. If a man was temporarily outlawed by his fellows Reiceys' was a reliable sanctuary until the passage of time softened or erased altogether his misdemeanour. To interfere with him while a boarder with the Reiceys was to interfere with Tom Reicey himself.

It was therefore much in demand for a variety of reasons. The food was plain but wholesome and if the rates were higher than most it was a small tax for the many important amenities the place afforded.

After two years the house was fully paid for. Tom was a general foreman and making money hand over fist in sundry other ways. Maisie finally announced that she was going to have a baby and one of the boarders mischievously remarked that the time of her conception coincided with the arrival of a Connemara buck navvy with a physique like a gorilla. The tale was carried to Tom Reicey and the unfortunate man who meant it as a joke was hospitalised for seven weeks with a multiplication of serious injuries. On the major building sites for years afterwards one might curse the queen or De Valera or even the Pope with impunity but if you were going to curse Tom Reicey it was safe to look around before you did so.

During the sixth month of her pregnancy Maisie gave notice to all the boarders except Joe. She was taking no chances. The doctor for whom she once worked called twice a week to carry out checks and to take occasional tests. During the seventh month on her doctor's orders she took to the bed. She wrote to Ireland for her mother and Tom went to Fishguard to meet her in one of the old Commer vans which he used for transporting his work force.

After nine months Maisie was delivered of a baby boy who was sound in wind and limb and who weighed seven pounds and four ounces. It went without saying that he would be called after Tom's late father whose name was Seán. Another year passed and she made her husband prouder still by presenting him with a baby girl.

Now nobody could say that the first child was a fluke. Two years were to pass before she gave birth again. It was another boy and much against Tom's wishes it was named for his wife's father Willie Greynie who was in Tom's opinion a drunkard, an idler and a general all round nuisance who was never done with begging for loans or gifts of money. If Tom had his way he wouldn't give the old wretch the light of day. If his wife wanted to send home a pound or two that was her business. God knows she had made a fair share of money for him and she never objected when he sent his own mother a few pounds. With three children to look after and an extra boarder in the shape of Tom's youngest brother Dicey she sought a change of locale and after months of fruitless searching for the house which would be ideal they finally, one evening, were shown round the Chelsea scene. House followed house. The inspections were brief till they came to one where Maisie intimated she would sit down and take a rest.

'This is the house I want,' she told Tom. 'Nothing else

and nothing less will do. It has to be this.'

'All right,' he had said. 'So be it.'

Before they left Tom told the agent that they had no interest in the house, that it was the type of building which would probably be demolished under a new local government order. He advised the agent to get rid of it as soon as he was made a decent bid. The agent was somewhat sceptical but Tom disclosed his identity and spoke with authority and pretence of being in the confidence of high-ups.

Tom allowed a fortnight to go by. He contacted an acquaintance who worked for a firm of valuers, a man of Cork extraction named Morrissey and sent him along to the agent for the Chelsea householder.

'I must know,' he told his friend, 'exactly how much the fittings are worth. I know what the house is worth. Bring me back the information I want and you'll have my cheque for twenty-five pounds in your arse pocket before you go to bed with your landlady tonight.'

Morrissey, who was nicknamed Red, went about his commission scratching his head. He had never been in bed with his landlady. He wasn't long enough in lodgings to chance his arm but the incredible thing was that he intended chancing it that very night.

So thorough was his examination of the house that he tested the patience of the agent. He made notes from time to time and spent periods of up to ten minutes examining bannisters and window-sills or it might be a fireplace or chandelier in an upstairs room. He spent three hours altogether and when he seemed satisfied that he had no more to see he turned to the agent and said 'You'll never get rid of this lot.'

'And why not if I may ask?'

'They're going to start knocking them any day now. Somethin' to do with the foundations. Still, I dare say you'll get somebody.'

When Red Morrissey left, the agent ejected his upper set of false teeth into the cup at his hand and wiped them with his handkerchief. This was the second time somebody had mentioned the possibility of the house being knocked. Could there be a grain of truth in it or were his two informants working in collusion? Quite possible but it was his duty to report the matter to the owner. Besides there was his own investment to consider.

A week passed and a softly spoken, cultured man asked if he might see the property. He did not seem to be greatly interested in details.

'My name is Nanty,' he said, 'Professor Percival Nanty.' The agent welcomed him with open arms. Here was the classic, myopic type beloved of all estate agents. Here was the surface examiner who purchased on whim and instinct. When his brief inspection was concluded the professor asked if there was a reserve. He was told yes but not to forget that reserves were there to be approached rather than reached.

The reserve was £14,000. There was a good deal of this type of property on the market at the time as the agent well knew. The owner had panicked and upbraided him for not accepting earlier offers which were only a trifle short of the reserve having heard his doubts about the soundness of the property.

'It was you who suggested the reserve,' the agent had reminded her.

'And it was you who refused to budge,' she countered bitterly. After a few more exchanges they decided not to withdraw the reserve but in the face of a reasonable offer that they should seriously consider lowering it

'£14,000 is a lot of money,' Professor Nanty said thoughtfully.

'Not really,' the agent said. 'Not with a valuable property like this. If you feel its beyond you I could always hear your bid and take it to my client.'

'It's not beyond me,' the professor said. 'I'll tell you what I'll do. I'll make you a bid of £10,000.'

'That is a most excellent bid sir,' the agent acted for a second as if he were about to slap him on the back.

'There is a condition,' the professor cautioned.

'What condition?'

'I would like to bring my engineer along to have a look.'

'But of course, of course you must bring your engineer.' Under his breath the agent uttered a swear word not in the least complimentary to the engineering profession.

The professor revisited Chelsea with Dicey Reicey after a lapse of three days. The youngest Reicey looked the part. Dicey, acting on Tom's instructions, tapped stairways and walls with his knuckles and listened as if he were a physician stethoscoping a patient's chest. Outside he used a slender steel rod and thrust it into the earth near the walls. He inserted it to a depth of a foot. He did this seven times in all and as he proceeded with his examination his face grew more serious. All the time the agent watched with great interest.

Without a word Dicey went to his car and returned with an instrument which the agent had not seen before.

'Nice sort of afternoon,' the professor said.

'Yes it is,' the agent answered.

'We may get rain.'

'Let's hope not,' was the reply. He wished the professor would stop talking about the weather. It upset his concentration. The engineer now lay full length on the ground. Pressed to the wall was the strange device he had brought from the car.

'What in blazes is that?' he asked.

'I'm sure it's some sort of seismograph,' the professor enlightened him.

'Ah! So that's what it is.'

'Damned expensive but deadly accurate,' Professor Nanty confided.

'I should think so.' The agent pretended he knew more about the instrument than he cared to divulge. In reality what Dicey was using was the speedometer from a five-ton truck. With the aid of a small battery it was an easy matter to send the numerals whirring around and around, increasing in speed until there was a protracted whine. This was exactly what was happening now. The agent craned forward, a look of alarm on his face. His lips posed a question but the professor motioned him to silence by bringing a finger to his own. Still the numerals whirred with the whine now at its highest pitch. Gradually it whirred to a stop.

With expressionless face Dicey looked at the professor, then at the agent.

'Is there something I should know?' the agent asked.

Dicey acted as if he hadn't heard. He returned his equipment to the car and called Professor Nanty to one side. Try as he might the agent could not hear a single word of the conversation. He waited impatiently while the colloquy went on and on. When it ended Dicey went towards the car and sat waiting, utter boredom and professional contempt written on his face.

'Everything all right?' the agent asked.

'Oh everything's fine. Just fine,' the professor smiled.

'Will I be having your bid then?'

'I'm afraid not. I'm genuinely sorry to have bothered you.'

'Is it because of something or other in the foundations?'

'All I am prepared to say,' the professor stated solemnly, 'is that I am no longer interested in buying the house. I am not at liberty to elaborate. I'll have to be going now. Good day to you sir.'

The agent sat on a bird trough near a gable and lit his pipe. Could it be a confidence trick? If it was then it must be one of the most elaborate on record. It couldn't be. The idea was nonsensical. Might it not be a good idea however to engage his own engineer? He drew slowly on the pipe and watched the smoke curl upwards where it disappeared wraithlike in the thin evening air. Suppose the second engineer condemned the house. What then? Who would compensate him for all his time, for the advertisements, for the sketch artist's outlandish fees, for the journeys to and fro. He sat in thought till his pipe went out. The house would go for the next reasonable offer. His mind was made up. The next reasonable offer.

Reg Noople, alias Professor Percival Nanty, site parasite and sometime conman gratefully pocketed the twenty-five pounds, fee in full for his part in the Chelsea scam. If Tom Reicey had but known the fee might have been nominal. Reg Noople liked to dress for the part and would have volunteered his services for nothing. Apart from being a natural shyster he revelled in a role where he could sport a pince-nez, a flowing silk handkerchief and twirl an ebony cane whenever the fancy caught him.

The next offer came the following day from a firm of solicitors. It was for £10,000 with the stipulation that it be accepted or rejected within 24 hours. It was not a standing offer. In a frenzy the agent contacted the other bidders to learn that they were not available or no longer interested for one reason or another.

The agent was in a quandary. He knew the value of the house to be at least £3,000 and possibly £5,000 more than what was being offered. He rang the owner and acquainted her with the most recent development.

This time she did not ask his opinion. She told him not to sell at the price but to wait yet a while to see if there would be an increase on the offer. The agent was determined to get rid of the property at all costs. His fee would be £500 if the house were sold at once. So what if he was losing a few hundred?

He told his client it was his duty to point out that there was a steady recession in the size of the amounts being offered. Houses of similar age and design were beginning to flood the market. If the declining price continued there was the danger that it could suddenly plummet to an all-time low. He had seen it happen with other properties. Then there was the danger of demolition or there might be a compulsory order for major repairs. In view of all these demoralising possibilities it would be the height of foolhardiness to hold out any longer.

A week later Tom Reicey moved in with a team of tradesmen. For the expenditure of a pittance he had saved himself £4,000. He realised he had been lucky but he had been largely responsible for the creation of that luck.

AFTER SYLVESTER and Joe had left, Dicey remained in the room.

'Christ Dicey I'm tired,' Tom pleaded. 'Can't it wait till some other time?'

'I want to become engaged for Christmas,' Dicey shot in quickly. 'I want to know if it's all right with you?'

'Is this the blood mare you've been chasing lately?'

'That's the one,' Dicey laughed, flattered by Tom's description.

'Have you asked her?'

'Not yet but if I had a good engagement ring I could.'

Tom Reicey sat up in the bed. Dicey solicitously patted the pillows and then placed them behind his brother's back.

'This girl,' Tom said, 'you're sure she's what you want?'

'She's what I want.'

'I've heard good reports of her. I hear she don't go with other fellows or never did. I also hear that she always goes to the Shillelagh. There's nothing but good girls goes to the Shillelagh. I think she's the girl for you Dice and I don't think you should wait too long. Decent girls are scarce.'

'This girl is pure. Believe me Tom.'

'So I'm told. I'm all for it.'

'Where am I going to get the price of a good ring?'

'Don't tell me you're broke.'

'You know damned well all my money is tied up.'

'A good job an' all. Still you have your pay. You have your director's fees and you have your cut out of the fiddle.'

'I have a horse in training remember.'

'Sell him.'

'Ah Jasus Tom don't make me do that.'

'I'll tell you what you bloody vagabond,' the laughter was breaking through Tom's rebuke, 'I'll stand you the bloody ring. It's my Christmas present.'

'Ah God you're better than a father to me.' Dicey knew that the paternal references always delighted Tom.

'Bring my trousers over here. It's hanging in the wardrobe.'

Dicey did as he was told. From the seat pocket Tom

withdrew a wallet. Inside were two wads of ten pound notes which were far from slender. Dicey estimated that there must be between £300 and £400 deposited in the pockets.

'And now what's the cost of an engagement ring?'

'About two fifty.'

'Two fifty what?'

'Pounds.'

'You're out of your shaggin' mind. No woman is worth that.'

'This one is.'

'Jasus when I made up my mind I bought Maisie a marriage band for fifty bob. I didn't know what an engagement ring was.'

'I want to do the thing right or not do it at all.'

Grumbling Tom counted the notes into Dicey's outstretched hand.

'I'll never forget you for this Tom,' Dicey was on the brink of tears. 'To the day I die I'll never forget you for this.' Tom was moved by his youngest brother's gratitude.

'Will you shag off outa here now and let me get some sleep,' he roared.

9

WHEN DICEY Reicey was twenty he grew restless with the passing of every single day. Neither Tom nor Joe would hear of his joining them in England until he was twenty-one. This was the excuse they offered whenever he started to chafe at the bit. What they really wanted of him was to keep his mother company until they could convince her that the only place for her was with her sons in England. The Reicey homestead was able to carry three milch cows and of course there was the old woman's pension. The money she received from England was hoarded about her person, most of it in a black cloth purse which was tied around her neck and which was never removed even when she washed.

The brothers also sent money to Dicey but it was never enough. In summertime he found life tolerable. There were a number of high class hotels in the district which catered for English and Scottish tourists. With a band of four others Dicey visited the seaside and lakeside resorts almost every night throughout the summer.

The barmaids in these hotels were drawn from the countryside around or if not they came north from Kerry and Cork or south from Donegal and Leitrim. The majority were scrupulously honest and would rather die than misappropriate a farthing of their employers' money. There were a few who were readily susceptible to the charms of the local boys, particularly to Dicey with his flowing tawny hair and bright blue eyes. He had a freshness and a pinkness which many girls found alluring. When a conquest was made it was a mere matter of form coming round the barmaid in question to supply drink and cigarettes to the victor and his friends without charge. Since he was seventeen there had always been some barmaid who had fallen for Dicey.

Dicey and his friends employed simple methods. Each

would select a barmaid from a different hotel or different resort. They would ask for a date and after the customary first refusal generally succeeded in getting the girl to agree to a meeting. The girls had little time off so that it would be the early hours of the morning when trysts took place. The managements frowned on all such relationships.

It was seasonal work and the season was short enough without the burden of sleepy barmaids. Sleepy barmaids were sharp with customers and they tended to make mistakes. When the bar closed around midnight they were expected to go to bed at once. They had a night off every week but this was hardly enough.

It meant that they stole from their beds when the other girls were asleep, often exhausted after the long day and night. The meeting would take place in a coach-house or outhouse or if the weather was dry and warm they might come together in a meadow where the freshly made cocks of hay would provide cushions of a kind. Dicey and his friends never chose pretty girls. It was too difficult to date them and half the summer might be gone before one consented. When they did they were niggardly enough with their favours. Rarely would they agree to defraud their employers and some went so far as to inform the management.

The plain girl was a better proposition all round. It often happened that she might not have dated before simply because she was never asked. Certainly a boy with Dicey Reicey's looks would be an exceptional treat and any offer from him would be seized upon at once.

As a rule the girls lost their heads and were agreeable to anything after a few illicit meetings. The combination of the hour, the secrecy and the summertime was difficult to overcome especially if a girl had been neglected all her life up till then. The procedure afterwards was that Dicey might present himself at the bar of the hotel a few nights a week with his pals. Almost always there would be a sing-song in progress. They might range themselves along the bar or if there was a table available take seats and join in the singing. None of the group had any money.

'What will it be lads?' Dicey would ask and rattle the

coppers in his trousers pocket. Memorising the different drinks he would make his way confidently to the counter where one of the girls would ask his requirements. If she wasn't the right girl he would turn towards his friends as though he had forgotten the identities of the drinks. The girl would move along to another customer.

Dicey would wait till his own girl was free to serve him. He would be greeted with a genuine smile. Not only was he her boyfriend but he was also bringing his business and the business of his friends to the hotel on her account. Willingly, casting smiles backward all the time, she would dispense the drinks on to a tray.

The first time Dicey tried it there had been shaky moments. When the girl had placed the tray of drinks on the counter she had said 'That will be five shillings and six pence please.'

'Very good,' Dicey had said and handed over the two pennies and half-penny which was all he possessed. The girl thought it was a joke at first.

'Ah come on,' she said. 'We're very busy.'

'That's all I have,' Dicey told her. The girl frowned and wavered between exposing him or becoming party to his thievery. With a sigh she put the money in the till and occupied herself with another customer, still frowning, unable to decide.

There was never any trouble after the first time. During Dicey's last summer in Ireland there came to one of the hotels a barmaid named Julia Dempsey. She was older and plainer than the usual run and when Dicey asked her for a date she agreed at once promising to meet him later. Dicey was by now an experienced hand with the opposite sex. After a few meetings Julia found that she could think of nothing else. He occupied her thoughts endlessly. When Dicey arrived at the weekend with his party of penniless rustics she waved in ecstasy in his direction as soon as he entered. The friends found a table and sat themselves down. Dicey memorised the order and approached the bar where she covered his hand briefly with one of hers. He named the drinks he required and turning to his cronies winked hugely. Julia Dempsey took her time about filling the order. All the while she kept up a conversation with Dicey.

'How're you after the last night?' was her first question.

'Oh great,' he told her. 'Great entirely.'

'I shouldn't have kept you out so late.'

'What late?' Dicey shrugged as if four in the morning was a normal hour.

'When will I see you again?' her expression was grave, graver than he had ever seen it.

'Tonight,' Dicey said and he noisily rattled the five coppers which represented the total wealth of the party.

'I'm delighted,' she said. 'I may be a little bit later over it being a Saturday night.'

'I don't mind,' he said amorously. 'I'd wait till cockcrow for you.'

'Oh go on,' she laughed but she was secretly elated by the compliment.

'That will be seven shillings and two pence please.' Her manner changed when she mentioned the money. Confidently he withdrew the five-pence from his pocket, held them for a moment in the palm of one hand and selected three with the fingers of the other. With a disarming grin he handed her the money. She accepted it with a smile and then looked at it.

'Hey,' she called. 'Wait a minute.' Dicey turned in dismay. The load almost fell from his hands. He decided against dropping the tray and clearing out as fast as he could. There were a number of people present who knew him.

'What's the matter anyway?' he asked innocently.

'Aren't you going to wait for your change?' she said.

'I'm very forgetful that way,' he said at once, the relief showing in his voice. He returned to the counter and waited while she went to the till. She returned and handed him four pounds, twelve shillings and ten pence. He was awe-struck.

'But this is the change of five pounds,' he whispered incredulously.

'I thought it was five pounds you gave me,' she said for the benefit of the other barmaid who was within earshot.

'Ah that's right,' Dicey said. "Twas five pounds all right. I remember now. There's been something else in my napper all day that has the memory rightly banjoed on me.' He winked at her and returned to the table. Dicey proudly recounted the change in the presence of his pals who could scarcely believe their eyes. Calmly he thrust the coins into a trouser pocket and the notes into the inside pocket of his coat.

'There's good times coming,' he said and they all laughed uproariously. The deception lasted all through the month of July and up until the night of 15 August when the bar was crammed with people. Locals had come out in force to celebrate the feast day which was also the local pattern day. On fifteen occasions in all since Julia Dempsey's first date with him he had been given the change of five pounds out of sums that never exceeded six pence.

He spent most of the money in other hotels further afield where he had the reputation of being a bit of a playboy.

As was her wont Julia waved enthusiastically in his direction as soon as he arrived.

'Spell it out boys,' he said. 'And don't forget the sky's the limit.'

He forced his way to the counter where he had to wait several minutes before she had time to serve him.

'See you later?' she asked hopefully.

'You're right you will,' he said. 'Why do you think I came?'

Satisfied she saw to his needs. When the drink was placed in front of him he handed her a few coppers. She deposited them in the till and withdrew the single pound notes one by one. She followed with the silver. As she was about to close the till her wrist was held firmly by the proprietor's wife.

Holding the hand rigidly the older woman made a quick inspection of the till's contents. What Julia Dempsey could not have known was that every time a five pound note found its way to the till on that particular night it was immediately taken out again by the proprietor or his wife. For long they had suspected deceit and now with no five pound note in the till to justify the amount she had withdrawn Julia was caught red-handed.

When the proprietress had time to look round there was no sign of Dicey or his companions.

Later that year when a district court justice was deciding sentence upon Julia Dempsey he was to remark that it was a mean type of offence, a betrayal of trust and all in all a very serious crime indeed. He sentenced her to twelve months in prison, the sentence to be suspended in view of the twin facts that she was pregnant and that her parents had undertaken to pay back the money.

Now more than a dozen years afterwards Dicey Reicey was preparing for marriage. Margo had insisted on a long courtship.

'I want to do things the right way,' she told Dicey who would have married her the day after they met. 'I want to be a good wife to you and the only way I can do that is by getting to know you. I want to give myself to one man and to do that I shall have to know everything about him. I want to understand him, to learn all his needs and to satisfy him in every possible way all the days of my life.'

'Jesus,' Dicey said to himself, 'what a woman.'

Now, a little over two years and two months after their first meeting at the Green Shillelagh the marriage was about to take place. Margo would have liked if the reception could be held at the Russell Hotel where she and Dicey frequently dined but when Tom Reicey offered a marquee in the grounds of his spacious home in Chelsea and insisted on paying for everything, she realised it would be foolish and ill-mannered to refuse such a magnanimous offer.

Guests were limited to 200. These would include many famous figures on the London/Irish society front. The Irish Embassy would be well represented and there would be two Roman Catholic bishops not to mention canons and monsignori. Two Irish rugby internationals, close friends of Tom's, had accepted. There was to be a police superintendent and an inspector. There were doctors and surgeons and nurses from the hospital. As far as Newsham General was concerned it was really a matter of who could be spared on the day.

'If it was any day but the day it is,' Tom Reicey told Dicey and Margo, 'the cardinal would do the job. The bother is he'll be in Rome all week. He'll send a telegram and look after a pontifical blessing for the two of ye.'

It was decided that a cousin of Margo's, a Father Monty Cullagan who was a curate in a nearby diocese, should be invited to perform the ceremony. There were no priests amongst the Reicey relations. Tom had already advertised for and decided upon a firm of caterers to look after the food and drink at the reception. His instructions were curt when they informed him that while they could quote a fixed price per head for food there was no possibility whatsoever that they could quote for drink.

'Let the damned thing flow,' he said, 'and let me worry about the cost.' Since Dicey first announced that he was going to marry Margo, Tom Reicey nourished a secret feeling of profound satisfaction at the way things were turning out. His relief was immeasurable when he found out that Margo was the very epitome of respectability. He had long been afraid that Dicey would be duped by a gold-digger or tramp. Now the reverse was happening and Tom was able to live up to the promise he had made his dying father. 'Keep an eye on that mad bastard,' Seán Reicey had implored his oldest son from his sickbed in the tubercular sanatorium. 'Yourself and Joe is fine but that cratur hasn't a spatter of sense to his name.' Tom assured the elder Reicey that he need have no worries. He was now relieved that his promise was on the brink of fulfilment. Marriage would be just the institution to house the turbulent and apparently sex-crazed Dicey. She was a fair-looker was this Cullagan girl. If it wasn't in her power to quieten him then it was in the power of no woman. Tom was certain that Dicey would settle into normal ways and pull his full weight with the firm now that he had the responsibility of a wife and please God a houseful of children in God's own time.

MARGO MADE things difficult for Dicey after the first night in the Shillelagh. In the beginning she allowed him to think that she was strongly attracted to him and then when she felt that her grip on him was sufficient to hold him indefinitely she played hard to get. She had him running around in circles.

After three hectic months of night clubs, race-meetings and a variety of other outings Dicey felt himself overcome by passion one night in his flat where he invited Margo for a cup of coffee. He also felt that his investment was deserving of some return. She showed no objection when he kissed her nor when he placed his hands on her yielding shoulders and drew her on to a couch. When he suddenly thrust a powerful hand up under the skirt of her costume she slapped him with all the force she could muster across the face. With his rude strength and her own natural inclinations he had almost proved too much for her. She slapped him a second time and screamed. It worked. He let her go and sat back on the couch making every effort to control himself.

He realised he had gone too far, that this was no fast and loose doxie from a Soho bar or shady nightclub. He was immediately contrite when he became aware of her heaving bosom and bloodless face. He could not know that she was also trying to control herself. He mistook her condition for one of shock and suddenly knelt on the floor imploring her forgiveness.

'I don't know what came over me,' he said.

Margo played her cards well. She had him where she wanted him and she had every intention of keeping him there till she was good and ready to marry him.

'You must think I'm an awful rat,' he whimpered.

'Please don't speak to me,' she said icily.

'Forgive me,' he begged.

'I've never been so insulted in my entire life.'

'Oh God, oh God I don't know what made me do it.'

'Take me home,' she said sternly. He got to his feet and stood at a distance unable to look her in the face, his head hanging.

It was a picture of Dicey Reicey which his friends would not believe had they seen it. She smoothed her costume and walked with her head erect to the doorway. Vainly he tried to reason with her promising on his dead father's grave that he would never do such a thing again. With broken voice he tried entreaty after entreaty but to no avail.

She could have burst out laughing but this would have been absolutely disastrous. There was only one way with a man of Dicey's instincts and that was to keep him at a long distance. She played it cool for the following weeks and relented at just the right time. To show his gratitude he bought her a gold charm bracelet and swore upon his most solemn oath that he would never molest her in any possible way ever again. He was to keep his word. After six months of going steady it was more or less taken for granted by both of them that eventually they would marry, but when? Dicey never grew tired of dropping suggestions and hints. Margo was too sure of her position to hurry things.

After the engagement, Dicey was the soul of attentiveness. He had changed from his old ways and of late was spurning the approaches of his more doubtful friends.

'In the honour of God,' he addressed Margo despairingly one March night, 'will you put a date on it and take me out of my misery?'

She had laughed. A good sign. It gave him encouragement.

'Just name a day,' he pleaded.

'All right,' she said at last, 'I'll be your bride in June.'

His first reaction was to whoop with joy. Then he leaped in the air and slapped his sides unable to control his delight. In the middle of it all he stopped.

'You're sure?'

'I've just said so.'

'You won't go back on your word and postpone it.'

'I would never do anything like that.'

'Of course you wouldn't. It's just that I've waited so long and I'd hate to wake up in the middle of a dream.'

They had kissed, a long tender kiss and he had released her reluctantly.

'I can't wait for the day,' he sighed.

MARGO CULLAGAN was happy. A fresh Nigerian intern had arrived at Newsham General and something told Margo that there were tremendous possibilities simmering underneath the rippling, ebony muscles. He was a very correct type, spotlessly clean and immaculately dressed as if the country from which he had come was dependent upon him alone to show that it was the equal of the best. Margo smiled to herself. For all his martinet-like manner and emendatory righteousness she would embed him in her own good time. Waiting and surmising would add to the pleasure.

She met him first in casualty. He was distant and unbending.

'What's your name?' she asked gently.

'I am Doctor Ngaya Lelumba.'

'I guessed you were a doctor,' she said soothingly, 'but what do they call you for short?'

'I am called nothing for short.' He was very precise.

'Didn't your mother have a pet name for you?'

'My mother is dead,' he said.

'Oh I'm sorry. Do you mind if I call you Guy?'

'I am Doctor Ngaya Lelumba.'

'I see. What part of Nigeria do you come from?'

'My home is Makurdi,' he said proudly.

'Is that east or west?'

'It is east,' he said fiercely. 'How can anybody think it is west?'

Margo felt a delicious shivery fear at his anger.

'I'm sorry. Do you feel lonely for home sometimes?'

'I am a doctor. We do not think of those things.'

'You're very serious aren't you?'

He chose not to answer.

'Have you got a girlfriend back home?' Unconsciously she fingered the fine solitaire on her engagement ring.

'I am still studying.'

'You're very handsome. Hasn't anybody ever told you?'

She watched for his reaction but there wasn't any. This was good. He might have frowned or grinned or even guffawed the way ignorant men do when they are complimented.

116

'Guy,' she half whispered the name, 'don't you like me?'

'I am Doctor Ngaya Lelumba.'

'Yes but don't you like me?'

She could sense he was relenting. She was running out of time. Dicey would be waiting and he didn't like to be kept waiting. She moved nearer the young intern. 'I only want to be your friend,' she said half petulantly, half tearfully. He averted his head in embarrassment.

'Won't you be friends with me?' She took one of his hands. 'Won't you Guy?'

She felt him tremble, almost like a child. He was lonely all right, lonelier than he would ever admit. 'I must go now. Before I go please say you'll be friends with me.'

He nodded without looking at her.

'And may I call you Guy? Not when there's somebody listening. Just when we're alone.'

Again he nodded.

He was no more than a boy really Margo felt but it was impossible to ignore that shining face and the gleaming rippling arms. Quickly she leaned forward and kissed him on the cheek. When she had gone Ngaya Lelumba found himself so weak that he felt his knees must betray him. He sat and tried to collect his thoughts.

In April Margo made an appointment with Ngaya to meet him for dinner in a hotel in south-west London. It was the first Tuesday of the month and the rain poured mercilessly from mid-morning. Ngaya knew all about her engagement to Dicey. In fact he had met him on more than one occasion.

The night before Margo had explained to Dicey that she would be visiting a married friend the following day and would probably stay the night. He volunteered to drive her but she declined.

'You mustn't devote so much of your time to me,' she chided. 'I would much prefer if you gave yourself to your work. It's the least you owe to Tom for all the kindness he has shown us.' He had asked if he might collect her in the morning but again she declined.

'I'd rather you didn't,' she said. 'You see this friend is in

117

trouble and she has confided in no one but me. She asked me to tell nobody. I'm not supposed to tell you even.'

'I hope it's not too serious,' he said.

'It's her husband.' Margo breathed a long sigh. 'For some time he's been seeing a woman, a married woman.'

'The dirty bastard,' said Dicey who if he were asked would not be able to remember the number of married women with whom he had slept.

'I've promised her with a long while that I would spend a night and talk things over. She's a dear friend really and it's the least I can do.'

'I understand,' Dicey nodded sympathetically. 'Will I see you tomorrow night?'

'You'd better be at the main gate of Newsham General at nine o'clock or you'll hear about it.'

'I'll be there on the dot. Have I ever been late?'

'Of course you haven't. I'd be lost without you.' They embraced and kissed before bidding each other goodnight.

Margo took a bus from near the main entrance. It was seven o'clock and the rain kept falling relentlessly, filling the gutters with brown floods of hurrying water. Ruthlessly the double-decker splashed everybody in the long queue without discrimination. There were curses but the conductor smugly pointed out that the fault lay with the driver who was inaccessible in the cab up front.

She met Ngaya at the hotel where they made love many times. Later that night as they lay side by side in the large, old-fashioned double bed there was silence between them.

'You're not lonely any more?' she asked.

'Not in the way I was,' he answered.

NGAYA LELUMBA ended his internship at Newsham General two days before Margo's wedding. He left for Nigeria one hour before she took the first steps towards the altar in Newsham parish church.

Ngaya felt no pangs of loneliness at the thought of losing her. He felt, instead, a keen sense of relief. Such a woman would make a poor wife for a doctor in Africa, or a doctor anywhere. He was grateful for the comfort she brought him at a time in his life when he was critically lonesome. Apart altogether from the sexual pleasure which she always afforded him up to their last meeting two nights before her marriage she had been good for him in countless ways. Their relationship gave him a sense of supreme confidence in dealing with white superiors in the medical world. There was a beautiful white woman always available to him, a woman more sought after than any in Newsham General. Their final meeting took place in his room at the hospital. By arrangement she tapped at the door gently three times. It was already open but the tapping was to ensure that he had no chance visitor. He embraced her hungrily and in a matter of minutes they were locked together in the narrow bed. They talked a lot, all the time in whispers since there was constant traffic all night long through the corridor outside.

'Will you miss me?' she asked.

'Oh yes,' he said, 'more than I can ever tell you.'

'I'll miss you too,' she said. 'You'll think of me won't you Guy?'

'Always,' he said. 'You are the brightest thing ever to come into my life, brighter than the stars.'

Ngaya did not see Margo again. He said his goodbyes that night in his room. He slept till noon of the following day. When he woke she was far from his thoughts. He could think of nothing but the prospect of home, the new status which he would occupy, the envy and the respect of man, woman and child in his native place and best of all the thought of the pride within his own family.

10

WHEN DAN went home for Christmas Willie was at the bus stop to meet him. Dan had driven without mishap to Fishguard and installed the van which Sylvester had borrowed for him in a garage near the harbour. He had said goodbye to Patricia Dee at Rosslare and taken a train to Mallow. On Christmas Eve Dan, his brother Willie and Murray senior went to the pub.

'I'm going back with you,' Willie had said.

Dan waited for his father's reaction. It was slow in coming.

'What do you think Dan?' Bill Murray asked.

'I'm alone in the bloody parish,' Willie put in before Dan could reply. "Tis all oul' men and oul' women. There's no one of my age left here.'

'Will you hold your tongue and let Dan talk,' his father said. Dan knew Willie exaggerated but there was more than a modicum of truth in what he said. Dan had seen for himself the boarded-up houses of the more isolated mountainy areas and the less arable cutaway. These decaying homes were becoming more and more evident as whole families left the Irish countryside forever to go to London or Manchester or Coventry. Desolation reigned where tiny fields and cultivated plots were abandoned as one by one the members of a family joined each other in exile. The wilderness soon claimed these hard-won plots. The plaintive cry of lapwing and curlew fell like a lament on the dreary landscape. Laneways where whole colonies of people once survived were now empty as deserts. No child's voice called. There was no sound of young folk at play, no crying, no laughter. The unchastised crow cawed raucously on ancient thatch and crumbling chimney. For young men like Dan who remembered these homesteads when they were filled with people the graveyard was a more attractive place to visit. There was no guarantee that life would be better in England. It was certain, however, from long experience, that it could not be worse.

'Well Dan?' his father asked. Bill Murray had a deep regard for his thoughtful son. Sometimes it showed. Most of the time it did not. He knew there was a strain of steel running through the older boy, that powerful possibilities lay fallow under the calm exterior.

'I don't know,' Dan said. 'If it's what he wants maybe it might be better to let him go. It's not as if he had no one there. I do well as it is and I hope to do better. From pure selfishness he would be a great help to me. I have plans to go on my own as soon as I have enough money put aside. Already I have two hundred pounds.'

Father and brother gasped but Dan continued, 'When I go back I think I'll ask Eddie Carey to come in with me.'

'He's as good a man as ever you'll meet,' Bill Murray said.

'I know. That's why I'm going to ask him.'

'You think that Willie should go?'

'Yes. I think he should. The only thing is will yourself and herself be too lonely when you have nobody?'

'That's the way we started out,' Bill smiled ruefully, 'and I suppose it's only natural that's the way we should finish.'

'I'll be back one day for good,' Dan said.

His father looked at him for a long moment and knew that he meant what he said.

No other Irishman spent that particular Christmas as Dan spent it. When business resumed after the short holiday he went to the nearest town with Willie and ordered a large quantity of bricks. There was no mortar available so he made do with sand and cement. It was delivered by truck that evening.

The following morning he took Willie aside.

'Willie,' he said, 'we're going to build a wall, a decorative wall in front of the house. Now I could build this wall in two, maybe three days if I had to but I don't have to so what I'm going to do is build a bit and take it apart, build another

121

bit and take it apart. All the time you'll be watching me, Willie. If you watch me carefully and do everything I tell you, you'll be able to build this wall yourself, under my supervision of course. We'll build dry to start with and then we'll build part wet, cleaning our bricks so we can start all over again.' Willie nodded eagerly.

'You never heard of headers or stretchers?' Dan said.

'No.'

'Well they're bricks and I never heard of them either till I went to England. You've never heard of English or Flemish bonding?'

'No.'

'There are different kinds of bricklaying. Before I'm through with you you'll know a brick from a scraw.'

They worked through the day from first light till dark. Mary Murray would sit at times near the front window watching her two boys. It took her back to the day when they made mud castles in the very same place. She watched the wall take shape and she saw the beautiful points of its structure. She sighed each time it was taken apart and the hope built in her when it was put together again. She saw what Dan was trying to do and she saw after the first week that Willie was learning. She wanted to see it take a form as much as she needed the arrival of Dan himself when he struggled and kicked in her womb.

Each night the three men would go to the pub. They rarely stayed late. Mary Murray wished in her heart that it might go on like this forever. She loved to cook for the boys. She knew what they liked and how they liked it.

It had to end. The time came for Willie Murray's solo flight. Dan would remain in the background and Willie had agreed that there would be no intervention except in dire emergency.

There were four days remaining, in which time the wall had to be built. During the first day Dan tackled the pony and common cart.

'We'll go to town,' he told his mother, 'I have business there.'

By this act he could not have shown greater confidence

122

in his apprentice. When they returned that night Dan brought with him a small, ornamental wrought-iron gate. He had been lucky to find it. It was second-hand but it would fill the bill. Willie's progress during the day had been exceptionally slow, slow but good, really good. On the third day the wall was finished. It was an admirable piece of work. Mary wept with joy and relief in the quietness of her bedroom. Dan hung the gate and greased the hinges with bacon lard which he heated at the fire to render it a little. The gate opened without the faintest protest and it closed as smoothly and silently as though it had hung there for years.

'A wall isn't much use,' Bill Murray announced, 'unless 'tis properly christened. We'll stay at home tonight and have a small party.'

Six days before a cock turkey weighing twenty-two pounds had made his farewell to the hen whose constant companion he had been since the rest of the flock had been disposed of to fill Christmas orders. Bill Murray had pulled his neck and plucked him in readiness for a farewell dinner to mark the boys' departure.

11

WHEN DAN and Eddie Carey started on their own they worked every day of the week often putting in as many as fourteen hours a day. It had been worth it. They bought a new Commer van between them just after Christmas. They had given a lot of thought to the venture and had also invested in new equipment, made new contacts and were furiously sub-contracting for brickwork wherever they could get it. Dan's brother Willie was also a member of the team.

The van was paid for in full and the profits were double the amount invested. In a matter of months Willie became a finished layer. He bought books on the subject and there was now no aspect of the trade unknown to him. He told Dan he would prefer not to be paid a wage, that he would ask whenever he wanted money. Carefully Dan lodged his brother's earnings in the Bertham branch of the Midland Bank in a separate account. The manager had been most helpful in the buying of the new van and with the setting up of the agreement with Eddie, giving Dan many useful hints and warning him to be sure to consult him whenever he found himself with difficulties.

Dan had now spent three full years and three months in England. He had prospered and so had Eddie. He still stayed in the lodgings in Bertham and when their work took them too far afield he still paid for the room which he now shared with Eddie and Willie. Gillian had agreed to a second bed after Dan's insistence that they would be quite comfortable.

The Murray outfit had built a good reputation during the short while they were established. If a job which normally took nine days had to be done in three, then Dan and his gang were the people to hire. They never dawdled, never took days off. Holy days or holidays never impeded them.

There was a six o'clock morning Mass in Bertham Parish Church on Sundays and Holy Days. Father Conners, the parish priest had agreed to celebrate the Mass at this unearthly hour when Dan, Eddie and a delegation of other Irish workers informed him that there was a need for such a Mass. They were right. A number of nurses also availed of it. Often there might be a policeman or maybe two but all through the spring, summer and autumn it was ideal for the Irish labourers. Dan, Willie and Eddie between them made up a gift of money for Father Conners but he refused it.

'I understand you lads have gone out on your own,' he said to Dan. 'When you are really on your feet and if you still feel so inclined you can give me an offering. Fair enough?'

'Fair enough,' Dan agreed.

'Work hard and never forget you're a Catholic and an Irishman,' he said with abrupt candour.

'I JUST can't accept this,' the special investigator from the internal revenue informed Sylvester.

'I knew it would happen sooner or later,' Sylvester said half to himself, 'and I knew it would happen just like this.'

'Did you say something?' the investigator asked.

'No. I didn't say anything. I think the best thing to do is see Mr Reicey.'

'I should certainly think so,' the inspector said snappily. In his hand was one of the cheques cashed by Sylvester and supposedly paid to casual workers. The cheque was four years old and it was made out to Sylvester O'Doherty, signed by Sylvester O'Doherty and drawn by Sylvester O'Doherty.

'This is a mess if ever I've seen one,' the inspector was saying. 'I mean you haven't got a thing, no stamps, no tax, no receipts, no anything. I'm afraid I shall have to notify the police.'

'Now before you do anything,' Sylvester told him, 'you're coming with me to see Mr Reicey. He can explain everything.'

'We shall see.' The inspector was grim-faced and taciturn. 'As far as I can see nobody can explain this. It's larceny pure and simple but as you say let's go and see your Mr Reicey.'

Tom Reicey refused to say anything in the presence of Sylvester. He neither confirmed nor denied the claim that the cash had been handed over to him as soon as the cheques were lodged.

'Tell him Tom,' Sylvester insisted. 'Tell him what happened after the cheques were cashed.'

'If you have any sense Sylvie,' Tom advised 'you will say no more. Just return to your books and leave everything to me.'

'I left everything to you for the past four years and see where it's landed us.' Tom Reicey rose to his feet and planted his two hands firmly on the desk in front of him.

'Sylvester,' he said calmly, 'do as I tell you.'

Sylvester was about to remonstrate with his employer but he noticed that Tom had winked an eye. This could mean that he had something up his sleeve. After all it was he who was answerable for everything. Sylvester took the hint and left the inner office. As he went out he heard Tom offering a cigarette to the investigator.

In the outer office the four typists and the two secretaries were whispering excitedly. Sandra allowed a few minutes to elapse before she approached the large desk which looked down on the others. As senior secretary she had the right to go and talk to the office manager any time she felt obliged to do so.

'What's happening?' she whispered urgently.

'There's nothing to worry about,' Sylvester assured her. 'Just a few items that need clarification.'

'I don't believe you.'

'I think you had better go back to your desk. The others are watching us.'

'I don't care. I want to know what's happening. If you don't care for yourself I do.'

'Look,' he said patiently, 'go and sit down. I'll meet you after work in the Leadlathe Arms. I'll explain everything.'

She had to accept this but when the investigator failed to reappear she cast worried looks at Sylvester and at the clock.

The Leadlathe Arms was a decent inn run by a landlord of Yorkshire extraction named Len Digby. Sylvester was well-known to Len and his missus. He had lunch in the place almost every day and sometimes if Tom and he worked late or if he was forced to stay on in the office he would adjourn there for a few pints of beer and maybe a sandwich if he felt too tired to prepare a meal in the flat.

Mrs Digby took a dim view of Sandra's intrusion into the lounge without an escort. Sandra was quick to notice.

'I'm waiting for somebody,' she explained. Mrs Digby had heard that one before too.

'Do I know him?' she asked icily.

'I'm sure you do. He's my boss down at Reiceys.'

'It's not Sylvester is it?'

'Yes it is.'

Mrs Digby came from behind the counter and sat with her till Sylvester arrived.

He seemed relieved when he arrived. Shortly before six o'clock the inspector left the inner sanctum accompanied by Tom who saw him to the door. He bade Sylvester good evening as if nothing had happened. Tom Reicey motioned Sylvester inside. The office clock was striking six.

'I think it's going to be all right,' Tom said.

'He seemed happy enough as he was leaving,' Sylvester declared.

'Musha he's not a bad fellow really. I don't think we have any more to worry about. Just keep your mouth shut.'

Suddenly it dawned on Sylvester that there might be buckshee involved.

'I'll be off so,' he said. 'I may tell you I was sweating it out here while he was inside with you.'

'Ah well now maybe that's an end to it thanks be to God and his Holy Mother.'

After he had told Sandra about the cashing of the cheques and the handing over of the money to Tom Reicey she made him repeat the whole story a second time.

'I think,' she said, 'that you should go to a solicitor this

127

very instant.'

'Oh come now!'

'Oh come yourself!' she exploded. 'You're in the middle of a bloody swindle. Even though I recommend a solicitor I don't see that he can be of any help now.'

'You're an alarmist.' He tried to gloss over the whole business.

'But you haven't a leg to stand on.'

'Haven't I now?' He was about to tell her it was his opinion that Tom had bought the investigator off but that would never do. Instead he told her that there was no reason whatsoever for worry.

'I hope you're right,' she said.

'Of course I'm right. Do you want to have supper somewhere?'

'I'm not hungry but I'll go along if you want.'

'Oh forget it,' he said unhappily.

'Sylvie?'

'What now?'

'I want you to do something for me.'

'What is it?' he asked guardedly.

'I want you to go to Luton this very night and stay with my mum and dad until I contact you. I don't like the shape of things. The Reiceys are sharp, too sharp for you Sylvie. If things clear up and if there's no more snooping by the tax people you can come back in a few weeks.'

'I can't just disappear. It's a busy time.'

'You can tell Mr Reicey you have to go visit your mother in that old people's home in Galway.'

'I can't do it.'

'You stay here in the pub and I'll find Dan. He'll drive you up in the van. You know how Mum and Dad like you.'

Sylvester laughed aloud. 'Will you forget it like a good girl? Nothing's going to happen.'

'Maybe not but it's better to be on the safe side.'

'Forget it. Go and buy a drink if you want to be helpful.'

'At least will you talk to Dan?'

A WEEK after the visit from the tax investigator Sylvester's worries concerning his position in the key role of the firm's accountant began to fade into the background. Dan Murray had agreed with Sandra that it would be wise for Sylvester to disappear from the scene until some acceptable development took place within the firm. In Luton he could change his name and get a decent job without difficulty. He would be another one of the many thousands of Irish who regularly changed names for a variety of reasons. In most cases names were changed to avoid military call-up or to elude probing tax men. The whole business was the essence of simplicity. What one did was to disappear altogether from the scene, go home to Ireland if necessary and then reappear in some other part of England with a new name. If, for instance, a man's name was Dan Murray he might change it to Donald Murray or Donal Murray.

Sylvester told Dan how much he appreciated his concern. Disappearing however was something he could not seriously consider.

'All right,' Dan said. 'Don't disappear. Just board a boat and go to see your mother. Stay a while. Sandra will contact you.'

Sylvester refused to yield.

'Listen Sylvie,' Dan pleaded, 'it's an even money bet that you'll wind up in jail. Tom Reicey is no fool. He's not going to take the blame when he can put it over on you.'

'I'm certain,' Sylvester said, 'that he bought off the inspector and that everything will be all right.'

Nine days were to elapse before the inspector visited the office again. This time he was accompanied by a heavily-built, over-coated man who he introduced as Superintendent Weyson. Instead of taking Sylvester's proffered hand Weyson nodded politely and held his tongue while the inspector addressed Sylvester.

'The superintendent's been having a look at the books over the past week.'

Sylvester was surprised. He had not seen the books leave the office. The superintendent must have come for them after office hours. They were kept with other records in a large filing cabinet to which Sylvester had little recourse unless he wanted to bring the large ledgers up to date. This he did about once a month.

'What can I do for you?' Sylvester asked hoping that his nervousness did not show.

'You can tell Mr Reicey we are here,' the inspector said.

'Of course.' Sylvester thought for an instant of making a dash for the door but he noticed that, whether by accident or design, the superintendent had conveniently placed himself between desk and door making it impossible for Sylvester to leave that way. Dammit he was letting his imagination run away with him. He chided himself and went into Tom Reicey. He was followed by both men. As soon as the inspector introduced the superintendent he excused himself and left.

'Would you be good enough to take a seat Mr O'Doherty?' the superintendent indicated a chair. 'It is my duty to inform you,' he said to Sylvester, 'that having carefully examined the books, cheques and bank statements of this firm, I find discrepancies too serious to be overlooked and I therefore hereby request that you accompany me to the charge room of the local police station where you will be formally charged.'

'What are you talking about?' Sylvester paled. If he had not been seated he would certainly have needed some form of support to help him remain on his feet.

'I am saying,' the superintendent repeated, 'that I must request you to accompany me to the nearest police station where you will be formally charged.'

'Formally charged with what?' Sylvester tried to implant scorn in his tone.

'I cannot say sir. That will be for the inspector in the charge room to decide.'

'This is bloody well ridiculous. I'm not a criminal. I've never in my life done any man out of a single half-penny.'

'I must ask you to come along with me now.'

'Suppose I refuse?'

'In that case I shall have no alternative but to bring you along by force. In case you think this may not be possible I shall call in my driver and have him clap handcuffs on you. Come along quietly like a good fellow. I'm sure a fuss is the last thing any of us wants.'

'Better go along Sylvie,' Tom Reicey advised. 'I'll get you a solicitor and I'm sure the matter will be cleared up in no time at all.'

'You know what you can do with your solicitor?'

'Now, now, that's no way to talk, I'm only trying to help. There's many a man in my position would pitch you to Hell.'

'Tell him the truth Tom.'

'I don't know what you're talking about. I've offered to help you. I can do no more.'

'Tell him the truth Tom or I will.'

The superintendent stood silently, legs apart, looking from one to the other. It had struck him earlier that Tom Reicey must be a very careless fellow indeed to allow his clerk such a free hand. It didn't add up properly when one considered the vastness of the Reicey empire. Such concerns were not built by men who were careless. Still it wasn't for him to decide. He had his duty to do and sympathy had no place in the execution of it.

'Are you going to tell him Tom?'

'For God's sake tell him what?' Tom Reicey sniggered.

'Tell him about the cheques.'

'There's damn-all to tell. I think you know more about cheques than me. God knows you've signed enough of 'em.'

'And I cashed them too didn't I Tom?'

'That will all come out in the wash as they say. Now be a good fellow and go away with the superintendent like he tells you. Don't be making the man's job any harder.'

Sylvester wheeled round and faced the superintendent.

'Don't you see?' he said. 'He's the man you should be charging. I cashed the cheques all right but the minute I drew the money I brought it straight back here and handed it to him. I often asked him for a receipt and he said not to worry.'

Sylvester faced Tom again.

'Isn't that what you said Tom? Not to worry. Those were

131

his exact words superintendent as God is my witness. Come on Tom. Tell the man the truth.'

By way of reply Tom Reicey shook his head and smiled ruefully. 'I wonder what you'll concoct next,' he said.

'Jesus, Tom I'll not go to prison for you. Get that into your fat head.'

'Please come along Mr O'Doherty,' the superintendent said yet he made no attempt to remove Sylvester. There was always the possibility that something of interest might emerge.

'For the last time Tom will you tell the man what happened?'

Sylvester advanced a step. Suddenly Tom Reicey lunged forward and seized him by the throat.

'You low down cur,' he shouted. 'How dare you accuse me of dishonesty after all I've done for you? Damn you, you hadn't a copper to your name when you came to me begging for a job.' He shook Sylvester with all his might. 'Is this to be my gratitude after all I've done for you, after all the fat bonuses, the use of transport, the gifts? I ought to belt the living daylights out of you.'

'Now, now,' the superintendent interposed, 'that's enough of that.' He broke Tom Reicey's hold on Sylvester.

Tom's outburst seemed a realistic one but it did nothing to convince the superintendent that he had the right man.

'I'll get you for this,' Sylvester yelled at Tom Reicey as he was being led away.

'Sure you will,' Tom called after him good humouredly.

In the charge room Sylvester was introduced to Inspector Brice.

'You are Sylvester O'Doherty of 117 Bachelor's Parade.'

'Yes.' Sylvester wanted to say more, to protest against the monstrous injustice, to shout out his innocence.

'You are in the employ of Reicey Brothers, the building contractors?'

'Yes.'

'I hereby charge you with larceny from the firm of Reicey Brothers for a period of four years up to and including this present time.'

'I'm not guilty.'

'That may be sir, I never suggested you were guilty,' Brice said evenly. 'I am merely charging you under the act. There is sufficient evidence to support the charge. I must also remand you temporarily and inform you that bail will be opposed. Do you understand the meaning of the charge?'

'Yes, I'm afraid I do, but what evidence can there be against me?'

'We shall see,' Brice replied. 'Now would you be good enough to place the contents of your pockets on this table? You shall have a receipt for any and every item.' So saying Brice produced a cloth bag from a drawer in the desk at which he sat. He commenced writing an inventory of the articles that Sylvester withdrew from his pockets, from loose change to the engraved cigarette lighter that had been a gift from Sandra.

'What's going to happen to me now?' he asked of the superintendent who was standing close by.

'Your solicitor will be notified of our intent,' he said stiffly. Then in a confidential tone he said: 'I imagine you'll be remanded for trial at the Old Bailey. Shouldn't take very long before the case will be heard. It isn't as if it were fraudulent conversion or embezzlement. These larceny charges are in and out before you can say Jack Robinson.'

'Thank you,' Sylvester said. 'May I ask what's the procedure from here on in?'

'You'd best be getting in touch with your solicitor. If you haven't got one or can't afford one we'll get one for you. He will be informed of the charge and shown the evidence against you. For our part I myself will prepare a full report and include photostat copies of all the exhibits. Then I'll send the lot to the Director of Public Prosecutions.'

'What do you think is likely to happen?'

'Oh come now. I've already said enough.'

Sylvester was remanded without the option of bail and when the first remand expired he was remanded again.

The trial at the Old Bailey was one of the most unspectacular and boring ever to come before the bench for those who were not involved. For his part Sylvester listened keenly to the exchanges. At times it seemed to him that he was outside the whole business, that it was somebody else who was on trial. In the gallery the three Reicey brothers sat side by side. Behind them sat Sandra and two other girls from the office who were there to give evidence on Sylvester's behalf.

Dan Murray and his brother Willie sat in the front bench. As soon as the trial ended for the day they would return to the site where they were sub-contracting the brickwork. There they would labour fiercely till dark. Eddie Carey was on the job with the labourers, Dan and Willie having worked from five till half-past ten in the morning. At half-three the judge declared a recess till the following morning.

Next day Dan came alone. It just was not possible to spare Willie from the site. The courtroom proceedings interested him the first day but he found the second day dull and dreary. He almost fell asleep once. The exceptionally early hours were beginning to take effect. He spent the whole afternoon yawning. He had partaken of a heavy lunch, not bothering to have breakfast that morning.

Dan looked around him in the courtroom. There were the same faces as the previous day. All the submissions for the defence and prosecution had been made. All that remained was for the judge to sum up for the jury. If they returned a verdict of guilty he would impose a suitable sentence.

The jury which consisted of two women and ten men were hardly an hour in recess. A number of damning facts had struck Dan forcibly during the summing up. The judge, an elderly and scholarly-looking man had referred to Sylvester's ingratitude to the firm. He had said it was a strange way of repaying his employers for the bonuses and other facilities of which he had availed freely over the years. Then there was the transfer of thirteen hundred pounds from his account to a place or person whose name the defendant would not disclose. The judge thought this a particularly significant factor against the defendant's case which seemed to him, in spite of strenuous denial by the defendant and a spirited and well-conducted defence by his counsel, to be one which deserved no verdict other than that of guilty. If there were any doubts still in their minds about his innocence then they would have to give the matter the most serious thought before returning a verdict.

As the jury returned Sylvester vainly searched their faces for a clue of some kind. All sat down save the foreman who looked grave and unhappy.

'How do you find?' the judge asked.

'My lord,' the foreman announced throatily, 'we find the defendant guilty as charged.'

'Will the defendant please rise?' The judge withdrew a spotlessly white handkerchief from his gown and blew his nose. Sylvester got to his feet.

'I sentence you to three years imprisonment,' the judge said, 'and I sincerely hope that you will make every effort to mend your ways when you rejoin law-abiding men and women.'

In the gallery a woman cried. It was Sandra. Sobbing helplessly her friends led her outside. Sylvester caught Dan's eye. He shrugged in despair. It seemed as if he had aged five years. He appeared to be greyer and there were dark hollows under his cheekbones. It was the look in his eyes that most affected Dan. It reminded him of what he had once seen on the face of a labourer who had fallen from a defective scaffold to his death. There was the tragic realisation of an indescribable loss. Part of Dan was destroyed too by the agony that came across to him when Sylvester threw his eyes in last and forlorn hope of redress, in his direction. Dan hurried from the court. He did not stop to console Sandra. He ran the last few steps to the van. Inside the tears flowed till the first terrible ache passed. Grimly he dried his eyes and drove back to his work.

DICK DALY, sometimes referred to as Crazy Horse, sat nursing a drink in the Irish Club in Eaton Square. He was puzzled. He had known Sylvester for ten years which was a while longer than he had known the Reicey brothers. He could not conceive of Sylvester's cheating anybody. His own wife had been a cheat. He discovered this to his cost after a year of marriage. His suspicions where fully confirmed when she left him for another. He had given her no reason to leave. No man could have been kinder or more generous to a woman. Similarly no employee could have been fairer to his employers than Sylvester. He had never at any time while Dick had worked at the Shillelagh been guilty of shady dealings and it would have been a simple matter for him, as Dick knew well, to line his pockets, with no chance of being found out. When the Shillelagh closed after a dance Dick and Sylvester would sit in the office drinking beer and conversing about the past.

The Reiceys must have framed him. Crazy Horse could form no other opinion on the basis of what he knew. He also trusted his own instincts. The only man Sylvester ever wronged was himself. He would give notice to whichever one of the brothers would come to the Shillelagh on Saturday night. He would give his reasons. He would tell whoever came that he could not work with anybody but Sylvester. He did not need the extra work. He already had a good job in the dispatch department of a wholesale drug company.

He would find out to what prison Sylvester had been sent and he would visit him. That was the least he could do for the man who had been his friend for so long.

12

IN JUNE the Maguire brothers Turlough and Shay returned to Ireland. For the quietly-spoken Cavan men England had proved to be the promised land. With theirs' and the Mulvanney sisters' savings, and a substantial loan, they purchased a large neglected farm in Cavan. This they would divide. The result of the division would be two viable parcels of good land. The farm was formerly owned by a Protestant family, descendants of Scottish planters who had been granted all the best farmland in the northern half of Ireland during the seventeenth century plantation of Ulster.

With the Maguires' departure Eddie was given their room. He had been the senior boarder since the Midlanders departed some months before. The Mulvanney sisters Rose and Bridie left London shortly after the Maguires. There would be a double marriage in early September in their parish church in County Leitrim. Part of their savings had gone towards the purchase of stock and up-to-date machinery which would make the land productive once more.

NOREEN CAREY was having her eighth child in the small district hospital which catered for the needs of five dispensary districts in that part of Kerry. Eddie had not come home, on her instructions. His work, she told him in a long letter, was too important and any slackening or cessation would only prolong the day of his return. Her mother had come from the south to look after the other children. It was her first visit. Noreen had not seen nor spoken to her in all her years of marriage until her father's death after Christmas.

'I was hard on you,' she said to Noreen between fits of crying, 'but they were hard times and others had to be fed.'

The eighth Carey child was a son. Now there were five boys and three girls. As the years had gone by Noreen missed Eddie more and more till she found it difficult to endure the long nights without him. In her letters she never told him how much she really missed him. Now at long last there was a real prospect of his coming home. Dan and he were making money steadily and increasingly. She deduced from hints and other subtleties in his more recent letters that once they were established in a fairly big way Eddie would offer his share of the business to Dan at a fair price. Then he would come home. She prayed for him and for the success of the venture every day and night. It was so vitally important that all should go well. The length of their future together dwindled with every passing year. Sometimes she worried that maybe the hectic pace they had set themselves was too demanding. She need not have worried. The partners were equal to the work and happy as children whenever they undertook a new sub-contract.

The child was called Hugh after his maternal grandfather. There was a widespread belief at the time among country people that no matter where the money came from, the doctor in charge of the hospital had to be presented with a confidential gift of cash otherwise he was likely to pay insufficient attention to patients without apparent means. The first thing Noreen did when she entered the hospital was to press a five pound note on the doctor. She did not want to fail Eddie at this stage and so sought the best possible attention. The doctor accepted the five pounds with a polite nod of the head. It was laid down at the Department of Health that he was entitled to take money from private patients only but as he so often said to his wife when she asked him if taking it from others was right: 'My dear old girl it makes them feel good. They would only throw it at me if I refused. I never ask. If they want to give, who am I to refuse?'

Noreen was well looked after. After a week she was on her feet and able to come to relieve her mother.

PATRICIA DEE had been on the night shift from eight in the evening until eight in the morning the day before Margo Cullagan's wedding. She was constantly on call. At eighteen minutes past eight the first case had arrived by ambulance. As sister-in-charge Patricia had to be present in a supervisory capacity when the casualty was delivered. It was a woman of forty, the mother of four children. She had swallowed fifty aspirins in a fit of depression when she discovered that her husband was being unfaithful to her. Patricia had her taken at once to the casualty ward where she would be submitted to cleansing by stomach pump. It was one of the frequent occurrences that Patricia liked least. The treatment was successful. No sooner was Patricia free of the casualty ward than there was an emergency call from the maternity wing. The two interns were already there but in the circumstances, with her wide experience, she was worth far more than the two. At the beginning of the week the hospital had had its first set of triplets in over five years. Tragically two were already dead, victims of bronchial pneumonia and now it seemed as if the third was about to succumb to the same malady. She called the medical superintendent. He had requested this if the third triplet seemed likely to expire. There was nothing however that anybody could do and with the passing of the third infant there was a general air of depression all over the hospital.

At five-thirty in the morning Dan Murray called on his way to work. The hospital was out of his line but it was a fine summer's morning and he reacted to a sudden desire to visit her. He could not stay long. They were flooded with work but he would be taking the coming Sunday off to visit Sylvester who had been transferred from Wandsworth to a minimum-security prison. Dan wondered if Patricia would like to come. He had applied for and received permission for the visit. Sandra would be coming too. Fortunately Patricia was free and would love to go.

He told her about the addition to the Carey family. There had been a telegram the evening before but there had been no time to celebrate. Dan had almost forgotten what a pint of beer tasted like. It had been a dry summer, a contractor's delight. There was no point at all in wasting it. There would be time for beer and recreation when the snow and ice of winter held up work in the building industry. He left in a hurry and as he sat listening on the bonnet of his van two hundred yards from his own site he remembered vividly Sylvester's talk with him about the 'sounds of the site'. There was no mistaking the chorus – it did his heart good.

TOM AND Maisie Reicey woke early on the morning of the wedding.

'Damn and blast it,' Tom said. 'I can't sleep.'

'Neither can I,' Maisie said.

'What time is it anyway?'

'It's not eight o'clock yet.'

Normally since he passed his fiftieth year Tom Reicey rose between nine and half-nine. He eased himself from the bed and looked out of the window.

''Tis one whore of a fine day,' he informed his wife.

'That's a Godsend anyway,' she returned.

'I'd better get dressed,' Tom said. 'The caterers will be setting up shop at eleven o'clock. I'll give a quick spin to the sites. 'Tis a morning they won't be expecting me.'

Driving across London in the new Wolsey his thoughts turned to Sylvester. After the trial Joe had managed to see him for a moment. On Tom's instructions he had told him that his job would be waiting when he got out plus two thousand pounds for the inconvenience caused.

His answer had been to spit past Joe's face. Bloody eejit. That was no way to act. With good behaviour he would be out in two years and four months and there were special cases where the sentence might be remitted when half of it was served. Of course it was hard to blame Sylvester. To be sentenced to three years for something he didn't do was no fun. Tom consoled himself by arguing that it was the Reiceys or Sylvester and any man in his sane senses would agree that the three brothers would be right fools to admit to the fiddle and wind up getting three years apiece. Even Sylvester must see that. He had made the sacrifice for the sake of the company only he was refusing to look at it in that light. He would be rewarded by the company for making that sacrifice. Any man in business must see that there could be no other possible outcome to the affair.

Some men were born to take raps or to be made into scapegoats. Sylvester O'Doherty was one. There were hundreds like him in every conceivable sort of business. What happened to him was happening every day somewhere in the world but, and here Tom Reicey hammered the point home to himself, the difference with Sylvester was that his employers had offered to pay cash for time spent inside. Tom's conscience was at rest. There was nothing more he could do unless go to jail and if he went to jail so would Dicey and Joe. This would not be at all practicable. Joe and he had families and Dicey was about to get married. Sylvester had neither chick nor child. There was his mother back in Ireland but she was well off and anyway he and the old woman were not on the best of terms. He had no dependents.

Tom's conscience would never again be bothered by Sylvester. He had thoroughly convinced himself that things could not have turned out otherwise and as for giving two thousand pounds to Sylvester when he would be released from prison his former accountant could now go and hump it as far as Tom was concerned. He put the whole unhappy affair from his mind. This was a day to be enjoyed. He would begin it by catching a foreman or two unawares.

JOE REICEY was worried. It was a terrible thing that Sylvester should go to jail. He had hoped the offer of the two thousand pounds would in some small way compensate for the severity of the sentence. The hate in Sylvester's eyes had shocked him. He watched the spittle scud by his face and returned to tell Tom and Dicey what happened.

'Ah musha' 'tis only all going through life,' Dicey said philosophically. Tom was quick to perceive Joe's distress. He decided against saying anything. Time would fix Joe. On the morning of the wedding Joe slept till eleven. He had drunk heavily the night before at a party given by some of Dicey's friends. Normally he drank little, a nip of whiskey followed by a few glasses of beer. Large quantities of intoxicating liquor made him sick. Feeling wretched he forced himself from the bed. He went to the bathroom where he washed out his mouth and cleaned his teeth. From downstairs came the smell of frying bacon. He felt like retching. He wished he could go back to bed and stay there for the remainder of the day. If only there had been some way of covering up for Sylvester or if money, no matter what amount, could have altered the situation. Anything but jail.

'Christ,' he said aloud. 'Three years is a long time.'

DICEY REICEY leaped from the bed the moment he awoke. He had spent less than four hours asleep. The party had not broken up till five o'clock in the morning. Discarding his pyjamas he stood under the shower and turned on the cold water. He yelled at the top of his voice as the chilling jets hissed against his warm flesh. Gasping for breath and savouring the mild shocks he rubbed the water into his chest and under his arms.

He tried not to think about Margo. For months he had tortured himself with erotic dreams of possessing her. He dared not dwell on any such thoughts now. He had an appointment for confession at eleven.

WILLIE AND Dan Murray, Eddie Carey and three labourers sat in the June sunshine at a corner of the building site in south London. Two of the labourers were brothers – Dave and Peter Costigan from West Cork. The other was a friend of Dan. He was, in fact, the man whose fine Dan had paid the morning after the Kilburn fiasco. Dan had forgotten all about him until one night he, Eddie Carey and Sylvester had paid a late visit to a pub in Hammersmith. Sylvester had been helping with some paperwork which had proved to be beyond Dan and Eddie. After he had shown them an easy way for surmounting such problems in the future they repaired to the most convenient pub. It was near closing time and for this reason Dan ordered three large whiskies and three pints of ale to follow. They were in the lounge and Dan could see into the main bar which was partly full despite the fact that it was only mid-week.

The barman informed him that the drink would be delivered instantly by the pot-boy. The friends sat chatting while the order was being looked after. It was decided that Eddie would have to learn how to drive. There was always the outside possibility that illness or mishap might confine Dan to his bed for a day or even a week and that would be disastrous since they were depending solely on him for transport. At first Eddie would not hear of it but eventually he promised to give it a try.

'How much is all that?' Dan asked the pot-boy, a podgy-faced youngster with a cheeky air who allowed some of the beer to spill over on to the tray. He placed the drink on the table without answering.

'I asked how much?' Dan said impatiently.

'You wot Paddy?' the youngster retorted cockily. Dan was forced to laugh at the lad's unabashed impudence.

'The drink's been paid for,' he announced.

'Oh,' said Dan. 'By whom?'

'Some big Paddy in the outer bar.'

'Point him out to me,' Dan said. The pot-boy dutifully led the way out of the lounge and into the public bar. Dan recognised the powerfully-built man whose head and arms had successfully withstood a dozen baton blows. He had been unconscious himself at the time but Sylvester assured him that it had been a magnificent performance by any standard. He was only half-drunk now as he stood swaying near the counter. Respectfully he saluted Dan who returned the salute and approached him.

'Thanks for the drink,' Dan said.

'That's all right boss,' the big man dismissed it. 'I'm waiting for change. I'll give you that thirty shillings I owe you as soon as I get it.'

'That's all right,' Dan countered. 'Forget it. The drink makes up for it.'

'Can't do that boss,' he said. 'A debt is a debt. I've been trying to find you this long time to pay you back.' He accepted the change of a ten pound note from the barman.

'Now,' the relief sounded in his voice as he handed Dan the money. 'That's a great weight off my mind.'

'Thanks,' Dan said.

'You might not believe it boss,' the big man said with a grim smile, 'but you're the only man I ever met in this vale of tears that ever gave me something for nothing.'

'Will you join us?' Dan invited.

'If I'm not butting in.' He followed Dan into the lounge.

'Listen Paddy,' the pot-boy snapped, 'you pay extra for your drink before you go in that lounge.'

'You have a father?' the big man queried.

'Yes,' the pot-boy answered.

'Why are you acting the bastard then?' The question set the pot-boy thinking. He withdrew deep in thought.

Dan introduced Eddie and Sylvester.

'My name is Richard Winterman but I'm nearly always called Dick,' the big man told them. They shook hands all round.

It transpired that Dick Winterman had been raised in an orphanage in Galway. After several years fruitlessly working for farmers he had abandoned Ireland for England. He admitted with a hint of pride that he never saved money. Instead he religiously drank his wages before each week was out. He lived in a rented room close by the pub. Before they had time to buy another round of drinks the last call of 'time' was shouted. Sylvester informed them that he had an adequate supply in his flat.

Later on Dick Winterman was hired by Dan as a charge-hand labourer. He was just the type of man they needed. His strength and experience would be invaluable assets on any site. He had no objection to the long hours. In fact they might be just the job to wean him off the drink for a spell. He would start the following Monday.

13

MARCH OF 1956 opened with temperatures which were below normal. The bluster of gusty, knife-edged winds was a familiar sound on the south London site. The Murray crew were engaged with the brickwork for a scheme of 24 houses which were being erected for a development company with headquarters in Central London. Neither the biting, snarling gales nor the driving hail which might suddenly pester every corner of the site impeded the work. The showers of hail were harassing but short-lived. Unless one was constantly on the move the cold penetrated the heaviest garments. Dan, Eddie and Willie found it difficult in the extreme since they were forced to stay in the same place for long periods of time, painfully laying brick upon brick, hour after hour without cessation.

It was less hard on the labourers. They were constantly on the move and when the supplies of bricks and mortar were more than adequate for the needs of the layers they could jump about or flap cold hands against their sides to keep warm.

It was Dan's fourth year in England and his third as a sub-contractor. Because of the furious pace at which they worked the labourers earned huge weekly wages and when work on a particular site was finished ahead of schedule Dan saw to it that they were rewarded with substantial bonuses. Between them in their joint names Dan and Eddie had succeeded in amassing over two thousand pounds in hard cash. The van and other equipment had been paid for in a matter of months. In a separate account at the Midland Dan was credited with eleven hundred pounds. These were savings out of his wages. Eddie Carey had more still while Willie too had a sum of six hundred pounds in his own account. Since they had started on their own the three bricklayers worked like Trojans and lived like Spartans. Dan had a long-term plan. He proposed in time to abandon sub-contracting altogether and to submit tenders for schemes of houses or flat blocks, for anything in fact in the building line. Smoothly as their every operation went there was one recurring snag which would have to be dealt with sooner or later. Although Dan was less than a thorn in the Reicey Brothers' side there was the inescapable reality that every time he won a sub-contract the Reicey Brothers or one of the smaller Irish firms lost it. While the size and number of the jobs Dan was undertaking were mere drops in the ocean to the big contracting firms there was always the danger that continued success at smaller undertakings would encourage him or his equals to expand and offer competition at the highest level. The tendency with small ambitious firms such as Dan's was to cut prices and work round the clock. There was no danger of dispute or strike since they themselves, their close friends or their families constituted the majority and often all the workers in the firm.

The Reiceys became aware of Dan's existence when he was but a fledgling in the dense and dangerous forest of sub-contracting. It happened when he and his crew finished a special job in less than half the time at their disposal. Ever greedy for worthwhile pickings the Reiceys realised that there was an enormous percentage of profit involved and small as the scheme was it showed that Murray might one day be a force with whom they would have to reckon.

There were many precedents for dealing with upstart firms who broke all the rules by flouting normal working hours and cutting prices to ensure that nobody else could possibly get the contract. They could be taken over at a price and things made easier for them by a guarantee of constant work. Another way was to underwrite them which was often a great relief to men whose literacy was questionable and who had poor heads for figures. While underwriting was not quite the same thing as a takeover it meant that the Reiceys were in charge and often drew handsome profits for agreeing to be responsible if anything went wrong.

The most obnoxious of all precedents was intimidation.

It was only used when all other methods failed. Feelers had been dispatched to Dan over a period through the general foremen, site engineers and even other sub-contractors to ask if he might be willing to be underwritten by the Reicey Brothers or if he would care to be apportioned regular work.

His answer had always been in the negative. When finally he succeeded in convincing them that he was determined to survive on his own a number of things began to happen, small things, none in themselves very damaging but the sum of the incidents served as notice for a possible major disaster unless Dan came to his senses.

On one sub-contract Eddie's bag of tools was stolen. On another Dick Winterman was struck in the back with a stone the size of a golf ball and when he turned to see if he could pick out the man who threw it every worker at his rear was preoccupied with one task or another, making conspiracy obvious. It was a frustrating experience for a big fellow like Winterman. When he turned again to go about his business there had been ridiculing laughter. The site had its quota of Reicey's Rangers and there was no doubt in Dan's mind that the stone thrower came from their ranks. There was a council of war at once and it was decided that the best thing to do was ignore what happened. It did not warrant further investigation. It was important, Dan pointed out, that they be on their guard at all times and that the provocation should be tolerated at all costs until the circumstances were more favourable.

On another occasion the Morrikan brothers who now worked full time for the Reiceys made things as difficult as possible for Dan and his men without an open declaration of hostilities. They would bump against Dan's labourers as they went back and forth on their business and when this failed they resorted to stone-throwing. On his way to the makeshift toilet one afternoon Willie Murray was struck on the back of the head with a carefully-lobbed missile which turned out to be an egg-sized lump of concrete. He fell to the ground at once and was semi-conscious when Dan and Dick Winterman came to his aid. Luckily the piece of concrete was not thrown with any great degree of force. As they lifted

Willie to his feet they heard the provocative laughter. The youngest Morrikan smiled and winked at Dan. His oldest brother Ruckard stood with his feet well apart, hands on hips.

'Well?' Dick Winterman posed the question. This was to infer that the answer lay with Dan and Dan alone.

'The bleeding is stopped,' Dan said.

'I know bloody well it is. What I want to know is how much more do we have to put up with?'

'It's not the time or the place. You know that as well as I do.'

'There's only the four of 'em.'

'No.' Dan was determined not to have his hand forced. 'If we start anything they'll be backed up. The influence of the Reiceys is strong here. When we fight the odds will have to be even or on my side. They have odds now. Whether we like it or not we're going to have to grin and bear it.'

Eighteen months had passed since then. There had been other mysterious happenings in the meanwhile. On two separate occasions when they finished work the air had been released from the four wheels of the van. After the second such happening they always parked their only means of transport where they could keep an eye on it. During a lunch break somebody poured a gallon of crude oil into the concrete mix. It took several hours to clean out the mixer. The best part of a day's work was lost.

In all there were over twenty incidents.

At three o'clock Eddie Carey started up the van and drove to a cafeteria where hot soup was available for take-away purposes. He was in the habit of doing this every day. He would return with three billycans full. It was a treat to which they all looked forward. In the first place they needed it to sustain themselves until they finished at dark and had their dinners. Secondly it provided a short break when they might talk and smoke. They invested their whole energy in the remaining hours and they always marvelled at the amount of work completed at the end of the day.

As Eddie was returning with the three full billycans Ruckard Morrikan suddenly appeared on the plank-constructed causeway which crossed the site. The planks were narrow and only wide enough to support one person. Eddie was not aware of Ruckard's presence until he was almost on top of him. Rather than risk a collision he obligingly stepped off the plank on to the muddy surface. Ruckard Morrikan stepped off at the same time, on the same side and made it impossible for Eddie to avoid him. Morrikan used his shoulder to send Eddie staggering backwards. In order to stay on his feet Eddie was forced to release his hold on the billycans. When they hit the ground the covers of each of the three fell off and the hot soup spilled out, forming small steaming pools on the uneven surface.

'Watch where you're going you drunken bowsie,' Morrikan feigned annoyance.

'Pick up the cans,' Eddie said. His voice was calm, his manner seemingly unchanged.

'Pick 'em up yourself,' Morrikan replied, ''twas your own bloody fault.'

'Pick up the cans,' Eddie said a second time.

'Make me.'

'I'll make you,' Eddie said. He did not notice the other Morrikan brothers and an assortment of workers noiselessly forming a circle at a short distance.

'For the last time,' Eddie was saying, 'pick up the cans.' Morrikan laughed aloud and turned to the ring of faces.

'Do you hear what he wants me to do?' he called. 'He wants me to pick up his bloody cans after he lettin' 'em fall through his own awkwardness.'

It was Dick Winterman who drew Dan's attention to what was happening.

'Whatever takes place,' Dan spat out the words, 'there must not be a fight. Get that into your head. No matter what they say or do there can be no blows. Clear?'

Winterman nodded reluctantly. Hastily Dan went to Eddie's side.

'You're not stopping me this time Dan,' Eddie informed him resolutely.

'You're mad if you raise a hand,' Dan whispered and attempted to lure his friend away. Eddie threw off the hand with which Dan would propel him back to their own corner of the site.

Suddenly Dan seized him by both hands. 'You're not going to ruin all we've worked for just because your pride is hurt Eddie.'

'He started it,' Eddie scowled.

'You are not,' Dan repeated emphatically, 'going to ruin all we've worked for. If you fight now you ruin us. I'll hold it against you for the rest of my life.'

Eddie was impressed, then uncertain. Dan stooped and picked up the billycans which he handed to Willie. Then taking Eddie by the elbow he led him away.

'Funky bowsies,' Ruckard Morrikan called after them. The taunt was ignored. When Dan returned with the second lot of soup he followed a more tortuous and circuitous path in order to avoid conflict with the Morrikans and their supporters. As they drank from tin pannies there was none of the usual wisecracking or banter. Eddie broke the silence.

'Dan,' he said and he shook his head solemnly, 'sooner or later we're going to have to fight. This just can't go on. A time is going to come when we won't get work unless we show that we are not afraid of them.'

'I thought you had more savvy Eddie,' Dan said.

'Dan is right,' Dick Winterman put in. 'Nobody likes a scrap better than myself but we'd be out-numbered five to one. I don't mind taking on two or three but any more and the fun goes out of it.'

'All right, all right,' Eddie agreed. 'But we all know if we're to survive at this game we're going to have to fight. If word goes out that the Morrikans and the rest of Reicey's Rangers can push us around at will no contractor is going to sub-let work to us. You can't blame the contractors. I've seen the acts of sabotage the Rangers pulled in other places. It's only a matter of time before they start on a big scale with us. From the looks of things they're building up to it. One of these mornings we'll walk in and find the work of the day before all smashed up or instead of letting the air out of our tyres they'll slash them.'

'That's the truth,' Dick Winterman said. 'I knew a bunch

of blokes just like us, quiet chaps. Always minded their own business. One evening when they were about to leave the site the van wouldn't start. The driver got out and lifted the bonnet. There was no engine.'

'I believe you,' Dave Costigan said. 'I've seen things happen too.'

'Even if we don't lick 'em in a scrap,' Eddie went on, 'so long as we give a bloody good account of ourselves they might leave us alone.'

'Don't misunderstand me boys,' Dan said. 'I'm not backing down from a fight. I was hoping against hope that it might not be necessary. I can see now that we will have to take a stand.'

'That's the spirit.' Dick Winterman patted Dan on the back.

'When?' Eddie asked.

'Very soon,' Dan informed him. 'I want to make arrangements. I want things to be right and I want the fight to be seen by as many Paddies as possible. I also want to make sure and certain we don't lose. If anybody wants to back out, now is the time because this won't be a pleasant business and a few people are bound to be hurt when it's over.'

Dan waited, giving them time to ponder but there was no dissenting voice.

'Tell us when,' Eddie pleaded.

'In a fortnight,' Dan said, 'it will be Saint Patrick's Day. That will be the date of our engagement with the Morrikans and any other Rangers who back them up outside the Green Shillelagh when the dance is over that night.'

'You're not making sense.' Eddie showed himself to be in complete disagreement. 'On Saint Patrick's night the Green Shillelagh will be mobbed. We'll be out-numbered. We'll be the laughing stock of the trade with the beating we'll get.'

'We might be out-numbered,' Dan spoke calmly, 'but we won't be out-classed. If we stick together we can make an example of them.'

'Why pick Saint Patrick's night?' Winterman asked. 'I mean if you wanted to pick a night to suit us you'd be better off to choose any other night in the year.'

'Let me explain.' Dan was patient. The others drew near and gave him their full attention. 'On Saint Patrick's night every county in Ireland will be represented at the Green Shillelagh. Reiceys' Rangers, even including the Morrikan brothers, will not number more than fifteen or sixteen. The rest of them will be scattered throughout London at the other Irish centres, although I'll grant you that their best men will be at the Green Shillelagh. At the moment there are 6 of us and there will be 15 of them. We don't need too many more. There is one man and if we had him on our side I think we might pull a surprise.'

'That's still 15 to 7,' Peter Costigan spoke doubtfully.

'Be quiet,' his brother told him. 'Let Dan talk.'

'The extra man I have in mind is Crazy Horse.' Dan let the name sink in.

'There's a good man.' Dick Winterman nodded his approval. 'A bloody good man.'

'I haven't got him yet of course but I think I might. I'm going to see Sylvester this weekend. I happen to know that Crazy Horse will do anything for him.'

'It's an improvement,' Eddie conceded grudgingly. 'But we'll still be out-numbered two to one.'

'It may seem that way but it's not the case if you look at it closely. It's worth the chance. The men we have are tried and trusted. Man for man we are better and there are some of us who could take on two or three. They have good men too but not as many. If we win we'll never be interfered with again. We'll have beaten them on their own doorstep against all the odds and before a big crowd. If we lose no decent man will laugh at us because we fought when the odds were stacked against us. Look at it like this, if we manage to lick them with a handful of men what might we not do if we mustered support?'

All murmured approval but again Eddie shook his head.

'It's a good idea,' he said, 'and I'm for it win, lose or draw but I can't see us winning.'

'I disagree with you entirely,' Dan spoke with such confidence that he surprised himself. 'We'll have a few secret weapons on that night. It could be the cause of our winning.'

'No weapons,' Peter Costigan said instantly. 'They're not for me.'

In saying this he was echoing the sentiments of all the thousands of workers involved in the building industry. A fight was an honourable thing but the use of weapons such as knives, coshes or knuckle-dusters was considered as despicable as it was cowardly.

'You misunderstand,' Dan smiled. 'Our secret weapons will be that not a man of us will put a strong drink to his lips on that night and that nobody outside our own circle will know our plans.'

'No drink on Saint Patrick's night. I never heard the like.' Dick Winterman's face was woebegone, his eyes semi-circling the gathering for sympathy and support. 'My ancestors would turn over in their graves if they heard this. No drink on Paddy's night.' He clucked his tongue in desperation.

'When we're finished,' Dan promised, 'there'll be enough drink to drown yourselves in. And now I want the word of every man here that no intoxicating liquor will pass his lips until our business is done.'

'I would imagine that one or two drops of the hot stuff would be a help rather than a hindrance.' Winterman looked hopefully at Dan.

'Not a single, solitary drink.' Dan was adamant. One by one they agreed until he had extracted a solemn promise from all.

'Now let's get back to work,' he said. 'And not a word to anyone or we're beaten before we begin.'

14

DAN WAS well known to the warders in the minimum security prison. It stood deep in a stretch of uninhabited moorland outside Liverpool. He was a regular visitor. He parked the van two hundred yards from the entrance. The first time he had parked it opposite the giant iron gate only to be told by a guard that he would do well to park it away from the prison. A twelve foot high stone wall similar to those which once surrounded the ancient demesnes of landlords and Protestant clergymen in Ireland enclosed the fifteen acres which the buildings and grounds occupied. Dan was to discover from Sylvester that the prison had once been the home of a Lord Somebody or other whose wife sold it to pay death duties. After an inspection by a prison reform committee it was decided that the location would be ideal as an experimental centre to help with the revision of the existing penal code. It was however, still a prison and there was no way out as far as Sylvester was concerned. Dan once suggested escape and he felt he could have easily organised a successful one but Sylvester frowned on the idea. Sooner or later he would be recaptured and, more important still, it would mean a harder time for his fellow-prisoners.

Unlike other prisons of the period it was possible for a number of visitors to see a prisoner at the same time provided that application was made well in advance and that the applicants were persons of good character. There was another advantage in that especially well-behaved prisoners were allowed to walk round the grounds in the company of their visitors. Among the prisoners themselves there was an unwritten law that no attempt would be made to escape. They had been told that the future of prisoners everywhere depended upon this experiment and others being carried out elsewhere. In spite of this escapes were made.

On this occasion Dan came alone. There was much he wanted to talk about. On the eve of the new year Sylvester's mother had died and left him a sum in the region of five thousand pounds. The money lay safely in Sandra's account in Luton. In the company of a warder Sylvester had been allowed home to Mayo for the funeral. The warder looked like a genuine mourner although everybody at the funeral suspected what he was. After the burial there was a brief meeting with the family's solicitor. While he had every right to be present the warder discreetly withdrew and allowed the pair the privacy of a secret meeting. During their return journey Sylvester passed his companion an envelope which contained a hundred pounds.

'Would you be good enough to post this for me?' he said.

'Certainly,' the warder had replied, taking not the least notice when he saw that the letter bore his own name but no address. Without another word he placed it in his inside pocket.

It was Dan's seventh visit to the prison and it was nearing the end of Sylvester's ninth month as a prisoner. All going well with full time off for good behaviour he would be released after eighteen more. It was agreed that no mention was to be made of the Reicey brothers during the course of their conversations but Dan knew that the name must come up on this occasion. There was a cold east wind to their backs as they set out from the prison proper on their tour of the grounds.

Sylvester was forbidden to wear an overcoat or any outer garment over the prison uniform although truth to tell it was not the type of uniform one would normally associate with the inmates of a prison. It was dark green in colour, a rich green like that of a chestnut tree's foliage in summer and there was a collar attached. There were two pockets in the coat and one in the trousers.

Sylvester shivered when they left the shelter of the buildings. Dan wore a heavy winter overcoat.

'The reason they don't allow overcoats,' Sylvester complained, 'is that they might encourage the weaker characters

155

in residence to take their leave of the place.'

As they walked Dan filled his friend in on the recent happenings on the London scene. He answered question after question and when Sylvester's appetite for outside news had been sated Dan launched into an account of his own activities, highlighting the acts of provocation and the other abuses he and his men had to endure. He told of his plan for Saint Patrick's night and of the absolute necessity for the presence of Crazy Horse. Sylvester listened carefully. He had no comment to make for a long, long time. This was good. Dan knew his friend's ways and he was happy that his plan was being given careful consideration.

'Here,' Dan said when a small knoll shut them off from the view of the prison, 'take a swig of this.' He handed Sylvester a noggin of whiskey. He had thought of bringing a larger bottle but he was afraid that the bulk might be noticeable. Sylvester took in a mouthful and withdrew the bottle from his lips, rolled the whiskey round in his mouth and swished it through his teeth before swallowing. As it coursed down his throat in its purity he gasped and shuddered.

'That we might never lose the tooth for it,' he cried gratefully between gasps. He disposed of the remainder quickly and returned the empty bottle to Dan. 'Next time you come bring two of those.'

Dan promised he would.

'I like your plan up to a point and I like the time you selected. If you have a pencil and paper I'll write a note to Dick Daly. I'm certain he'll want to have a say in the proceedings.'

Dan handed over a notebook and a pencil. While Sylvester wrote he spoke.

'As good as the plan is it has a flaw and while one flaw might be nothing much in other situations you can afford none at all when dealing with the Reiceys. They have an animal cunning for sizing up situations. Don't doubt me when I say they'll size up this one. Some one of the three will be in the ticket office of the Shillelagh supplementing the normal staff on Saint Patrick's night. It's big business and you may be sure that whichever one it is will have his eyes open for signs of trouble. The dance-hall itself has a trouble-free re-

156

cord fight-wise and they want to keep it that way.'

He continued to write and talk at the same time. Then he tore a page from the notebook, folded it and handed it to Dan.

'Give this note to Dick Daly. You'll find him most nights in the Irish Club in Eaton Square. If he's not there he'll be at the Old Capstan close by. If he's not at either place enquire for him. I'm sure you won't have any difficulty finding him. I'm equally certain that he'll back you up. Now about your plan.'

Sylvester returned the notebook and pencil and folded his hands in deep thought. He made Dan repeat everything he had already told him. Sometimes he would interject a question but would not pass comment when it was answered.

'Listen carefully,' he said when Dan had told the whole story for the second time. 'Your stay is nearly up so I won't go into details. Your plan is a fine one and will work if you do what I tell you. The most important thing is to stay sober. You'll win the fight if you all do this. It's towards the end of the trouble that your problems will begin. I think we can take it for granted that Dicey will be the Reicey representative in the ticket office on the night in question. The minute the action starts he'll size up the situation at once. There's a phone in the ticket office and he'll use it. Because the call is from the Reiceys the police will be there in a flash. If, however, he thinks his side are likely to win he won't pick up the phone. If he has the slightest doubt about the outcome he'll use the phone and you must be prepared for police intervention. If you're still there when the police arrive they'll arrest you and your men but not before they really do a job on every one of you. These custodians of the law won't be the same as the men who batoned you outside the pub in Kilburn. These will have been well treated by Tom Reicey in the past. Remember they've never been given the slightest trouble by the Shillelagh. They've always been respectfully treated by the Reiceys. Dicey will put the finger on you and yours unless the phone is disconnected. A small wire-cutter will do the job easily. I've drawn a little map in the notebook and marked with an X the best place to cut the wire so that you won't be observed doing the job and so that the disconnection won't be found easily. You'd want to cut the wire about five minutes before the dance ends.'

Dan promised to carry out the instructions in detail.

'One final thing,' his mentor laid a hand on his arm, 'don't divulge your plan to anybody and be certain you have a good diversion lined up.'

'Diversion?'

'I'm sure you have friends you can trust outside of those who'll be involved in the fight?'

'Yes.'

'You know a vacant lot on the left as you pass Lade's Hotel in Hammersmith. It's about three miles beyond the Shillelagh and a mile and a half beyond the police station.'

Dan pondered a moment before replying.

'Yes,' he said after a while. 'I know the place.'

'Could you arrange for your friends to be there at one o'clock? That's the time the dance ends at the Shillelagh. It's a well appointed spot, ideal for the kind of diversion I have in mind.'

'Go on.' Dan listened carefully.

'If these friends of yours could manage to explode a Molotov Cocktail or two just before one o'clock in that particular place it would ensure that no police car would accidentally pass by the Shillelagh while the fight was in progress. As soon as the explosions are heard in that very quiet and purely residential area the phone in the nearest police station will start to ring. If you have any problem with the cocktails Dick Daly will solve it for you. In fact it might be in the best interests of all concerned if there were a few rehearsals elsewhere beforehand.'

'I'll do everything you say.'

'I'll be most anxious to hear how things work out.'

Although there was a strict rule that inmates were allowed to receive letters only once a month Dan and Sylvester used a simple system which was foolproof. Dan would address the letter to a friendly warder who knew Sylvester well enough to be certain nothing underhand was involved.

At the first suitable opportunity the letter was handed over. It was worth the few pounds expense involved. It also meant that Sylvester heard regularly from Sandra.

They returned to the prison where Sylvester was forced to submit to a thorough search after taking his leave of Dan. In the early days he was humiliated when the questing fingers felt under his arms and between his legs. He had grown to accept them although the searches were never perfunctory. When his hair was cut there was the same sense of humiliation. His preconceived ideas about prison life had been near enough to the mark.

There was the degrading association with convicted criminals during meals and breaks. He would never grow used to the overpowering intimacy. The food was not bad, just dull and there was enough of it but never more than enough. He made a few friends, one in the prison library where he worked and another younger character who was serving a five year sentence for embezzlement. He had succeeded, despite his tender years, in bankrupting a large, well established company. In a desperate bid to avoid being found out he had gambled four thousand pounds of the company's cash on a horse called Red Eleven which was contesting a modest race at Epsom. Aided by an accomplice he had done a competent SP job. The horse was beaten by a head at odds of one hundred to six against. If the animal had won he would have drawn over seventy thousand pounds. He could have replaced the money he had already stolen and kept over ten thousand pounds for himself. Fate decreed otherwise.

Most of all Sylvester missed the company of women. His longing for female companionship was a persistent agitation so piercing and so penetrating that it often knotted him up into a twisted and forlorn spectacle in the privacy of his cell. He smothered many a cry of deep and insatiable longing. There were times when he would have grovelled at the feet of any creature that resembled a woman. It was not a calculated torture devised by the authorities. It was for many of the victims the ultimate in human suffering.

There were many female visitors to the prison. One of

159

these, the wife of a forger who was serving a three year sentence like Sylvester, wore tight-fitting skirts and jumpers and always took off her coat as soon as she entered the prison. Whenever she moved the enclosed flesh rippled underneath her clothes. When she walked her breasts bounced up and down and her buttocks hither and thither proving a distraction above and beyond the commonplace in that bleak establishment.

'When I see her pass by,' Sylvester once told Dan, 'I'd be prepared to serve another three years for one crack at her.'

There were other women too, attractive and unattractive but none so ugly that she was not capable of disturbing a prisoner's thoughts for the day and night. In his imagination Sylvester had ravished, in the close confines of his cell, most of the female visitors. The prison had a large representation of homosexuals and he had received several invitations. He was not flattered although he had been tempted. So inexpressibly dreary was the routine that anything would be an uplift from the oppressive barrenness.

There were some advantages. His health was restored completely and physically he never felt better. There was also the prison library which, although by no means up to date, gave him the opportunity to read books he certainly would never have read otherwise. These were nearly always ancient and gnarled editions of the English classics with very fine print but without them life would have been intolerable.

The outcome of Dan's forthcoming confrontation with Reiceys' Rangers would be something to look forward to. He had no doubt in his mind about the likely result. Dan was a cool one. He would leave nothing to chance. That he also possessed the necessary ruthlessness Sylvester had no doubt either. For once the Reiceys might have been better advised to leave well alone. If Dan succeeded on Saint Patrick's night it would be the first real kick in the teeth the firm received since its foundation. Sylvester winced at the thought of defeat for Dan and his men. No. Dan was no fool. If things did not appear to be favourable he would postpone his vendetta until things were.

It would be something new for the Reiceys. It was never

pleasant to be at the receiving end moreover if one was unaccustomed to it. It would make it doubly hard if one's pride took a knock as well. Sylvester had not prayed since he left Maynooth. He made the sign of the cross and entwined his fingers.

'Incline to my aid O Lord, O Lord make haste to help me.' The introduction to the Rosary came to him at once despite all the years of neglect. He would pray now as he never prayed before, with that fervour and ardour he failed to imbue into his entreaties for a vocation. His armour of devotion would be impervious to all assaults. He would pray every hour of every day till the morning after Saint Patrick's Day and unless God had turned completely deaf he would be moved by the passion and consistency of his pleading. God would see to it that Reiceys' Rangers got the father and mother of all beatings, that the bejasus might be kicked out of every one of them and that their sores might never heal.

DICEY REICEY'S marriage to Margo had been working out well and she had lived up to all his expectations. Recently, however, it had been marred with tragedy. Margo, nine months to the day after the wedding was whisked away to Newsham General when the labour pains she was experiencing became more frequent, taking on a predictable pattern. Dicey had driven her to the hospital himself and Patricia Dee who was on night duty was there to receive them. Margo arrived at half-one in the morning. Her own doctor arrived shortly after and at her insistence promised he would stay on till the child was delivered. Hour followed hour with Dicey pacing the corridor filling the traditional role of worried father-to-be. Finally Patricia persuaded him to go home promising to ring him personally as soon as there was news.

'You're doing nobody any good here,' she told him, 'and Margo would much prefer if you went to bed. Don't worry I'll call you immediately there's news.'

Reluctantly he left. Margo's doctor was well known in maternity circles in London. Second generation Irish, his name was Willie O'Sullivan. He was in his late fifties and enjoyed a high reputation among his colleagues. Patricia and he had a cup of tea together in the dining-room. He regaled her with tales of the medical circles in which he moved. She found him unpretentious and good-humoured. From time to time Patricia would look in on Margo. The delay was unusual. The child should have been safely delivered an hour before. Slightly puzzled Doctor O'Sullivan decided upon inducement. Patricia stood by in the labour ward preparing the swaddling clothes.

'Suffering Christ!' The exclamation came from the Doctor. Patricia was by his side at once.

'Is there anything the matter?' she asked.

'I should think so.'

Patricia could not bring herself to look down.

'What is it?' she asked.

'You might say we are on the verge of medical history,' Doctor O'Sullivan commented wryly.

'I don't understand.'

'This must surely be one of the first black Mayo men to come forth into the world.'

Suddenly the truth dawned on her. The pity welled in her heart for Margo. Dicey Reicey would kill her.

'Oh dear,' Doctor O'Sullivan said.

'What now?' Patricia asked. The doctor indicated the cord round the neck. The child was dead, a victim of asphyxiation. They tried in vain to restore it to life. Patricia placed the infant in a cot nearby and looked to the doctor for instructions. He was deep in thought.

'I'll get a box,' Patricia suggested.

'Do that,' he said.

When Patricia returned Margo was in a daze and had no idea of what happened.

'We want to tread lightly here sister. You know what's involved?'

Without answering the question Patricia placed the infant in the little white box and covered it lovingly with a white embroidered shawl. Then she put the cover on.

'Is there a burial place near?' Doctor O'Sullivan asked.

'The porter will show you.'

'Don't ring her husband till she comes to and knows the score.'

Patricia nodded.

'And till the day you die let this be our secret.'

'I swear that to you,' Patricia said.

'Good.'

Doctor O'Sullivan put the box under his arm and departed. Patricia sat near the bed where Margo tossed and turned in an effort to regain full consciousness. She mentioned names and places which were all meaningless to Patricia. As the minutes went by she came nearer and nearer to reviving. At length she opened her eyes but unable to focus them and not having the strength to persevere she closed them again. Patricia wiped the perspiration from her forehead and throat.

'The devil's children have the devil's luck' – the old saying occurred to her when she tried to conjure up a picture of Dicey Reicey's face upon beholding the black baby. She shuddered at the thought of it. With luck he would never see it, would never know that he was not the father of his stillborn son. He might request a look but Doctor O'Sullivan would be in a position to veto any such demand on the grounds that there might be after effects which could, more than likely, affect Dicey's relationship with his wife. This would be true but not in a way that Dicey could possibly comprehend. He would hardly insist. If he did the consequences would be tragic.

Margo opened her eyes a second time and fixed them on one position. She lay perfectly still for several minutes then looked about her slowly and carefully. Her eyes met Patricia's and for a long time she allowed them to remain settled there in the hope that a message might be forthcoming. She looked round the room hopefully, not daring to speak. She craned her head forward but fell backward again.

Her eyes questioned Patricia and when no answer came alarm spread across the beautiful face. The alarm changed to fear and the fear framed a question on her lips.

'Where?' she asked weakly.

163

Gently Patricia took both her hands and covered them with her own.

'Where?' Margo's weak voice grew shrill. 'Where is my baby?'

'It's dead.'

'It can't be.'

'It's dead.'

'How?' she gasped, her face ashen with the shock.

'Cord round the neck,' Patricia explained trying not to show emotion, hoping that the nurse in Margo would bring about the beginnings of resignation.

'What was it?' she asked pitifully.

'It was a boy.

'Prepare yourself for a shock Margo.'

'What now?' She tried in vain to rise but she was firmly pinned down.

'The child was black.'

Patricia said it reluctantly but time was running out and Dicey Reicey would want to know why she hadn't rung at once as she promised him she would as soon as something happened. .

'What did you say?' Margo was incredulous.

'I said the baby was black.'

The expression on Margo's face changed again. Then cold reality had dawned. It was replaced by an expression of pitiable fear.

'Dicey!' she cried. 'He'll kill me.'

'No he won't. He doesn't have to know.'

'But the doctor? He's his friend.'

'He's out burying the child now.'

'Suppose he wants to see it?'

'Hardly. You tell him that you wanted the child buried, that it upset you. Do you think you can do that?'

'Oh yes. Yes I can,' she replied fearfully, the terror now fully apparent in her eyes. 'Do you think he'll believe me?'

'There's no reason why he shouldn't.'

'Will you stay a while when he comes?'

'Yes. I'll stay a while but he'll want to be alone with you. His only concern will be your wellbeing. He won't miss the

164

child. You can't miss what you've never had.'

'You don't think he'll notice anything?'

'How can he? Now for his sake tidy yourself up. I'll go and ring him.'

15

DICEY REICEY sat in the ticket office of the Shillelagh waiting for business. He occupied himself with reading through the London evening papers. Outside things were quiet. It was only half-nine. In another hour things would begin to hum. The admission fee had been raised to six shillings. It was Saint Patrick's night and nobody would mind. From the direction of the bandstand came the music of the specially engaged orchestra. They had been brought over from Dublin for the occasion and were charging a hundred pounds for the night. As far as the Paddies were concerned this particular band was one of the biggest attractions in town. Dicey figured that 2,000 patrons would somehow be crammed in to the inadequte ballroom.

He put the paper aside and asked the girl who assisted him if she had the correct time.

'It's almost ten o'clock,' Tilly Atkins said. 'It won't be long now sir.'

Dicey nodded. 'I think I'll take a turn outside, I won't be long. If there's any problem call the doorman.'

He walked across the forecourt to the main thoroughfare. It was pleasant and peaceful with a rural undertone that he had almost forgotten. He would pop over to Lade's Hotel in the car and have a drink or two before the big business of the night began.

On his way to the Shillelagh that evening he had called to the police station where he had been most cordially received. He deposited a case of whiskey in a corner of the day-room without saying what it was or referring to it in any way. The police car would look round regularly. There was nothing to worry about. Every police station in London had extra men on duty because of the night it was. Dicey accepted a cigarette from the orderly and they sat a while smoking, each trying to prophesy how the night would turn out. Early reports had it that things were quieter than usual. There were less than a dozen arrests and with only three hours to go till midnight it could well prove to be the quietest Paddy's night on record.

Dicey returned to the dance-hall. The doorman was a well made fellow of over six feet with a scar on his cheek and a disfigured face generally. In his day he had been a fair to middling heavyweight. He was no Crazy Horse but Dicey had no doubts about his ability to quell a row. The usual score of girls sat hopefully near the bandstand while on the floor several couples, all girls, waltzed to the catchy music of the imported band. Everything seemed to be in order.

The Shillelagh was bursting at the seams when the Commer van pulled into a dark alley two hundred yards from the ballroom. The alley was deserted. At the end was a sharp turn which expanded into a cul-de-sac. Into this the van was reversed until it was no longer visible from the entrance. The parking spot had not been chosen at random. Dan had chosen the area after nearly a week of reconnoitring. On Saturday and Sunday nights there was an old Ford truck parked there but on the other nights there was nothing.

Its most obvious asset was that they could shoot straight out on to the highway without the aid of lights. These need not be switched on until they were established in the weak flow of traffic which would be moving towards the city at that hour of the morning. Secondly, it was near enough to the Shillelagh when the time would come to beat a hasty retreat. Thirdly, if by some mischance they had to scatter they could easily rendezvous there or thereabouts when it would be safe to do so.

Nobody, not even a senior police sergeant would believe that anybody could be so unthinking as to make a getaway into a cul-de-sac. Its fourth advantage was that the spot was sufficiently off the beaten path to ensure that the sound of the explosions would not be drowned out.

At exactly one o'clock there would be two bangs, one hard upon the other in the vacant lot suggested by Sylvester. This would be the signal to move in on the forecourt of the ballroom. In the event of there being no explosion the assault would be abandoned and a second attempt made on some other night.

When the van rolled to a stop it was exactly ten minutes to one. The headlights were turned off and after a five minute interval a man emerged from the driver's side. He went to the rear and opened the door. One by one, purposefully and without hurry, six shapes alighted. Noiselessly the door was closed behind them. They were the Costigan brothers, Dave and Peter, Dan's brother Willie, Crazy Horse, Dick Winterman and Eddie Carey. No one spoke. They stood in a group without moving or making the least sign to each other.

Further away to the south the Dubliners, Willie Hunt and Neal Rohan cruised along the almost deserted streets of the sleeping suburbs. Willie had had some misgivings when Dan had put the proposition to them. Neal had none at all. He had suffered more than once at the hands of Reiceys' Rangers and here was an ideal opportunity to get his own back. Willie sat comfortably on the pillion of the ancient but high-powered motor cycle which carried them to and from work. As they neared their destination a grim smile of satisfaction hardened Neal's goggle-covered face.

'Are yez all right back there?' he called over his shoulder. The answer was a reassuring pressure on his shoulders. Willie Hunt did not feel in the least assured. He still had the same misgivings. If it had been anybody but Dan he would have told them where to go. On his back was a bulky haversack and he silently prayed that the time for deliverance of its contents would come. It was all right for Neal. The bloody fellow was behaving as though it were to a picnic they were going.

'It won't be long now,' Neal called back. 'We're almost there.'

Turning off the headlights he slowed down to a snail's pace. Then he suddenly whirled the machine into a vacant lot almost dislodging Willie in the process. Quickly they both dismounted. Neal checked his watch. He had, earlier that night, set it by Dan's who had checked with the BBC's time signals. In less than four minutes the bombs must go off. There would be no damage, merely a deafening explosion followed at once by another. Willie had taken the containers from the haversack before returning it to his back. They stood on the ground glinting ominously in the poor light.

'Right,' Neal's curt order was issued hoarsely.

Trembling, Willie lifted the first cocktail. Outwardly calm and indifferent but with a hidden feeling of immense satisfaction Neal struck a safety match against the side of its box. The flame flickered and almost failed then tongued its way exultantly upward.

'All set?' Neal held the flaming match stick in readiness.

'All set,' Willie whispered. Suddenly he found himself with the flaming bomb almost ready to go off. With a terrible cry he flung it from him with all his might. It smashed against the ground with a deafening crash. The flames shot viciously upwards highlighting the roughness of the brick walls that enclosed the lot. Shaking all over he lifted the second cocktail.

'All set?' from Neal.

'All set.' He managed to get the words out. In anger he flung the flaming missile high into the air. Again the deafening crash and the surging flames.

'Come on out of it.' Neal dragged him towards the bike. In two minutes they were a mile and a quarter from the scene.

'There's no mistaking that,' Crazy Horse whispered to Dan when the first bomb exploded. Dull as was the sound and distant as it was it had nevertheless the depth and volume of a major explosion. The second bang seemed to be louder than the first.

By this time the telephone wires from the Shillelagh were severed. This job had been entrusted to a friend of Dick Daly, a linesman who worked for a local telephone company. He had asked no questions but for a modest fee had undertaken the job. With a man of his experience and professionalism there would be no slip-up.

Unobtrusively the seven men made their way towards

the Shillelagh. They had made no positive plan. The idea was for Willie to bump accidentally into the youngest of the Morrikans with all the force at his disposal. From then on they would play it by ear.

Their timing could not have been more accurate. From their vantage point at the side of the forecourt they could hear the strains of the familiar waltz 'Goodnight'. Traditionally this was always the last melody played at the Shillelagh. Inevitably the national anthem would follow and then the crowds would come pouring out. They would come slowly, lingering about the forecourt or the street beyond, delaying departure till conversation had worn itself out and it was certain that absolutely nothing was to be gained by further delay.

Sure enough as soon as the waltz ended the band struck up the national anthem. At the same time the light in the box-office went out. This did not mean that Dicey was leaving. What it meant was that he would be able to see without being seen.

'A last word lads,' Dan addressed his followers. 'We have only one enemy here tonight and that's not the Morrikans or the Reiceys. We can take these in our stride. Our enemy is panic. The first man to lose his head loses the fight and remember that no matter how poorly things may be going with you yourself, there are six others who will be faring well. Just hold till one of us is free to help you.'

Crazy Horse spoke. 'I've been in many a mix,' he said. 'I've killed Germans and Italians, even comrades of mine by mistake. I've fought my way from one end of Kilburn to the other and what Dan says is true. Panic and we're done. If you find your knees knocking and your teeth chattering don't let it worry you because mine are doing the same thing. You wouldn't be any use if you didn't feel nervous. Just remember. Don't give in. It's when you think you're beaten that victory is at hand. Always remember that. Never lose sight of it tonight.' Crazy Horse looked upward slightly and blew a kiss into the night. 'The first blow and the last blow are for you Sylvester,' he whispered.

'Right boys,' Dan commanded. 'Here they come. Mingle

with them. Don't scatter too widely.'

One by one as if they were casual strollers they moved towards the emerging crowd. Scarcely a yard divided one from the other. If Dicey noticed he was not showing alarm. They need not have worried. His head was craned out of the office window watching the ballroom's main exit. Dan felt his arm being tugged. It was Crazy Horse. He pointed to an insignificant figure scurrying towards the outer part of the forecourt where one electric light bulb shone ineffectively. It would serve its purpose when the ballroom lights went out. Willie Murray, who also spotted the youngest Morrikan, was about to follow when Dan restrained him. Dame Fortune was about to take a hand in the proceedings. Young Morrikan had found himself a victim. This was nothing new. It was just that Dan had mistakenly felt he might have foregone such a luxury on the feast day of the great Irish apostle.

Taking their time the seven converged on the lamp-post. Young Morrikan had waylaid his man. He berated him loudly, obstructing him whenever he made a move to pass by. The victim was of the classic mould, gangly and in his teens. Dan noted with relief that the youth was taller than usual with good shoulders. He did not seem in the least perturbed by the abuse Morrikan hurled at him. Dan noticed Ruckard Morrikan and the other brothers moving nearer the scene.

In a matter of moments a large crowd had gathered. The youngest Morrikan was now sparring with his opponent. Suddenly the strange youth erupted into action and with a smart spattering of blows drew blood from several different parts of his assailant's face. Ruckard Morrikan lunged forward swearing loudly. The alarm showed for the first time in the youth's face.

'Now boys!' Dan shouted.

Just as Ruckard Morrikan contacted with the youth's poll Dan struck him smartly between the eyes. He struck a second time and a third time always on the same place. Ruckard lifted his left hand to ward off the blows. Dan finally hit him with a blow which began at his own shoulder bone. He met Ruckard dead on the jaw and felt the jarring shock in every joint of his right side. Miraculously Ruckard did not fall. He was stunned but somehow managed to keep his footing. He fell forward on top of Dan and held on to him as if he were drowning. In vain Dan tried to shake him off but his hands were pinned under the great weight. Ruckard held on to him desperately, trying to regain his strength. Dan brought up his knee but the heavier man instinctively arched himself out of harm's way. Dan felt the smashing fist on Ruckard's ear. Then a second, harder blow. It was his brother Willie. Ruckard was forced to release his hold in order to defend himself. Dan drew back his right hand again to administer the *coup de grace* but before his clenched fist was half way to its target he felt as if his whole mouth had caved in. Spitting out a tooth and part of another he slumped to his knees and then to the ground. It was a disastrous moment. The man who struck Dan was the second Morrikan brother, Shamus who was reputed to be the best of the four. Immediately Willie engaged him. He caught Willie with two sharp lefts in the face. Both made him gasp but he did not retreat. He dared not with Dan on the ground. Willie feinted and landed a blow on Shamus Morrikan's mouth. It had no effect whatsoever. As Dan attempted to rise, Ruckard Morrikan, half-stunned, was rapidly becoming aware of the situation. With his right foot he felt along Dan's bent form. Satisfied that he had located the most vulnerable area he drew back his leg. Willie seeing his intention butted him into the face. Furious at being caught napping so easily Ruckard flung Willie aside. Again he drew back his leg. Dan was barely conscious but he was aware that he was in mortal peril. He rolled over, narrowly avoiding the heavy shoe. They he heard the voice of Crazy Horse.

'Don't get up!' it said. 'Keep your head.' Grimly Dan nodded to himself. He was semi-conscious. He sensed the legs of the big man astride him. One huge foot was firmly planted at either side of his defenceless head. Dick Winterman smashed his way through a crowd of opponents who clawed at him like terriers baiting an old badger. He stood back to back with Dick Daly. Eddie Carey and the Costigan brothers, heavily out-numbered, were fighting for their lives.

None of the three knew that their leader was out of the contest.

Sensing that Dan would be all right Willie rushed to Eddie's aid. He did not come a moment too soon and his arrival made a difference. They were still fighting a retreating battle but when they least expected it they were aided by another powerful ally. He was the youth who had been waylaid by the youngest Morrikan. The minute he saw Ruckard Morrikan bearing down on him he knew he was in the middle of a set-up. He ran for all he was worth but he had gone only a few hundred yards when his conscience started to prick him. The man or men who had joined in when he started to run? What was likely to happen to them? Conscience got the better of fear and he returned slowly. Cautiously he approached the forecourt. A savage free-for-all, the likes of which he had never seen before in his life was in full swing.

Defending themselves desperately were Willie Murray, Eddie Carey and the Costigan brothers. Instinct told the youth that these were the men he should fight for.

'I'm Lynch from Tipperary,' he explained to Eddie who was trying to contain two different barrages at the same time.

'Good God man I'm aisy where you're from,' Eddie wheezed. 'If you're half a man you'll back us up.'

'I'll do that all right,' Lynch said and without further preamble caught Eddie's nearest opponent with a bony right knuckle just under the eye.

'Come on the Rangers,' a voice shouted. 'We have the bastards.' This taunt and the arrival of the Tipperary man were just the tonics Willie's side needed. Led by Eddie Carey they scorned the flying fists and tore wildly, savagely into the opposition.

'Up Ballynahaun,' Eddie roared at the top of his voice. Heartened they held fast, not retreating an inch. Instead they forced the foe to give ground. They were out-numbered two to one but for the first time they were bringing the fight to the other side.

Dan still lay huddled on the ground. His mouth was a bloody mess and with his tongue he could feel the gap where he had forfeited a tooth and a half. He shook his head and spat out the mixture of blood and spittle but he was still too groggy to risk rising. Overhead, it seemed an awfully long way off, the giant heads of Crazy Horse and Dick Winterman ducked and dodged and weaved as from all sides their attackers kicked, clawed and sent out wallop after wallop. It was Crazy Horse's greatest hour. He accepted everything that was offered. He never winced nor sacrificed a single fraction of an inch as the blows rained in on him from all sides. The attackers were fully aware as he was that if they could get at the huddled form the battle would be over.

Winterman fought gallantly but it was on Crazy Horse that the brunt fell. A reputation to last a lifetime would be the reward of the man who struck the blow to bring him down. Here indeed was a chieftain worth deposing. There were many too who had felt his ire in the early days of the Shillelagh and now like a wolf pack they fought viciously to tear him down. Time after time he sent men spinning. Some were a long time in returning. Others stayed where they fell. The three older Morrikans battled relentlessly egging on the four other Reicey Rangers who were still active. There seemed to be no bottom to the reserves of strength in Crazy Horse. A number of onlookers who had no part in the fight stood at a respectful distance and marvelled at this mighty man who seemed to absorb blows and kicks as if they were meat and drink to him, whose mighty arms never seemed to tire. At his back Dick Winterman was more content to take punishment than to administer it. The truth was that he was tiring and only barely managing to stay upright. His years were a disadvantage. Still on the ground, well protected, Dan found a little of his strength returning. He was slightly concussed without being aware of it. He was still dazed but he knew he would come round fully if one extra minute of breathing space were afforded to him. He knew too that Dick Winterman was nearing the end of his tether and that even Crazy Horse could not last forever. Great as he was there were too many good men lined up against him. Dan could hear his breathing grow heavier yet still not an inch of ground did he yield.

Dan placed both hands on the ground and raised himself with difficulty. He sunk back to his former position, rested a moment and tried again. The second attempt was better than the first. He was fully aware now of the extent of the fighting around him. He felt the shame and frustration of being out of things when he was most needed. Again he shook his head before attempting to rise. Again his legs failed him.

Then drifting inward from a great distance the voice of Eddie Carey came to him poking into his subconscious, alerting him, waking him fully to his obligations.

'Up Ballynahaun!' A wave of fierce and passionate anger sent the life surging through him. He flexed the muscles of his wrists and arms and for the first time he knew that his strength was almost fully returned. His brain was not fully alerted to what was happening overhead but he knew he was wanted up there and wanted sorely at that.

'Up Ballynahaun!' he shouted. 'Up Ballynahaun!'

Crazy Horse helped him to his feet. The moment he found his footing he was at the receiving end of a vicious blow to the head. All it succeeded in doing was angering him further. With a snarl he charged into the man who had struck him. Like flails his arms worked the unfortunate fellow over. He turned on Shamus, second oldest of the Morrikan brothers. Shamus was the most respected of the foursome and the most feared. While the others instigated and incited it was Shamus who finished what they began. The others, however, were well able to look after themselves and Ruckard in particular was possessed of immense strength but it was to Shamus they always turned when the chips were down and chastisement seemed imminent. The taste of defeat was unknown to him.

Dan took him by surprise. It was fortunate that he did. Dick Winterman had fallen and was out of the fight. Crazy Horse still stood his ground, backed up now by Eddie and Willie, the Costigan brothers and the man from Tipperary. It seemed when Winterman fell under a rain of blows from a much smaller opponent, a squat, red-haired man, that

175

Reiceys' Rangers must overwhelm the remainder of Dan's force.

It looked like the turning of the tide and the Rangers sensed it. They redoubled their efforts so that even Crazy Horse was obliged to give ground. Irresistibly Dan waded into Shamus Morrikan. He knew that everything now depended on him. Such was the frenzy of his onslaught that the others paused unconsciously to watch. Like one gone berserk he rained blow after blow upon the head and body of his foe. He brought his blows from everywhere, from the ground in looping uppercuts, from his right and left shoulders in savage crosses, from wide arcs which swung his body fully around. Not all of the blows landed but those that did sent Shamus Morrikan backward. Shamus scarce had time to fight back so busy was he trying to defend himself.

Fight back he did, however, and now the pair stood toe to toe too exhausted to attempt anything fanciful, determined to bring the affair to an end.

There is a time in every fight when the tide of battle, though churning and swelling, neither ebbs nor flows. That is the time when an act of greatness can swing the issue one way or the other. It is a time for superhuman effort and as Dan Murray and Shamus Morrikan stood slugging it out every man present knew that this was a battle of chieftains. The others had all but expended themselves and now they stood and watched as their leaders drew upon their ultimate reserves. Of the two Dan was smaller by three inches but he was more agile and for every blow Shamus Morrikan delivered, he returned two and often three. Then came his supreme effort. Almost doubling himself into a steel-like spring he absorbed three blows without endeavouring to reply. Imperceptibly, his legs inched themselves apart and his shoulders seemed to swell. Then the spring uncoiled and with a smashing series of vicious lefts and rights to the face he sent Shamus Morrikan reeling. He followed up to the cheers of his companions and mercilessly rained blow after blow upon his staggering adversary.

When Shamus fell he fell heavily and as he fell Ruckard Morrikan drove forward at Dan. He was followed by his brothers and by the rest of the Rangers. From deep in Crazy Horse's chest came a noise that resembled a squeal. It was followed by a great roar. He went forward taking Ruckard Morrikan in his stride.

'Come on boys!' Dan shouted. 'We have them.'

They swept away the remaining opposition as if it didn't exist. Only one man still stood up to them. He was the red-haired man who had knocked down Dick Winterman.

'Take off Ginger,' Crazy Horse called to him.

'Never,' said the squat, red-haired man.

'Let him be then,' Crazy Horse commanded. He stood with his hands on his hips, his great chest heaving, waiting for Dan's command.

'All right,' Dan said, 'let's move.'

Quickly, without breaking into a run, they moved silently from the scene. As they moved out of the danger zone Dan ordered the others to wait for him at the van. With them went the Tipperary man. Dan merged with the shadows at the entrance to the forecourt.

There were eight shapes huddled on the ground. All seemed capable of movement save one. He noticed a figure emerging from the main entrance of the Shillelagh. It was Dicey Reicey. Dicey bent and took off his shoes. Noiselessly he ran to where Dan lay in wait. He would want to see which way the attackers went, follow them and hopefully take the registration number of their transport. As he edged around the corner his head craned forward, Dan stepped out and caught him flush on the jaw with a well-aimed clout. Dan ran for the first time that night.

As they drove towards the city and to an appointment with Sandra in her Kilburn flat they heard the distant wailing of several police sirens. 'They've just stopped at the Shillelagh,' Dan said.

'By Christ I could do with a drink.' Dick Winterman spoke with feeling.

'So could we all.' Dan spoke for everyone.

Everything would be taken care of by Sandra.

On his return from the prison Dan had told Sandra about his conversation with Sylvester and outlined for her

177

the full plan of campaign for Saint Patrick's night. She had asked if there was some way in which she might be of assistance. Dan had told her what she must do.

She gave him her undivided attention and grasped everything down to the last detail. He gave her a bundle of notes and told her to invest in food and drink, advising her not to skimp. Also she must make her flat available and have a supply of medicaments handy. All going well she could expect them at two o'clock. If there was a delay she was to wait. If there was a long delay she was to forget everything and go to bed.

'I'll prepare a hot meal,' Sandra had promised.

'No. You mustn't do that.' He warned her against it but she insisted.

'It may go to waste.'

'It won't,' she replied confidently. 'We'll have a victory dinner. Don't you fret.'

Dan had not told Patricia Dee about his plans for Saint Patrick's night. For a while he contemplated telling her but a sixth sense told him she might not altogether approve. She had been keenly disappointed when he told her that he would be unable to take her out. She did not tell him that she had spent the previous weeks, when she had been on night duty, looking forward to it.

FOR DICEY Reicey the night had been one of the most catastrophic of his life. At midnight he was prepared to gloat. The box-office receipts had broken all records and in addition he had managed a nice personal fiddle for himself. He had every reason to be pleased. At half past twelve he invited the chuckers-out in to the office for a drink. It was a quiet time with nobody going in or out. Later when the band sounded the national anthem he had turned off the light in the ticket office. There was bound to be some sort of scuffle. One could hardly expect otherwise with such a large crowd.

Nobody could blame Dicey if he wasn't prepared for what was to follow. The first inkling he had of forthcoming disaster was when one of the chuckers-out was floored. Up to then it had looked like a normal row which any experienced doorman could handle without difficulty. A few of the Rangers taking it out on some poor latchiko who wasn't long out of the bogs! He had learned that it was wiser to let the Morrikans have their bit of fun provided they didn't overdo it. It was following the usual pattern. He turned off the main lights in front of the ballroom and was about to lock up for the night when he sensed that it was more than a run-of-the-mill brawl.

'Better put an end to it Pete,' he called to the head bouncer.

Dicey remained where he was but first he made sure to lock the doors in case they should attempt a return to the ballroom. With nearly nine hundred pounds in cash resting in the safe it was the sensible thing to do. If the doorman got into trouble that was his look-out. He was getting paid for it. It was Dicey's job to look after the interests of the Reiceys. He returned to the ticket office where he saw with alarm that the fight was a serious one. He was just in time to see his doorman succumb to a right cross from Crazy Horse. This was too much. He recognised others in the crowd, Dan Murray and his brother, the Morrikans and several other Rangers. He hesitated. In spite of his doorman's being out of it there seemed to be more than enough Reicey men to handle the situation. He would wait a while. No point in creating an alarm which might result in embarrassment for Tom at a later date.

'Just remember Dicey,' Tom had once explained to him, 'every time somebody gets seriously hurt in or near the Shillelagh it costs me money, big money.'

Dicey remembered Tom's other injunctions: 'If a row looks like getting out of hand ring the police at once. There's nothing the equal of a police siren for putting an end to a row.'

Dicey hesitated no longer. He caught the phone and dialled. It was some minutes before it dawned on him that the line was dead. It took still longer to discover that the wires had been cut. If only he had parked his car elsewhere. It would be impossible to drive it through the mob in the

179

forecourt, that is if he ever succeeded in getting into it. Still all was not lost and as long as nobody was seriously injured there was, as yet, no call for serious alarm. He drew across the shutter of the ticket office, uncorked a bottle of beer and waited. After ten minutes he drew back the shutter. All seemed quiet. A group of men had just turned the corner. Several lay scattered on the forecourt. He would follow the fleeing group at a safe distance. It was possible they might have transport. In a matter of minutes he could have a fleet of patrol cars on top of them. He appeared round the corner. Stars exploded before his eyes. He remembered no more.

16

DAN MURRAY and his men did not work for the remainder of the week. Some were not capable of doing so, like Dan himself whose face was swollen beyond recognition and Dave Costigan whose ribs were so painful that he dared not move. Dick Winterman, Crazy Horse and Eddie Carey were unable to work because they drank themselves into stupors when they arrived at Sandra's flat. No one ventured out till the following night. Dan, because of his grotesque appearance, decided to stay indoors for a longer spell.

Peter Costigan and the newcomer Larry Lynch were chosen to reconnoitre Kilburn and Cricklewood. They were to make themselves inconspicuous and to pay heed to the crack. They were bound to pick up bits and pieces about the aftermath. Under no circumstances were they to ask questions. If they were identified which was highly unlikely it might suggest that the Murray outfit was worried or nervous or still uncertain about the extent of their victory. They would be in little danger of assault for two reasons. The first was that Dan felt nobody would want to fall foul of the element which accounted for Reiceys' Rangers and the second was that the Paddies in the mid-week were always a morose lot, unwilling and unable to fight because of the after-effects of the previous weekend.

On Dan's instructions his brother Willie took a cab to Bertham. Dan had previously told Sid and Gillian that they might not be returning to the digs for a few days; that there might be a visit from the police. In the event of this happening they were to say that he and his men were working in the far south of the city on a contract and were unlikely to be back until the weekend. They would have no idea where the site was. Dan had already decided that he would see the police of his own accord. It was likely to make an impression for the better if he called to find out what they wanted. He had been briefed by Sylvester about how he should comport himself with the law. He would take his time. If the law liked to move majestically then he would move alongside complimenting rather than obstructing. At half-past ten all the reports were at hand. The fight was the talk everywhere. As far as Peter Costigan and Larry Lynch could deduce, from listening carefully on their separate itineraries, there was no mention of revenge. Everybody felt that the Rangers received no more than was their due. Nowhere was there sympathy for them. One man with whom Peter Costigan had joined forces for a few drinks had released some discouraging news. He had heard that a man was in a coma after the fight. He did not know which hospital.

This was disquieting news indeed but not necessarily true. With misgivings Dan recalled seeing one unmoving figure as he quitted the forecourt of the Shillelagh. Could this be the man or was it just a wild story? There would be many exaggerated accounts of what happened in the weeks and months to come.

Some buck-navvy balladeer was certain to make a song about it. The story of the song would be far from the truth. The man with whom Peter Costigan had been drinking said he had been present at the scene of the battle.

'I am twenty and five year in this place,' he told Peter in his clipped County Louth accent, 'twenty and five year and I never seen the like of it. The Murray men was the freest-fightin' latchikoes I ever did see twenty and five year man and boy in this place.'

He had no further information about the man who was supposed to be in a coma. From what Peter could gather there were several who had undergone medical treatment. It was rumoured that there were a few in hospitals. These were in no danger, just routine strapping and stitching.

Dan had guessed rightly that the victory would be a popular one. The police would never admit it but this fact would weigh heavily against an all-out investigation. The only outcry would be from the Reicey Brothers.

Larry Lynch had visited several pubs. In the Volunteer he had caught a glimpse of Ruckard Morrikan and the third eldest brother, Mick. From what he could gather Shamus was confined to quarters and the youngest Morrikan was in hospital with a fractured jaw. In all the pubs visited by Lynch there was no other subject mentioned. It was an extremely popular win. The underdogs had triumphed against all the odds. It would be talked about for many a day. Larry Lynch spoke with several young men, never soliciting information. He didn't have to. Everybody wanted to talk about the fight. Some had it that the Murray gang numbered only four while others put the number as high as six. There was an estimated forty in the Reicey outfit. Upon such wild speculation were legends founded. The real truth never made for fanciful retelling.

Lynch dared not stay long in the Volunteer. If the Morrikans recognised him he would be in a tight corner. He visited three other premises frequented by the Irish. He always sat on his own as soon as he received his half pint of ale. In one establishment a man sat alongside him and asked him if he had heard about the fight. Larry replied that he had.

'It was goin' to them so-an-so bullies for many a day,' the man said. Larry agreed and offered to buy a drink. The offer was taken up. While they drank the stranger gratified him with accounts of terrible deeds over the years perpetrated by the Morrikans and their fellow Rangers.

'God's blessin' be on Murray or whatever his name is,' the man said. 'He surely put down great blackguards last night.'

Dan was heartened by these accounts. A victory so popular could not possibly result in attempted retaliation.

The mustering of sufficient support would be difficult in the extreme. Few would want to be in Dan Murray's bad books after the way he and a handful of allies had dealt with the biggest body of thugs circulating in the Irish environs of London.

The Reicey Rangers had a bad name from the outset. Their laurels had always been won under questionable circumstances. Their foes had been drunk, heavily out-numbered, more inexperienced. There was no known instance of a heroic victory. Dan's triumph was the very opposite. He had delivered a blow for small men and lone men everywhere. His name would be highly respected from that day forth. There was not a shred of suspicion attaching to his achievement. Evermore it would be thrown in the faces of Reiceys' Rangers. Let them start their shenanigans again and the taunt would be flung at them – 'Dan Murray softened ye,' or 'Remember the Shillelagh!'

A vital inroad had been made into their dominance of the building scene. All seemed well save for the disturbing news of the comatose casualty who was reported to be still in hospital. Dan had a nagging suspicion that there was more than a grain of truth in the story brought back by Peter Costigan.

When Willie returned from the digs at Bertham he told of his interview with Sid and Gillian. The police had called twice. There did not seem to be any urgency on their part when told that Dan and his work mates were away. They asked if the luggage was still in the rooms. Gillian assured them that it was. They did not ask to see it. They promised they would be back but offered no information as to why they wished to interview the absent lodgers. Gillian hoped everything would be all right. Willie assured her that everything would be, that they would be returning without fail at the weekend.

Dan was pleased. He gave Sandra sufficient money to replenish the stocks of beer and spirits. Only one question remained unanswered. This was the one concerning the man reported to be in a coma.

To put his mind at rest Dan gathered everybody into the sitting-room of the large flat. When each had been supplied with the drink of his choosing Dan insisted that everybody take a seat. For his part he sat on the floor with his back to the wall.

'I want all of you to go back over the happenings of last night,' he stated. 'As you do I want it to be quite clear that no matter how you answer the question I am now going to put to you I will never forget your courage last night especially when things were going against us. I am proud of each

184

and every one of you but this question has to be asked.' He took a long swig from his bottle of beer. 'Does any man recall during all the excitement to have used the boot. Remember what I said. I won't hold it against you. I have to know because I need to be prepared.'

After a moment or so a hand was raised. Immediately two others raised theirs too. The first hand raised was Willie's. Dan signalled him to proceed with his version.

'He drew his boot at me,' Willie said, 'and I lashed out at him.'

'Where did you kick him? What part of the body?' The question came from Crazy Horse.

'In the shin,' Willie replied. Crazy Horse and Dan exchanged satisfied looks.

The second hand raised was that of Dave Costigan.

'Yes?' Dan urged.

'I lost my head towards the end of the row. There was this fellow I was trying to get at all night. When I got my chance I let him have it.'

'Where?' Again the question from Crazy Horse.

'In the arse,' Dave answered.

Everybody laughed. The answer relieved the air of tension and men took time off to refill their glasses.

Dick Winterman was the third man.

'Right.' Dan indicated that he was to proceed.

'I couldn't help it,' Winterman declared defensively. 'He had a hold of my leg and his teeth were sunk in my calf. Here. Look at this.' Hastily he pulled up the leg of his trousers and pointed to where the marks of the teeth were visible on his right calf. 'The bloody fellow just would not let go of me. I hit him three or four times but he held on like a bloody bulldog.'

'Where did you kick him?' Crazy Horse asked.

'I don't know for certain,' Dick Winterman's voice was hoarse now. He was forced to swallow before continuing.

'Think,' Crazy Horse's voice was toneless.

'I'm sure it was somewhere between the balls and the navel.'

'Nearer to which?'

'Nearer to neither. I'd say it was dead between the two.'

'Did you kick him hard?'

'Yes, I kicked him hard. I had to. He was trying to bring me down. It was him or me and by Christ it wasn't going to be me.'

'Did he let go his grip at once?'

'Yes.'

'It fits,' Crazy Horse addressed himself to Dan.

'Jesus I'm sorry Dan!' Winterman rose to his feet clutching the bottle of beer supplicatingly to his belly. 'I hope I didn't bitch it.'

'Don't worry Dick,' Dan spoke reassuringly. 'You did what you thought best. I don't blame you.'

Relieved, Dick Winterman sat down.

'You think he could be the man in the coma?' Dan asked.

Crazy Horse deliberated carefully before answering. 'There may not be a man in a coma. We may be making mountains out of molehills. What I'm saying is that when a man is kicked with more than average force between the pubis and the naval his bladder might easily sustain a rupture. I saw it often enough in the army. It follows that such a rupture would result in a coma.'

'Could it be fatal?' Dan asked.

'It always is. I wouldn't worry too much about it. At least I wouldn't allow my conscience to bother me. In all probability he would have done the same to one of us in similar circumstances. When you become involved in all-out fight you take your chance. That's the way I look at it.'

Dan said nothing. For the next hour they reminisced over the many incidents of the night. They praised each other's prowess and sought easily-forthcoming confirmation of personal actions. All were agreed that the highlight was Dan's two-fisted attack on Shamus Morrikan. Dan would have preferred them simply to gloss over it but they were enjoying themselves immensely and he hadn't the heart to interrupt.

The Tipperary youth, Larry Lynch told his version. It had been his first night at the Shillelagh, his first night in any London ballroom. He was out of Ireland a week. He had nothing to drink. He was dancing with a good-looking girl from Cork when he received a hefty thump in the back. It knocked him off course. He turned to see an impish, ferret-faced, young man smiling villainously at him.

'Cut that out,' he had said. He thought no more of it until later during another dance he was tripped. He fell heavily bringing his partner with him. He looked up to see the same individual grinning down at him. He knew him now to be the youngest of the Morrikan brothers. At the time he could not understand the fellow's motives. The girl insisted she did not know him. He was tempted to retaliate but decided against it on account of it being the night it was. Still he was worried. He knew all about the set-up situation from friends who came home on holiday. All night the youngest Morrikan annoyed him. Larry Lynch had decided positively that he would not be provoked. After the dance he half-expected to find his tormentor waiting.

He was not in the least surprised when he was challenged. After he had accounted for young Morrikan he knew exactly what to expect. He intended to fall down and roll over. Then a quick burst through the crowd and after that he would trust entirely to his feet. He was an accomplished cross-country runner. He had been so determined to get away that it was only when he was over two hundred yards from the scene he remembered that somebody had gone to his assistance. Reluctantly he had turned back. He was glad now that he had done so.

Dan sat slightly apart, watching and listening. They were like schoolboys after a successful prank. It was just then that he remembered he had neglected to call Patricia. He had promised he would. He went to the phone in the hallway and rang the hospital number. She would have been on duty since ten o'clock. It was now almost eleven. He did not have long to wait. She came to the phone at once.

'Hello,' he said. She did not answer at once. When she did he could not help but notice the chill in her voice.

'Is there something wrong?' he asked.

'I don't know,' she said in a way that wasn't in the least like her. 'Maybe you're the one to answer that.'

This was a puzzle.

'I don't understand,' he said. 'Have I done something to offend you? Tell me what it is.'

'I know all about last night.'

'I'd be surprised if you didn't,' he laughed. 'Every Irishman and woman in London knows about it.'

'Is that all you can do? Laugh?'

It was a different Patricia. He had never heard her like this. She would have to understand that the fight was an absolute necessity if he was to survive. Everybody with an inkling of knowledge about the building trade recognised this. He set about explaining his position but he could sense her impatience.

'In the name of Christ,' he shouted, suddenly losing his temper, 'will you tell me what's wrong?'

'Don't raise your voice with me.'

'Oh God!' He said it half to himself.

'Just now,' Patricia intoned bitterly, 'there is a man dying in this very hospital. His name is Walsh and he comes from the West of Ireland. I have been told that he has a wife and five children and I understand the wife is on her way here.'

'All right, all right,' Dan shouted, 'but what has all this to do with me?'

'It has everything to do with you.'

'Oh?' He was suddenly on his guard. A picture was beginning to take shape. It quickly dawned on him that the rumours he had heard were true.

'Do you know what I'm talking about now?' The same merciless attitude from Patricia.

'All right,' he said. 'Tell me the worst.'

'He won't be alive when his wife gets here,' Patricia said.

'I'm sorry to hear that.'

'Are you?' The relentless hammering at his conscience was beginning to annoy him.

'Dammit, you know I am.'

'He is dying from uremia. Somebody kicked him in the stomach.'

'You're blaming me?'

188

'A man is dying.'

'It was entirely his own fault.'

'No it wasn't. His friends say he was drunk, rotten drunk. They say he was caught up in the row by accident. Don't you realise the gravity of what you've done? Can you be so callous as to try and justify the murder of an innocent man?'

'Don't put all the blame on me.'

'But I do. I put all the blame on you and your thugs.'

'Don't say that.'

'I will thank you to ring me no more. I don't want to see you again.'

'I hope you don't mean that.'

'I mean it. I never realised the kind of person you were. I suspected you were a hard worker and that you were ambitious but I still find it impossible to believe that anybody could be so ruthless.'

'It was an accident.'

'No Dan. It was no accident. You started the whole thing. Everybody says so. I'm hanging up now.'

He stood for a while holding the phone in his hand. There was no mistaking her determination. He knew her well enough to comprehend that she never said anything lightly. Carefully he replaced the phone and returned to the sitting-room. An uproarious sing-song was in progress. Nobody noticed the set expression on his face. He called Crazy Horse aside.

'Do me a favour.'

'Name it.'

He thrust a ten pound note into the big man's hand.

'Before you come to the traffic lights as you go down the street to the left there's an off-licence. Bring back as much whiskey as the ten pounds will buy.'

Crazy Horse closed his hand upon the money, was about to say something but changed his mind.

'Everything will be all right,' Dan said reassuringly. 'It's just that I've suddenly developed one right whore of a thirst.'

'I know what it's like,' the big man said. 'Believe me Dan

I know what it's like.'

A WEEK after the Shillelagh affair, Dan went voluntarily to
Hammersmith Police Station with his brother Willie, Crazy
Horse and Sandra. He made a voluntary statement saying
that on the night in question he was nowhere near the Shillelagh. Neither were any of his friends. They spent the night
having a small party in Sandra's flat. They had not stirred
outside.

What of Dick Winterman? The police were curious. Was
he also at the flat? Dan answered in the affirmative. Then
why did he not come along as Dan had done and volunteer a
statement? Dan explained that they could not all absent
themselves from work together. The truth was that he did
not know the extent of police interest in Winterman. What
about Edward Carey? Yes. He was also at the flat but could
not come to the station at this particular time. Winterman
and he would be along later. The interviewing inspector
seemed relieved. No charge was proffered. The inspector
rose as they were about to leave and asked them one by one
if they would be available for future questioning and if they
would be good enough to notify the station in case of a
change of address. He then apologised to Dan for any inconvenience caused.

'If you like,' Dan said, 'I can return with the other two
right away.'

'That won't be necessary,' the inspector had answered.
'So long as we know where they are, we can always contact
them. Perhaps you would be good enough to furnish the
address and phone number of the site?'

The inspector could not have been more apologetic. Dan
provided him with the information required and left. He
drove straight to the Midland Bank and withdrew a hundred
pounds in five pound notes. He placed the money in an
envelope and pocketed it.

The inspector knew far more than he pretended. That he
knew the names of Eddie Carey and Dick Winterman surprised Dan. Somebody, hostile to Dan to say the least, must

have volunteered the information, but who? Certainly none of those involved. It would have to be Tom Reicey, anonymously of course. There was no need for secrecy since all in the district knew of the fight. There was no point in keeping it quiet when every policeman in that part of London and indeed all over it knew that the fight of the year had taken place outside the Green Shillelagh on Saint Patrick's night.

The incident would do the Shillelagh no good. The police were annoyed. They had been embarrassed. If the Reiceys had undertaken to provide proper and adequate supervision there would not have been a fight and consequently no death. Three days passed before the inspector put in an appearance. His manner was most deferential. If he proceeded with the investigation it was certain that Dan and his men would be charged and tried. The inspector did not want to go ahead because the damned Paddies, once they got wind of danger, would take off for the bogs of Ireland or join up with the long distance men who might be in Dorset today, Devon tomorrow and Durham the week after. Name, identity, everything would be submerged and a new person replete with all the characteristics of a fresh arrival from Ireland would emerge instead.

Dan never ceased to be astonished at the attitude of the police towards the Irish. Let an Englishman do injury to another Englishman and he would be hounded relentlessly until he was brought to justice. The same applied to the Welsh and Scots but let an Irishman do one of his fellows to death and all the police wanted was to gloss over it. They showed genuine appreciation when the Paddies involved made things easier for them.

When the inspector called at the site it was approaching evening and already growing dusk. He beckoned to Dan who hastened to his side.

'Are your friends available?'

'Yes of course,' Dan replied with what he hoped was guilelessness. 'Do you wish to speak to them?'

'I'm not sure that I do,' the inspector answered and he looked quizzically at Dan like an actor who has forgotten his lines and desperately needs a cue.

Dan gave him no assistance whatsoever.

'The superintendent seems to think I should press on. It's really up to myself.'

'I see,' Dan said and he placed his hand in his pocket. 'I wonder,' Dan continued and he withdrew the envelope, 'if you could help me in a personal matter.'

'I'll do what I can,' the inspector said.

Dan thrust the envelope at him and allowed it to slip into his hand. The inspector was forced to clutch it or allow it to fall.

'I want you,' Dan mustered all the sincerity within himself, 'to hand this offering to a suitable charity, the family of a deprived policeman or some such worthy cause.' At Sylvester's insistence he had memorised every word.

The inspector pocketed the envelope gratefully. 'I know just the family,' he said.

'Good.' Dan was relieved in more ways than one.

'Goodbye sir.' He extended a hand. Dan accepted.

'I don't expect to see you again.' The inspector sounded confident. Without another word he disappeared into the deepening dusk.

SYLVESTER RESOLVED to investigate the possibility of improving the quality and range of books in the prison library as soon as his term ended. At present his job was to catalogue the existing stocks, a task to his liking. He was assisted by his young friend Bert Edgecombe. Bert greatly admired Sylvester. Every day he learned a little from the older man. Bert was aware that Sylvester was serving his sentence unjustly, not that it would have made any difference to their friendship had it been otherwise.

'How's the investment going?' Sylvester asked. Every inmate knew of the investment. With an imaginary capital of a thousand pounds Bert operated a non-stop betting system in an effort to vary the depressing routine. The newspapers, when they received them, were a fortnight old but the sports pages were intact and when a fresh supply arrived there was tremendous interest.

'As far as I can make out,' Bert replied, 'I'm winning very nearly seventeen thousand pounds.'

The prison bookmakers were two convicted forgers whose integrity was considered to be above reproach. Every day Bert would place a wager with the pair while a number of specially chosen colleagues would act as witnesses. Bert's opening bets resulted in heavy losses so that after a few days half of his capital was dissipated. After this he pulled in his horns and changed his betting procedure. Instead of investing heavily on one fancy to the tune of fifty pounds or a hundred pounds he invested smaller amounts ranging from ten shillings to five pounds. Always he chose long-shots, compounding his fancies into each way doubles, trebles and occasional accumulators.

His bad luck continued until all that was left in his imaginary kitty was a solitary five pound note. He decided upon an ultimate plunge on five one pound accumulators. Advisers and friends disagreed. They advised him to back money-on shots in a bid to increase his diminishing capital. He was adamant. It was to be all or nothing. As if it ever needed to be proved his long drawn out fluttering showed more clearly than ever that only the bookmaker won.

Then there was a dramatic change in his luck. One of the accumulators, consisting of five, moderately-priced, second favourites, came up. At first he could scarcely believe his good fortune. It was true however and the winners ranging in price from two to one to seven to one brought his capital to six hundred and seventy-two pounds. After that he could do nothing wrong. Now with seventeen thousand pounds to his credit he thought bitterly of the cruel luck which had led him to his present impasse. Without luck he felt a man might as well be dead. Bert did not subscribe to the belief that a man made his own luck. He knew from bitter experience that whoever coined such a phrase had never been reneged on by good fortune. On this point Sylvester would agree with him. So would every other prisoner. Each one was capable of making a classic case whereby it could be clearly shown that nothing but bad luck was responsible for his incarceration.

'There but for the grace of God go I,' one of the warders suggested in the course of a conversation with Bert and Sylvester during the night of a particularly bad storm.

'That's one way of putting it,' Sylvester agreed, wanting the conversation to go on.

'Call it what you like mate,' Bert argued. 'It still boils down to luck and if the old lady don't smile on you all the hard work in the world and all the honesty in the world won't save you.'

The others nodded, forced to agree in spite of themselves. It was the governing philosophy of prison life. The warders were lucky. They had not been found out. The scale of their misdeeds might be relatively small but illegality was involved nevertheless. The prisoners were the unlucky ones. There was not one who could not name ten so-called, respectable business or professional men on the outside who deserved prison far more than themselves. According to the prisoners the judges who sat on their crimes were fully cognizant of this. The judges salved their consciences by stressing that they could only judge on the quality of the evidence presented to them but no sane prisoner was prepared to accept this monstrous duplicity.

Judges were lucky to be where they were. They were lucky to be born of parents who could afford to educate them. They were lucky to be born with higher intelligence and better powers of application than their unluckier fellows who were currently serving long sentences. One took a different view of the entire situation on the inside. Every man who breathed freely and who was permitted to go his own way in the outside world was born under a lucky star. To tell a prisoner otherwise was to invite the laughter of ridicule. Should not, and nobody knew better than he himself, Sylvester be a free man and Tom Reicey the occupant of his tiny and unspeakably lonely cell? It was the luck of the game. Being good or bad or mediocre had nothing to do with it. Most of those on the outside were aware of this although not fully. It had never been brought home to them. One would have to be tried and found guilty to appreciate it.

Bert Edgecombe would be a free and possibly a wealthy

man if a certain stable had not succumbed to an onslaught of coughing on the night before a certain race and if a certain trainer had not broken all the rules and run the horse in the vain hope that the animal would win.

Joe Scalman, a seedy, withdrawn individual, who was a friend of Sylvester's and whose job it was to pack and unpack the incoming and outgoing books would not be serving a sentence but for a stroke of bizarre and unfortunate ill-luck. Joe who was in his fifties had, all his life, been inordinately shy of women. His only contact with the opposite sex was under cover of semi-darkness. In the cinema he would allow his hand to wander on to the lap of a woman who might be seated near him. It never worked. In most cases the woman would remove herself to another seat or firmly push his hand away but on the odd occasion a woman would report him to one of the usherettes. As a rule Joe recognised when the writing was on the wall and while the offended party was in the act of making the complaint Joe would be making tracks for the nearest exit.

One night it was his misfortune to be seated near a neurotic. The moment his hand alighted on her exposed knee she screamed and screamed thereby attracting the attention of every usherette in the cinema. Joe panicked and bolted but all he succeeded in doing was running into the arms of a giant doorman who had appeared suddenly from nowhere to cut him off. Prosecution followed and there was a suspended sentence. A week passed and Joe found himself seated near an attractive female in one of the more exclusive types of cinema, a far cry from his usual preserves. Half way through the film he allowed his hand to wander in the direction of the woman's lap. Then with fluttering heart he decided to rest it on her stockinged knee. There was no response whatsoever. He hesitated and moved his hand above the knee. Still no response. Never before had he been so fortunate. Always at this stage the woman either vacated the seat or slapped his hand. Not daring to breathe he felt the soft outline of her thigh. He caressed the silken flesh gently and murmured an endearment. His hand probed further and then it happened. He should have guessed. His experience

195

should have forewarned him. Firmly a strong hand covered his slender wrist and held it as though in a vice. He tugged for all he was worth but there was no breaking the hold. The woman lifted her free hand as if by arrangement. Suddenly the houselights went on and he found himself the centre of attention.

'That's 'im,' one of the usherettes cried and covered her mouth with her hands as though she had indicted Jack the Ripper.

'It looks like 'im,' another said doubtfully. What Joe Scalman could not possibly have known was that for several weeks two police women dressed in civilian clothes were occupying separate seats in this particular cinema as a result of complaints made by women who had been molested. Joe was not the man about whom the complaints had been made. He felt there would be no real point in a denial. He knew he would make no impression.

He was remanded and returned for trial. It had been a cruel slice of ill-luck. He had never forced himself upon any woman. At the first sign of rejection he had kept his hands to himself, thankful not to be given away. Joe was amused when his counsel stood up to defend him. Did his Lordship understand the need and the loneliness which had driven him to do what he did? If his Lordship did he never showed it. He listened with the bleakest of faces. He was there, he explained later, to administer the law and not to sympathise. He had a good look at Joe Scalman. Silly bugger. Why didn't he get a tart like any normal chap? He thought of a particular one and with difficulty brought his mind to bear upon the proceedings.

It was Joe's fifteenth offence. There was also the ominous fact that he was serving a suspended sentence.

This would have to be taken into account. The judge was painstaking. He explained that it was expected of him to provide adequate protection for unsuspecting and unescorted women who wanted no more than a simple night at the cinema. He would be failing in his duty were he not to convict. The defendant had already taken advantage of one judge's leniency. He had promised to behave and for this

196

reason the sentence which had been passed had not been implemented. The defendant had broken faith. Eighteen months might seem a long time now but if the defendant took into consideration the fact that he would have time to contemplate the gravity of his transgressions it would be no time at all before society accepted him once more. He would emerge a better man and there was no reason why he should not thereafter be a useful member of the community.

It was tough luck on Joe that he happened to be at that particular cinema at that particular time. It was the essence of ill-luck to have chosen a seat next to a policewoman.

There were some who might say that Joe's luck had run out on him, that sooner or later he would have to pay the price. Joe would laugh at this as would every other prisoner. How come then that the luck of some people never ran out? How come they passed happily from cradle to grave without being found out? No matter how you examined it the answer was that some people were luckier than others.

Sylvester was concentrating on the historical section of the library when the warder entered. He handed Sylvester a book and with a knowing wink said, 'Have a look inside before you put it back. You might find something interesting.'

Sylvester opened the book and found the letter. He opened it and withdrew the single sheet of notepaper. It was no more than a few lines. It had Dan's signature at the bottom.

> *It was a good night. You should have been there, I don't expect we will be troubled again from that quarter. The youngest of the three divine persons got his fair share too. See you shortly.*

Sylvester knew what Dan meant, Dicey had been among the casualties. God but this was sweet news. Sylvester started to whistle, tunelessly but exultantly. He slapped Bert Edgecombe on the back and claimed the attention of a convenient warder. He wanted to relish the note in solitude, to gloat over it, search every word for hidden meanings. He wanted to laugh out loud. Permission granted he hurried to his destination fit to burst with laughter.

17

JUNE OF 1958 saw the commencement of Dan Murray's first comprehensive building contract. It was a modest undertaking involving the construction of 24 houses on a developed site a stone's throw from Mitcham Common in south London. It would be to south London with its immense development possibilities that Dan would turn during the years to come. The undeveloped fields in the southern perimeter of the great city were, to young and ambitious building contractors, what the tang of salt air is to the restless mariner. There was the same urge to be up and away, the same desire to explore further and further till nothing worthwhile was left undone. With his heart in his mouth Dan opened the foundations for the scheme at six o'clock on a June morning of rare beauty. His team were as eager as he that the effort should be a success. Since the defeat of Reiceys' Rangers as the bully boys of the construction scene, more and more Irish workers looked to Dan and his circle of cronies for employment and protection.

Not all of Dan's eggs were in one basket. On the same morning Eddie Carey, with another smaller team, was putting the finishing touches to the brickwork for a new school less than a mile away. Almost everywhere one turned there were new factories going up and this spelt housing. As long as there were factories the demand for houses would always exceed the supply. Even when the erection of factories ceased and production was at its apex in the fully operational plants there would be demand for better houses.

Three months before that important June morning Dan had never seen, much less heard of, Captain Dingley Bates-Beary. Dan and Eddie Carey had spent a Sunday afternoon surveying the new developments in the district of Mitcham. Having satisfied themselves that their standards would match up to anything they had inspected they stopped to look at the window of a prominent development office close by a cluster of new sites. Displayed on the window was a sketch drawing of 24 new houses which were to be built on what was once the kitchen garden of a country house.

The sketch was at the lower corner of the window and they had to squat in order to examine it closely. It had some interesting features but it was plain to be seen that there was no builder present during its conception. It was altogether too theoretical although there was nothing basically wrong otherwise. They were so absorbed with pointing out to each other the various refinements that, unknown to them, a very old Rolls drew up right at their backs outside the door of the office. Its sole occupant was a dapper, moustached, sprightly man of fifty. From the way he stepped on to the street and consciously straightened himself upwards to his full height, it was obvious that he was ex-army and most likely an officer. Noiselessly he closed the car door behind him and with a trace of a smile watched the excited pair examining the sketch. He was about to pass them by when it occurred to him that nothing could be lost by having a word.

'Good afternoon chaps,' he opened politely.

Surprised, Dan and Eddie got to their feet.

'Afternoon,' Dan replied.

'I see you've been examining the sketch drawing,' Bates-Beary spoke encouragingly.

'Just plain curiosity,' Dan said with a laugh.

'You chaps Irish?' Dan nodded.

'In the building?' Again the nod from Dan.

'And pray what do you find wrong with the sketch?'

'Not an awful lot,' Dan returned.

'Yes, but I have the feeling that you do not altogether approve.'

'Well,' Dan hesitated, 'I hope you don't think I'm forward and it's really none of my business but there would seem to be room for another house.'

'There always is,' Bates-Beary agreed, 'but the more houses on a site the less room on the outside. Still let's have a look.'

He squatted on his haunches bidding Dan and Eddie resume their original positions. With his index finger Dan traced a rough outline of what he had in mind.

'Let's go indoors,' Bates-Beary suggested. On the inside he withdrew the sketch from the window. He handed it to Dan. From his lapel pocket he took a pencil which he also handed to Dan.

'Show me,' he said, 'and take your time.'

Laboriously Dan repeated the tracing he had outlined at the window bottom. Painstakingly he pointed out that with slight alterations and minimum rearrangements by cutting off a yard here, by shaving a foot there, yet without any significant change in the general picture there would be no difficulty in allowing for the extra house.

Bates-Beary looked at him with a mixture of respect and pleasant surprise. He begged him to go over the sketch again. When Dan had concluded, the drawing was returned to its original position in the window.

'Should I know you chaps?' Bates-Beary asked.

'I doubt it,' Dan replied.

'Are you with Murphy's?

A shake of the head from Dan.

'McAlpine?'

Again the shake of the head.

'Reiceys then?'

'No.'

'But you are Irish and you are obviously in the building line?'

Dan introduced himself and then Eddie. Briefly he outlined his position in the building world and suggested hopefully that he would not turn his back on an opportunity to build the proposed houses. He stressed that he had not previously negotiated a large housing scheme.

'My name is Dingley Bates-Beary,' Bates-Beary informed them, 'Captain of the same name.'

Dan repeated the full name and title so as to affix it firmly in his memory.

'Right first time,' Bates-Beary said approvingly.

'Good,' Dan said, 'but you aren't called all of it surely?'

'No indeed,' Bates-Beary assured him. 'Those who work for me call me Captain.'

'And those who don't?' from Dan.

'I wish I knew. I really do.' They all laughed at this.

On an impulse Bates-Beary looked at his watch. 'How about a drink?' he said.

A fortnight later Dan was asked to submit figures. Although still in prison but nearing the end of his time Sylvester supplied them with the aid of a freshly drawn-up sketch plan.

'You've got everything going for you,' Sylvester told Dan. 'It's the ideal time of year. You have your own workpool and you have me. There shouldn't be the slightest problem.'

Sylvester, of course, was right. In the building business fine weather is everything and, anxious to earn substantial bulk sums for late summer holidays, tradesmen and labourers alike work longer hours of overtime than at other times of the year. As the work progressed Dan or Willie would pay regular visits to Sylvester. His advice was invaluable. There was nothing he did not know about the building trade. In the finer points of costing and estimating he proved to be a wizard. It occurred to Dan, not for the first time, that without Sylvester in the formative years, there might never have been a Reicey empire. He was due to be released in August and it was agreed that, after a few week's holidays, he would come into the firm. Dan realised that without Sylvester's guidance he would never arrive at where he really wanted to be. Eddie Carey was reliable and the best friend a man could have but like Dan he was wanting in education and had only a modest head for figures. If Dan lacked education he wanted for nothing else. He had the necessary drive, energy and brilliance to out-pace his contemporaries. He had courage and the requisite proportion of recklessness which would be needed when greater undertakings would be involved.

They worked throughout that month of June as if their lives depended on it.

Eddie finished the school contract towards the end of the

month. All their combined resources were then flung whole-heartedly into the major effort. Dan had no problem acquiring plasterers, painters, carpenters and other tradesmen whenever he wanted them. He was Dan Murray, the hero of the Shillelagh. Some considered it an honour to work for him. Most of the sub-contractors he approved rearranged their sub-contracts in order to facilitate him. Another factor in Dan's favour was that there was no ceiling to what a man might earn. There was no time limit, no union interference, no income tax. It was lump and leave. The tradesmen upon whom Dan depended from time to time were here-today-and-gone-tomorrow men. One had to be really in the know to locate them. They owed allegiance to none but once they gave their word it was never broken. Furthermore Dan never refused a man who might have financial trouble at home. Without preface or condition he asked the amount required. Later it could be deducted on a weekly basis when the borrower was back at work.

The relationship between Dan and his labourers was built on absolute equality. For Dan's part this was never put on. Any pretence was easily detected by buck-navvies who were reared and weaned on the ideology of subservience. From an early age this attitude was forced upon them by their parents whose whole thinking processes were geared to simple survival. The hat was to be lifted at all times to the priest, the teacher and the shopkeeper, in fact to all who wore collars and ties. These were the people who controlled the jobs and the money. This attitude bred a fierce and often dangerous contempt in the offspring. They did not have to be told they were the equal of Dan Murray or the president of Ireland or the queen of England. They knew it. Dan was the boss because they wished it so. If, in concert, they ordained otherwise it might not be so. Luckily for Dan he understood them. There was no leaning over backward, no going out of the way to ladle out pleasantries. It was to be natural, unaffected equality pure and simple. With attitudes like these, Dan was to control a powerful work-force. It could and would be explosive at times but he would always be on top of it.

Captain Dingley Bates-Beary was impressed by Dan's methods. The dynamic young Paddy over-rode all the conventional snags, tore through red tape and succeeded in outstripping all the other established contracting concerns in the district. As soon as Dan got through ten thousand pounds worth of work the Captain handed over the same amount. Dan needed the first ten thousand pounds desperately as his own and Eddie's money was almost gone. They had used it to carry the job for the first month. In the last month they would be able to pay themselves back in full and return the repayment to the joint account which was the sole capital of the company.

At the conclusion of the work on the 24 houses, having paid all bonuses including a special one to Willie, they realised a profit of five thousand pounds. Four thousand of this was lodged in the joint account and the remaining thousand pounds divided between them. They were hardly finished when Bates-Beary offered them a similar scheme at exactly the same terms. He had already found purchasers for the first 24 houses and the demand for more of the same was unprecedented.

Shortly after the commencement of the second scheme during the last week in August Sylvester was released from prison. Dan took Sandra to Liverpool where he left the pair to their own devices. He did not see or hear from either for three weeks. When Sylvester showed up at the site he was greeted like a soccer star who has just scored the winning goal in the last minute of extra time. First there was hand clapping, then cheers and finally a triumphant tour around the site on the shoulders of Crazy Horse and Dick Winterman. When the reception ended and everybody returned to work Dan showed him to a freshly painted office with the word PRIVATE printed on the door. It was in reality only a dressed-up garden shed but it was comfortable and there was excellent light from an outsize window inserted in it by one of the chippies. Inside was a large filing cabinet, a desk, typewriter, two chairs, an oil heater and a three-foot high heap of span-new ledgers.

From the top drawer of the filing cabinet Dan withdrew

a bottle of champagne and two glasses.

'Welcome to the firm,' he said. He had handed Sylvester a brimming glass of champagne.

'It's good to be here.'

Sylvester fingered equally brimming eyes.

'It's good to know I'm going to be useful again.'

'In time, provided all goes well,' Dan told him, 'you'll have a real office and suitable staff to go with it.'

'I have no earthly doubt about that,' Sylvester said. 'In fact we'll drink to it.'

'Let's sit down and talk,' Dan suggested, 'while we're finishing the bottle.'

'You took the words out of my mouth,' Sylvester said.

While they sat and sipped Dan did most of the talking, reversing for once his accustomed role of listener. There was a lot Sylvester wanted to hear. Did any suspicion still attach itself to Winterman from the Shillelagh fight and the subsequent death of the casualty in Newsham General? Was it true Patricia Dee married a doctor? What were Dan's immediate and most important of all what were his long-term plans?

First tell me about Patricia Dee.'

'There's nothing to tell. She married a few months ago.'

'Who?'

'A doctor.'

'Ah! He would be fat of course.'

'Yes.'

'And bald!'

'Slightly. How the hell did you know?'

'I know,' Sylvester grew serious, 'because it's the way of things. Did she ask you to the wedding?'

'No but I went anyway. I shaved, put on my best suit and sat where she would have to see me as she came down the aisle on the return journey. She looked lovely. He was twice her age. When she saw me she faltered. Then she gasped. The groom was full of concern. She almost fainted but he got her out quickly into the fresh air. Then I left.'

'If,' Sylvester sounded undetermined, 'he is twice her age, of what use will he be to her?'

'I hear he's very wealthy.'

'His wealth won't buy him a new penis.'

'She was never greatly interested in that sort of thing.'

Sylvester guffawed at this. 'She wasn't because she never had it,' he said.

'You asked about my plans,' Dan said, anxious to move away from the subject.

'Have you been out with any girls since Patricia?' Sylvester persisted.

'Several.'

'Yes, but have you slept with any of them?'

'No.'

'We'll have to remedy that.'

'My short-term plan,' Dan went on, 'is to continue building for Bates-Beary until I have the feel of general contracting. I need the experience before I tackle the big time. I'll also need money but that doesn't worry me.'

'I have some.'

'I know you have and when the time comes I'll want you to come in.'

'You have a long-term plan then?'

'Yes but it's not fully formed. Don't worry. You'll be the first person to know. If we're to be partners you'll have to know everything.'

'I'll drink to that. Tell me about Dingley Bates-Beary.'

'Retired Guards' captain. Served in Korea. Got himself the DSC. If you want details he was educated at a public school. Graduated from Cambridge. With his army gratuity he started a development company. He borrowed most of his needs from a small commercial bank, private of course, in Throgmorton Street. I may look in there some time.'

'Who did the dossier on Bates-Beary?'

'Nobody.'

'You mean he volunteered the information?'

'Yes.'

'Why?'

'Because he's that sort of man. With him everything is above board. All is cut and dried. Of course I checked out his credentials, just to be sure.'

205

'Does he know you plan to go on your own?'

'Yes, I told him.'

'And what did he say?'

'He asked me to come in with him.'

'How did you get out of that one?'

Sylvester filled his glass and looked in the bureau drawer to see if there might be another bottle. There wasn't so he sat down again and sipped from his full glass.

'I got out of it,' Dan replied, 'by telling him I'd think about it. I wouldn't mind going in with him. He's likable and we're making money. He plans another scheme of 48 houses after these are finished and he's offered me the job, provided of course that the price is near enough. We're on safe and solid ground and if we go along the way we're going we'll all wind up rich men.'

'But this isn't what you want?'

'Not quite. While I like Bates-Beary I feel he has no vision, that he'd hinder me if I went after the big time. He's happy the way he is, leasing small fields and cabbage patches, then taking up the options when the time to build comes, always playing it cautiously.'

'You want to be as big as the Reiceys?'

'No.'

'How big then?'

'Bigger than the Reiceys. I don't see what's to stop me.'

'Neither do I.'

'You'll string along then till the time is ripe?' Dan asked anxiously.

'Of course.'

'The pay won't enable you to drink much champagne and you'll have to work hard, harder maybe than you've ever worked before, for several years at least.'

'I have no objection to that. How soon do you think you'll be making your move?'

'It won't be more than a year.' Dan did not confide to Sylvester that he had taken an option on a 20 acre field less than a mile from where they were seated. He had told nobody. It was nobody's concern, at least not yet. He had scouted Mitcham and the other south London suburbs relentlessly whenever he found spare time. The field was out-side the present perimeter of development but it was Dan's guess that in less than five years at the present rate of land consumption it would be priceless for building purposes. He would buy it or attempt to buy it within the next few weeks. He had no idea what price the owner might want. The own-er didn't really want to sell but Dan felt that if he made a sudden, dramatic and magnanimous offer it would not be turned down.

'What are you doing tonight?' Sylvester's question cut across Dan's thoughts.

'Nothing.'

'Good. I took the liberty of booking a table at the Colo-rado. We'll get pissed and stay the night.'

'What's the point in staying the night?'

'Humour me will you. Just humour me.'

'Will Sandra be coming?'

'Sandra will be coming.'

'All right we'll stay the night but you needn't expect to see me in the morning. I like to be on the site at six o'clock.'

'I'll personally see to it that you get to bed early. I can see you've missed my guiding hand while I was inside. All work and no play makes Jack a dull boy. It's a fine thing to get ahead in the world but if you don't get in a bit of living in the process what's it all for?'

18

TOM REICEY'S wife Maisie read the telegram for the second time. Her face registered neither surprise nor shock. She returned it to its envelope and went indoors, ignoring the delivery boy who waited patiently in the vain hope of a tip. She had been dozing in the garden when the persistent ringing of the front doorbell disturbed her. It was a sultry August afternoon and she had felt drowsy after the washing-up. She never kept a maid, priding in the fact that she was capable of running her home without help from anybody. The year before her mother had died in Kerry and a bare month afterwards her father passed away. Maisie was fond of telling her friends that her father had died of a broken heart, that he had found life intolerable without his darling wife. What happened was that he succumbed to the month-long bout of intensive drinking in which he indulged after the old woman was safely interred. Without his wife there was no one to care for him or no one to check his drinking. There was also the fact that her insurance money was burning holes in his pocket. Clutching the telegram in her palm she went to the phone and dialled Tom's office number.

'Who's that?' His voice was gruff.

'It's Maisie, love.'

'What does Maisie love want?' He forced the tolerance into his voice.

'Prepare yourself for a shock.' She allowed this to sink in before breaking the news.

"Tis the old lady, isn't it!' Tom forequoted her.

'How did you know?' Maisie was genuinely surprised.

'Well, she couldn't live forever. She's dead, isn't she?'

'Yes. She passed on this morning, the poor creature.'

'I'll be home right away. Get the children from school

and start packing. I'll tell the others.'

Without delay Maisie collected the children and placed them in care of a friend. She packed what was needed and waited for Tom.

Old Mrs Reicey's funeral was large and representative. Many of the mourners came specially from England. There were prominent architects and engineers who had never seen the old lady, who if they had would have been amused or slightly shocked but these were indebted or obliged to Tom.

There were builders' suppliers from London, Manchester, Coventry and elsewhere who had never been to Ireland not to mention Mayo. Word had spread. The Irish were impressed when people went out of their way to attend the funeral of a loved one. They tended to remember such gestures. No Irish politician would dare miss the funeral of a constituent who had living relatives. Attendance at funerals meant votes and it was good for business.

There was a large number of clergy, several from England. Before the requiem Mass, prior to the burial, the three brothers, dressed in black suits and wearing black ties which contrasted sharply with new white shirts, stood outside the little parish church of Mulvinney where sympathisers came forward to offer their condolences. One by one the hundreds present shook hands with the brothers and any others who looked like kin. Most of the people present were women from the district and from neighbouring townlands. It would never do to miss the funeral of the Reiceys' mother. Their husbands and sons were sending home sums of money undreamed of by the poorly-off folk of the neglected countryside. The bishop was not present due to an indisposition but the bishop of a neighbouring diocese was prominent.

It was a dignified procession which set out for Mulvinney graveyard. The motor-driven hearse at the head was without a coffin since it was still the custom in Mulvinney to shoulder the remains to the last resting place. The three brothers and a first cousin on the old lady's side took the first turn. They were quickly relieved by another foursome

209

anxious to impress. These again were relieved after a short distance. This was an indication of the measure of respect in which the Reiceys were held in the district. Men vied with each other for the right to shoulder the remains. The clergy in white soutanes, numbering more than thirty, walked in double file intoning Latin as they proceeded, true resignation evident on their faces and in their bearings.

At the entrance to the graveyard the brothers again accepted the burden of the coffin. This was the custom. Preceded by the priests they proceeded to a corner of the ancient graveyard where a mound of broken earth slanted upwards from a freshly dug grave. Gently the coffin was lowered to the ground. There was a short lull while the undertaker and his minions, all appropriately sober-faced, took charge. When the grave was filled the presiding cleric asked the concourse to kneel.

The obsequies over, Tom Reicey spoke briefly to each of the cross-channel mourners. He thanked them for coming, patting them fraternally on the shoulders. Most had arrived by taxi from Dublin airport and were anxious to be away again after the unexpected disruption of everyday affairs. Tom was followed by Joe and Dicey who did exactly as he did.

Tom's wife Maisie, Joe's wife Dora and Dicey's wife Margo stood together. Only Maisie showed signs of emotion. Her eyes were red and swollen but this could easily have arisen from frequent applications of her stiff linen handkerchief. She had cried out shortly after the first clod fell on the coffin simply because it had not occurred to anybody else to do so. Some vocal manifestation of grief was vital to the proceedings. Several of the local women joined her but their cries had none of the anguish of a tragic bereavement. From the moment the green scraws were rolled over the grave-mound Margo Reicey was the centre of attention. She wore a simple black costume and a black hat with a wide sloping rim. No one present begrudged her the beauty which made the most obdurate and exhausted countryman look a second time. Stealing a march on Maisie and Dora she moved among the local women. It was a tribute to Margo's charm and ease of manner that they spoke freely to her. They curtsied first and she accepted these obeisances without embarrassment as if they were no more than her natural due.

The local women were delighted with her. They had heard of her and word of her beauty had spread. There were some in fact who would not have bothered to attend the funeral that day but for the fact that it would give them an opportunity to see if she was as beautiful as was rumoured. She left no doubt in the mind of every man and woman present.

Only a churl would deny that she turned the sombre setting into a brighter place. She was still without child. Since the birth of the still-born son of Ngaya Lelumba she had suffered three miscarriages. Not once since her marriage to Dicey had she been unfaithful to him nor had she once contemplated it. Margo was never less than honest to herself. Before marriage she got everything or nearly everything she wanted. She was content enough with Dicey. She did not love him. She never would but he would never know. He was as insensitive to the subtleties of a loving relationship as a prize boar. Since the last miscarriage, which had taken place six months previously, he had been drinking heavily. He was always fond of drink but now he had a daily intake of two bottles of whiskey. Tom had spoken to him and Joe had spoken to him but to no avail. One night as they lay together after a session of lovemaking, Margo suggested they adopt a child. Adoption she pointed out in the case of a person like herself, was often the prelude to a successful conception. Dicey would not hear of it.

'Me,' he scoffed, 'me feed and clothe another man's bastard!'

'It could be the child of somebody we know,' she pleaded, knowing how desperately he wanted children.

'Look,' he shouted and he clouted the pillow, 'a bastard is a bastard and it can't be changed.'

'But it could be the child of dead parents.'

'No,' he said doggedly, 'if I can't have one of my own I'll do without.'

211

Margo had not pressed the matter. They were happy enough although by any stretch of the imagination it could not be said that they were deliriously happy. He was never deliberately cruel and he was a fairly effective lover but he had no sensitivity. Money-wise he could never give her enough. He never tired of taking her places although he might have no interest whatever in the goings-on. She loved the theatre and he went along whenever she asked. Later however he would not return from the bar after the first act no matter how interesting the play might be.

He would be waiting for her in the foyer after the final curtain. Then to a West End night club for a meal and a drinking session which might last till two or three in the morning. He did not keep drink in the house. This was a rule to which he adhered rigidly. It was in a sense his inherent admission to a dependence on alcohol. Neither did he drink by day. No matter how much he desired it and regardless of how he might feel as a result of a punishing session the night before, he always managed to hold out till the working day was at an end.

Margo suspected that he might be having occasional affairs but these most likely would be chance tarts and therefore could not be regarded as competition. It had happened first during her last pregnancy when the doctor insisted that lovemaking be suspended. She knew from his breathing when he fell into a heavy sleep. She had not minded. It was a purely animal thing. She confidently felt she could not be replaced.

Immediately after the funeral, having first settled with the undertaker, Tom and Maisie drove south and west to Connemara where a luxury hotel owned by the Reicey brothers had been recently opened. They arrived at seven o'clock and spent a short period resting in the double room which had been booked in advance before going downstairs for dinner. From his window Tom looked out across the endless reaches of the Atlantic. It was calm and still with an attractive white border of foam where the waves spent themselves. Further up the coast he could just barely discern the imitation turrets of the only other hotel within miles. As a boy Tom had worked there for part of the summer but was sacked when it was discovered that he and another youngster were stealing cigarettes from the store room.

'Get out of here you snot-faced prick,' the manager of the time had screamed at him. No proceedings had been brought for the simple reason that nothing whatever would be gained by such action.

For a time Tom had toyed with the idea of buying that hotel but decided that building a hotel of his own was a far better way of getting even. By all accounts since the new hotel opened the other one might as well be closed.

'That's a fierce good view,' Tom Reicey called to Maisie who was changing into a new frock. She came to his side and looked out of the window.

'Did you see her today and she makin' free with them rotten devils in their shawls?'

'What in the name of the long-suffering Jaysus are you on about now?' Tom was mystified.

'Did you see her and she guffin' with the labourers' wives? You'd think she'd know her place at this time of her life.'

'Is it Margo you're talking about?'

'Who else would I be talking about?'

'Listen here to me,' Tom Reicey placed his hands on his hips. "Tis talking with labourers and their wives that has us here in this hotel this night. We were all labourers not too long back.'

'I know, I know,' Maisie endeavoured to mollify him, 'but one can overdo a thing.'

'Yes, yes. Come on now and we'll eat a bite, I'm starved.'

AT THE same time in another part of the world, the Colorado Hotel to be exact, another party was about to sit down to dinner. It consisted of Sylvester O'Doherty and his girlfriend Sandra, Dan Murray and a girl he had not met before. She was a student of architecture who had come along at the invitation of Sylvester. At first Dan was annoyed but the more he looked at the girl the more he appreciated her youth and good looks. She was only twenty and she lacked nothing by way of womanly embellishments. A waiter arrived with two bottles of champagne for Sylvester's approval.

'They'll do grand,' he assured the waiter as he absently confirmed his choice.

Dan was hard put to unravel the mystery of the girl. As the meal wore on he slowly realised that she was no ordinary date. His first impression was that she must be a tart but he ruled this out the moment she opened her mouth and made her first contribution to the conversation. She was quite beautiful with white even teeth and a ready smile.

What was Sylvester up to? Where did he find her? Why had he not informed Dan that she would be coming?

Her name was Phyllis something or other. He could not quite catch it when Sylvester introduced her. He made no effort to conceal the fact that he was puzzled. From time to time he caught the girl's amused expression and was not slow to perceive that she exchanged mischievous looks with Sandra from time to time.

'I have booked you into no. 34,' Sylvester informed him. 'It's on the second floor. You can't miss it. I also told the girl at reception that you wanted to be called around five. That should get you on the site for six o'clock.'

'I don't know what I'd do without you,' Dan said.

The girl had a red tint to her hair at certain times when the light caught it. Her best feature was her smile. There was also her readiness to laugh. It wasn't easy to remain serious for long with Sylvester at the top of his form, relating yarns about prison life. The girl's eyes were grey or at least they seemed to be. Again Dan thought it was a matter of how they reacted to the light.

He felt himself becoming mildly intoxicated. He ordered more champagne. The talk ebbed and flowed. Sometimes it was mere banter and sometimes a serious note prevailed. A word or a look was sufficient to set the laughter going again. Parties at other tables smiled in spite of themselves. The hilarious foursome were obviously celebrating something, perhaps a win at the races, a business deal. Whatever it was it did not lack in merriment. Towards the end of the meal Sylvester, now well fortified by a long day's drinking, got to his feet and proposed a toast.

'To open spaces,' he said.

'To open spaces,' the others raised their glasses.

'To beautiful women,' Dan said, at which the ladies had the modesty to bend their heads.

When the meal ended they repaired to the bar and later to the residents' lounge after the call of time in the public bar. Dan, looking at his watch, noted that it wanted only a few minutes to midnight. Unsteadily he rose to his feet.

'Well folks,' he announced and he swayed from side to side. 'I'm afraid I'll have to be saying goodnight.'

A look of alarm crossed Phyllis' face. Sylvester shook his head and from this she took her cue.

'See you some time tomorrow,' Dan said to Sylvester.

'I'll be late,' Sylvester told him, 'but I'll catch up in due course.'

'Don't I know it,' Dan said and he swayed again.

'A stranger watching me would think I have drink taken. Goodnight,' he said finally and made his way out of the room.

At the door he turned. 'I'll see you some time soon,' he said hopefully to Phyllis. 'We must do this again.' Then he was gone.

He found his room without difficulty. Thoughtfully somebody had left the door ajar and the light on. In a matter of minutes he was undressed. Kneeling at the bedside he mumbled a prayer and then gratefully eased himself into the bed. His thoughts were a jumble, inclined to maudlin.

He promised himself he would go home soon and then there was confession. After all the promises he had made his mother that he would always perform his Easter duty he had failed her. He had never missed Mass deliberately. At least that was to his credit. There was a phone in the room but how in the name of God would he contact his mother at this hour of the night. The post office phone in Ballynahaun back in Kerry was out of action after nine o'clock and did not operate until nine in the morning. Anyway what was he thinking about. Phoning home at this hour of the night! Now

for sure he was drunk. Still the loneliness for home persisted. What use was all the success if there was nobody around
with whom he could share it, in whom he could confide. He
sighed self-pityingly and turned over on his side. What was
that? What was that? It sounded as if somebody had turned
a key in the lock. He opened his eyes. The lights were still
on. Somebody was opening the door all right. He collected
his thoughts. What if it were a thief? Who else could it be?
The door was fully open now and framed there in the doorway against the darker light of the passageway was a girl.
Her auburn hair was tousled and there was a smile on her
face. She stood with her legs apart. It was the same girl with
whom he had spent the earlier part of the night or was it?
Yes. It was she all right. What's that her name was? Phyllis.

'What are you doing here?' he asked foolishly.

'Don't be alarmed,' she said. 'I'm only a girl.'

'Is there something the matter?' Dan asked with concern,
sorry now that he had not worn his shirt or singlet going to
bed. The girl came into the room closing the door behind
her. Dan sat up in alarm clutching the sheet to his chin.
Words failed him. He tried to say something but the protest
died on his lips. How foolish and idiotic it would have
sounded.

'I'll freshen up,' the girl said. 'I won't be long.' Opening
her vanity bag she entered the bathroom, closing the door
behind her.

Dan was mystified. He had not asked her to his room
but it seemed obvious that she meant to stay the night unless
of course it was for a conversation she came which seemed
doubtful. Still she did not look like the kind of girl who
would jump into bed at a moment's notice. Was he being
made the butt of a practical joke rigged by Sylvester? For a
moment he contemplated dressing hastily and leaving. He
had never been involved with a woman at this level. The
girls with whom he had gone out on dates and particularly
Patricia Dee were virgins and dead bent on remaining so. At
thirty-one it was an odd admission. The fact that he had
never made love to a woman was in part due to the influence of his mother, partly to his religious upbringing but

principally because of an innate reticence and what might seem to be old-fashioned guilt-ridden reservations. He would never confess his position to any of his friends.

He was in a quandary. Maybe he was just being an alarmist. He had no longer any doubt about the role the girl intended playing when she appeared in the doorway of the bathroom. She was absolutely naked except for a charm bracelet which hung from her left wrist. Dan found himself swallowing.

'Well,' she said, 'aren't you going to say something?'

Dan felt his mouth go dry.

'Don't you like me?' She placed a hand on the crown of her head and another on her hip. This is a dream Dan thought. It's all that bloody champagne. There is not a beautiful girl in the doorway of the bathroom. She is not beautifully designed and she is not smiling seductively. It is all in my imagination.

'If you wish I'll leave. There is no obligation,' the girl said.

She seems to be there, Dan thought. If I leaned out of the bed and touched her I would know soon enough whether she was real or not. He would not bring himself to move a single inch.

'If you could give me some indication,' the girl was saying, 'I would know where I stood.'

Dan directed his full gaze at her and nearly choked. He recovered and looked into her eyes.

'You do like me, don't you?' the girl said.

Unable to manipulate a solitary word Dan nodded.

'That's a double bed, isn't it?' the girl said.

Dan looked at the bed at either side of him and nodded.

'If,' the girl said in a tone that made Dan swallow again, 'you were to move over a little the two of us might fit. Or would you rather sleep at this side.'

Dan shrugged and moved over. He lay on his back looking at the ceiling.

When she did not get into the bed at once he listened for her breathing but could hear nothing. He had been right. It was his imagination. He raised his head. She was bending to draw back the clothes, her full firm breasts quivering gently as she knelt on the edge of the bed. Dan extended his arms. At once she sprung into them and wrapped her own around the small of his back with the faintest of cries.

'I like you,' she said, 'I liked you from the first moment I saw you tonight.'

Dan's only acknowledgement of this compliment was a stifled groan.

'Look at me,' the girl said.

Dan forced himself to look at her face.

'You moan as if you were in pain,' she said, her grey eyes laughing.

'Have pity on a poor exile,' Dan whispered.

They both laughed. He kissed her lips gently, then her face all over. The yielding and incomparable softness of her body excited him more than he thought possible. He kissed her neck and breasts and then without effort or embarrassment or difficulty, but with the utmost pleasure, he found it happening. At his climax he cried aloud. With infinite understanding she responded to his release.

Afterwards he lay on his back, one hand round her bare shoulders, the other supporting the back of his head.

'Why did you cry out?' she asked, feigning innocence.

'Where I come from back in Ireland,' Dan said, 'all the menfolk do that.'

'Go on,' she said. 'Do they really?'

'It's a fact,' he said.

'You mean they roar out loud?'

'Yes.'

'And what if somebody's listening?'

'We live in the hills,' Dan explained. His tone was serious. 'The people in the valleys make no noise when they do it. Often they wake up in the night when they hear the roaring of the hill men. "That's Jack Moynihan", a man might say to his wife, "that's the third time this week".'

'You mean they can identify the man making love by his voice?'

'Oh yes. Except when two or three roar together. Then it's difficult.'

'Go on,' she said, 'you're having me on.'

'You want me to roar again?' Dan suggested.

Soon afterwards they slept. When the phone rang Dan dragged himself from the deepest sleep he had ever experienced.

'It's five o'clock Mr Murray. You asked to be called.' It was the voice of the night porter.

Sleepily Dan thanked him.

'Will you be wanting breakfast sir?'

'No thank you,' Dan answered. 'In fact I think I'll sleep it out this morning.'

'Very good sir.'

Dan looked at the girl. She was fast asleep, her rich reddish hair profuse on the pillow, her young breasts rising and falling as she breathed deeply and quietly. In sleep she looked younger. There was a childish innocence in her abandonment. Nurturing fond thoughts for later when she would be awake Dan drew the bedclothes about him and lay on his stomach. Sylvester the old sonofagun was responsible for the girl being by his side. He had chosen well. The only regret Dan felt as he fell asleep was that he had not interested himself sooner in this business of sharing beds with girls.

When he awoke the girl was gone. There was no sign of her clothes. He looked in the bathroom but there was no sign of her. He looked at his watch. It was almost ten. He would have a hasty breakfast and hurry to the site. No time to shave or bathe. In the dining-room Sylvester sat at a table reading a newspaper. Dan joined him.

'Where is she?' was Dan's first question.

'Gone,' Sylvester informed him. 'She left with Sandra.'

'I know she's gone.' Dan sounded impatient. 'What I want to know is where she's gone.'

'What the hell do you want to know that for?'

'I have my reasons.'

'I fixed up everything if that's what's worrying you.'

The waiter arrived and handed each of them a menu. Both ordered bacon and eggs. Dan fidgeted while the waiter repeated the order. When he had gone Dan removed the newspaper from Sylvester's hands.

'Let me get this correctly.' He raised both hands palms outwards and spoke slowly. 'Did I hear you right when you said you fixed up everything?'

After a while Sylvester answered. 'Yes,' he said, 'you heard me right.'

'What is meant,' Dan phrased the words carefully, 'by fixing up everything?'

'Exactly what it's supposed to mean.'

'That doesn't answer my question. I'd appreciate it if you were to tell me exactly what you fixed up.'

'I paid the girl her fee and she went about her business.'

'Fee?' Dan was staggered.

'But of course my dear old segocia. You would hardly expect her to do it for nothing.'

'I can't believe it. She was such a nice person.'

'I agree with you. She was a nice person.'

'But she took money.'

'What's wrong with that?'

'She's a whore.'

'No. She's a student. She needs the money badly but she didn't want to charge you which does you credit.'

'A woman who charges for it is a whore.'

'Wrong again. I asked the girl to dinner to view you. If she hadn't approved she would have gone her way after eating and that would have been the end of it. The fact is that she liked you. If she hadn't liked you she would not have gone to bed with you. A whore could hate your guts but for the money she would be prepared to overlook her dislike of you. You will never see this girl again. She will never do it a second time with the same person no matter what she's offered.'

'I find all this very confusing,' Dan said.

'That's because your pride is hurt. Just remember that she is only one of many. I can always put you in touch with another until you get to know the score for yourself.'

'How much did it cost?'

'It was my treat.'

'I accept that. I'm asking out of pure curiosity and for future reference.'

'Twenty pounds.'

'Will she be with somebody else tonight?'

'No. Not tonight. Probably next week. She only does it when she wants the money.'

'How did you get in touch with her?'

'The night porter.'

'Here at the Colorado?'

'Yes. He costs another five pounds but he's a discreet chap and his contacts are always sound.'

Dan was silent for a long while.

'Is something the matter?' Sylvester asked.

'No,' Dan assured him, 'it's just my mother. I'm wondering how she would react if she knew.'

'She wouldn't blame you, not even if you raped the girl. In the eyes of an Irish mother the screwed party is always the villain. Here comes our breakfast.'

They both ate hungrily.

'It's a pastime that gives you the hell of an appetite,' Sylvester announced.

'I always eat a good breakfast,' Dan said.

'It saps a lot of energy and the body needs extra food,' Sylvester persisted.

'Speak for yourself.'

On his way to the site Dan wondered why he had not slept with a woman before. Most of his friends went into Soho on Saturday nights and sometimes succeeded in getting away with the hostesses and hustlers who frequented the doors of clip-joints. Wiser ones surveyed the ads in the glass cases which were to be found outside many shops. A phone call and an appointment was made without any fuss any time from two in the morning until two in the afternoon. Three pounds for a short time or ten pounds for the long-lie-down as the navvies dubbed the all-night session which included a cup of tea and a sandwich in the morning.

The more sophisticated girls cost more and could cost a small fortune if one was to maintain one exclusively. It wasn't lack of knowledge which prevented Dan from gratifying any overwhelming desires he may have had from time to time. His reluctance was tinged with superstition.

There was the fear, instilled by his religious upbringing, that he would have no luck were he to fornicate. That was only part of it. Ignorance also had a little to do with it, ignorance and not a little fear, the fear of being knifed or mugged by a pimp. Basically it was his upbringing. As he drove through mid-London he felt relieved that he had tasted the forbidden fruit. He was even more relieved that he had liked it. While he didn't feel exactly triumphant or exultant, there was a warm glow nevertheless. He had always presumed that he would feel terrible afterwards, filled with guilt and debased from sating his basest desires. It wasn't like that at all. Sylvester was the only one of his friends who had guessed the truth about him. The others would hardly have believed it. Almost eleven years in England and no notch on his gunstock. He wondered if he was unique. It would be inconceivable to some. Back at home it would have caused little surprise. The non-availability of consenting women would be the prime cause.

When he arrived at the south London site he stole a glance in the mirror. He looked no different except that he had not shaved. He would work till dark tonight to make up for his lapse that morning.

19

CAPTAIN DINGLEY Bates-Beary sat by the fireside in the living-room of his luxury flat in Kensington. He put aside the *Financial Times* through which he had been browsing and turned to his wife. Early in their marriage he had decided that he would never burden her with business matters. However, something of serious import had come up and he felt that it might be wiser and more equitable if he took her into his confidence.

'You've never met Dan Murray, dear, have you?'

'No,' his wife replied. 'Although I've heard you mention him often enough. Why do you ask?'

'Because I face a crucial decision,' Dingley Bates-Beary answered, 'and I would like to know what you think.

'Murray started to work for me two years ago. Since then, I have prospered in a very substantial way. In fact my bank balance is such that I could bow out of business in the morning and survive without difficulty.'

'In the style to which we are accustomed?'

'You could say that,' Bates-Beary replied after he had carefully considered the question.

'I didn't know you had that much money.'

'Let's just say that if I were to retire I would have enough.'

'What's the problem?'

'The problem, my dear, is that Dan Murray wants to buy me out.'

Mavis Bates-Beary was more than surprised. 'Wherever did he get the money?'

'Oh, he's not alone. There's his brother and his clerk, O'Doherty, not to mention a chap called Eddie who is already his partner. He has money because he worked hard, unbelievably hard. His credit rating is high and that's what really matters. He's a ruthless competitor although I must say I have always found him to be above board. You have no conception of the way these chaps work. It's almost inhuman.'

'So Dan Murray wants to buy you out. I don't know what I should say. Why don't you tell me exactly what you're selling while I pour a drink?'

Mavis Bates-Beary chose two ornate crystal glasses and poured a large quantity of Scotch into each. She filled them up with soda from a fresh siphon and returned to the fireplace. She handed a glass to her husband who sipped and nodded.

'It's an odd thing,' Mavis Bates-Beary said, 'but I know absolutely nothing about your business. I suspect, of course, that you felt one worrier in the family might be enough.'

'Exactly. There was no point in giving you a headache too.'

'Was it that bad?'

'Not exactly but one had to be on one's toes.'

'Please tell me about Dan Murray.'

'Two years ago he went along to one of the bigger farms in South Mitcham and offered the owner twenty thousand pounds for a 20 acre field, no staggered payments, just twenty thousand pounds straight on the noggin. The farmer accepted. The field is now worth ten times what Murray originally paid for it.'

'Where did he get the twenty thousand pounds?'

'He and his brother had most of seven thousand pounds between them. O'Doherty had five thousand and Eddie Carey, who is Murray's partner, invested two thousand pounds. A man who works for them and whose pet name is Crazy Horse invested a thousand. It was a simple matter to borrow the remainder. He shortly proposes to build 125 first class houses selling at nine thousand pounds apiece on the twenty acres.'

'That's over a million,' Mavis Bates-Beary calculated.

'Exactly. He has long since paid back the money he borrowed to buy the field. He has offered me twelve thousand pounds for the house and office in Mitcham and for the options on two five-acre fields.'

'Is it a fair offer?'

'It is. The house and office are worth no more than four thousand and the options two thousand pounds more. That's only six thousand pounds.'

'Then why is he offering twelve thousand pounds?'

'Because very soon he'll be selling 125 expensive houses and he needs a reliable estate office to get rid of them.'

'And yours is a reliable estate office?'

'Yes. Most reliable. We are part of Mitcham. Mention us and we're at once identified with the local scene. We contribute to local charities and take an interest in local affairs. We have an excellent reputation and it is for this that Dan Murray is willing to pay the extra six thousand pounds. There is an alternative. I can, if I chose, become a director of Murray Brothers which is the name the new firm has adopted.'

'But you don't think it would be wise.'

'I think the firm is destined to make millions with a man like Dan Murray in the driver's seat. I think that in ten years you would be a millionairess.'

'Me?'

'Yes, you, because I doubt if I could survive the strain of dealing in millions with the awful possibility of bankruptcy always lurking in the background. Bankruptcy and building are synonymous. I have a neat, tidy, profitable business which has been good to me and to my wife. However, I think it has reached its limits so I have decided to accept Dan Murray's offer. I think it would be wise to sell.'

Then as an afterthought Bates-Beary added, 'with your approval of course.'

'I think you're doing the right thing,' Mavis said. 'Does it mean we may have time to travel?'

'It certainly does.'

Mavis Bates-Beary placed her drink on the mantelpiece.

'Come here,' she told her husband, 'and let me show you how much I appreciate your good business sense.'

DAN HAD gone to the bank in Throgmorton Street, the same one frequented by Bates-Beary. He had asked for the manager but been told it would not be possible to see him unless he had an appointment. He made an appointment for the following day. He was received coolly. The manager's name was Slater, the same as that which belonged to the bank. Dan presumed that the present Slater must be a descendent of the man who founded it. Instead of being shown in to the manager's office Dan was asked to wait. Several minutes passed before Slater appeared. He did not ask Dan to sit down.

'What can I do for you sir?' he asked, placing his hands behind his back indicating that he had only so much time to spare. Dan became suddenly annoyed.

'I am not in the habit,' he said, 'of baring my soul in a public place.' The words were out before he had time to think.

'I don't understand. What exactly are you trying to convey?' the manager made no attempt to hide his irritation.

'I'll tell you what I'm trying to convey,' Dan said. 'I made an appointment yesterday. I arrived punctually just now. Yet for some odd reason you seem to resent my presence.'

'Oh come now.'

'It would be a very simple matter for you, Mr Slater, to ask me into your office, that is if you have an office. The only reason I don't walk out of here and take my business elsewhere is that I don't think you really are the ill-mannered prick you seem to be. I'm prepared to give you a second chance.'

Slater's puffed face turned abnormally white with mounting temper. He glared at Dan as if he were about to strike him. Dan absorbed the look without flinching. For a long while Slater tried to cow him.

'Come into my office,' he said. Dan followed him along a carpeted corridor at the end of which a heavy ornate door stood partly open to reveal a luxurious room dominated by a gleaming mahogany desk. The carpet here was thicker and of a deep green. On the walls were two large oil paintings of goateed gentlemen clad in morning suits.

'The gentleman on the right is my grandfather Reginald Horatio Slater,' the manager said. 'It was he who founded this bank on his ill-gotten profits from investments in Bengal. He had no faith in other banks so he founded his own. The party on the right was his brother Nathaniel. You know you have a neck to address me the way you just did.'

'If I didn't,' Dan pointed out, 'would I be in your office now?'

'Touché,' Slater said. 'Now perhaps you will be good enough to tell me why you forced your way here.'

'I need money,' Dan confessed, 'and I need it in a hurry.'

'Nothing unusual about that,' Slater retorted. 'Why don't you tell me the story of your life? Then we shall see what can be done.'

Dan launched into a brief account of the firm's activities and brought Slater up to date. He outlined his future plans, produced the deeds for the twenty-acre field and laid them on the desk. He gave him an exact account of his financial position. Slater listened carefully. He asked no questions until Dan had finished.

'Nine thousand pounds is a lot of money for a house,' Slater argued.

'Not for these houses,' Dan assured him. 'Each will have a large garden. Each will be detached. Each house will have every possible amenity. This is the kind of house suited to today's executive type.'

'One hundred and twenty-five,' Slater said doubtfully.

'The demand is there,' Dan said.

'You may be right,' Slater grew more interested. Dan handed him the letter from Bates-Beary. Slater read it carefully.

'Why the devil didn't you give me this at the beginning?'

'He told me you were short-tempered,' Dan replied without a trace of a smile. 'I wanted to see how short-tempered.'

'I see,' Slater said thoughtfully. 'To be truthful with you Mr Murray your sights are dead on target and I personally think you have a good thing there. What you need is some bridging finance. You won't need a terrible lot if you get your deposits well in advance. Again purely from a personal point of view the houses seem most attractive. You may not believe it but by a strange coincidence a friend of mine has been thinking of investing in such a house for some time now. He doesn't own the house he lives in and the rent is a drain really. The only snag is that he has a number of extras in mind.'

'Such as?' Dan prompted.

'Well for one thing a tennis court and possibly a small pool. He has a growing family. I don't see how the plots you offer would embrace the two extras.'

'There are plots and plots,' Dan said.

'But your plots are uniform, and big as they are I doubt if they would fill his requirements.'

'I think we might just manage to accommodate him,' Dan said. 'You see there will be an end house in the front terrace which will have more ground than the others. This is due to the irregularity of the plot. Because of this there will be a triangular piece of ground, in addition to the normal plot, going with this particular house.'

'Exactly how much extra ground?'

'One-third of an acre.'

'You think with the existing plot,' Slater asked eagerly 'there would be enough ground for what my friend has in mind?'

'There would be more than enough,' Dan assured him.

'You say in the front terrace?'

'Yes. In the front terrace and not overlooked by any other house in the entire estate.'

'Sounds almost too good to be true,' Slater said. 'The trouble is that with these extra amenities the price would probably be away over the heads of most people.'

'A good deal would depend on who wanted it.'

'Quite candidly old boy,' Slater lowered his voice, 'I

want it.'

'In that case,' said Dan, 'and in view of the fact that we will probably be doing business together from now on the price will be the same as the others.'

'But what about the pool and the court?'

'Compliments of the firm.'

Dan extended a hand which Slater grasped readily.

'My friends call me Tommy,' Slater said.

'They call me Dan.'

Dan stood up ready to leave. Even if he had not volunteered the concessions to Slater there was every likelihood that he would have succeeded in negotiating the loan or bridging finance as Slater called it. Slater was a greedy man but in spite of this Dan could not help liking him. The brusqueness was authentic and Dan knew that in spite of the concessions Slater was quite capable of changing his mind if there was the slightest suggestion of patronage.

'There is one other thing,' Dan said as he was about to leave. 'My partner is anxious to return to Ireland. There's a distinct possibility that he will suddenly announce that he wants out.'

'I see no problem,' Slater said, 'so long as he wants out of his own accord. The ball is in your half of the court. He'll be obliged to accept whatever you feel like giving him. It's most fortunate for you that it's not the other way round. If you wanted him out he could call the tune and a very expensive one it might prove to be. I get the impression that you don't want to take advantage of him and that you feel conscience bound to pay a fair price. This is most worthy but you must remember that it is he who will be seeking the concession and moreover he may be seeking it at a damned difficult time for you. Nobody could possibly blame you if you arranged conditions of sale to suit yourself. However, there is the matter of goodwill and there is always the reputation of your firm to be taken into account.'

'What do you suggest?' Dan was impressed by Slater's appraisal of the situation. Here was a man who had a very important sense of values.

'Since you don't have any definite idea of when he proposes to leave you you can only wait and see with the very important insurance that you know it is definitely going to happen. When it does happen let him fix the price. Under no circumstances must you make any bid. If his price is reasonable accept at once. Don't try to beat him down. He's your friend and as such he's not likely to consult with an auctioneer or solicitor about the exact value of what he has for sale. If he did you could find yourself in very deep water.

'If his demands are reasonable I'll advance you the money under the head of bridging finance. Better that he should collect the money here where our solicitors will make the deal legal and binding.'

'I'm deeply grateful to you,' Dan said.

'Thank you,' Slater smiled triumphantly. 'You have shown your appreciation. Perhaps,' he laughed, 'when the house is complete you will come one day for a swim in my pool or perhaps a game of tennis?'

'I'll look forward to it,' Dan promised. They shook hands. Slater placed his free hand paternally on Dan's shoulder.

'I'll be keenly interested in your progress,' he said. 'You mustn't fail me. If you do it is more than likely that I'll be out of a job. It could be just the opportunity my directors are looking for.'

20

NOREEN CAREY mounted her bicycle and set out for the farmhouse of Tom Joe Scanney. The time was three o'clock in the afternoon. After Mass at the church in Ballynahaun she had given the children their midday meal and hurried through the day's chores. Wisely she put the whole flock out of doors before she left. They would do less harm out in the open and her habitual fear of fire would be diminished. She placed the boys in charge of the solitary milch cow whose sustenance for the afternoon would be whatever she came across in the Long Acre which was the name given to the grass margin of the public roadway by the cottiers and small-holders who allowed their cattle to forage abroad when fodder was scant on the home pasture. She tucked the baby in its pram, charging the girls with its safe-keeping.

Noreen Carey was in a hurry. She had heard disturbing tidings on her way out from Mass. The news had not been meant for her. However, she could not help but overhear since not just one but several groups were airing the same topic.

It was the first inkling she had received of Tom Joe Scanney's intention to sell his farm. The word was that he intended to buy a small house in the nearby town where he and his wife could live in retirement. He had grown too feeble of late to manage the numerous acres and since there was none of his own brood inclined towards the land there seemed no point in holding on to it.

'I believe,' the man who made the original disclosure was saying, 'that he's finding great trouble getting good men. They can earn five times the wages in England for half the work.'

'I'd well believe it. My own lad is knockin' down twenty pounds a week there.'

Noreen followed at a discreet distance pretending to be on the lookout for a friend.

"Tis a great country surely. Then of course Tom Joe couldn't get a milkmaid to work for him if he offered a hundred pounds a week.'

'Would you blame them? Sure the man would screw a cat goin' out a skylight.' They both guffawed loudly at this.

Behind them, her head bent, her family in tow, Noreen Carey smiled grimly. She could not catch all that was being said but she heard enough to be able to piece the whole story together.

'It'll make a quare penny,' the first man said.

'Don't you doubt it,' said the second. 'There's no one around these parts would rise to the price anyway and that's for sure.'

'There's many a Ballynahaun man in England it might not be beyond.'

'Five thousand pounds wouldn't buy it.'

'No nor seven thousand. I'm thinking it would be nearer to ten thousand pounds.'

Noreen Carey paused, deep in thought. The men were now out of earshot. It might be possible. It might just be possible. There was only one way to find out and that was to see Tom Joe. He would have been at Mass and if she was of a mind to scout around there was no doubt she would find him in a pub but this was not the way she wanted to go about it. Her business would be private.

As she cycled along the dry road her determination grew. This was her first real opportunity of bringing Eddie back permanently. There was fifteen hundred pounds in the post office in Ballynahaun and as far as she knew Eddie had two thousand pounds in the Midland Bank in Bertham. That was three thousand, five hundred pounds. It now depended on Dan. How much was Eddie's share in the firm worth and how much could Dan afford to pay? She needed time and her sole reason for calling on the Scanneys was to ask for that time. She chided herself for not having noticed the ad in the local paper but then she had little time for papers.

When she arrived at the farmhouse Tom Joe was asleep in front of the kitchen fire. His wife shook his shoulder gently and he opened bleary eyes. When he recognised Noreen he got to his feet and offered her his own comfortable chair. She accepted the seat and Tom took another at the other side of the hearth.

'Why didn't you tell us you were coming and I'd have something nice?' Mrs Scanney reproved. She busied herself with the ritual of tea-making while Tom Joe enquired after Eddie and the family.

'I was often meaning to call,' he said, 'but I used put it off and then when I got into the habit of not calling it hardened that way.'

'Well you're always welcome and you know that,' Noreen told him.

'I hope there's nothing wrong below?' Tom said with some concern. 'You hardly came cycling up here for the good of your health with eight young children behind you.' It was the opportunity she had been waiting for.

'Is it true your farm is for sale?' she asked.

'Yes. It's true.'

'I want you to do me a favour.'

'If I can.'

'Don't sell a while yet.'

'You can't be serious.'

'But I am. I'll be writing to Eddie this very night and if he says it's all right I'll be making a bid.

'I don't know,' Tom Joe shook his head doubtfully.

'The whole business won't take a week and I'd be forever beholden to you,' Noreen said cajolingly.

'That may be,' Tom Joe agreed, 'but you see there is a bid of eight thousand pounds since yesterday. That's fifteen hundred pounds up on the last bid. You couldn't expect me now to hold out after an offer like that.'

'But you haven't taken it?'

'Not yet but I will. Don't have any choice Noreen.'

'Couldn't you wait a week? Just one week?'

'You can't expect me to. I couldn't gamble on the offer

233

standing that long. Anyway where in the name of God would yourself and Eddie come up to money like that?' Tom Joe Scanney laughed but his wife spoke from the table where she was laying out the tea things.

She had heard stories. The Murray brothers were doing well and wasn't Eddie Carey in some sort of partnership with them? She had always liked and respected Noreen. When Tom had misbehaved himself years before Noreen hadn't noted him around the countryside the way other girls had.

'Don't say no to Noreen Tom. It's only a week.' Mrs Scanney came close to her husband's chair.

'I don't know.' He was still in doubt.

'You owe it to Noreen Tom,' Mrs Scanney said with finality. Tom Joe bent his head and did not commit himself for a time. The women exchanged hopeful looks.

'I suppose I do,' Tom Joe said lamely. 'If the truth was told I suppose I do.'

Later as she cycled down the hillside on her way home she felt like singing but then the hard facts started to present themselves. What if they could not raise sufficient money? There were banks in the town and they would surely loan them part of it. The banks were doing it for everybody else and particularly for those who were buying farms. Somehow they would manage to raise the money. Beg, borrow or steal she would bring her husband home. They were too long apart. It wasn't just nor was it natural that people who needed each other so desperately should be made to suffer so much.

EDDIE CAREY read and re-read his wife's letter. It was almost too good to be true. Here at last was the long-awaited chance of a lifetime. He read the letter for the last time, returned it to its envelope and took a notebook from his pocket. In the crowded pub nobody took any notice. He might be a punter making out the returns on a successful each-way treble for all anybody cared.

234

Eddie knew the Scanney farm like the back of his hand. As a young man he had worked there seasonally at the threshing and the hay-making. It was by far the best farm in Ballynahaun and possibly one of the three best in that part of Kerry. Naturally it contained unproductive patches and some acres of scrub. Much of it was bog and there was an area densely wooded with stunted, native oak and pine but the important thing was that it contained one hundred acres of arable land as good as could be found anywhere in the country. To stock it fully would cost in the region of four thousand pounds but that problem could be tackled piecemeal and easily surmounted in time. The house and outhouses were in excellent repair. The dwelling house was known locally as the 'Great House'. This was the name given to the outsize habitats of the Protestant ascendancy, now no longer to be found in Kerry. Making a go of it would be a formality. His eldest boys were almost men.

He entered several sets of figures into the notebook. From time to time he would cross a set out and replace it with another. He might just manage it. He would see Dan that very night. He knew where to find him. Of late during weekends he had taken to staying overnight in the Colorado Hotel in Newsham. If he wasn't there he would be with Crazy Horse or Sylvester at the Leadlathe Arms. It wasn't the best time to present his proposition. The firm was entering a period which would tax every resource they had. Let them think him selfish. Let them think what they liked. He had spent long enough away from his wife and family not to mention his country.

In addition there was the fact that he had been seeing a woman. Her name was Eleanor Apley. She worked as a part-time barmaid in one of the bigger pubs in Bertham. It had developed slowly, inevitably over a period. Eleanor was married with three children. After the birth of the third child her husband had disappeared without trace. Since Dan had started to interest himself in women Eddie was more or less left to his own devices over the weekends. He worked long hours and this helped dispel some of the loneliness. Eleanor

Apley was quick to notice that he was a lone wolf. She took a special interest in him whenever her duties permitted. She would lean across the counter polishing a glass while Eddie spoke about his work or about home. After a few months he knew all about her. He was familiar with the ailments of the children and the idiosyncrasies of Eleanor's mother who looked after them and who had lived with her since her husband's departure. After a few months they went to the cinema on one of her night's off. After that it became a regular thing.

Eleanor Apley was forty-three, attractive, with a good figure. After that first visit to the cinema they more or less took to going steady when their workbreaks coincided. It made life bearable for Eddie. He had started to grow desperate for home. He realised he was not getting younger and that most of his life would be wasted unless he made a dramatic change in his way of living.

After some months Eleanor Apley invited him to her home. The mother took to Eddie at once. He had brought her a present of a noggin of whiskey and she appreciated it. It was inevitable that Eddie and Eleanor should make love. They both hungered for a closer relationship. It was she who made the proposal during his third visit. The old woman had gone to bed and was sleeping soundly. They sat by the dying coal fire in the tiny sitting-room.

Eddie had looked at his watch and conveyed the pretence of a yawn. 'Time to be going,' he had said.

He meant otherwise but he could never get up the nerve to say so. He was about to leave. Indeed Eleanor had come with him to the hall door where they stood exchanging a few final words. There had been a lull and suddenly without the least trace of emotion Eleanor had met the situation squarely.

'Would you like to come upstairs love?' she had said.

'I'd love to,' Eddie had replied. That had been three months ago. Now almost every Sunday night and sometimes on other occasions they were in the habit of going upstairs. The old woman and the children were always asleep.

Eddie took out his notebook again and quickly scanned the page on which he had made the entries. He rose and went to the bar counter. It was Saturday night. By agreement they never dated on Saturday nights. He caught her attention after a while.

'I've got to go,' he said.

'Oh,' she exclaimed surprisedly.

'Something's come up,' Eddie told her. 'Something to do with the job. Nothing serious, just routine.'

'Have you made up your mind yet?' Eleanor asked. A week before she had suggested he give notice to the Hubards. The idea was that he should come to live with her. The old woman was agreeable. Eddie had been taken completely by surprise. He stalled for time explaining that all his workmates stayed together of necessity. He had promised to think about it.

'I know you'll do the right thing,' she had smiled.

He had never realised at the outset that he would become so involved. He supposed that sooner or later it would come to an end but now he wasn't so sure. He had grown fond of her but the thought of a permanent relationship frightened him. For some time his conscience had been bothering him.

Although he was glad of Eleanor's company he was far from happy in the situation where he now found himself. The affair was interfering with his work. He was continually uncomfortable and was really upset when he found himself alone and thinking of his wife and family.

His brief affair with Eleanor ended without difficulty. Gillian Hubbard had been of immense value to him when it seemed that he might not be able to shake himself loose. After he had failed to show up at the pub for over a week Eleanor had come to the digs. Gillian had politely shown her into the small sitting-room and had gone upstairs to call Eddie. It was a wet Sunday afternoon and he had gone to bed after his lunch. Desperately he explained the position to Gillian.

'You should 'ave looked before you leaped,' she said but

237

then her soft spot for her star boarder declared itself.

'You stay where you are,' she ordered. 'You've done enough 'arm as it is. I'll go downstairs and see if I can't reason with 'er.'

Eddie was not troubled by Eleanor again and in atonement he rarely stirred out nights. His one desire was to be safely back in his birthplace with his wife and children.

WHEN HE left the pub he hailed a passing taxi and informed the driver that he wished to be taken to the Colorado Hotel. Traffic was dense and the journey took time. There was no trace of Dan in either of the bars in the Colorado. Hopefully Eddie looked in the dining-room. Sure enough his friend was seated at a table for two in a dimly-lighted alcove. His companion was an attractive black-haired girl who could not have been much more than twenty. Quietly Eddie closed the door gently and retired to the bar where he could see the comings and goings of the diners. In this way Dan could not leave without his knowing it. He decided to allow his partner finish his meal in comfort.

He would have much preferred if had Dan been alone. This would be the most important conversation of Eddie Carey's life. From landless labourer to estate owner! It was possible, really possible. By Christ let them say what they liked, England was a great bloody country. Eddie called for a whiskey and soda. He felt out of place in the high-ceiling-ed, beautifully draped bar with its vigorous baroque settings and quaint plush covered spidery seating. There were uni-formed porters and numerous other white-coated attendants floating all about. They made Eddie nervous. He had been to the Colorado before but the team had been with him.

Another thing that annoyed him was that everybody spoke in whispers. It was not the sort of place where you would be likely to meet a gang of hard-drinking Paddies on a Saint Patrick's night. To hide his embarrassment he took the notebook from his pocket and commenced a study of the freshly entered figures.

Time passed and it must have been a good half-hour before Dan and the dark-haired girl emerged from the dining-room. The girl was a looker if ever Eddie saw one. Taking her gently by the arm Dan steered her towards the lounge bar. If anything, although smaller, this was more elaborate than the public bar where Eddie sat. He allowed a few minutes to elapse before following. Dan could scarcely conceal his surprise when Eddie touched him on the shoulder.

'What in God's name are you doing here? Is anything wrong?'

Dan's concern was immediate.

'Everything is fine,' Eddie assured him. 'It's just that I want to speak to you privately for a few minutes.'

'Of course, of course.' Dan put him at his ease. 'But sit down and have a drink or is it a matter of life and death?'

'I imagine 'twill keep a few minutes,' Eddie said, sorry now that he had not waited till morning.

'What will it be?' Dan asked.

'Whiskey,' Eddie answered gratefully.

Dan ordered brandies for himself and the girl and a large whiskey for Eddie. He introduced the girl as soon as they were seated. Her name was Sally Bowersbee. She was a second year art student studying in London, hailing originally from Reading.

'Now,' Dan invited when the drinks were delivered. 'Tell me all about it. You don't need to take any notice of Sally.'

Uncertainly Eddie began with the news contained in the letter. He was apologetic for not choosing a more appropriate time especially since Dan was about to begin on the biggest contract so far. When he finished Dan swallowed some of the brandy.

'Exactly how much money would you need?' he asked.

'Well there's the stock to consider and stamp duty and of course there will be auctioneer's fees. I'm almost afraid to say.'

'Come on,' Dan encouraged him. 'I won't stand in your way if the farm is what you want. What worries me is that you might be leaving at once.'

'Oh God no. I'll give you three months notice. I realise it's a bad time and I realise you're just starting to go places in a big way but I have to get back. I've been away too long.'

'All right. How much?'

'To be on the safe side, eight thousand pounds. I have the rest.'

'It's a bad time,' Dan hesitated, 'but don't worry. I'll have your money next week. It means that you'll no longer have claim of any kind in the firm and you promise to stay for three months till we get off the ground with the new project.'

'I agree on each count.'

'You'll have to sign a statement to that effect.'

'I'll sign anything if you give me the eight thousand pounds.'

Eddie left in a mood of extreme jubilation.

Dan apologised to the girl for the interruption.

'Are you a millionaire or something?' she asked.

Dan laughed.

'Just now,' he said, 'I don't know exactly what I am.'

'Perhaps I could help you find out,' Sally Bowersbee said.

21

DAN'S IMMEDIATE objective, once work began to move smoothly on the first group of houses, was the completion and furnishing to the finest detail of a show house. Builders providers, furnishers and decorators in that part of Greater London signified their willingness to look after the loose ends in this connection, free of charge. For them it was a heaven-sent opportunity to display their wares and a chance to prove conclusively to prospective customers that it was no longer necessary to visit metropolitan London in order to secure the most modern in house fittings and furnishings. In the Mitcham office, where Sylvester was now permanently enthroned with Sandra, there were models of the houses on display. In less than two months, deposits had been received on 50 homes and it was patently evident that, with the completion of the show house, demand would exceed supply. After the first two months Dan no longer worried about money. He visited Tom Slater regularly in his Throgmorton Street bank but only for advice or to discuss long-term plans. At one of these interviews Slater was quite outspoken.

'Dan,' he opened, 'you are either going to be a very big fish or you are going to be a fair-sized minnow.'

Dan had enough common sense and experience to give Slater free rein.

'I mean,' the banker elaborated with an outgoing gesture of both hands, 'that it is not enough any more to plan for next year and the year after. If you are to reach the heights where I can already envisage you it will be necessary to plan five and even ten years ahead. Remember, however, that I am merely a salaried underling with nothing to lose. Yet here I am laying out a course which could eventually lead to your bankruptcy. If only this particular industry did not depend upon so many factors. I hope I am not dispensing worthless advice.'

'Not you,' Dan assured him.

'It is very easy to make plans with somebody else's money or rather somebody else's credit rating. Even if I had the money myself I doubt if I could ever plan successfully. I lack the courage and the detachment and I have a wife who likes to breathe over my shoulder. Dan you must stop thinking about the houses you are building now. They no longer present a problem. You must start to think about those two fields you took over from Bates-Beary. Next year the houses you are currently offering at eight thousand pounds will be making ten thousand and maybe eleven thousand pounds. You must move now and I think I may be able to arrange the necessary backing. How is my house coming along?'

'It will be among the very first. The pool is sunk already.'

'You have been more than generous with me so now I'll let you in on something. You must never say where you got your information. The borough council plan an intensive and all-out campaign of high density housing and flat dwellings. This will not affect the type of housing you specialise in. Quite the contrary, it will make your sites more valuable. This scheme will mean a population increase of roughly 20,000 in the next few years. How are you geared to meet this increase?'

'I'm not sure I understand.'

Slater was at pains to elaborate. 'What sort of amenities will these people need apart from the normal playgrounds, parks, schools, churches and what-have-you?'

Dan considered the question carefully. 'Cinemas,' he answered, 'dance-halls ...'

'To mention but two,' Slater said.

'Now that I know what you're driving at,' Dan confessed, 'it's only fair to tell you that I've considered the possibility of building a dance-hall but I had second thoughts because a dance-hall becomes old-fashioned the moment another is built unless you're lucky enough to have one situated near the heart of the city.'

'Have you considered leasing a building?'

'Yes. I've thought of it and I've looked over a number of places.'

'And?'

'I found nothing suitable.'

'How well do you know Mitcham and the area round it?'

'Reasonably well. Naturally there would be places I haven't seen.'

'You know the old drill hall near the new cafeteria?'

'I pass it every day.'

'The Territorial Army used to drill there. It's used for nothing just now. In fact it's an embarrassment.'

'Its nicely situated and it's big enough,' Dan spoke thoughtfully. 'What about fire hazards?'

'It was good enough for the army. If you like I can see about a lease.'

'Yes,' Dan agreed after a pause. 'I'd appreciate that.'

'Your main problem,' Slater struck a note of warning, 'would be hiring worthwhile bands. As far as I know all the good ones are tied up with the bigger halls on a percentage basis. It's not the sort of situation that encourages new enterprises in this particular sphere.'

'In my case,' Dan assured him, 'there would be no such problem.'

For a number of years Dan had been seriously considering renting a number of suitable buildings in the city with a view to converting the more ideal ones into dance-halls. Having toyed with the idea for a lengthy spell he decided that the competition was too keen, not that he wouldn't have made a go of such a venture but thorough investigation had convinced him that the margin of profit would be too small for the risk and the amount of time involved. The old drill hall was the perfect centre. Instead of engaging bands from the London scene he would engage Irish bands. These would be better known to the recently arrived Irish emigrants who would be the nucleus of his support. There were hundreds of these in the Mitcham district alone and there were thousands within a cheap bus ride. With the aid of a

243

good start, in other words a glittering opening with one of the big Irish bands, the pickings thereafter would be easy and considerable.

'Get that lease for me,' he told Slater, 'and you won't be sorry.'

'I shouldn't worry,' the banker replied confidently. 'I don't expect it to be anything more than a formality. In fact I'll see to it this very evening.'

'Good,' said Dan and added, 'there's another thing. As you know, a builder without his own land is at the mercy of exploiters. The reason I stand to make such a substantial profit on the present scheme is because I had already purchased the land. Well there are other reasons but the land is the chief one. I'd want to buy more land and I'd want to buy it now.'

'I take it this would be in Mitcham or south of it.'

'No,' Dan replied. 'It would be in Dublin, at least south of Dublin city where land is still cheap and where there will be an insatiable demand for houses very soon.'

'We have an agent in Dublin,' Slater put in.

'I'd want quite a lot of money,' Dan continued as if he hadn't heard. 'Land will never again be cheap to the south of London but there are substantial farms for sale from time to time outside Dublin.'

'Exactly how much would you want?'

'I honestly don't know,' Dan answered. 'I wouldn't want to be restricted if I saw the makings of a good investment. I'll have the money myself in two years, maybe less. Meanwhile I'd like to avail of some of your bridging finance.'

'Mention a figure. It doesn't have to be spot on, just something to give me an idea.'

'A quarter of a million,' Dan said and he looked at his watch.

'Good God!' Slater exploded. Jumping to his feet, he slammed the table with both hands and sat down again.

'With a quarter of a million I can buy land which will be worth millions in ten years time, in less than ten years time. Things are changing fast in Ireland. Dublin will swell beyond recognition. I must get in now. It has to be now.'

'What do you propose to do with the land in the mean-time, that is provided you acquire it.'

'Put cattle on it. Then when the time comes I'll sell it piecemeal to builders. Without soiling my hands I can make a million. What are my chances of getting the money?'

'Couldn't you wait?'

'No. It has to be now. I've waited too long already. What do you think of my chances?'

Slater rose, thrust his hands into this trousers' pockets and jingled the change therin. He cleared his throat.

'Everything is in your favour except the amount. Person-ally I approve but if I approved in the presence of my direct-ors they'd look for substantiation. I couldn't justify a quarter of a million. If you will forgive the abominable expression they would think we were in cahoots. Hard to blame them. To qualify for bridging finance on such a scale you would need immense securities. I'll do what I can but meanwhile I suggest you look around. I can recommend a finance com-pany. The interest rates are not too crippling and if you're so sure that the land value will multiply to such a degree it would be well worth it.'

'I don't like finance companies but if I have to I will. Can't you point out to your board of directors that they can't lose? They can hold on to the titles of the farms as security.'

'They would be doing that anyway. However, I will pre-sent a strong case. It would help if you held yourself avail-able in the building during the next board meeting.'

On this promising note they parted, Slater to an appoint-ment, Dan to London airport where Sandra awaited him. They sat together on board the Dublin-bound plane.

Not long after the commencement of work on the new houses Dan had foreseen that there would be a shortage of labourers and skilled workers from time to time. To offset this he placed advertisements in all the provincial papers in the south of Ireland under a caption which called upon tradesmen and labourers alike to avail themselves of a new and splendid opportunity. In brief the opportunity was an invitation to workers to become part of a work pool from which Dan would draw when necessary. This system suited married men with families who did not want to settle permanently in England. It suited younger men anxious to get married in Ireland but lacking the finance to do so. What Dan offered was the opportunity to work for short terms of three months at a time. He would notify willing workers as soon as he required them. They would come at once, draw a fixed weekly wage, enough to support themselves and their families and allow the remainder of the wages to accumulate. This, together with the substantial tax-free bonus which Dan promised at the end of the prescribed period, guaranteed them a handsome sum at the end of their labours.

Dan paid no more and no less than other London contractors but his single workers escaped income tax by claiming fictitious wives and children and in most cases the married men had gone home before tax was demanded of them. The remainder did not exist as far as the authorities were concerned. Some who did pay tax were able to claim it again when they became redundant. Most of what they had paid was sent on to them in Ireland by the super indulgent income tax system prevailing in England.

The Murray lump system was well-known to Irish workers. It never failed to entice men who wanted money in a hurry.

On that very night Dan was due in a Limerick city hotel. Indications were that at least 200 assorted tradesmen and labourers would show up out of curiosity if nothing else. The following noon he was due at a hotel in Tralee and at half-past seven in Cork city. The next day he would take in Mallow and Nenagh. That would wind up his itinerary. In between he would make a dash to see his father and mother and spend a night with them. There would be no time for sightseeing or relaxing. When the business was done it would be straight back to London.

On the plane they conversed little till they neared Dublin.

'When are you and Sylvester going to get married?' Dan asked.

'Whenever he asks me.'

'When will that be?'

'Whenever he gets around to it. At the moment he's too busy hating the Reiceys and trying to make a multi-millionaire out of you. I'm happy enough. We're together. I have no right to expect any more.'

Dan did not force the conversation. At the airport they rented a car and drove directly to Limerick where they had a meal. Later, in the hotel's function room 115 workers ranging in ages from eighteen to sixty presented themselves to hear the proposals. Dan sat at the rear of the room.

Sandra mounted the small stage and sat at the table which had been provided by the management. She outlined the full facts briefly and efficiently. Murray Brothers needed workers and were prepared to pay full transport costs in addition to an advance of wages. Accommodation would be provided. Already Dan had four large caravans on the major site. Those interested were invited to supply their names and addresses. The firm would notify them as soon as work was available. Sandra explained that the firm was in the market for all kinds of tradesmen, plumbers, plasterers, carpenters etc. She would be only too happy to answer any questions. These came one on top of the other and were mostly concerned with union membership and tax evasion. She managed to satisfy nearly everybody.

The idea of maintaining a labour pool in Ireland was unprecedented in the English building world. Its real value lay in the fact that there would be no necessity for holding on to tradesmen when there was no longer any work for them. Other contractors were content to pay full wages just for the sake of holding on to skilled labourers from job to job. It was easier and safer than trying to recruit labour from a pool which, particularly in summertime, might be dried up. Dan dared not chance to pot luck. Although his stock was high there was still the danger that work would be held up while the search for skilled workers was in progress. In a smaller contract one could make up for a scarcity of suitable workers by the simple expedient of working long overtime with the promise of fat bonuses. This had always worked for Dan in the past but so great was the scope of his latest project that labour scarcity could prolong the conclusion of the full con-

247

tract by months. Finishing ahead of time was the difference between giant profits and small. With any luck Dan hoped to clear a quarter of a million. Maximum profit was ensured by the fact that his sites were already paid for. Add to this the very tangible asset that Dan was his own general foreman.

'No matter how far we go or how high we climb,' he told Sylvester, 'my overalls stay on while there's work to be done.'

Crazy Horse, Eddie Carey, Dick Winterman and Willie Murray acted as unofficial charge hands. There was little pilfering on the site. When there was, Dan's attitude depended upon the ability of the man responsible. If it was a good man and if the pilfering was reasonable he closed his eyes, at the same time letting the culprit know that there was a line of demarcation. If the pilferer was expendable he was thrown off the site without as much as a day's notice.

Right from the beginning every man pulled his weight. A busy building site offers no camouflage for a slacker and those who joined up in the early stages in the hope of making soft money were bitterly disappointed. With no union to cover for them they were given short shrift by the charge hands.

On their way out of the hotel they saw a man who had earlier made himself objectionable. He was a sorry sight. He had not yet risen to his feet but sat propped by the corridor wall with his bloodied face half buried in his hands. Nobody attempted to help him.

'Did you do that?' Sandra asked while they waited at reception.

'Yes,' Dan said. Then by way of justification: 'I didn't travel several hundred miles to be kicked in the balls by a dosser. I hope you're not upset.'

Sandra laughed.

'You forget,' she said, 'that I was there when you and your men came back from the Shillelagh. You don't upset easily after a night like that.'

'Why are you laughing then?'

'It's just that you don't expect such behaviour from a

millionaire.'

'I'm not a millionaire yet but remember that an Irishman with my qualifications doesn't become a millionaire by sticking to the rules laid down by the Marquis of Queensbury.'

There was no reproof in Dan's tone, merely a reminder that he was not prepared to offer apologies for being what he was.

He decided to drive to Ballynahaun that night. It would never do if his father and mother heard of his visit secondhand. The name of Dan Murray was a household word in his part of Kerry and further afield. His photograph appeared regularly in local papers at functions organised by the various Kerrymen's associations in England. He was a good mark for local charities and if a man was prepared to work Dan Murray was not the one to turn him down.

They drove by the coast road past Askeaton and Foynes until the great Shannon river appeared on the right hand, its flat, unfractured expanses shining like gold in the sunset. To the far west the Atlantic shored itself peacefully to the crimson horizon. Dan sensed that Sandra's interest was aroused. A pair of cormorants flew low over the water almost within reach and further out a gull cried raucously, disputing a speck of flotsam with its greedy brethren. An ancient castle appeared on the left and old forts stood stark and bare on the promontories that thrust themselves discreetly into the shining river.

'Scenes like these,' Sandra said after a while, 'are they what make Sylvester and you so lonely sometimes?'

'Me?' Dan disclaimed. 'I never said I was lonely.'

The river sped by. A grey freighter slowly moved upwards towards Limerick, its shapely prow gently ploughing the still waters.

'You're right,' Dan acquiesced. 'We can never rid ourselves of pictures like these.'

'I'm beginning to understand,' she said.

'You'll find my mother old fashioned,' Dan warned.

'I'm sure we'll get along. Eddie Carey told me all about her.'

'He's a man who's got what he wanted.' Dan sounded wistful.

'When is he leaving?'

'Three weeks time. No one deserves it more. He worked long and hard for what he has now.'

They drove over the Kerry border and south towards the distant mountains. As darkness fell they entered the narrow, undulating road which led to Ballynahaun. High on either side of the roadway the whitethorn hedges in luxuriant green gave the impression of driving along an endless avenue. Hundreds of white moths drifted by like snowflakes.

'We're almost there,' Dan said. In the distance the headlights of the car highlighted the long, low, whitewashed house with its roof of thatch.

'What a quaint wall,' Sandra enthused as the brick wall Willie had built years before came into view. Dan smiled to himself in the darkness of the car. Willie had wanted to knock the wall on several occasions and use his new expertise in the rebuilding of it. His mother would not hear of it.

'Dammit,' he had said. 'I can build you a wall that will be the talk of the countryside.'

'I don't want it.' His mother had been adamant. 'This wall is of sentimental value and I don't want it touched.'

She had been equally firm when Dan had suggested that they remove the thatch from the roof and replace it with slate.

'The thatch will remind us of who we are and what we are,' Mary Murray had said. 'It will be a good reminder in case any of us starts to fly too high.'

As usual Bill Murray had said nothing. Mary had consented gladly to the installation of hot and cold water and to the bathroom which the boys had built during their second holiday.

As soon as the car pulled up the front door was thrown open and Bill Murray followed by his wife came to the small ornate gate which opened on to the roadway.

'You're welcome,' Bill Murray said as he shook Sandra's hand. Mary Murray threw her arms round her older son, then held him at arm's length and with penetrating eyes

250

searched his face for signs of change. She embraced Sandra and led her by the hand into the kitchen where a bright fire burned despite the time of year.

'You were expecting us,' Dan said in surprise.

'Willie rang the post office,' Bill Murray explained. They sat by the fire and talked. The main topic of conversation in Ballynahaun and the surrounding districts for the past several weeks had been the surprise purchase of the Tom Joe Scanney place by Eddie Carey.

'They're saying,' Bill Murray said, with a wink at Sandra, 'that if Eddie Carey could afford to buy a farm of that size then Dan Murray should be able to buy the whole of Ballynahaun!'

'They might be right at that,' Sandra said.

When news of Eddie's purchase had leaked out the first reaction was one of disbelief. Where in God's name would he muster that kind of money? Smaller farmers who themselves had eyes for Scanney's verdant acres scoffed at the story. That the product of a labourer's cot in Ballynahaun could buy the biggest farm in the district was beyond their comprehension. As the days passed and the rumour remained unrefuted they began to have second thoughts. There was no doubt but that Dan Murray was placed very high across the ocean and wasn't Carey in with him? The fact that there was truth in the tale began to take root. It was true that wages in England were at least twice as good as they were in Ireland. A man was paid for the amount done not because of who he was or what he possessed. These were old truths that not even the most outspoken enemy of England would deny. Many of the smaller farmers despised the roots which held them in the same place generation after generation. They would never have enough, never be truly independent. They cursed the ill-luck that shackled them to small-holdings of rushy land and an outlook that never went an inch beyond the udder of a milch cow.

Later that night when Dan and his father went to the pub in Ballynahaun the after-hours customers wondered at Dan's expensive suit, his suede shoes, his immaculate white shirt and silver grey tie. They pondered the exposure of white cuff, the teeth obviously well cared for, the unconscious ease and air of opulence that exuded from the man. Dan stood a round of drinks to the house and placing a twenty pound note on the counter instructed the publican to keep refilling as required. In whispers, the locals boasted about him to each other. A decent man. One of the richest men in the country. England must be a great bloody country. They listed off the other Kerrymen who had become millionaires from humble beginnings, who had boarded the emigrant ships at the North Wall, Dún Laoghaire and Rosslare with worn suitcases, no money and limited education.

Yet they had succeeded. There was luck in it. Of that there could be no doubt. Still and for all, luck was only part of it. There was many a man tending to seven or eight cows, slaving to support his wife and family, who had the capacity to be a success likewise but circumstances kept him chained to his heritage.

All of the pub's occupants had brothers or sisters or sons or daughters in England. They might not be as well off as Dan Murray but at least they had holidays every year and they were never without a roll of notes in their pockets. Yet for all the easy money there was not one who would not come back, who would not swap places at that very moment with those who manned the pub counter. Thus consoling themselves they quaffed their porter and toasted Dan Murray. Dan and his father sat in a corner where they could converse freely. In a low voice Dan filled him in on his and Willie's progress. Bill Murray listened eagerly, from time to time sipping the double whiskey his son had thrust upon him. He was at times bewildered and amazed. The sums of money mentioned made him swallow in astonishment. Dan only told him so much. There was, Dan honestly felt, only so much he could absorb. They had several drinks. It may have been the extra drink that prompted the question which was uppermost in Bill Murray's mind.

'Have you any notion of coming home?' he asked.

'Not at the present time,' Dan told him honestly.

'We're getting old you know, your mother and I, and we don't see much of yourself or Willie. This is your country

252

Dan. All the money in the world won't buy you the right to belong to a country, I mean really belong.'

'I know,' Dan said. 'I know what you mean. There are a number of targets I have to strike. I just couldn't turn my back on the opportunities facing me at this time. I'll be back and I promise you it won't be too long.'

'Eddie Carey will have a right hold here when he comes home and he has less than you,' Bill Murray pressed his claim.

'I agree,' Dan said, 'that's exactly what Eddie Carey always wanted but it's not what I want. I'm pretty sure I can be the best at what I'm doing Dad. I think I would be failing myself if I stopped in midstream. This is the way I'm made. This is what I'm designed to do. Other men could never do it just as I could never do what some men do easily. I want to reach the limit. That's the time I'll stop. I'll know when I have enough. Let others take over then. The main thing is that I'll be all right. I'm seeing to that. I don't want you or mother to worry and I promise you here and now that Willie and I will come home very often from now on. My business will bring me more regularly to Ireland anyway so you can expect to see me fairly often.'

'Have you any notion of getting married?' Bill Murray shot the question out of the blue.

'Not at present,' Dan replied.

'You're shoving on Dan. There's men of your age with three or four children by them.'

'I know. I know,' Dan said.

'What about the girl with you?' Dan was half expecting the question.

'What about her?' he countered.

'Is she your girl or what?'

'Or what,' Dan echoed and laughed out loud. 'No, she's Sylvester O'Doherty's girl. She's just acting as my secretary.'

'No man should be without a secretary,' Bill Murray said with a straight face. By this Dan knew that the interrogation was over. They relaxed over their drinks and in a short while were respectfully joined by the other customers. Predictably the talk turned to Eddie Carey's purchase. Dan, they all knew, was the man to answer the many questions which had been troubling them. As the session, maintained by Dan's money, wore on he let it be known that the money paid by Eddie Carey for the Scanney farm was only a fraction of Carey's real resources. He also let it drop that it was only one of many Carey enterprises.

'That should give the bastards something to think about,' he whispered to his father. The dawn was beginning to break along the eastern ridges of the mountain range when they left the pub. Dan wondered how Sandra had fared with his mother.

She would be questioned closely about Dan's love life. That seemed to be his mother's greatest worry. In all her letters there would be a reference to the necessity for settling down with a nice girl. She never said so directly but her meaning was always clear enough. There would be references to other men of Dan's age who had entered the matrimonial stakes without any obvious depreciative effects. Also outlined, although vaguely, was the value of a wife as a housekeeper if nothing else. Since Dan had left Bertham and Sid Hubbard's to live permanently with Willie, Crazy Horse, Dick Winterman and the Costigan brothers in the roomy upstairs of the estate office his mother was continually worried about the conditions in which he and Willie lived. She need not have concerned herself. They partook of the major meal of the day in a nearby restaurant where they were well treated. Sandra and Sylvester lived in the top storey and between the lot they employed a local woman on an hourly basis to do the housekeeping and take charge of the laundering. Eddie Carey, for a variety of reasons, stayed on with Sid and Gillian Hubbard in Bertham.

As they walked along the mountain road under a paling sky from which legions of stars were vanishing with every passing minute Bill Murray pointed out the many deserted houses which seemed to Dan to have doubled in number since he first left Ballynahaun.

'Imagine any man in his right mind abandoning a countryside like this forever,' his father said with a shake of the head. They stood silently at the margin of the roadway.

Overhead the sky whitened and from everywhere came the first overpowering chorus of newly awakened songbirds. Down below where the rocky fields sloped outwards for miles the silver grey sea swept away into infinity. Around them the uplands of the mountains were turning to a purplish blue.

'Maybe,' Dan said, 'a day will come when they'll be glad to come back.'

'Maybe,' his father said wistfully. Then in a sobering tone: 'Whatever you do don't delay too long Dan. There's only so much to a lifetime and often it lets you down when you're best geared for going on.'

The birdsong was now almost deafening and from the chimneys of the surrounding farmhouses wisps of smoke rose in immaculately straight lines. From a distant valley came the morning's first cockcrow. Bill Murray stole a look at his son. The lines of care showed at the corners of his eyes. The mouth had hardened but this would be apparent only to someone who knew him well. It was still the face of a young man. He thrust his hands deep into his trousers pockets and walked slowly towards the farmhouse.

'Your mother will murder us,' Bill Murray said.

22

MARGO REICEY raised the phone from its crook and, after an initial moment of hesitation, rang Tom Reicey's number. His secretary answered and on hearing the caller's name asked Margo to hold on while she went in search of him. It had taken a great effort on Margo's behalf to get in touch with her brother-in-law.

What she chiefly regretted was not being able to cope with the situation herself. She had never rung Tom before, although lately Dicey had given her sufficient cause to seek outside aid; not that he ever molested her in any way but he was now in the habit of coming home helplessly drunk at all hours of the morning. Mostly he was deposited on the doorstep by taxi drivers or occasionally by a band of revellers with whom he had been drinking. Last night he had arrived home on the stroke of midnight. Without a word he had struggled upstairs, spurning her offer of help. He had locked himself into the guest room and in a matter of minutes was snoring loudly. She had made herself a cup of coffee and idly glanced through a magazine whiling away the time until she was absolutely certain that he would be overcome by a deep slumber. He would fall asleep with his clothes on as he was in the habit of doing lately, unless she intervened. She would undress him when there was no fear that he would wake up. It was never an easy task, getting his clothes off when he was drunk.

On this occasion she had listened for several minutes outside the guest room door. The snoring, though fitful at times, was deep and sustained. When she turned the door handle she discovered that it was locked from the inside. Sometimes when he had a headache, in addition to being drunk, he would lock the door. She listened for a further period and satisfying herself that he was all right she went to bed. In the morning, as usual, she had gone to call him but there was no response. She had knocked loudly as was her wont when he chose to sleep behind closed doors before this. There was no reply. She knocked again but still no answer came. Not unduly alarmed she went downstairs. There was a phone in the room. Yet in spite of repeated ringing there was no indication that he was awake. She replaced the phone and went upstairs. She began by calling his name but this proved equally futile. Again she smote upon the door but it was a waste of time. She knelt and listened at the keyhole. She could hear nothing. This was not unusual, however, as Dicey often slept with the clothes over his head, making it impossible for his breathing to be heard. Another consoling aspect was that he never snored in the mornings, only at night when he had a large quantity of drink taken.

'Yes Margo, what can I do for you?' It was the deep voice of Tom Reicey.

'It's Dicey,' Margo explained.

'What's he done now?' The weariness was unconcealed.

'Nothing,' Margo replied, 'except that he isn't up yet, the door is locked and I can't seem to wake him.'

'Was he drunk going to bed?'

'Yes he was,' Margo confessed.

'Listen,' Tom Reicey said. 'You go and get the coal bucket and stand well back from the door. You let the door have it five or six times with the bucket, as hard as you can mind you, and I guarantee you that Dicey will get up and get out of it.'

'I'll do that,' Margo responded hopefully. 'I'll do it right away but what if it doesn't work?'

'It will work,' Tom assured her. 'Just keep banging till he answers you. I'll hang on here just in case. If there's no answer I'll be right over. I wouldn't worry about him. A drunken man never comes to harm.'

Greatly encouraged Margo went upstairs a second time. She swung back the heavy coal bucket and cracked it against the guest room door. There was a sickening plunk from the bucket and from the door a loud deafening bang. She persevered with the formula till she was almost out of breath. In between she called her husband by his name. When there was no reply to her repeated assaults, she became genuinely frightened and abandoning the bucket on the stairway ran downstairs to the phone. Tom was still waiting as promised.

'It's no use,' Margo said breathlessly. 'He doesn't answer.' The the fear showed in her voice. 'I'm worried sick Tom,' she told her brother-in-law. 'It's not like him.'

'Now, now,' Tom spoke patiently. 'I told you not to worry. Just don't get excited and I'll be over in a matter of minutes.'

Returning the phone to its resting place she sat nervously on a settee. She was now afraid to go upstairs, almost afraid to stay in the house alone. She had a premonition that the worst had happened, that Dicey had succumbed to a heart attack and was lying dead in his bed. She could not bring herself to go upstairs and repeat the knocking. Suddenly she knelt on the floor and started to pray. She did it she told herself because there was nothing else to do.

If she had but known there was no way just then of assisting Dicey Reicey. He was quite dead and had been for several hours. He lay only a few inches from the door of the guest room. The front of his white shirt was soiled with vomit. So were his coat lapels. There were also traces of it around his open mouth. It was this same vomit which was responsible for his death at roughly half-three in the morning. He had inhaled part of it into his lungs while half asleep. He had managed to struggle from the bed to the door. Collapsing he had endeavoured to call out but the sounds were suffocated in his throat. He died almost at once from asphyxia.

EDDIE CAREY died later that same day in different circumstances. It happened because of the silliest of errors. The awful irony was that it was his last working day in England. At nine o'clock Dan Murray was to drive him to London airport to catch a flight to Dublin, where he was to meet his wife. She would travel by hired car and then by train to Dublin.

Eddie Carey should never have died. Everybody said so.

He was killed by the carelessness of a fellow worker, a hod-carrier recently hired, fresh from Kerry, a rough fellow willing and eager to please but careless and thoughtless with little experience of building. With his hod full he was about to mount the second storey scaffold when the electric bell, signalling the lunch break, sounded below him. Normally he would place the bricks in the innermost part of the scaffolding where they would not impede the comings and goings of the brickies and their mates. When the bell rang he saw no need for doing this at once – wouldn't they all be eating? Instead he deposited the fully-laden hod in the centre of the scaffolding and hared it down the ladder as fast as he could.

Working nearby was Eddie Carey who had not seen him come or go. He was in a happy frame of mind. That night he would be meeting Noreen and the following evening, all going well, he would be walking the clover-covered pastures of his newly acquired farm. At long last, after the lonely and often bitter passage of so many wasted years he would be home, home for evermore. There was nothing in the world to compare with the springing summer grass under a man's boots when he walked the land.

Eddie did not immediately leave the area where he was working at the sound of the bell. A few finishing touches were needed and he saw to these before descending. He cleaned his trowel and took a step backward to inspect the work he had just completed. It was then the calf of his leg came into contact with the unexpected object. Eddie cursed under his breath. Whatever the obstacle might be it should not be where it was. He lost his balance. A loud cry escaped him and he stumbled backwards, helpless and unable to control his movements. Vainly he clutched at the nearest pole of tubular scaffolding but it was out of reach. Both his hands clawed the empty air looking for a hold. Then he fell over and downwards with a sustained, despairing cry.

There were many on the site who recognised the import of such a cry. They had heard its like before. To men who had spent their lives on building sites and construction works it was a familiar one. They abandoned everything and

259

converged on the area from which the call of distress had come.

Eddie Carey fell astride a small mortar mixer almost directly underneath where he was working. It was an auxiliary mixer and would not have been there at all but for the fact that the big mixer, which was a regular fixture, was giving trouble. At the time of the accident, Dan Murray and his brother Willie, were working at the other side of the building.

'Christ,' Willie Murray exclaimed loudly. 'That sounds like somebody's fell.'

Dan recognised the cry for what it was. At the time he could not know that it was his friend.

'Come on,' he called to Willie.

Further away Dick Winterman was talking to Dave Costigan about a soccer game they planned to watch the coming Saturday. 'That's a fall!' Dick Winterman said when he heard the cry.

Dan was one of the very first on the scene. 'Don't touch him!' he called when some of Eddie's work-mates attempted to remove his body from the top of the mixer. They held back at once, terrified lest they do harm.

'Somebody get a doctor,' Dan ordered. 'And a priest,' he called, 'don't forget a priest.'

Men rushed to do his bidding. Cautiously, filled with a fear he had never before experienced, Dan went around the mixer to where Eddie's head hung slack. Gently and slowly Dan lifted the head and listened for signs of breathing. He heard none. He put an ear to Eddie's chest. Vainly he listened but there was nothing to be heard. Crazy Horse was pushing his way through the crowd. He came to Dan's side.

'You look like a ghost,' he said. Then he looked at Eddie and shook his head sorrowfully.

'What do you think?' Dan asked though he already knew the worst.

'He's dead,' the big man replied.

'You sure?' Dan asked, a tremor in his voice.

'His neck is broken. Let's get him down off it.'

Between them they lifted the body from the mixer and

laid it on the ground. A man stepped forward and taking off his coat moulded it into a pillow to lay under the head. Another folded the dead man's hands and entwined a rosary beads between his fingers. The whisper went round that Eddie Carey was dead. Hard faces softened and paled with the impact of the news. He was one of themselves. In his early days he had been a long distance man and a buck navvy. These were attributes of which a man might never be ashamed. Caps were taken off and a man knelt down. He was followed by others until every man on the site was on his knees.

'The Lord be good to him,' the first man to kneel said. 'He grafted hard and he never turned his back on it.'

'No better man,' a number of respectful voices whispered.

'I believe in God, the Father Almighty,' a grey haired, elderly labourer, with a face marked and scarred, intoned the creed. A great volume of men's voices answered him. On Saturday night they might maim each other or drink themselves into varying stupors. Some would lie with prostitute and hustler and others sleep in prison cell but, in this thing, this calamity they were one. For a long time they prayed in quiet resignation.

Although Eddie's death had been an accident there were few of the kneeling men who inwardly accepted it as such. To them Eddie Carey's death was the toll for the money they earned and the drink they consumed. It was the Paddies' tally. Every tunnel Paddy dug was a toll-tunnel, every bridge a toll-bridge. Every road had its toll-booth and the toll-man was death. They accepted it as part and parcel of the game they played. Where men worked in a frenzy of hurry for quick money there was bound to be carelessness. There had to be accidents. In that year there were ten times more Irishmen killed on building sites in England than in Ireland. It was an astounding figure but it was a true one. It was a conservative figure compared to bad years when cruel ill-luck would dog the building industry.

Almost every week the provincial papers in the south and west of Ireland carried accounts of fatal accidents on

British building sites. Mostly the victims were labourers, men in their forties who were losing the sprightliness so necessary for surviving without mishap. Often they became careless, taking situations for granted. Protective headgear was unknown where the Irish worked. There were few, if any, safety regulations. All was to change in a few short years, the stamp-dodging, the tax evasion, the name-changing. It would spell the end of the small sub-contractor. It would mean that Irish contractors, for the first time, would have to compete on an equal basis with their English counterparts. It was not to happen all of a sudden but slowly and surely there would be parity at every level of the trade.

Less than an hour after Eddie's death Sylvester, acting on Dan's instructions, had rung the presbytery in Ballynahaun and asked the parish priest to break the news to Noreen. Dan was not sure whether she would be at home or whether she would be already on her way to Dublin. The priest promised to contact her at once. She was not at home. A friend was looking after the children. She had no idea where Mrs Carey would be staying in Dublin. All she knew was that Mrs Carey was meeting her husband at Dublin Airport that night. There was no way of contacting her before then. For Dan it was a horrible dilemma. It was Sandra who solved it. She had already met Noreen during her visit to Ballynahaun. She would take the next flight to Dublin

'I don't envy you,' Sylvester confided as they waited at the airport for the flight to be called.

'It has to be done,' Sandra replied. 'I don't like doing it but I'm sure I can do it better than any of you. If it were you I don't know what I should do but bad as it would be for me, look what it's like for her. They were husband and wife and then there are the children. It doesn't bear thinking on.'

The inference about marriage did not escape Sylvester.

'Why the hell are you so anxious to get married?'

'Who said I was?'

'You can't open your mouth without dropping a hint.'

'Why shouldn't I want to get married?' She was on the verge of tears.

'We're all right the way we are. Marriage would only

262

complicate things.'

She started to cry. Embarrassed, Sylvester looked around the lounge to see if anybody noticed. She dried her eyes quickly and without a word produced some makeup which she applied with the aid of a small hand mirror. There was no further conversation between them till the flight number was called. He kissed her goodbye.

'See you when you get back,' he said.

'Don't strain yourself on my account,' she flung back at him as she swept out of the lounge. It was a good curtain line. It left him perplexed as intended. This was a new bitchiness he had not encountered before. It disturbed him.

NOREEN CAREY'S grief was terrible to behold. She could not be consoled. Her distress was enormous. Mary Murray was constantly by her side on the day of the funeral. She became so distraught towards evening that the doctor was sent for. Heavily sedated she had her first hours of sleep since the night before Eddie died. Dan could not bring himself to speak to her at length. He held himself guilty. He should have released Eddie at once. He knew nobody would blame him, least of all Noreen, but he was nagged by the thought that if he had sent Eddie back the moment he bought the farm the tragedy would not have occurred.

He could argue that Eddie himself had insisted on staying on for the extra three months. He recalled that he had suggested to Eddie that there was no obligation on him to stay. On the other hand he had not told him to go. He might have but it was a critical time. Yes but a critical time for whom? Not for Eddie surely. It was a critical time for Dan Murray and the future of his firm. No matter how he slanted the evidence in his favour he could not but reproach himself.

After the funeral he dismissed the matter from his mind and called Crazy Horse.

'Let's get back,' he said. 'Time's a wasting.'

He bade a speedy goodbye to his parents. 'When Noreen comes round,' he told his father, 'you can tell her that all the funeral expenses have been paid, that if there's anything in the world I can do she knows where to find me.'

'I'll tell her,' Bill Murray said, 'but I'm afraid it will be some time before she recovers enough to realise her loss.'

Dan nodded grimly and sat in the front seat of the car. Crazy Horse turned the key in the ignition and in seconds they were lost in a cloud of August dust.

DICEY REICEY was laid to rest on the feast of Saint Bartholomew, less than 24 hours after the burial of Eddie Carey. The funeral was delayed for a day because of the absence in Ireland of his brother Joe and Joe's wife Dora. They could not be located and eventually it was only through the emergency message relayed from Radio Éireann that they were contacted in a hotel in Donegal. They returned at once.

As they drove south and west Joe Reicey would shake his head in disbelief every few miles.

'Christ almighty he had the health of a horse,' he said.

'He had the health of a horse,' she echoed.

'He had the heart of a lion,' Joe said.

'He had indeed, the heart of a lion,' Dora chimed in obediently. Years earlier she had been quite a chatterbox. No sooner would Joe open his mouth than she would improve upon or contradict his pronouncements. This had little effect on Joe so long as Dora had some idea about the subject under discussion. For the most part she had not. Joe endured her harmless chatter for the first year of marriage but it came to a stage where he could not open his mouth without an embellishment or detraction from Dora. He spoke to her about it and for a while it stopped. It started again and he remonstrated again. This time she denied that she was contradicting him. A more patient man would have taken no notice but Joe Reicey was far from being a patient man. One night after a few drinks he beat her up. Thereafter she faithfully parroted all of Joe's opinions. Never once did she contradict him. Joe was grateful for the change. Sometimes he was annoyed by her faithful interpretation of everything he said but it was better, anything was better than the maddening contradictions.

Sometimes he felt sorry for her. He felt pity at the abject repetitiveness.

'I just cannot understand it,' he bellowed as they were forced to slow down by a large herd of cattle. 'The man was like a bloody stone wall. He had the health of a salmon. It couldn't have been the heart.'

'Oh no,' Dora said. 'It couldn't have been the heart.'

'There's no need to go repeating every word I say.'

'No need, no need at all,' Dora said. Once, while on an afternoon visit to Margo, the latter had remarked how placid and even the course of Dora and Joe's marriage seemed to be. She had asked Dora for the formula. She was somewhat taken aback by the answer.

'Never question,' was Dora's formula for the successful marriage. 'No matter what he says or what he does never question or you'll wind up sore.'

Margo was on the point of seeking elaboration but the air of nun-like resignation on Dora's placid face forestalled her.

Dicey Reicey's funeral drew a large crowd. The cortege that proceeded from his home to the Catholic graveyard in North London numbered 190 cars. At the graveside it was estimated that there must have been a hundred wreaths. Someone said this was a record for the funeral of an Irishman in London. Dan Murray stood at the edge of the crowd. He missed nothing. From time to time Tom Reicey would lift his head and allow his eyes to sweep the crowd. The size and quality of the attendance was some consolation in this time of great grief. Dan knew how Tom's mind worked. Near Tom stood Joe and next to Joe stood Tom's wife Maisie. Dora Reicey stood at one side of Margo Reicey and her cousin Father Monty Cullagan stood at the other. No grief, no weight of sorrow, no amount of crying or sobbing could make Margo Reicey anything but beautiful. Dressed all in black she stood out in shining contrast to those surounding her.

When the burial ceremony was over those who had not previously done so formed in a queue to shake hands with the widow and the chief mourners.

'I'm sorry for your trouble,' Dan said as he took Margo's hand in a gesture of sympathy. For a moment the surprise showed in her face.

'Thank you,' she said. 'It was good of you to come.'

Tom and Joe Reicey limply acknowledged Dan's handshake. Both bridled but preserved their calm. With proper funeral faces they stood grimly side by side without moving. They would stand there till the last condolence had been tendered. In between Tom leaned over and whispered to Joe, 'It's a great funeral. I never saw such a crowd.'

'He had no enemies,' Joe said.

As he left the graveyard Dan heard his name being called. He was almost certain he knew the voice. He turned to see Patricia Dee bearing down on him. She had not changed in the least.

'Any chance of a lift?' she asked with a laugh.

'Sure,' Dan said. 'I'm parked just outside the gate.'

It was a full five minutes before either of them spoke. It was Patricia who broke the silence.

'You never married,' she said.

'No,' he replied. Again there was a long silence.

'When we get to the Strand you can drop me,' Patricia informed him. 'I can get a bus from there.'

'Whatever you like,' Dan said agreeably. 'Your husband is a doctor, isn't he?'

'Yes and a very successful one, so successful that he couldn't find time to come to the funeral. We have two children, a boy and a girl and my husband has one of the finest collections of antique silver in England.'

This was the old Patricia. She spoke as though she were reciting the history of somebody else's family.

'He never misses an auction. Most of his fees are in cash and it's a good way to dispose of the money. If he were to pay tax it would be enormous so every Saturday morning he strikes out for the antique shops with the week's take.'

'You approve?'

'Of course not. I wasn't brought up that way. I think its perfectly disgusting but I never say anything. I'm too good a wife for that. Dan, there's a question that's plagued me for

266

some time. I hope you'll answer it for me. It's caused me some trouble. Why did you show up at my wedding?'

'To get even with you.'

'If it's any satisfaction to you at this late stage you succeeded. You really bowled me over. I was sick all that day and night. It wasn't a nice thing to do.'

'I know it wasn't but at the time it was the only way I could protest.'

'Was it that bad?'

'It was bad enough.'

'You got over it quickly.'

'I plunged into my work.'

'You're not in the least like my husband,' she said. 'He's an extremely fastidious man. He's also extremely mean, not to me. I get what I want. He knows better than to refuse me anything but at the same time I have never seen him perform a generous act. His mother is still alive and from what I can gather she is not too well off. He never sends her anything although it was her sacrifices that paid for his education. Sometimes I send her a few pounds unknown to him. We were only married a month when he questioned me about the price of a joint I bought for the Sunday lunch. "If," I told him, "you persist with these petty questions you can do the housekeeping yourself and I'll go back to work." He's very careful since, careful to see that I'm never short of money. You haven't changed at all Dan. Are your father and mother still alive?'

'Yes, they're in great health. Eddie Carey died a few days ago. I'm only just back from his funeral.'

'He was one of your closest friends wasn't he? I'm so sorry. I really am. He was such a kind man. His poor wife and family. Oh that's a terrible thing. Was he long ailing?'

'He wasn't ailing at all. It was an accident.'

'The Irish have no luck on building sites,' Patricia sighed. Dan did not comment on this. At the entrance to the Strand he asked her where she would like to be dropped.

'Oh anywhere,' she said. 'Before you do Dan I want to tell you how sorry I am for what happened between us. I know better now. Will I see you again?'

'Why?'

'I don't know why except that I'd like to meet and have a chat now and then. We were very close once.'

'No,' Dan said. 'We'd better not.'

'For God's sake why not?' Patricia was peeved.

The car came slowly to a halt. Dan opened the door on the passenger's side.

'Come round to the house then for a meal some evening? We'd love to have you.' She eased herself from the seat on to the thoroughfare.

'Think about it,' she called after him but he was out of earshot. As he drove away he chided himself for not having persisted when she had stated her resolve to have no more to do with him. 'I wouldn't have been mean with her,' he spoke aloud.

IN THROGMORTON Street Tom Slater was waiting. 'Follow me,' he said. Dan followed him along the carpeted corridor.

'I got the lease,' Slater called over his shoulder. 'It's in my name but that makes no difference.'

They stopped outside a door with Boardroom written on it. Slater knocked. A cultured voice invited them in. Three men waited for them, two elderly and one middle-aged. The middle-aged man sat at the head of the table. He bade Dan to be seated indicating a vacant chair at the bottom. Slater sat near the top where he would be available with information from a dossier which he placed in front of him. Slater performed the introductions. The man at the top of the table was Mr Roundwood, the chairman. It was he who did all the talking.

'Mr Murray,' he announced gravely, 'we are approving a loan of two hundred and fifty thousand pounds on the advice of our manager Mr Slater and on the strength of other information available to us.'

'Thank you.' A huge smile crossed Dan's face.

Roundwood raised a finger. 'Before you enthuse Mr Murray, you had better hear our terms. The loan is for a period of two years after which time it must be paid in full. If not there will be a forfeiture by you on our terms. The rate of interest is nine and a half per cent. Should the loan be paid off before the specified time the interest will still remain the same.'

'I find the terms acceptable,' Dan said.

'In that case,' Roundwood beamed, 'Mr Slater will let you have a cheque for two hundred and fifty thousand pounds as soon as you sign certain papers.' He inclined his head and made the faintest of nods in Slater's direction who in turn nodded towards Dan. The interview was over.

23

THE EARLY winter was milder than usual so that work on the houses proceeded ahead of schedule. The first group was now finished and the deposits for the entire 125 were paid up. Dan learned, not for the first time, that people were prepared to pay for quality. He knew from experience that there was incessant haggling over cheap houses, houses which cost only one-third of what his were realising. The income group at which he aimed were convinced that house purchase was the safest and most rewarding of all investments. The better the house and the bigger the site the easier it was to dispose of it. While work on the drill hall progressed he flew to Dublin to finalise the purchase of two farms for which he advertised in the daily press in Ireland. He made it clear in the ads that he only sought land within a 10 mile radius of the city and preferably in the south.

There were 10 replies. Two had asked for outrageous prices but the rest had seemed reasonable enough. It was November. As yet the big building fever had not gripped Dublin. There was widespread development but money for investment was still scarce. He spent two days in Ballynahaun before inspecting the Dublin properties.

He inveigled his father into making the Dublin trip. They both arrived in the city around midnight, had a few drinks and went to bed. In the morning they drove southwards to look over the acreages on offer. In most cases the land was down, in dire need of drainage and fencing and already heavily mortgaged. He liked none of the places he saw. They were wrongly situated and he doubted if 50 years of continuous development from the city outwards would enhance their worth. Neither were the situations pleasant but on the credit side there would, he believed, be little difficulty in securing planning permission for mass building.

Disillusioned they returned to the city for lunch. During

the meal his father expressed the opinion that in order to acquire anything worthwhile one had to lay out big money. Dan had at his disposal a sum of two hundred and ninety thousand pounds. There was the loan of two hundred and fifty thousand from Slater's of London and there was an extra forty thousand which Sylvester had conjured seemingly out of nowhere but basically it came from site deposits and the temporary withholding of certain payments to builders' providers.

It was almost three o'clock in the afternoon when they visited the first of the two high-priced farms. Most of the property skirted one of the main Dublin roads and was only 2 miles from the nearest built-up area of the city. The land was good and consisted of 75 acres. The house was old and in need of repair. It had once been the country seat of a distinguished Protestant family. There was almost no really good land in Ireland which had not been in the possession of Protestants. The owner was away for the day but his sister, a sprightly and talkative octogenarian took them on a tour of the 6 fields and small paddock which comprised the estate. There were outhouses and a large hay-shed and the old lady was surprised when Dan evinced no interest in these.

When they finished Dan asked if she or her brother had considered lowering the price. She assured him they would not consider any such move.

'But you're asking eighty thousand pounds,' Dan pointed out. 'That's over a thousand pounds an acre.'

'It's worth every penny of it,' she said stoutly. 'There's no day but there isn't an enquiry. Why only yesterday there were 3 Englishmen here and they promised to let us know shortly whether they would buy or not.'

Dan had already made up his mind.

'You'll think I'm mad,' he said to his father as they drove from the old house on to the roadway.

'No,' his father said. 'I think it's one of the most sensible things you ever did. Land doubles in value every few years and the way things are going its likely to treble.'

This coming from a Kerryman as cautious as his father served to strengthen Dan's determination to buy. They arrived at the second farm at five o'clock. The owner was a widowed Protestant gentleman who told Dan that his only reason for selling was pressure from creditors particularly the banks which held substantial mortgages. Another stimulus was the urging of a daughter who was married to a solicitor in the city. Her children were approaching university age and the money left over would help with their education. Of course he would go to live with her. Originally the place had consisted of 250 acres and had thrown up many a fine hunter as well as a winner of 13 steeplechases. Dan paid little heed to the old man's ramblings. He took stock of all he saw. In a few years it would be priceless building land. For the ninety-five remaining acres the price was one hundred thousand pounds.

Later when it was made public that the two farms were sold for sums of eighty thousand and a hundred thousand pounds the news was considered to be of sufficient importance to merit inclusion in the front pages of several daily and evening newspapers. The name of the purchaser was not disclosed. The transactions were carried out by a firm of London solicitors, Seymour, Seymour and Wiley. They would be involved in other land purchases for Murray Brothers.

DAN HAD given much thought to the selection of a suitable name for the converted drill hall. Already the city of London and suburbs had seven dance-halls with Irish names. Dan wanted something distinctively Irish yet something which would not appear too obtrusive in a south London setting. Names like the Kathleen Mavourneen and the Maid of Erin came to mind but he dismissed these as being too redolent of the sloppy sentimentality of earlier generations. Such names, no doubt, would go down well in America where the Irish tear was nearer the surface. He doubted very much if they would ring any bells in the Mitcham surrounds.

Sylvester had suggested 'The Four-Leaved Shamrock' and Sandra 'The Four-Leaved Clover' but Dan wasn't satisfied with these either. He felt that they were too commonplace. It would have to be something vastly different from its predecessors yet retaining an Irish flavour. The backbone of its support would come from Irish emigrants and from the first generation Irish in the catchment area.

In the end he was on the point of drawing a name from a hat when Dave Costigan asked what was the matter with 'The Molly Malone'. Dan mulled it over and decided that there was nothing wrong with it. By the time the legal ends were tied the summer had passed and it was well into autumn. The Molly Malone needed surprisingly little by way of repair. A new stage would have to be erected and a ladies' toilet installed. Parts of the floor would have to be replaced. Because it was composed of genuine maple this would prove costly. Most of the repairs were carried out by night except the paintwork which was the greater part of the undertaking.

The Saint Stephen's night opening of the Molly Malone was widely publicised. Dan personally visited every presbytery in south London where he had interviews with the parish priests. He explained that this was an Irish ballroom with a difference. There would be no exploitation of Irish boys and girls. Drunks would be excluded and anybody with the remotest sign of intoxication would be refused admission.

There would be strict surveillance during the actual dance and there would be stricter scrutiny at the door. He gave each priest a substantial Mass offering and was promised that the opening would be publicised at all Masses for weeks before the event. He advertised in local cinemas and in the local newspapers. He sent out no invitations. It was not to be a gala occasion. It would be strictly business from the outset. For the opening he engaged the most popular band in Ireland. The hall was able to accommodate 1,500 dancers but on the opening night more that 2,000 were admitted. Among those who paid for admission were many known blackguards and county gangs who had made ugly reputations for themselves at other venues. On Dan's instructions nobody was to be refused except those who might be helplessly drunk. Deliberately he chose to admit those who were likely to cause trouble. He was well equipped to deal with it and if there were disturbances, the opening night was the proper time to quell them ruthlessly. At the entrance immaculately rigged out in evening dress was Crazy Horse. There was no other evidence of house control but only a fool would be taken in by this. In the background were the Costigan brothers and Willie Murray. By arrangement they made themselves as inconspicuous as possible. In the box office where Sylvester and Sandra had their hands full Dick Winterman was seated where he could not be seen by the patrons. Just inside the door of the ballroom was Dan himself. Mingling with the dancers was the Tipperary man, Larry Lynch, who had fought at the Shillelagh. There were others of Dan's work force in well-appointed places all over the hall. Dan was determined that the night should be a success and he was more determined still that any display of thuggery should be dealt with discreetly, severely and instantly.

With this in mind he briefed his staff beforehand. Under no circumstances was Crazy Horse to leave the entrance. If there was any attempt at gate-crashing Dick Winterman would come to his aid. Between them they should be able to manage the most difficult situation. Lynch was placed in charge of the ballroom staff. At the slightest sign of trouble he was to report to Dan who would enlist the aid of his brother Willie and the two Costigans. Those responsible for the trouble would be rushed quickly to the main door where their exit would be hastened by Crazy Horse and Dick Winterman.

Those with good memories would think twice before risking a confrontation with Dan Murray and his men. Unfortunately there were some with not so good memories and there were others recently arrived from Ireland anxious to test their strength. These were the cockerels of the fighting game whose pin feathers were beginning to show and who were not able to cope with strong drink. At midnight the hall was packed to capacity. From then on the *House Full* sign was displayed in the foyer. Many were turned away. Some protested but Crazy Horse quickly convinced them that they would be better off elsewhere. His method was to seize the more belligerent by the shoulders, spin them around and boot them in the behind down the steps which led up to the entrance. One foolhardy fellow produced a knife. Crazy Horse feinted with his left hand and suddenly seized the knife hand with his right. He applied maximum pressure. The knife fell to the ground and the youth screamed in pain. His elbow was dislocated.

'I hate bastards who use knives,' Crazy Horse whispered fiercely. With the back of his hand he struck the offender across the mouth. At once the blood appeared and the knife wielder spat out two broken teeth. At that moment Dick Winterman appeared. He lifted the semi-conscious youth by the coat collar and trousers seat and rushed him down the steps. He ran him for about two hundred yards until they came to an alley. Steering him into this Winterman rammed a huge fist into the bleeding face. He then removed trousers, coat and shoes and tied them into a neat bundle with the aid of the coat sleeves. As his victim began to show signs of consciousness Winterman left the alley with the bundle under his arm. Just then a truck passed. He lofted the clothes into its rear and with a grim smile returned to the Molly Malone where Crazy Horse was waiting.

'I'll kill the next bastard who pulls a knife,' Crazy Horse said. Winterman told him what he had done with the clothes. Crazy Horse, not much given to mirth, threw back his great head and roared with laughter.

'It's a good job,' he cried between peals, 'that I left him a hand to cover his jewel box.'

The only other outbreak took place in front of the bandstand. It could have developed into a full scale melée with disastrous consequences for the future of the Molly Malone but for the prompt action of Dan's men. It began when the leaders of two groups from different counties started an altercation over an excuse-me dance. The girl involved stood with her hands folded hoping they would fight over her. Dan's men pounced at once. One after the other every youth involved was expertly rushed to the exit where he was soundly booted down the main steps by Crazy Horse or

Dick Winterman. None was neglected.

As the dance wore on it became clear from the atmosphere of gaiety and abandon that the night was going to be a howling success. Ninety per cent of the customers were not even aware that there had been disturbances so speedily and effectively were they dealt with.

With a new dance-hall a good beginning was everything. When word spread that the opening night was an outstanding occasion it was hard to check enthusiasm for the new ballroom. When parents discovered that there was no rowdyism and that their offspring were in no danger of assault from gangs of young thugs the future of the ballroom was assured. So it was that the Molly Malone deservedly won a reputation for being one of the best run ballrooms in London. It wasn't a reputation which was won overnight.

For the first year of its life while its character was being formed the Molly Malone was never without a strong force of experienced emergency men. Dan never engaged second rate bands and if his admission prices compared unfavourably with prices elsewhere there was always a guarantee of good music and an opportunity for good dancing at the Molly Malone. That at least was something. After two years the ballroom became a landmark and a successful future seemed ensured. When older married couples, keen on dancing for dancing's sake, started to patronise it the box office receipts rose dramatically and subsequently the profits were enormous. A time was to come when there would be dancing almost every night.

DURING THIS time he began to take an occasional close look at himself. He was in his mid-thirties. His brother Willie, after a short courtship, married Nellie Costigan, a sister of Dave and Peter, in June of 1963. The brothers themselves married shortly afterwards as if their sister's binding had been the cue they were waiting for.

The year 1964 was a notable one for the firm. The two five acre fields, on which Dan had taken up the options, were used up and it was necessary to buy more land south of London. Dan already had an option on a 35 acre farm a few miles south of Mitcham. He purchased it for fifty thousand pounds. He would begin his biggest undertaking later that year. Dan's Dublin farms were long since paid for and he had several smaller interests in London. Slater was continually putting him on to new investments.

At night when he left the sites he would visit the Molly Malone. He would talk with Crazy Horse or sit awhile listening to the music. Sometimes people would join him for a chat. He was Dan Murray the millionaire but he was also, ask anybody, the very same Dan Murray who had arrived penniless at Fishguard in the early 1950s. The success had not gone to his head. Dan was aware of what was being said about him. Maybe this was his problem. He had the sort of money mostly found in the upper echelons of society but he was moving in circles nearer the bottom. This was partly from choice but also partly from habit. There was also a small part which consisted of uncertainty. He sometimes wished fervently that he had a better education. He tried reading books but frequently found them tedious and time-consuming. He realised the fault was in himself, not in the books. He began to feel that he had missed many things which other men took for granted, belonging to a set for instance, being in demand for parties. He had never put himself in the way of such things. Business associates had often invited him for weekends to places in the country. Slater had once asked him to join an Ascot-bound party but Dan gave the excuse that the notice was too short. He had been sorry afterwards. He decided to accept if a second invitation should be forthcoming. He thought of having a heart-to-heart talk with Sylvester but Sylvester had his own problems.

WHY THE hell was Sandra always on about marriage? They had a perfect arrangement. In marriage people were inclined to take things for granted. They grew tired after a few years and the relationship grew listless. At least that was what he gleaned from observing married friends of his. He could not bring himself to propose marriage to her. For some reason that he could not fully explain to himself the thought of matrimony sickened him. In an effort to be honest with himself he frequently wondered if it had something to do with his parents and their relationship. Prison had nothing to do with it. He had the same feelings before he was convicted. Could it be that the years in the seminary were the cause of deterring him? Was there a basic insecurity in his make-up, an underlying belief that he would not be able to make a go of it?

What the prison psychiatrist told him might be nearest to the truth, that he was a natural loner. He was not a lonely person by circumstance or environment. There was in him an unshakable desire for loneness. So he was a loner. Of course he could marry Sandra. There was nobody of whom he was fonder save Dan Murray whose friendship he considered incomparable. From now on he would attune his instincts to the suggestion of matrimony. He would gear himself so that he would become accustomed to the idea. It was the least he owed her. It would not be easy but he would make the effort. The thought of the final irreparable step was enough to make him want to change his mind. That emphatic yes in front of the altar of God left no loophole. A man became committed for eternity in the sight of his friends and in the presence of God. He dismissed the finality of it from his mind and brought his new thinking into the conflict. He could not know it then but he would never see Sandra again

Without a word and without advance notice of any kind she disappeared. There had been no row, no obvious justification – a marriage proposal apart – that Sylvester could think of.

When she did not show up after a fortnight he began to worry and when, after a month, there was no word he went to see her parents in Luton. Yes she had come home and she had stayed a week but then she left and they hadn't heard from her. Sylvester fretted more and more as time went by and she failed to put in an appearance.

'I'd marry her in the morning if she returned to me,' he

confided to Dan. 'I'm lost without her.'

There was nothing Dan could say to lift his friend's depression. He knew it was inevitable that Sandra would leave. What amazed him was how and why she had endured the relationship for so long when she knew in her heart that Sylvester had no notion of marrying her.

Sylvester was never to hear from her again. Less than a year after she left him she married. Dan heard news of it in the Colorado from an Irish waitress whose sister had seen a photo of the wedding in some newspaper or other. Dan conveyed the news to Sylvester having consulted with Crazy Horse. The big ex-Commando argued that Sylvester had gone into a decline since the girl had left. Therefore there was nothing to be gained by not telling him. Sylvester's reaction was to embark on a methodical and monumental bender.

'I have no luck with women,' he confessed. 'Maybe I should have become a priest after all.'

A few months after Sandra departed Mrs Dick Daly wrote a long letter to her husband asking if she might return. She regretted all that happened and confessed that she had an awful cheek but she explained that she had been young when she left him. She had been impressionable and easily led. She would make it all up to him. There was no reference to her paramour. She insisted however that she had not experienced real happiness since she left. Crazy Horse showed the letter to Sylvester.

'You're asking me?' Sylvester said bitterly.

'Give me your opinion,' Crazy Horse said.

'You must decide for yourself,' Sylvester told him, 'but if it was me I'd bloody well take her back. I would go on my knees and beg her to come back. Life is no good without someone to care for you. Look at me. Did you ever see a more disconsolate wretch, a more woebegone example of my species.'

Crazy Horse did not answer the letter at once. Acting on Dan's advice he went to see the parish priest of Bertham, Father Conners.

'What was she before you married her?' was Father

Conners' first question.

Crazy Horse did not understand.

'Was she a Catholic or a Protestant?' Father Conners simplified matters.

'I don't know what she was,' Crazy Horse answered truthfully.

There were many other questions. When he had satisfied himself that there was nothing further he needed to know he pursed his lips and bent his head in thought. Eventually he said, 'I would take her back. First and foremost you are a Catholic and the marriage ceremony took place in a Catholic church. You will no doubt still be familiar with that part of the catechism which states that what God hath put together no man dare put asunder. In the sight of God she is your wife and she will always be your wife. I am also sure that she has learned her lesson.'

That night Crazy Horse drove northwards to Leicester where his wife worked in a café. They returned to London together and spent the night at the Colorado. In less than a week he found a cottage for rent in Mitcham. They settled in and seemed to be happy together. That was in January. In June she disappeared without notice taking with her the contents of his wallet which amounted to five hundred and fifty pounds. He was never to see her again.

Dan would often consider the cheerless existence of Crazy Horse and go back over the wasted years of Sylvester's life. They were good and loyal companions but they were incapable of setting a gathering alight. Often they had the opposite effect. They always looked as if they were in need of cheering up. He wondered if he was like them or was turning out that way. Much as he admired them he shuddered at the thought. He resolved to escape the rut.

ONE JUNE morning in 1964 Dan drove into the city and made his way to the Jaguar showrooms in Picadilly. He spent a long time examining the two main exhibits, one a yellow E-Type and the other a Mark Ten. From time to time others would stop to admire the latest models. There were

Americans, turbaned Indians, Malayans, Africans and many others. Again Dan was aware of a deficiency in relation to his appreciation of London. The great city concealed so many different worlds. His own was one of the least colourful and least sophisticated. It did not have to be so.

Symbolically his first step across the threshold into the Jaguar showrooms was the first into a new world and the first out of his own. There was a short waiting list for both E-types and Mark Tens. The senior salesman informed him that the delay would not be overlong but he did think it only fair to warn him. Dan sat himself into the yellow E-type and wondered if hands as calloused and horny had ever before clutched such a steering wheel. Gently he let his fingers play around the frame of the wheel. He sat for several minutes and then sat in the Mark Ten.

He motioned to the senior salesman to come to the driver's window.

'I'll take one of these,' Dan said. 'This colour will do nicely if you don't mind.'

'Very good sir,' the salesman announced blandly.

'I'll let you have a cheque for the full amount right now.'

'As you wish sir,' the salesman showed no surprise. One's reactions had to be guarded with the type of customer one met at this level.

Dan filled out the cheque and asked when he might expect delivery. In less than three months, the salesman assured him, the car would be his. Dan handed over the cheque and walked out of the showrooms into the blinding June sunshine. The streets were busy. Mostly the pedestrians were tourists. He strolled along clean pavements now and then pausing to inspect a shop window. He looked at his watch. It stood at a a quarter to eleven. He had an appointment with his solicitor at eleven. Afterwards if he so desired he could catch a plane for Shannon or Dublin. It would be incredibly beautiful and balmy now in any of the resorts of the west coast of Ireland or he could fly to the Canary Islands or indeed to anywhere in the world and the expense would hardly dent his capital. He would think about it when his business was concluded. Half the enjoyment was savouring the prospect of where he might travel to.

Edwin Seymour of Seymour, Seymour and Wiley rose from his desk when Dan was ushered into his office. They had known each other for a number of years now, ever since Tom Slater had suggested to Dan that he retain the firm to protect his interests. Edwin Seymour was a florid-faced, grey-haired man in his fifties. He looked the sort who was born to wear tweeds. Indeed he wore them most of the time and they suited him as no other materials did.

'You got my note?' he said to Dan.

'Yes,' Dan answered when he had taken a seat.

'Good,' Edwin Seymour said and he settled comfortably into his chair. 'We have quite a busy time before us. First of all there is the business of Patrick Aloysius Moroney and Brendan McNamara.'

Dan listened intently. The two men, employees of his, had died within a month of each other. Moroney had died two days before Christmas of the previous year when the pick he had been industriously wielding came into contact with an underground cable. The shock had killed him instantly and rendered unconscious another worker who went to his aid. The fixing of responsibility for the accident proved to be a tricky problem since compensation would have to be paid in full by whoever was at fault. The cable was originally laid by a power company and after lengthy negotiations it was made clear that the onus rested fully on them.

The second employee of Dan's, Brendan McNamara, was killed when a trench caved in on him. He was not insured. In fact he was one of the specially imported workers who had come in answer to Dan's recruiting campaign of a few years before. As far as the British government was concerned Brendan McNamara did not exist, neither was there anything the Irish government could do to make Dan pay compensation. They had no jurisdiction. Dan was prepared to pay the dead man's widow a sum of two thousand pounds but he wanted to be absolved of all responsibility.

Edwin Seymour, after long and careful consideration, had come to the conclusion that it would not be feasible for Dan to pay anything. To do so would be to admit responsibility. There was an alternative. When McNamara died his workmates had made a collection to have the body flown home to Ireland. Seymour decided that the sensible thing to do was for Dan to subscribe to this collection however belatedly. This would ease his conscience and at the same time benefit the widow. Edwin Seymour suggested a sum of a thousand pounds.

The third piece of business was to discuss an offer of two hundred and fifty thousand pounds for one of Dan's properties in Dublin. It came from a Dublin based company called the Green Valley Trust. This was a recently formed development company of which Dan had heard. They would have no way of knowing that he was the owner of the Dublin property which, incidentally, was less valuable than the other.

'It's three times what you paid for it,' Seymour reminded him, 'but unless you need the money I think it would be unwise to sell.'

'I have no notion of accepting such an offer,' Dan told him.

A number of minor matters had to be cleared away before their business together was finished.

'Well now Mr Murray,' the older man rose and extended his hand, 'till we meet again.'

'There's just one thing before I go,' Dan said. 'I want you to buy me a racehorse.'

'Please sit down Mr Murray and tell me what kind of racehorse?'

'A chaser,' Dan said. 'A promising novice chaser.'

'A promising novice chaser will cost you a good deal of money Mr Murray.'

'I'm aware of that,' Dan said.

'Steeple-chasing is a wonderful sport Mr Murray,' Edwin Seymour told Dan warmly. 'As you may know I have a horse in training with Len Ricketts of Basingstoke. I've never been without one. All we owners really do is keep the trainer in bread and butter. You must never expect to make money out of racing. A win now and then is desirable and if this offsets the expenses a whit then that's a good thing. Len Ricketts' is not a gambling stable. I doubt if he ever placed a shilling on a horse in his life but he is a good trainer and he is a very honest man. I'll entrust the transaction to Len. How much are you prepared to go?'

'I'm prepared to go to ten thousand pounds,' Dan said.

Edwin Seymour looked at him with respect.

'You believe in having a good one or nothing,' he said. 'When everything is arranged you must come with me some weekend to Basingstoke.'

'I look forward to it,' Dan said.

DURING HIS weekend visit to Basingstoke with Edwin Seymour they had stayed at a small but exclusive hotel called the Winchester Willows. After an inspection of the Ricketts' stables Len had returned with both men for a night-cap at the hotel. Len confided in Dan that Firearm would shortly win a novice race valued at three hundred pounds. He should have a small wager but he was not to tell any-body. One drink borrowed another and they stayed long after midnight. Shortly before they retired an imposing mat-ronly woman and her attractive daughter registered for the night. It transpired that they had motored from London and had some business with Len Ricketts concerning the sale of a horse on the following morning. Ricketts insisted they re-main on for a drink. The night porter was summoned and sandwiches ordered. The matronly woman was a Mrs O'Lully. Dan guessed that with such a name her husband or his antecedents must have been Irish.

The husband, poor fellow, Len Ricketts informed Dan and Edwin Seymour, had died some months before and much as he personally objected to it the widow insisted on selling the horse Len Ricketts trained for him. The horse was an average seven year-old hurdler with one win, two plac-ings and several appearances which left him out of the frame.

When Mrs O'Lully eventually spoke at some length the very Englishness of her accent convinced Dan that she was British but he was somewhat surprised to learn from the good lady herself that she was none other than one of the

Kildare O'Garans while her husband who had been an eye specialist in London was one of the county Dublin O'Lullys.

Could it be possible she asked that Dan was one of the Kilgunney Murrays of north county Dublin?

'I'm a Kerry Murray,' Dan informed her.

When Edwin Seymour went searching for the night porter to order a round of drinks Dan found himself seated near Miss O'Lully. She turned out to be a quiet and rather shy person but with Seymour's vacant chair like a duenna between them it was difficult to converse without raising their voices. Dan guessed that Iris O'Lully, like himself, was not in the habit of raising her voice. This was not the case with her mother who was unfolding a long tale at the top of her voice to a constantly nodding Len Ricketts. Iris O'Lully's charming smile decided Dan's next move. He vacated his own chair and sat in Seymour's for the remainder of the night. A few trips to the washroom aside, he never left her side. By consent, as it were, they were left to their own devices while the oldsters were careful to keep to theirs. It was an enjoyable night.

Dan and Edwin Seymour were on their way to London the following morning long before Mrs O'Lully and Iris were out of bed. Edwin was able to furnish Dan with the missing details of the general O'Lully canvas. Unable to earn a five figure annual income in his native Dublin, Doctor Kenneth O'Lully transferred himself, his wife and two-year-old daughter to London shortly after England's declaration of war on Germany in 1939. He surmised correctly that there would be much need of his specialised talents in a private capacity in the sprawling, spirited city. He succeeded in making a great deal of money but he spent most of it. He always kept a horse or two in training, a house in the country which he seldom visited and a good-looking barmaid in Chelsea, whose flat, generously paid for by himself, he often visited. Mrs O'Lully did not look too unkindly on Kenneth's deviations. When his Chelsea excursions were reported by a friend she used a phrase she had heard her maternal grandmother use once; to spare his wife a thorough gentleman always keeps a good hack. Time slipped merrily by and eventually Kenneth died unobtrusively in his sleep. He might have left his wife and daughter better off but considering the pace of his gallop through life the story might have been worse.

'If Iris was two years of age in 1939 it would mean that she is now twenty-seven,' Dan calculated.

'It would indeed,' Edwin Seymour agreed.

'How come,' Dan asked, 'such a nice and such an attractive girl never married? I mean I cannot see her having the slightest problem in getting a husband.'

'The same thought had occurred to me,' Edwin Seymour confessed.

'Could the mother have anything to do with it do you think? Dan asked.

'It is easy to see why a suitor would be repulsed, that is a suitor who would not know the mother well.'

'Yes,' Dan said and he closed his eyes. Edwin Seymour looked briefly if askance at his client. He wondered what ran through the mind behind the hooded eyes. Imperceptibly he shook his head and smiled. The busy road which opened continuously before him was sufficiently taxing.

24

MARGO REICEY made no effort to conceal her annoyance when the phone rang.

'I'm sorry darling,' she apologised to the young man who sat at his ease in an armchair near the sitting-room fire. It was a cold April day. Outside there was a driving wind often filled with rain. It howled in the chimney and rattled the window panes. The young man snuggled deeper into the chair and lifted his glass from the floor. The whiskey was still hot. On its surface a dozen cloves, surrounding a large slice of orange, floated like insects. He sipped it gratefully.

'Better answer it,' he said to Margo. 'It might be important.'

She looked at her watch. The time was a quarter to eleven. Who on earth was likely to be ringing so early in the day? It could be one of her in-laws. On the other hand it might be the agency. To pass the time since Dicey died nine months before she frequently took part-time work. The money meant nothing to her. Her husband had been insured for fifty thousand pounds and there was his interest in the firm. The house was paid for and there were several thousand pounds still in the bank from a joint thrift account. A month after Dicey's death she had gone home to Wexford for a long rest. The family home in Drumlee was less than a quarter of a mile from an extensive and unfrequented strand. Here she would walk morning and evening by herself. She missed Dicey more than she ever imagined she would. After a month she felt an improvement within herself. Her depression lifted and she decided to visit Europe. After a long, conducted tour she returned to London and at once registered with a nursing agency.

The young man who occupied the armchair was deep-chested, dark-visaged and in his prime. He had been aware of these assets for a considerable time and when he set eyes on Margo as she crossed the site to Tom Reicey's temporary office a week before he resolved to train every resource at his command on this incredibly alluring creature. All his instincts told him it would be worth while. Finding out who she was took less than an hour. Finding out where she lived was a formality.

'You're wasting your time there,' the office girl who had given him the address informed him. What she implied was that he would have less difficulty with herself.

Paddy Joe Doolin was a Dubliner. He had left the city of his birth for two reasons. The first was his family. His wife had, as the neighbours put it, let herself go. By this they meant that she no longer looked after her appearance and that she was running to fat. When they married, in a hurry, Paddy Joe had been 20 and she 17. Now 7 years later there were 7 children. Paddy Joe's second reason for leaving Ireland was that he did not feel obliged to answer a court summons for assault. He broke bail and fled on the eve of the court. The assault consisted of an interference with a thirty-five year old housewife who lived in a nearby flat. The woman might have charged him with more than interference but she dreaded the effect the publicity might have on her school-going children. All she wanted she told the civic guard who took her statement was an assurance that he would never interfere with her again.

Paddy Joe's first glimpse of Margo Reicey affected him profoundly. He was completely overcome. The following weekend when he drew his weekly wages of twenty-five pounds he placed three pounds in a registered envelope. In a short note he explained to his wife that a concrete block had fallen on his foot and left him idle for four days. He explained that the three pounds he was sending her was all the money he had left after paying for his digs. Dressed in the one good suit he possessed he repaired to the precincts of Margo's house and waited. He arrived at half-past six and from then till a quarter to eight he walked up and down the long street. At quarter to eight she appeared. She wore a light white mackintosh and carried a frail umbrella. Without hesitating for the barest fraction of a second Paddy Joe Doolin accosted her a few yards from her door. He was fully aware of the fact that she would probably be frightened but that she would, if his intuition was right, be impressed by his rugged good looks and physique.

'Excuse me,' Paddy Joe Doolin spoke in a subdued tone and ventured a smile which spread from one side of his face to the other. He knew his teeth would not let him down in the circumstances. 'You're Mrs Reicey aren't you?' he said respectfully and politely. Surprised and puzzled Margo nodded.

'My name is Paddy Joe Doolin,' Paddy Joe announced earnestly. He thrust forward a hand. In spite of herself Margo took it. He shook her hand briefly and gently and let it go. 'I'm honoured to meet you,' he said.

'Who are you?' she asked. 'How come you know my name?'

'Oh God but that's a long story,' Paddy Joe Doolin said. Margo took him in with one swift experienced glance. He was a good-looking scoundrel all right but she was on her way to the Old Vic and all that sort of thing was long behind her.

'You must excuse me,' she said curtly, 'but I have to be on my way.'

'Please let me come with you,' he said.

'What you ask is impossible,' she replied as determinedly as she could. She hoped he did not notice the tremor in her voice.

'Please,' he begged. 'Just as far as the corner.'

'Now look here,' Margo's voice was suddenly firm. 'Don't put me to the embarrassment of calling a policeman.'

'Sorry,' Paddy Joe Doolin said. 'There's no need for that. I'd never embarrass you.' He could hardly restrain his triumph. He knew he had come up with a winning line. Apologetically he stepped out of her way and as humbly as he could bent his head in atonement.

'Look,' Margo said when she saw his utter dejection, 'I don't know you from Adam and I don't want to seem unkind but you must realise that I am a defenceless woman and you're a black stranger, a very powerful black stranger.'

Again the disarming smile from Paddy Joe. 'Have one drink with me and I'll explain everything,' he said.

'Indeed I won't,' Margo said crossly.

For reasons that she could not fully explain later she allowed herself to be propelled along the street into the main thoroughfare and thence to a lounge bar while all the time her escort kept up a flow of humorous chatter. In the pub he bared his soul. He had seen her for the first time in his life as she crossed the site. He used various ruses to find out who she was and where she lived and now here he was with his heart in his hand. His very audacity brought a smile to Margo's face.

'Don't ever stop smiling,' he said. In all she made three serious attempts to tear herself away to visit the theatre as she had planned but each time he cajoled and wheedled her into staying. After the third gin she gave up and told herself that it could do no harm. He was such a frank person. He went back over the poverty of his youth reminding her every few minutes that he could not believe she was really having a drink with him. All his clothes until he was eighteen, he told her, were bought by his mother at jumble sales all over the city of Dublin. They were always too big for him. She listened fascinated. Suddenly it was closing time. He walked her back to her home. On the stone steps that led to the door she stood fumbling through her handbag for a key. Impulsively he took her in his arms and kissed the nape of her neck. She trembled but did not respond otherwise. Neither did she try to break away.

'Don't send me away,' he whispered fiercely.

That had been the previous weekend. He had suggested towards mid-week that he leave his digs and move in with her. She convinced him it would be out of the question. The mention of Tom Reicey had helped. She did not want him living in the house and yet she did not want to break with him. From the beginning her hunger had been unappeasable. She was slightly afraid of him, slightly uncertain but she yielded to him without demur whenever he demanded it. She craved such demands incessantly. During the week he came and went. She wondered if he was working.

When the phone rang for the third time she decided to answer it.

'I think you had better leave now,' she told Paddy Joe Doolin. 'If you like you can come round tonight. I never can tell who's likely to call during the day.'

'I'll go after you answer the phone,' he said.

Margo was surprised when she learned who the caller was.

'The last time we met,' Dan Murray told her, 'was at your husband's funeral. I hope you've recovered from the ordeal by now.'

'Oh Lord yes,' Margo answered. 'The worst is over this long time.'

'I'll tell you why I rang,' Dan said. 'You see I have a horse running at Stokely this afternoon and I've been told by the trainer that bar a fall he's going to win. My problem is that when he wins I'll have nobody to lead him into the winners' enclosure to accept the plate. I thought about it a lot and I'm convinced that you are the one person who could do a good job on it. Sorry the notice is so short.'

From the long silence which ensued Dan was certain she must have hung up. Dammit, he thought, the least she might have done was answer. Minutes passed and finally she spoke.

'You couldn't have rung at a worse time,' Margo said. 'I have a friend here at the moment and I have an appointment tonight.' Margo would have liked to go to Stokely but she had long since lost her appetite for the sort of respectable relationship which might lead ultimately to a proposal of marriage. She knew that if she accepted there was every likelihood it would be difficult to avoid seeing him regularly. She had what she wanted. She had long since decided that if she were to marry again it would be an Englishman, somebody a good deal older. In fact there was a number of such prospects hanging around, well-off respectable fellows who sometimes squired her to hospital dances and other functions which demanded partners. She had met these in her capacity as a part-time nurse.

'Just for this evening,' Dan Murray persisted. 'He's a good horse and it would be a terrible shame if there was nobody to lead him in. There's also the fact that you can back him and make a few quid for yourself ...'

While he spoke she tried to recall all the things she knew about him. He was, there was no denying, one of the most successful builders in London and didn't he have a dance-hall and heaven knows what else? He was quiet and inward-looking as she recalled and he had been friendly with Patricia Dee but that hadn't come off because he had waited too long. In fact that could well be the story of his life as far as acquiring the right woman was concerned. He was anything but a gay card. The most truthful thing that could be said about him was that all work and no play made him something of a dull boy. She had liked him when they met first at the Shillelagh.

'It's a lovely afternoon for racing,' he went on.

'I'm sorry,' Margo responded earnestly, 'but it's out of the question just now.'

'Some other time then?'

She had been right from the beginning. His perseverance convinced her that he would be playing for keeps. She decided to adhere to her resolve. Never again would she be permanently tied to an Irishman.

'Yes then. Some other time,' she said politely.

Dan lowered the phone slowly and thoughtfully. He had felt certain that the lure of leading in a possible winner and the fact that she once liked him would have resulted in her accepting. There was also her love of money. Hadn't she married for it! He was disappointed, far more than he had a right to be. At once he dialled Sylvester – he had told him about Firearm a few days before. Sylvester had begged for permission to contact Bert Edgecombe. Since their release from prison Bert and Sylvester had seen a good deal of each other.

'He'll do a thorough SP job,' Sylvester had promised Dan. 'He knows the ropes.'

'No, no, no,' Dan had said. 'I promised Ricketts.'

'If you lay the money SP he won't know.'

As he waited Dan became slightly embittered towards Margo Reicey. He could have asked several girls but he had been fool enough to choose her.

'O'Doherty speaking.' It was Sylvester's voice.

'Contact Edgecombe,' Dan told him.

'Yes sir,' Sylvester replied gleefully. 'Right away I will. Might I ask what led you to change your mind?'

'We must make the most of our opportunities,' Dan said.

Laying down the phone Dan dialled a third number. As he waited for a reply he was tempted to ring Margo Reicey a second time to ask her for an explanation. He was on the point of doing so when a woman's voice answered at the other end. It was Iris O'Lully. Dan laid before her the proposal he had put to Margo Reicey. The response was the opposite of Margo's.

'I can't believe it's me you want.' Iris O'Lully could hardly conceal her surprise. 'Are you sure it's not somebody else?'

'Well it's the number you gave me that night at the Winchester Willows,' Dan told her. 'That means it would have to be you.'

'The answer is yes,' Iris O'Lully assured him.

WHEN MARGO returned, having disposed of Dan Murray Paddy Joe stood with his back to the fire.

'You were a long time,' he said.

She shrugged an apology.

'Who was it anyway?'

'Somebody I used to know.'

'What did he want?'

'Oh come now,' Margo retorted with a sternness she instantly regretted. 'I must have some privacy.'

Paddy Joe stood sullenly with his back to the fire. Margo mistook his anger for hurt.

'I'm sorry,' she apologised.

'You wouldn't by any chance have any money?' he asked. He chose his moment well.

'Were you not working this week? Of course you

weren't. I'm sorry.'

She left the room for an instant and returned with her handbag. Rummaging through its contents she could produce no better than a solitary pound note and some change.

'This won't do,' she said looking at him and shaking her head. He shook his. From the handbag she took a key. She went to a sideboard where she knelt preparatory to putting the key in the lock.

'There's some cash here,' she explained. 'I keep a little reserve. I don't like going to the bank.'

She turned the key in the lock and opened the door of the sideboard. She withdrew a larger, older handbag. Holding it close to her breast she withdrew two ten pound notes. She returned the handbag and rose to her feet.

'You'll have to do better than that,' Paddy Joe pleaded. 'I need more. I have to pay my digs. I have to send money home.'

Margo withdrew two extra ten pound notes and was about to return the bag when she looked up in alarm. Paddy Joe was standing over her, feet apart.

'I think,' he said matter of factly, 'you had better give me the lot.'

'You've had all you're going to have,' Margo snapped. She thrust the bag inside and turned the key. Paddy Joe lifted her firmly to her feet.

'Now don't be mean,' he cautioned. 'You won't miss it.'

'Maybe not,' Margo said, 'but you're not getting any more. I've given you forty pounds.

'Give me that key,' he said and attempted to prize it from her clenched fist. She managed to struggle free. He seized her from behind as she attempted to run from the room. He spun her around and slapped her face. The force of the blow sent her staggering across the room. Vainly she looked around for some sort of weapon. He stood between her and the fire where the coal shovel stood invitingly in its bucket. Suddenly he lunged forward and brought her to the ground. Getting astride her he hit her twice with clenched fist on the face. The second blow was unnecessary. She lost consciousness after the first. The key had fallen from her hand on to the carpet. Fumbling and panting he turned it in the lock. Greedily he opened the handbag. All that remained was another forty pounds. He tried all its crevices. Disgusted he stuffed the money in his pocket. Bending over Margo he seized her by the shoulders and shook her violently.

'Is there any more?' he shouted.

There was no response. The lovely head hung limply to one side, its beautifully coiffured black hair trailing on to the carpet. He slapped her sharply twice but she failed to recover consciousness. Hurriedly he rose. As he left he heard her moaning faintly. He was relieved that she had regained consciousness. It was his guess that she would not call the police. It did not occur to him that there might be other lesser-known agencies available to her free of charge.

PADDY JOE Doolin was well-known to Dan and to Crazy Horse. He had once patronised the Molly Malone. He would never do so again and, should he try, there would a special reception awaiting him. On his only visit a young country girl, fresh from the west of Ireland, had been foolish enough to believe that he was single. After considerable persuasion over several dances she consented to be escorted as far as her bus stop. On the way she resisted several amorous advances by Paddy Joe. When she told him she wanted to return to the ballroom he struck her on the face, almost knocking her. She screamed and he struck her again but before he could harm her further a running figure hove into view. Paddy Joe was well used to taking care of himself but the size and the dogged lumbering gait of the oncoming giant sent him scurrying out of danger. Crazy Horse lifted the girl in his arms and brought her back to the Molly Malone. He had seen her leave with Paddy Joe Doolin. Something told him that it was an unlikely partnership. Doolin was a marked man from that night forth. Some night in some pub there would be a phone-call and two, maybe three capable men would repay him for his assault on the girl.

AS HE stood in the owners' and trainers' stand in Stokely Racecourse he watched her in the distance as she made her way from the tote where she had placed a modest wager. She was one of the most attractive and well-dressed women at the meeting. Iris O'Lully was the sort of girl it would be impossible to dislike. Dan guessed that his mother would be very much on this girl's side. Her quiet and easy-going disposition would impress Mary Murray. As she came towards him she waved and he descended the concrete steps to join her. He had not, as yet, placed a wager of any kind. It was the fourth race of the day, the Stokely Novice Chase with an added purse of three hundred sovereigns. The distance, over fences, was three miles. Firearm was installed as favourite although by no means a firm one. There were 11 other runners. Taking Iris by the arm he escorted her to the parade ring. The horses were being led in when they arrived. They both leaned over the white timber railings.

'Do you know anything about gambling?' Dan asked.

'Enough,' she returned.

'I'll let you in on something,' he informed her. 'A friend of mine is doing an SP job on Firearm.'

'Len Ricketts won't like it.'

'That may be,' Dan said with a smile, 'but if he has his rules and regulations I also have mine. Will you help me?'

'Was this the reason you invited me?'

'No,' he replied truthfully. 'I'm sorry you should get that impression. I invited you because I like you and for no other reason.'

For this she pressured his arm gratefully.

'What do you want me to do?' she asked.

'Let's have a look at the bookies' boards and see what's happening.'

Together they moved slowly along the line of raucous bookmakers. Firearm was being offered at odds of 3 to 1 but there was no evidence of support even if he was the shortest-priced entrant on view. It was a race which attracted little or no betting. Dan noticed that there seemed to be some interest in the second favourite, a mare called Greasy Joan. She had been backed from 9 to 2 down to 7 to 2. He made up his mind quickly. He was certain that Bert Edgecombe's team and Sylvester's contacts would be laying the money on Firearm just about then. Without flurry he extracted his wallet and handed two hundred pounds to Iris.

'Start further down,' Dan ordered, 'and at my signal lay this money on Greasy Joan. It's unlikely that any one bookmaker at that end will take more than fifty pounds at this stage but get on all you can at the best odds available.'

'But Greasy Joan isn't going to win,' Iris O'Lully protested.

'I hope not,' Dan said, 'but if we succeed in making her favourite it's just possible that Firearm's price will go out. Now move down the line and act when I signal.'

Dan moved in the other direction and stood in front of the busiest board at the meeting. By a stroke of good fortune the bookmaker in question suddenly made Greasy Joan a joint favourite by extending Firearm's price to seven to two. Furiously Dan signalled to Iris. Then he waited for the first faint wave of alarm. It came at once. Bookmakers further down were slashing Greasy Joan's odds. Dan suddenly thrust a sheaf of notes upwards.

'Fifty pounds on Greasy Joan,' he called. Reluctantly the bookmaker accepted the money and confirmed the bet to his clerk. A number of observers sought the same odds but the price was slashed to 3 to 1. At the same time Firearm was being offered at fours. The general support was steady for Greasy Joan. Dan invested another fifty pounds and the odds on the mare were shortened again. She was now a firm favourite at 5 to 2 while the odds on Firearm varied. Some offered him at fours, others at fives and yet some, anxious to balance their books, shouted sixes.

Quivering with excitement Iris O'Lully clutched Dan's arm. The conspiracy had moulded them into a team. Together they ran to the stand which was already filling. The horses had left the parade ring and were cantering past towards the start at the far side of the course.

'God,' Iris O'Lully whispered, 'this is awful.'

'What's awful?' Dan's query was indulgent.

'The excitement. What happens if Greasy Joan wins?'

'I lose thousands,' Dan said.

'Oh God,' she said again. 'And if Firearm wins?'

'I'll win an awful lot of money.'

'Suppose neither wins?'

'You cheer for Firearm and don't you forget it.'

'Oh I will, I will,' Iris whispered enthusiastically.

There's no doubt but she is a very charming girl, Dan thought. Inevitably he compared her with Margo Reicey. Iris O'Lully had beauty but she did not radiate it the way Margo did. Margo stood out in a crowd. Iris became part of it. Margo forced people to look at her. Iris was demure. Dan could not be absolutely certain but it seemed to him there was much to be said for the latter.

25

DAN MURRAY sat in the front office of the Mitcham estate. His head throbbed slightly but he smiled to himself as he went back over the events of the day and night before. Firearm after a shaky start when he nearly came down at the first soon asserted himself and won comfortably. Dan well knew that in the mail in the very near future there would be a letter from Len Ricketts asking him if he would be good enough to seek alternative arrangements for the training of his horse. What matter. It had been well worthwhile. Sylvester's squad managed to lay fifteen hundred pounds and Bert's team almost two thousand pounds. They might have had more but if word reached the course there was no telling what Ricketts might do. Most likely if he thought he was being used in a gamble he would withdraw the horse. He would have the power to do so. Firearm was returned at 5 to 1 which left the syndicate with a gain of seventeen thousand pounds.

After the last race at Stokely, Dan and Iris decided not to return to London at once. With the silver trophy safely tucked away in the locked boot of the car they drove to Guildford and had dinner at a small hotel. Understandably there was champagne and as Iris laughingly pointed out, once a person started the evening on champagne it was next to impossible to change to anything else.

The dinner had been excellent. As soon as they had finished Iris excused herself in order to phone her mother.

'It's not that she'll be worried since she knows who I'm with,' she explained to Dan, 'but she's so alone since Daddy died.'

'You can tell her,' Dan had insisted, 'that I'll have you home straight away. I have a feeling she might like to join in the celebrations.'

While Iris was phoning her mother Dan sought out the manager of the hotel and told him he needed a case of the very best champagne. On the road back to London they had conversed non-stop. When she asked him if Firearm's winnings meant much financially she was quite staggered at his rough estimation of what the winnings were likely to be.

Between the effects of the champagne and the intimacy of the car Iris O'Lully was tempted to ask questions she would not normally ask. The truth was that Dan fascinated her. His decisiveness at the race meeting and his almost total disregard for money made her even more curious. She was careful, however, not to appear nosy or crudely inquisitive.

She began by asking him if his parents were alive. It was a good opener because, generally speaking, in mentioning parents one was certain to arrive at beginnings.

'Yes,' Dan assured her. 'They're both alive and well and I have one brother younger than I am who is married in London.'

Iris laughed.

'Serves me right for being so nosy,' she said.

'No you're not,' Dan contradicted. He went on to tell her about his first night in London and of his interminable wait at Bertham railway station. 'It's quite a change from now,' he said wistfully. 'There I was with my lone suitcase and a few pounds between me and the poorhouse. Look at me now, driving a Jaguar with a beautiful girl from another world by my side, a successful racehorse owner and with more money than I'll ever manage to spend. I'd better pinch myself and make sure I'm not dreaming.'

They laughed. At her insistence he elaborated on his early days in London. She was an appreciative listener and he knew from her occasional responses that she was keenly interested in his narrative. He told her of his first contract, of the nights without sleep, about Sylvester and his term in jail.

He told her about the fight at the Shillelagh although he had not intended to. He had never mentioned the fight to any other woman. The woman who mattered most at the time had heard it from the wrong sources and had disapproved altogether. Just as well he thought. He imagined it would be hell to be married to her. Well maybe not for him since he had been very special to her. At the time he had considered himself unfortunate to have been let down. Later when he had time to be honest with himself he was forced to admit that it was this letdown that really started him on the road to success. It had been partly to spite Patricia that he had worked so hard. It had also been partly to forget her. The end result was success long before he thought it possible on such a scale.

Iris O'Lully listened fascinated. She had never met any-body quite like Dan Murray. She admired and respected him all the more for his candour. She was not a snob and his beginnings did not matter in the least to her; she was certain that he was the kind of man who would be proud rather than self-conscious of them. When he had finished she sat silently huddled in the front seat looking thoughtfully in front of her.

'What a sheltered and absolutely useless life I've led,' she sighed.

'That's nonsense,' Dan said.

'Compared to you and people like you,' Iris said sadly, 'I am a totally ineffective person. I also think there's something else you should know about me.'

'What would that be?' Dan asked.

'Think what you will of me but I've never had an intimate relationship with a man.' She laughed awkwardly.

'I expected that to be the case,' he said with a smile.

'You still want to spend the remainder of the evening with me?'

'Indeed I do,' Dan assured her. 'I very much do.'

He had spent the night at the O'Lullys. It was an old house tucked away in a quiet backwater of Chelsea. He had been unable and unwilling to leave the comfortable sitting-room where Iris, her mother and himself had drunk bottle after bottle of champagne. He had to be helped upstairs to bed at an hour which he could not recall. He certainly recal-led most of the conversation which had been monopolised by Deirdre O'Lully, Iris' mother, not that he had objected to the monologue. Far from it. She had regaled them with stories of her youth and of the free-swearing, wench-struck, colourful, Anglo-Irish Protestant classes who hunted and drank their way out of generations of supremacy.

Irish independence had ended all that although it would never be quite dead. The native Irish still looked on in quiet amusement at the far flung hunt balls and coming-out parties. They listened patiently to the outrageous ascendancy accents. It was all a harmless relic from the past. It was a question of enjoying rather than tolerating. One could afford to be indulgent towards a relic.

A FORTNIGHT to the day after Firearm's win Dan called to the Mitcham office and enquired after Sylvester. He had failed to locate him at any of the sites.

'I don't think he'll be in today,' the receptionist informed him.

'Did he say so?' Dan asked.

'No,' the girl said, 'but he wasn't in yesterday or the day before.'

He found his friend at the Colorado. He was very drunk and quite maudlin. Sylvester looked at Dan for a long while.

'I meant to tell you before this,' Sylvester wept as he spoke. 'I suppose I should have told you at the beginning.'

'Told me what?' Dan put the question sympathetically.

'I'm not at all well.'

'I've known that for some time my friend,' Dan informed him. 'Don't you think it's time we did something about it?'

'Something about what?' Sylvester focused bleary eyes on Dan.

'Whatever it is that's wrong with you.'

'Do you know what's wrong with me?'

'No but I know that it's nothing that can't be set to rights.'

'I have what doctors call carcinoma of the lung. That's the medical name for it. Laymen like you and I would call it cancer of the lung. It's a dirty, rotten, stinking, loathsome bastard. It's foul and it's filthy and the man that has it is a walking corpse.'

Sylvester's drunken voice rose shrilly. 'That's what I am. A walking bloody corpse. I never had an ounce of luck since I left that accursed seminary. It's God's final fling at me.' Sylvester clenched both fists and beat on the bar counter.

Gently Dan grasped him round the shoulders and steered him into the lounge. They sat in an alcove, Sylvester with his head buried in his hands

'How can you be absolutely sure that it's what you say it is without a second opinion?' Dan asked.

'I've had a second and a third opinion. All the tests were conclusive. I insisted on finding out the truth. As a matter of fact I knew it was something malignant from the beginning. I always knew that I'd fall foul of some terrible bloody disease. It's my luck.'

Sylvester told Dan he had felt the first searing stab under his left shoulder blade several weeks before he decided to go to a doctor. He dismissed the isolated dart of pain but when it returned a week later he became worried. Yet he was reluctant to do anything about it. He theorised that if it was something bad there could not possibly be a cure for it and that if it was nothing serious it would go away when it felt like it.

From time to time the pain would visit the same area. He purchased a bottle of liniment at a chemist's thinking it might be no more than an arthritic twinge. He had Crazy Horse apply it. For a day there was no sign of the pain and then suddenly as he sat in the Irish Club one night it came back with a vengeance. He almost doubled over. After that would come uncontrollable fits of coughing and on a few occasions when he was alone in his room he thought he would surely smother. He decided as a last resort to visit a doctor. There followed a series of tests at a nearby clinic and one fatal morning he was summoned before his physician.

'I would like very much,' the doctor said, 'if you sought a second opinion. I would like it to be an independent one.'

Sylvester did as he was told. Similar tests followed and after three days he was summoned by the first doctor.

'I'm afraid you'll have to go to hospital,' the doctor said

with a professional smile. There was something in the smile that put Sylvester on his guard.

'Fair enough,' he said, 'but you'll have to tell me why.'

'Can't be sure,' the doctor said blandly, 'a few weeks in hospital will tell all.'

'I have no intention of going to hospital until I find out what's wrong with me. You must tell me. I have a right to know.' Although he persisted he knew at the back of his mind that the doctor was hedging desperately and that there was bad news in the offing.

'Mr O'Doherty you are a sick man and it's imperative for your own good that you go to hospital at once. Won't you accept my word as your doctor that it's essential for you to go?'

'No,' Sylvester said angrily. 'I can't. Look doctor you'll have to stop treating me like a child and tell me the worst. I have no kith or kin. There's only myself.'

As if he were himself in pain the doctor sighed.

'It is never the function of a doctor to burden a patient with news of the worst kind. The patient already has enough on his plate by virtue of his illness. I just can't say to you that you have a fatal disease because if I did I would be discounting all the great day-to-day advances in medicine. I would be discounting God. I would have no right and certainly no authority to make such a statement.'

'You're beating about the bush,' Sylvester said.

'No,' the doctor denied the charge. 'I am not. I am your doctor and you are a very sick man. All I am trying to tell you is that we must hope for the best. We must never lose hope and as surely as I sit here there is the possibility that you could get better. I've seen such a case. What I want to impress upon you is that your condition is unsatisfactory and that you must go to hospital.'

'In the name of Jesus will you tell me what I've got?' Sylvester rose from his chair and placed his hands on the doctor's desk. 'I'll walk out of here and I'll never come back if you don't tell me.'

'If you did,' the doctor's face grew suddenly wan, 'it would be easier on both of us.'

'Oh,' Sylvester exclaimed and he fell back into his chair.

'I'm sorry,' the doctor bent his head. During that long moment of truth he could not bring himself to look at his patient. He had conveyed the terrible tidings before to other men but there was no way in which one could grow used to it. It was an awful realisation. He could not know the full extent of the awfulness but he could guess.

'All right,' Sylvester gritted his teeth. 'Is there a name for it?'

'Carcinoma of the lung.'

'You mean cancer of the lung?'

'Yes.'

'How much time?'

'With the proper use of drugs and care I would say that you have a lot of time.'

'How long exactly?'

'I would rather not say.'

'A year?'

The doctor shook his head.

'Six months?'

'It is possible that there is six months left to you.'

'How much is due to you?' Sylvester asked casually.

'You'll have my bill at the beginning of next month.'

'I'll be seeing you,' Sylvester said as he got to his feet.

'Where are you going?' The doctor rose to his feet too.

'To get pissed,' Sylvester said. 'Can you recommend anything better?'

The doctor shook his head.

Sylvester walked quickly out of the room.

Slowly in whispers Sylvester intoned the name of Jesus over and over. In his eyes was the same despairing look which Dan had seen when the verdict was announced in his trial at the Old Bailey. Dan turned his eyes away.

'Be thankful Dan that you have your health,' Sylvester whispered. 'Be thankful every hour and minute of the day.'

Suddenly Dan rose to his feet. 'Let's get out of here,' he urged.

'Where to?' Sylvester asked suspiciously.

'We'll have to go to hospital or at least to some sort of

home where you'll get the best possible care.'

'Not me,' Sylvester said firmly.

'You can't stay here,' Dan said with equal firmness.

'Maybe not but by the Lord God I am not going into a hospital to be confronted by other zombies like myself. What do you take me for?'

Vainly Dan searched for something suitable to say. It was an awkward situation.

'Look,' he said trying to be cheerful, 'there are new cures coming out every day. Any day you pick up a paper there's an announcement about a cancer cure. You mustn't give up hope.'

'Balls,' Sylvester submitted drunkenly.

'At least come back to the flat,' Dan said. 'You'll give yourself a chance to get sorted out.'

'All right,' Sylvester agreed weakly, 'but don't pull any hospital tricks on me Dan. The doctors said that I had between 4 and 6 months. When I find it unbearable I'll sort things out in my own way if you don't mind.'

'No,' Dan said, 'I don't mind.'

'Most chaps when they find out say they won't end up like living skeletons, an embarrassment to everybody, a stinking, decaying, helpless wretch. Yet with all the sworn promises they make to themselves they cling on and on and they become content to hang on to the slimmest, foulest breath of life. I'm not going to do it. I want some shred of dignity attached to my departure and it will have to be pretty soon because by all accounts the mind goes towards the end and the body is purely animal, rotten animal.'

'Let's go,' Dan repeated.

'Let's stop on the way for a quick one,' Sylvester pleaded.

'Of course. Where would you like it to be?'

'The Ritz. Where else?'

DAN WAS by his bedside before he died. He did not die from carcinoma of the lung as the doctors had foretold. He died from barbiturate poisoning as a result of swallowing 40 sleeping capsules. There was an envelope addressed to Dan. In it was a short note which asked him to call to a solicitor in whose care there was a will he had made a few days before. There was also a short farewell message in which he thanked Dan for his long friendship and warned him to take care of his health. It concluded with a request to bury him with his father and mother. The will was vintage Sylvester:

> *Most of my fortune I have already left to mine host of the Leadlathe Arms and to other gentlemen of the same calling ...*

This was far from being true. He certainly drank his wages and his share of the company's profits. His interest, however, in Murray Enterprises was substantial. Dan estimated his share at roughly two hundred and fifty thousand pounds. The will continued:

> *To my friend Cuthbert Edgecombe affectionately known as Bert, I bequeath two thousand pounds to be paid out of my shares in Murray Enterprises by the managing director, Dan Murray. To my friend Richard Daly, alias Crazy Horse, I bequeath the sum of one thousand pounds to be paid by the same Dan Murray. To the right honourable Dick Winterman the sum of a thousand pounds from the said Murray. For the eventual repose of the souls of the living dead, Thomas and Joseph Reicey of Reicey Brothers, I bequeath the sum of ten pounds for masses. The remainder of my worldly goods I bequeath to my dearest friend Daniel Murray. And so the time has come close the book. 'Farewell sweet friends till we meet again'.*

There was no more. Dan saw to it that the mass cards were sent to Tom and Joe Reicey.

Bert Edgecombe, Crazy Horse, Dick Winterman and Dan accompanied the remains to Mayo. After the funeral they went into a public house where Dan ordered four large whiskies. It was to be the start of a three-day drinking bout which would tax their utmost physical reserves. It was, they felt, the least they owed to Sylvester.

MAISIE AND Dora Reicey sat uneasily in the lounge of the Colorado Hotel waiting for Tom. From the moment they left the hospital where they had been to see Margo his mood had been sullen. He had excused himself to make a phone call.

'What do you make of it?' Dora Reicey asked Maisie.

'She was flyin' her kite of course. What else?'

'I wouldn't put it past her,' Dora agreed.

'And to look at her,' Maisie said viciously, 'you'd swear that the jig-a-jig was the last thought in her mind.'

'Those kind are always the worst,' Dora prompted.

Maisie ground her teeth in agreement.

'What made her say 'twas a burglar?' Dora asked in puzzlement.

'Burglar my arse,' was all the answer Maisie supplied. She sat silently taking stock of the others in the lounge. Dora had enough wisdom to remain silent.

In the booth Tom Reicey waited impatiently. He had not believed a word of Margo's tale about her surprising a burglar. He had not been able to question her at length the night before. Her jaw was fractured and her nose broken. She had agreed to a visit by two detectives but merely nodded or shook her head to confirm or deny suggestions. Tom knew instinctively it was a lover. What he desperately wanted to find out was who the lover was. He did not altogether blame Margo. He was disappointed, bitterly so, to think that his brother's wife should so quickly forget her dead husband. Still that was life and Margo was a Reicey whatever else. He redialled the number and waited. Finally there was an answer from the called number.

'Superintendent Telley please,' Tom spoke sharply, 'and tell him it's Tom Reicey will you like a good man.'

'Tom.'

Telley was through almost at once.

'Sorry for the pressure Bill.'

Tom Reicey did not sound apologetic but he was anxious to let Telley know that he did not regard him as a mere lackey.

'Any news?'

'Yes,' Telley answered. 'We apprehended the suspect at

308

half-past three in the morning.'

'Great, great entirely,' Tom thumped the metal coin box with clenched fist. 'Who is he?'

'He's Irish,' Telley informed him. 'His name is Patrick Joseph Doolin and from what we can gather you were his last employer.'

'Ah indeed,' Tom said with what he hoped was normal interest. As it was he trembled violently at the thought of Doolin's assault on his sister-in-law, on a woman who carried the tag of Reicey.

'What will you do with him?' Tom asked.

'We'll hold him of course and charge him.'

'I want you to release him on bail.'

'I'm afraid that's out of the question.'

'You'll have to release him if I get my sister-in-law to say he's not the man. Look Bill this is important to me and when something is important to Tom Reicey the cost doesn't matter at all.'

'I think it might be arranged.'

'Good,' Tom could have shouted with joy. 'God but I appreciate this Bill.'

'I'll let him go at once then.'

'No, not at once.' Tom was insistent. 'Release him at exactly ten o'clock tonight. Can you arrange that?'

'I think that will be all right Tom.'

TOM REICEY sat at the wheel of the large Commer van. By his side sat his brother Joe and seated behind them sat the brothers Ruckard and Mick Morrikan. The time was five to ten and already the street lights were switched on. It was not yet dark and a slight drizzle of warm rain moistened the pavements. The police station was no different from any of the well-preserved, three-storey, Edwardian houses that lined the wide thoroughfare on either side. It was not until one was upon it that the royal insignia intimated what sort of business was conducted behind the large, oaken door.

'What time is it Joe?' Tom Reicey's voice was calm and business-like.

'I make it two minutes to ten o'clock,' Joe answered.

'Same as me,' Tom said. 'How about you Ruckard?'

'I'm only a minute away from it Tom.'

Ruckard Morrikan always used his employer's Christian name. Tom Reicey was such that it would sound ridiculous if a workman of Ruckard's skills called him by anything else.

'I make it down on top of the hour.' Mick Morrikan slowly returned the heavy Ingersoll to his pocket.

'All right then boys,' Tom Reicey moistened his lips. 'It's hard telling whether he'll come this way or whether he'll go down the road into Hammersmith. Better for us he should come this way. It would spare us having to follow him.'

'Renting the van was a good idea,' Mick Morrikan said. 'If it was one of the firm's vans now he'd spot it right off.'

'Boys,' Tom Reicey cautioned, 'this is a dodgy merchant. Let's go over it once more. Proceed Michael.'

'The minute he leaves the police station,' Mick Morrikan repeated his instructions for the umpteenth time, 'I quietly open the back door of the van and when he passes I jump out in my socks and rap him on the head with this.'

He held the old police truncheon aloft. 'A good smart rap, enough to bring him down. Then Ruckard and myself lift him between us into the back of the van where we keep him subdued till we get into the country.'

'That's lovely, lovely entirely,' Tom Reicey said. Tom did not ask for a recapitulation of the alternative plan should Paddy Joe go into Hammersmith. Tom knew that Paddy Joe would not be that foolish. At five minutes past ten by Tom's watch the figure of a man emerged from the police station. It was Paddy Joe Doolin. He looked up and then down. His eyes took in the parked cars and vans along the avenue. He stood still for several minutes looking up and down. Then he moved quickly in the direction of the Commer van. Tom and Joe Reicey had removed themselves into it's cavernous interior so that there was no sign of life evident to anybody approaching. Paddy Joe Doolin had a jaunty walk and he moved quickly. He was superbly fit. As he passed by the van the door opened noiselessly and Mick Morrikan, without his shoes, leaped out.

Instinctively Paddy Joe turned but as he did the truncheon was already swinging in its unstoppable arc. It came down smartly on his head right over the forehead. He fell at once. Without hurry Ruckard Morrikan stepped from the van. With Mick's aid he lifted the semi-inert form into the back. Tom established himself once more in the driver's seat. He drove slowly down the road past the police station where he turned the van and drove back the way he had come. Then he veered left after a mile and crossed the city through its main artery. After a half an hour they found themselves on the road to Chatham.

'Where are you taking me?' Paddy Joe Doolin had been awake for some time. Ruefully he conceded to himself that escape was out, at least for the present. 'Where are you taking me? In the name of God tell me.' There was a plea for mercy concealed in the question.

'Quieten him,' Tom Reicey commanded.

Immediately Mick Morrikan applied the truncheon. They drove silently for several miles and then turned off into a by-road. They drove for a further two miles and branched off again on to a little used track.

'This is as good a place as any,' Tom Reicey announced. 'Is he fully conscious?'

'Yes,' Ruckard answered. 'He's his sweet self again.'

'You know why you're here, Doolin?' Again it was Tom who put the question.

'Whatever it is you have the wrong man.'

'You assaulted a woman yesterday. Don't deny it.'

'No. No. I did not. You have the wrong man. Even the police cleared me.'

'They did,' Tom Reicey informed him, 'because I told them to do so.'

Paddy Joe Doolin gasped. Only then did he become fully aware of the deadly peril in which he found himself. It had been too easy. He had suspected nothing when he was told that he had been bailed out. He should have guessed. Who would redeem a person like himself, unless it was to wreak vengeance?

'Are you going to admit it?' Tom Reicey asked with

311

growing impatience.

'How can I admit something I never did,' Paddy Joe lied.

'Search him,' Tom Reicey commanded. Roughly the Morrikan brothers went through his pockets. It was easy to locate the seventy and odd pounds which were left over from the eighty pounds. Without further talk they led him out of the van. When he attempted to break loose Ruckard Morrikan lashed out with a huge fist. There was a sickening thump. Paddy Joe slumped against his captors.

'Hold him upright and hold him firmly.' There was a note of merciless authority in Tom Reicey's tone. Taking his time he struck Doolin twice with clenched fist on each eye. He struck him in the pelvis with left and right fists. Doolin was held fast by Joe Reicey and Mick Morrikan.

'Get his legs apart,' Tom called to Ruckard Morrikan.

Ruckard went to the rear of Doolin and kicked the legs apart. Tom Reicey stood back a yard and swung his right boot at a point between the victim's legs. There was a despairing groan from Paddy Joe Doolin. It was faint but it was unmistakably agonising.

'Keep him standing,' Tom Reicey called out. Again he drew back his boot and aimed at the same target. This time there was no response from Paddy Joe Doolin. Luckily for him he had lost consciousness.

'Get his clothes off.'

At Tom's command the Morrikan brothers stripped the lifeless form down to the last garment. Joe Reicey made a neat bundle of the clothes and tossed them into the van. The naked shape of Paddy Joe Doolin lay huddled and white in the faint moonlight. Tom Reicey drew a last savage kick which connected with the bloody mess under Doolin's arched rump.

'Come on,' he said, 'before I do him in.'

'He'll not mount anything for a bit,' Ruckard Morrikan tried to force the laughter into his voice. The joke fell flat and the four men silently returned to the van.

In less than an hour Paddy Joe Doolin regained consciousness. He could not believe that he was alive and able to move his limbs. Then came a burning bolt of excruciating pain. He looked at the source and vomited in disgust.

WHEN MARGO left the hospital she phoned the number of an apartment house off Hammersmith, Broadway. No, Henry Wilkes was not in. Yes, she would see to it that he got her number. Margo was not in the least startled when the telephone rang on the stroke of midnight. It was Henry Wilkes, the bus-conductor from Salford, gentle Henry, ever-tender and understanding and the only man who had consistently infiltrated Margo's intimate fantasising from their first meeting onwards.

26

DAN, IRIS O'Lully and Noreen Carey sat in the sun-drenched garden in front of the long, low farmhouse. It was mid-June. The air was fragrant, almost heavy with the scent of countless blooms. Faintly from a distant meadow came the drowsy monotone of a mowing machine. The birds, so vocal all morning, were now silent, completely overcome by the noonday heat. Iris O'Lully excused herself and went indoors.

'I'm glad all is going well for you,' Dan said.

'Yes it's a good farm,' Noreen admitted.

'But nothing could ever replace Eddie?' Dan suggested and he scrutinised her face carefully for reaction.

'There is somebody,' Noreen said and she had the grace to bend her head. 'I haven't told anybody. You're the first to know and I need to know what you think.'

'Do I know him?' Dan asked.

'Hardly. He's a widower with two grown-up sons, both done for. He's a middling-sized farmer over Ballylicken way. He's a very quiet man. I think I could be happy with him. The loneliness has been unbearable since Eddie died. Our oldest lad is ready to take over the farm. I hear he's courting strong and I have a feeling that one of these days he's going to come to me and tell me he wants to get married. One day they'll all be married and where will I be then?'

'I think you're doing the right thing,' Dan counselled.

'I spent most of my married life alone. I never had Eddie when I really wanted him. I feel I'm entitled to the companionship and love that I know this man can give me.'

'Let me know the day,' Dan said, 'and I'll be there to give the bride away.'

'You were always a dear friend, Dan.'

Noreen laid a hand on his, squeezed his palm and drew the hand away again. There was no more than the suggestion of a tear in her eye but he felt she was relieved that she had confided in somebody.

'You won't say a word to anyone just yet, will you Dan?'

He shook his head. 'You'll hear nothing after me,' he assured her.

'Tell me about yourself or rather tell me about yourself and Iris.'

'What do you think of her?'

'She's a beautiful girl. How long have you known her?'

'Nearly two years now.'

'And do you have an understanding.'

'Well I asked her to marry me after Sylvester died but she asked me to wait. I'm afraid I didn't press her very hard.'

'And did you ask her again?'

'More or less.'

'I have the feeling Dan Murray that marriage is the last thought in your head. I think you're very foolish not to marry this girl. Does your mother like her?'

Dan nodded his head.

'Your father?'

Again the nod.

'What's holding you back then?'

'She mightn't have me and besides she has a mother.'

'You ask her Dan and you ask her soon or it'll be too late. I hate to say this but remember you were late before. Don't let this opportunity go Dan. I promise you'll be happy.'

Iris returned from the house stopping on the way to admire the surroundings. Catching Noreen's eyes she waved and smiled.

'She's beautiful,' Noreen whispered.

'Yes,' Dan said. 'There's no one could deny her that.' He got to his feet. 'We'll have to be going,' he said, 'but we'll come again before we go back to London.'

'I'll look forward to it.'

Noreen took Iris's hands in hers. 'I hope we'll see much

315

more of each other,' she said.

'I hope so too,' Iris responded warmly.

As they drove down the hillside Iris looked out of the window across the wild, heather-covered slopes. The scene changed dramatically as they neared the valley floor. They passed the brook where generations of lovers had dipped their feet in the pool under the tiny waterfall.

'Stop. Please stop here a moment,' Iris appealed.

Dan stopped and reversed the car. They walked across the mountainside until they arrived at the watercourse. The stream was crystal clear. The cascading drops of tumbling water glittered in the sunshine.

'It's a little paradise,' Iris declared. 'Did you come here when you were young?'

'No,' Dan told her, 'but it was a favourite haunt of courting couples.'

'You mean people like us,' Iris O'Lally said and she smiled.

Iris grew suddenly serious. She knew the question he was framing in his mind and she did not know what her answer would be. She loved him as she had never loved anybody but her fear was that he did not love her. The first time he had asked her to marry was after the death of his best friend. She felt honestly that what he really wanted then was her sympathy. She could have married him but the thought lurked in her mind that there might come a time when he would think that she had taken advantage of him.

He had been shattered then, so shattered that he had been ill and run down for months afterwards. These factors, Iris felt, would have made the conquest too easy and she was honest enough to admit to herself that this was hardly the best foundation on which to base a successful marriage.

There had been other snags. There always would be.

Suddenly Dan was standing very close to her. His hands caressed her face and gently encircled her head.

'You must marry me,' he said earnestly.

'I want to Dan. Oh God I want to.' She threw her arms round his neck and clung to him. He kissed her passionately and she responded. It was the first kiss he had given her that was imbued with any degree of deep feeling.

'Say you'll marry me,' he whispered.

'You've never said you love me, never once.'

Iris wept against his chest. She looked up into his face. 'Do you Dan? Do you love me?'

'Yes,' he said. 'I know now I do. I know that I always have and I was a damned fool not to tell you.'

He held her gently at arm's length and allowed himself a long appraising look at her.

'I should have told you a lot of things,' Dan said tenderly, 'but I'm afraid I've been blind and stupid.'

'I hope I'll be all right for you. I used to believe I was frigid and cold but I don't feel that way anymore.'

The words gushed out revealing facets to her character that made him wonder if she was the same girl, the same quietly-spoken, unemotional creature who liked to hug the background, afraid to disclose her slightest feeling.

'You must always tell me you love me,' she said. 'You see what it does to me.'

They sat on the flat slab of rock which overhung the pool and held hands. They took their shoes off and immersed their feet in the cold water.

'How soon will it be?' Dan asked after a while.

'Next month if that would be all right with you?'

'The sooner the better,' he said and he placed a protective arm round her shoulder.

'It's better than I thought it would be,' he said.

'It always is,' Iris O'Lully replied, 'when it's the right person.'

Suddenly the practical side surfaced.

'I'll have to tell my mother,' she said, 'and bridesmaids? I'll have to choose bridesmaids. We'll marry in white won't we? I'm so happy.'

She rested her face against his shoulder.

'We've wasted so much time,' Dan said reproaching himself.

'No,' she said. 'We have the rest of our lives together. There's plenty of time to catch up.'

Later that night as he lay in bed in Ballynahaun his mind

ranged back to their first meeting. She occupied the room next to his. It was the room where Willie and he slept when they were boys. He felt happier than he had ever been. He had not realised until the episode near the waterfall that he could desire anybody so much. Physically and mentally he longed for her. This then had to be the love that was always absent before. He eased himself from the bed and tiptoed into her room. She lay on her back with her eyes open. She did not act in the least startled when he sat on the side of the bed and kissed her.

'I only came to tell you how much I love you,' he whispered. She nodded without a word and raised herself to a sitting position. He placed an arm round her shoulders and another against the outline of her breasts. They kissed and she lay back against the pillows.

'I'd better go,' Dan whispered.

'It might be best,' she whispered in return. There was laughter in her voice. He laughed aloud and returned to his room. He lay awake a long time. He would be eternally grateful to Edwin Seymour for inducing him to pay that visit to Basingstoke. He thought of Sylvester O'Doherty and of the ill-luck that dogged him compared to his own, wonderful, good fortune. He would never forget Sylvester.

He thought of Eddie Carey's tragic end, so sudden and so cruel at a time when all his woes had disappeared, when love and happiness beckoned for the first time with a promise of fulfilment. He remembered how he himself might have expired while he lay semi-conscious on the forecourt of the Green Shillelagh. Surely, at the very least, he would have been maimed for life had he not been succoured by friends encountered through outrageous chance.

He would never forget the innocent man kicked to death before his time in a vendetta about which the poor fellow knew nothing. He would be haunted forever by that look in Sylvester's eyes, by its anguish and torture and lack of resignation when he knew that he must release forever his hold on life. 'There,' he thought to himself as he stood by the grave in Mayo, 'lies the best man I ever knew.'

'Walk aisy when your jug is full,' Dan repeated the

familiar adage used faithfully by his father whenever he confided a fresh success. On that score the elder Murray need not worry. He had always walked aisy and from now on would do so more than ever.

He knelt by the bed and said his prayers. He thanked God for the good luck which had accompanied him to this point in life. He would say, if asked, that luck was the be-all and end-all of life.

From next door he could barely discern the deep breathing of his wife-to-be. From its regularity he knew she was asleep. From a far-off farmstead came the faint barking of an alarmed hound. Dan turned over on his side. It seemed only a short time since he turned restlessly in his bed the night before he first set sail for England. It was, however, all of seventeen years and, as he recalled, a dog had barked its alarm too on that far-off occasion. From memory he placed his hand under the pillow. There had been three shillings spending money and that would have to do him until Eddie Carey found him a job.

DURANGO
John B. Keane

Danny Binge peered into the distance and slowly spelled out the letters inscribed on the great sign in glaring red capitals:

    'DURANGO,' he read.

    'That is our destination,' the Rector informed his friend. 'I'm well known here. These people are my friends and before the night is over they shall be your friends too.'

The friends in question are the Carabim girls: Dell, aged seventy-one and her younger sister, seventy-year-old Lily. Generous, impulsive and warm-hearted, they wine, dine and entertain able-bodied country boys free of charge – they will have nothing to do with the young men of the town or indeed any town ...

Durango is an adventure story about life in rural Ireland during the Second World War. It is a story set in an Ireland that is fast dying but John B. Keane, with his wonderful skill and humour, brings it to life, rekindling in the reader memories of a time never to be quite forgotten ...

IRISH SHORT STORIES
John B. Keane

There are more shades to John B. Keane's humour than there are colours in the rainbow. Wit, pathos, compassion, and a glorious sense of fun and roguery are seen in this book. This fascinating exploration of the striking yet intangible Irish characteristics show us Keane's sensitivity and deep understanding of everyday life in a rural community.